FIONA ERSKINE

Losing Control

Terror in Teesside

First edition

ISBN: 978-1-7385120-7-2

This book was professionally typeset on Reedsy.
Find out more at reedsy.com

Foreword

Between the extremes of TV drama and real-world paperwork lies the fascinating world of investigation and detection. *Losing Control* is a work of fiction, not a documentary. Neither the fictional characters nor the organisations they work for nor the rules they follow represent real systems, real police forces, or real people.

Chapter 1

ALF

Alf opened the door of his Portakabin and sniffed the air outside.

The nightwatchman's nose was finely attuned to the scents on his patch. He smelt the weather, the direction of the wind and chance of rain. He tracked the passage of time by the estuary odour. At low tide, exposed silt and mud released the aromatic legacy of decades of heavy industry. At high tide, the salty tang of seawater dominated. In between the two extremes, the briny interface ebbed and flowed with the moon. When the River Tees hit the North Sea, the change in temperature, salinity and alkalinity released most of the bounty picked up along the way. Eighty-five miles it travelled, from the peat bogs of the Pennines, meandering past farmland, tumbling through ancient woods, wiggling round villages and towns before greeting the sea at the mouth of the Tees.

Alf sniffed again.

A sharp sense of smell came in useful at the scrapyard. In winter, it was already dark when he arrived at work, and still dark when he left in the early morning. There's only so much you can see in the beam of a torch with all the colour and depth washed out. His ears weren't so good these days, even with the new hearing aids, and he didn't bother to put them in at work, what with the cost of batteries and the noises in his ears. The vibrations told him all he needed to know: freight trains rattling along the branch line – fewer now the steelworks had closed; lorries thundering up the trunk road; the thrum of tugboats and sloosh of river wash as the big ships came in and out of the container port. Over time, he'd even come to terms with the quivering ghosts. There were a few malevolent ones, the broken spirits of men who'd once toiled here, on this very site, but mainly gentle ones, like Grace, his late wife, who he talked to every night.

Alf worked alone. He preferred it that way. Four men worked on site during the day when it was busy with the scrap coming in and out, all needing to be sorted and weighed. There used to be two men at night. One to patrol the perimeter fence while the other manned the cabin at the gate. Then the management hired a new security firm who installed cameras, linked them to a control centre in Wilton and dispensed with the night shift security guards. Until the incident, after which they sacked Tiger Industrial Security and hired Alf. Bosses don't like mysteries; they always need someone to blame. Welcome to Teesside, where there are more mysteries than you could shake a stick at. They never got to the bottom of the cable kerfuffle. What did he care? It got him this job.

Some nightwatchmen managed to sleep, but Alf preferred to keep busy. He washed and dried the dishes left by the day shift, swept and mopped the filthy cabin. He allowed himself forty winks – his Australian son-in-law called it a power nap – after his mid-shift sandwich. A man was entitled to a proper break. Afterwards, he'd mark the new day by going for a walk down to the river to talk with Grace.

It was just before his midnight walk, as Wednesday turned to Thursday, that Alf noticed the unusual smell. A bonfire, but it wasn't wood that was burning. He smelt petrol and charred feathers.

The wind was gathering strength as Storm Babel approached, no moonlight or stars visible through the thick cloud. Alf checked the torch. The beam was weak, so he unlocked the store cupboard to get new batteries. No batteries. Bloody typical of the day shift to nick them.

He zipped up his waterproof jacket, pulled on a hat and set off in the

2

direction of the smoke. Despite the perimeter fence, it wasn't hard to break in to the scrapyard if you were determined enough. All you needed was a pair of wire cutters.

As Alf moved east, towards the boundary shared with the container port, the terrain got rougher, and the smell became stronger. He raised his torch and raked the fence line. The weak beam of light caught a curl of smoke. Something moved behind it, a single shape dividing in two and running away into the darkness.

'Oi!' Alf yelled and increased his pace.

By the time he reached the fire, there was no one there.

Probably just kids causing trouble again. Not that he could entirely blame them. There was nothing for them around here. He'd been a wild lad too, once upon a time, but his uncle had swung him a job when Alf was aged fourteen. Alf had laboured until his back gave way. He'd been lucky. Not like the kids today. Idle hands become mischievous hands and eventually criminal hands.

Alf thought he saw a flash of flame, but it was only the tail-lights of a car on the other side of the fence. As it passed under a halogen light on the far side of the dock, he caught sight of a taxi logo on the side.

He was out of breath when he reached the perimeter. As he feared, the fire was on his land. Someone had thrown a few rubbish bags over the chain-link fence before setting them alight with petrol. He almost tripped over the remains of a jerry can. Judging by the ragged metal tear down its seam, it had been capped and thrown onto the fire where it had exploded.

He used his stick to scatter what was left of the bonfire. The wind whipped the ash away. Underneath were beads of melted plastic, scraps of charred cloth, leather and a single metal button glowing red in the ashes.

As Alf was walking away, the torch went out. He hit it with the back of his hand, and it flashed on. On the ground, something flashed back. He bent down and picked it up. The torch went out again and nothing he could do would bring it back to life.

'Grace,' he called out. 'I haven't forgotten about you.'

The wind was picking up. The TV weatherman had warned of a storm moving in from the west and it smelt to him as if it was coming faster than predicted. It was too dark to go down to the river without a torch. Grace would be furious with him if he fell in and drowned. However much he longed to see her again, it wasn't a great idea to start the afterlife in her bad books.

'Been a bit busy tonight, love,' he said. 'I'll make up for it tomorrow, OK?'

Grace understood that work came first. She'd always given him that. He'd take her something extra special tomorrow.

As Alf trudged back towards his cabin, he spotted the fox and her two cubs outside the door. She always waited until he set off on his nightly walk. In his haste to find the fire, he'd forgotten to put out a can of dogfood and a saucer of milk. She'd punished him by tipping the dustbin over and tearing the rubbish bags to find something to eat. He hoped the cubs hadn't swallowed any plastic.

Alf added a note in the log, pinpointing the exact location of the fire. He didn't bother calling the police.

They had better things to do.

Chapter 2

JULIE

Hartlepool – Thursday, 7 November 2024

Detective Inspector Julie Cadell shivered on the cobbled wharf of Hartlepool Historic Quay as the police divers extracted the body from the water.

Last night's gale, Storm Babel, had blown itself out through the morning, creating a wall of obsidian cloud, dense and black, heading east.

At the sound of heavy footsteps, Julie turned, shading her eyes against the low winter sun. DS Iain Wharton emerged from the museum gift shop. His silhouette, square and solid, cast a long shadow.

Julie dabbed a drop of camphor oil at the base of each nostril before offering the little pot to her colleague as he drew level. He raised his eyes heavenward before shaking his head and walking on. DS Wharton had a way of turning the smallest gesture into a rebuke, a comment on her lack of leadership experience, a slur on her competence, a predictor of failure. What in heaven's name had her boss been thinking of to add him into her team on this, her first major case as Senior Investigating Officer?

At least she had an ally in the Crime Scene Manager. CSM Adrian Prosser stood beside the tarpaulin, as the divers laid the corpse at the feet of the attending medic.

Julie joined the CSM. She stared down at the dead man and shuddered.

Floaters were often hard to identify, but it didn't look as if he'd been in the sea for very long. Under the dark hair and full beard, it was just about possible to imagine the man he'd once been, poor sod.

'Who spotted him?' she asked.

'Group of primary school kids visiting the HMS *Trincomalee*,' Adrian replied.

She followed his gaze, taking in the restored sailing frigate, built in India for the British Navy in 1805 and now the main visitor attraction in the outdoor section of the National Museum of the Royal Navy.

'A fine day out.' DS Wharton let out a low chuckle. 'One they won't forget in a hurry.'

The doctor pronounced the man dead – it didn't take decades of medical training to make that call, but protocol must be observed – and Rosie, the police photographer, came in close to take pictures.

The victim was wearing trainers and a thin tracksuit, the jacket zip halfway down revealing a T-shirt with a reflective logo. The letters Y and W glittered under the flashlight of the camera.

DC Gibson, the third member of Julie's team, hurried down to the quayside. DS Wharton elbowed him in the ribs. 'One less drug dealer to worry about, eh, son?'

Julie clicked her tongue. 'Let's not jump to conclusions,' she warned. 'Do we have a name?'

DC Gibson shook his head.

Julie turned to the CSM.

'Any ID?' she asked.

'Leave it with me.' The CSM pulled a pair of long-sleeved, heavy-duty gloves over the nitrile ones. His assistant taped them to the white Tyvek suit. He knelt beside the body and began rummaging inside the man's clothes.

'Turn him, please?'

His assistant tilted the waterlogged corpse, and Adrian continued his search in the back pockets of the trousers.

'OK. I'm done.' The CSM stood and displayed empty hands, holding them out for his assistant to sluice them down with seawater then disinfectant.

'No wallet. No phone,' he reported.

Lights bounced off the water as Rosie turned her camera to the area where the body had been found.

The CSM called to the lead diver.

'Can you search the water before you go,' he asked. 'See if anything fell out of his pockets?' He pointed to the rubbish that had kept the corpse company. 'And bag up all that stuff, too, in case it has something to tell us.'

'Are we treating this as a potential crime scene?' Julie asked.

The CSM peered down at the lights under the water as the two divers went down again. 'Until further notice.'

Julie pointed at the cameras. 'Looks as if we've got good CCTV cover.'

'They're loading up last night's recordings,' DC Gibson said. 'I'll go and check if they're ready.'

'Has anyone called the coastguard?' Julie asked.

'I've spoken to the harbourmaster,' Adrian said. 'They liaise with all the maritime agencies.'

Julie nodded. 'Tell them I want to speak to someone with local knowledge of wind and tides.'

The two divers surfaced, and DS Wharton hurried over to speak with them. Julie hesitated, then followed, her feet leaden, each step slower than the last. She could have recused herself from this investigation – she had ample justification. But it was her first opportunity to lead as SIO. And what use was a Hartlepool DI who couldn't stand the sea? She could do it. She would not mess this up.

The lead diver ignored the sergeant and addressed her directly.

'Nothing obvious down there, Detective Inspector,' he said. 'We can net the lock gate, so nothing more comes in or out of the quay tonight, and then do a full search tomorrow when it's light.'

She tried to return eye contact, but her gaze kept straying to the air cylinders on his back, the instruments and dive computer at his shoulder, the mask that hung from his neck. Had he checked the cylinder valve, the pressure controls, the weights and buoyancy? Of course he had, he was a professional diver. Not a naive holidaymaker with more confidence than skill.

The lump in her throat strangled her voice, so she simply nodded.

'Don't be so bleeding soft,' hissed DS Wharton. 'They've got lights. There's no reason for them not to finish tonight.'

Julie stared at him, temporarily tongue-tied. Was she hearing right? Had her second in command called her soft in front of colleagues? What had got into the man? The anger would come later, first came the paralysis: a prickling of cold sweat, a metallic taste on her tongue and white noise in her ears.

The divers were watching her. Even the crime scene team had stopped work to listen in.

It wasn't new, her hatred of conflict. She'd been learning how to overcome it, to do the job that was expected of her. But the sight of the breathing apparatus, those air cylinders and masks, the wetsuits and flippers, all those things brought back other memories.

A sandy beach. A blue sky. The gentle lapping of the waves.

Julie pressed her fingernails into her palms and took a deep breath.

'On the contrary,' she said. 'There's every reason to pause. I want the search done properly. In daylight.'

Julie turned back to the divers. 'Thanks, guys – that was a horrible job. I appreciate it.'

'Better than the rigs,' the lead diver joked. 'At least I get to sleep in my own bed tonight.'

'I bet your missus isn't so keen,' DS Wharton sneered. 'She led the life of Reilly when you were away. I should know.' He made an exaggerated wink. 'Now it's more husband, less money.'

The lead diver made an obscene gesture and moved away.

'DS Wharton,' Julie beckoned.

Her sergeant turned slowly. 'Ma'am?'

How could someone put so much venom into a single word? She was aware the CSI team were observing them, hoping for fireworks. As if they hadn't all had enough drama today.

DS Wharton had made no secret of his frustration when she'd been brought in from another force and promoted above him. If they were going to work together, she needed to address his attitude, but best wait until they were back in the privacy of headquarters. Until then, she needed to isolate him, avoid further public damage to her already fragile authority.

'Check in with DC Gibson,' she said. 'See how he's getting on.'

His lips curled into a nasty smile. One that suggested he'd been expecting, even hoping for a bollocking and knew she'd bottled it.

'Yes, ma'am.' He started to saunter away.

Julie's intestines twisted, the nagging discomfort building into a sharp stab of pain. Why saddle herself with an openly hostile second in command when she had a junior team member ready and willing to step up? Chris Gibson was young and keen. Leading a team meant you got to choose who did what.

'In fact, take over on the CCTV, will you? I need DC Gibson at the post-mortem.'

She waited for Iain to protest, but he simply carried on walking.

'You're the boss,' he said.

Julie walked over to the waiting ambulance.

'I'm all done here,' the CSM said. 'Anything else before they take him away?'

'Not from my side,' Julie said.

Adrian beckoned the paramedics. 'Let's bag him up,' he said. Together they manoeuvred the corpse into the body bag. Adrian attached a label to the outside of the bag and then sealed it.

There was no need for a flashing blue light as the ambulance made its way from Hartlepool Historic Quay to the morgue of James Cook University Hospital.

Julie stopped off at the office in Middlesbrough to file an initial report. She'd barely logged on to the system when her phone rang.

'Ma'am, I have the coastguard on the line for you.'

Julie closed her office door and picked up the desk phone.

'DI Cadell, Cleveland Police.'

'Evening, Inspector, this is Sienna Sutton from HM Coastguard. The harbourmaster asked me to call you.'

'Are you based in Hartlepool, Sienna?'

'No, ma'am. The Hartlepool station operates with volunteers during rescue operations. Permanent staff for the north-east of England work out of the Humber office.'

'Hull is what? Eighty miles south of Hartlepool as the crow flies?'

'We cover more than six hundred miles of coast stretching from Berwick-upon-Tweed to Colchester.'

'I really need someone with local knowledge.'

'Try me.'

Julie sighed. 'We recovered the body of a man from the water in Hartlepool this afternoon.'

'I'm sorry to hear that.'

'We'd like to get an idea of where he may have drifted in from.'

'Where exactly was the body found?'

'The Historic Quay. Under the bow of HMS *Trincomalee*.'

'Well then,' Sienna said. 'That's relatively easy to answer. Anyone or anything found within the quay must have entered the water within the quay.'

Julie scratched her head

'Why do you say that?'

'Because there's a lock gate between the Historic Quay and the marina. The gates stay closed unless the museum is moving something in or out.'

Julie closed her eyes and pictured the scene. She tried to focus on the lock gate, but it remained obstinately in the shadow of the arc lights. Some discrepancy niggled at the back of her mind, something just out of sight, out of reach, too slippery to get hold of.

'We'll check the CCTV,' she said.

'Is there anything else?' Sienna asked.

'I'll call you if I need anything,' Julie said. 'Thanks for the help.'

Julie filed her initial report, then sent a summary and link to her boss, Superintendent Graham Chalmers, a man who liked early warning of anything likely to attract press attention.

DC Chris Gibson appeared at the door.

'Just had a call from the hospital,' he said. 'They're ready to make a start on the post-mortem.'

'Let's go, then.'

In the car Julie checked her calendar. The weekly shop was due to be delivered this evening; she'd booked a late slot to be sure not to miss it, but heaven knew how long the PM would take.

She texted her son Arni.

What time will you get home?

One tick. Two ticks. Blue ticks. Typing . . .

BCK NW

What was it about teenagers and vowels? Was there some reason they avoided them? If Arni was home now, then at least he'd be in for the food delivery.

I'll be late tonight.

One tick. Two ticks. Blue ticks.

An OK emoji appeared.

She sent a blue heart back.

Chapter 3

Julie quickened her step as she entered the hospital atrium. On the upper floors, doctors were diagnosing and nurses tending to the sick. Machines were whirring and beeping, keeping patients alive. Until there was no hope left.

She took the stairs down to the mortuary. Some police officers dreaded a post-mortem, found the dissection of human bodies distressing. Julie, on the other hand, had always found it fascinating. So much of police work was slow and tedious, a process of elimination, trudging down one blind alley after another. Post-mortems were different, a concentration of clues. Even after death, the victim could point the investigation to the correct starting point. In the hands of an expert guide, the deceased had much to reveal.

'Good evening, DI Cadell.' Dr Sandy Armstrong met her outside the briefing room. 'And what puzzles do you have for me to solve this evening?' A tall, thin man with a shock of red hair and twinkling green eyes, he prided himself on extracting secrets from the dead through scientific enquiry. The Home Office-registered forensic pathologist was one of the best in his field, and he knew it.

'Floater,' Julie said. 'Male. Identity unknown. Removed from the water at Hartlepool Historic Quay two hours ago.'

Sandy opened the door to a windowless office where police photographer

Rosie Patton had hooked up her camera to a screen for the briefing. CSM Adrian Prosser and DC Gibson were the last to arrive.

'Sorry I couldn't make it to the scene,' Sandy said.

'I'll summarise what we found,' Adrian clicked through the photos until he found a wide-angled view of the Quay showing the position of the body before extraction. 'Rosie will stay here to document the autopsy and can provide any additional detailed images you need.'

Sandy nodded. 'Time is of the essence if our man's been in the water.'

Once the briefing was complete, the CSM left and the rest of the team moved swiftly to the changing room to scrub up.

The examination room was a cold and clinical place. Smooth walls in shades of pale blue met the tiled floor in a cleaning curve. A row of stainless steel tables, each with trough and drain, shone under the recessed ceiling lights. Only one table was occupied. A black body bag lay on the centre table, a trolley loaded with ferocious surgical instruments at its side.

'Everyone ready?'

The pathologist read out the label.

'Unknown male recovered on the seventh of November 2024 from the water at Hartlepool Historic Quay,' he said. 'This our man?'

'Yes,' Adrian confirmed.

The pathologist broke the seal and the mortuary technician removed the bag.

Sandy walked round the body, dictating into a microphone on his lapel.

'Deceased is male, wearing a shell suit and trainers. He has a full beard and long hair.'

'The uniform of a drug dealer,' DC Gibson muttered.

Julie gave her constable a withering stare. DS Wharton was a bad influence on the younger man. She was going to have to get him away from the sergeant's festering prejudice.

'Let's remove his clothes first,' Sandy said.

The mortuary technician tugged at the trainers. Even though the laces were loose, it took a concerted effort to remove the shoes.

'Photograph the feet and hands, please,' Adrian instructed and Rosie moved forward.

Sandy moved up to the chest. The plastic zip on the jacket opened easily.

'Under the jacket is a T-shirt,' he dictated. 'Embossed gold logo says *My Way*.'

'Not to be recommended, then,' chirped DC Gibson.

Julie sensed nervousness under the braggadocio. Was this his first post-mortem? She should have checked before snubbing her sergeant.

Sandy found the label and described the size and make, then the mortuary technician peeled the T-shirt over the corpse's head before removing the trousers. Each item of clothing was photographed, bagged and labelled before being sent to dry.

Sandy walked slowly round the gurney.

'Deceased is male. Circumcised. Maceration visible on palms of hands and fingers.'

Sandy continued his dictation.

'No maceration on soles of feet. Skin elsewhere is wrinkled, opaque and whitened but has not delaminated.' Sandy paused and looked up. 'What time was he found?'

DC Gibson checked his notes.

'First report was twelve twenty-three in the afternoon, but it took a while to assemble the marine team, and we got him out at two fifty-one.'

'Water temperature?'

'Eleven degrees centigrade.'

The pathologist put his gloved thumb and forefinger together and pinched at the skin on the left forearm. 'I'll need to do some tests, but judging by the good state of preservation, he went into the water less than twenty-four hours before you pulled him out.'

'Time of death two fifty-one yesterday afternoon?' DC Gibson asked, pen poised.

The pathologist gave him a withering look. 'I most certainly did not say that. All I said is that he was in the water for less than twenty-four hours.'

'How can you tell, Doc?'

'Washerwoman's hands,' Sandy said. 'The keratinocytes in the stratum spinosum produce a water-repelling glycolipid . . .' He looked up to see DC Gibson's jaw had dropped. 'In layman's terms, when we're alive, the skin is constantly producing a waterproofing oil. As it gets washed away, the keratin in the skin starts to react with water and decompose.'

DC Gibson wrote something down. 'Thanks, Doc.'

'That timing matches the witness statements,' Julie said. 'Staff are certain the body wasn't there last night. One of the museum guides said that yesterday was quiet and they used the time to clean the quay. He was sure he'd have noticed a body under the bow of HMS *Trincomalee*.'

'Our man was most likely already there when the museum opened this morning,' Adrian added. 'Witness said it was busy with a school visit and someone would have noticed him falling in.'

'So, he entered the water between five o'clock last night - when the museum closed – and ten o'clock this morning when it opened?' DC Gibson asked.

Sandy ignored him, continuing his detailed inspection, lifting the scrotum and then palpating the stomach. 'Who found him?'

'Some kids from Haverton Hill on a primary school visit to the HMS *Trincomalee*.'

Sandy looked up and frowned. 'Have they had counselling?'

'According to the teacher they're enjoying the spotlight,' DC Gibson continued. 'Minor celebrities now.'

'Don't be fooled.' Sandy wagged a gloved finger. 'Shock can be delayed. Make sure they get a referral.'

Julie made a note. 'On the case,' she said.

Sandy returned to his inspection.

'Light ecchymosis looks to be post-mortem.' He beckoned for the CSM. 'We would normally expect to see the bruising reveal itself over several days,' he added. 'But it's always more complicated with bodies that have been in water.'

'It wasn't easy getting him out.' Adrian shook his head at the memory.

Sandy continued his inspection. 'Hair long but styled, beard trimmed, nails manicured, teeth . . . mmm, that's interesting . . . A young man in general good health.'

'Not now, he's not,' muttered DC Gibson.

The pathologist returned to his inspection of the chest.

'Rosie, get a close-up here.' He pointed to a puckered area just under the collarbone.

Rosie took pictures, showing them to the pathologist in the viewfinder until he was satisfied.

'OK, let's turn him,' he said.

The mortuary technician deftly rolled the dead man onto his stomach.

'Dark and mottled patches on back, buttocks and backs of legs where blood has pooled. Pattern of lividity suggests he lay where he died, on his back, for several hours.'

'In the water?' DC Gibson scratched his head. 'He was found floating face down.'

'Patience, Constable,' Sandy said. 'First we observe, then we test and eliminate hypotheses – what definitely didn't happen – and finally we discuss possible conclusions.'

He parted the hair at the back of the cranium and explored it with his fingertips.

'Feels like a swelling,' Sandy said. 'Can you shave a patch of hair here?'

The technician used scissors and then a cut-throat razor.

Once the wound was visible, Rosie took close-up pictures as directed.

'Blunt force trauma to the back of the head,' Sandy said.

'Enough to kill him?' Julie asked.

'Difficult to say from the outside,' Sandy said. 'Let's get his height, weight and the toxicology samples, please,' he ordered. 'Then it's time to open him up.'

The mortuary technician helped to roll the corpse back to face the scalpel.

Sandy selected a blade from the trolley and placed the tip of the knife at the centre of the collarbone.

'First Y incision,' Sandy said, glancing at DC Gibson who had turned a little green. 'From each shoulder to the tip of the xiphoid process. Write that down.'

'Yes, Doc.'

The pathologist made the first two cuts, then drew the blade from the sternum to the pubic bone, cutting through fat and muscle until he could fold back a triangle of flesh to cover the face, exposing the chest cavity.

'The human body is a thing of wonder.' Sandy whistled as he removed the pectoral muscle to reveal the ribs. 'See this, here?'

He pointed to a damaged rib on the left side of the body. 'Picture, please, Rosie.'

After approving the images, Sandy swapped the scalpel for a circular saw and cut through the breastbone. He returned the power tool to the tray with a clatter and then used both hands to crack open the ribcage to expose the organs beneath.

With a series of swift slices, he removed them for inspection and weighing one by one.

'Not much water in the lungs,' Sandy said.

'He didn't drown?' Julie asked.

'Exactly. And the blow to the back of the head didn't kill him either.'

'So, what did?'

'Take a look.'

The sac which surrounded the heart was torn and beneath it the heart muscle had a single laceration.

'Stabbed?' Julie suggested.

'Exactly.'

Sandy continued his dissection, using a pair of tweezers to remove something from the wound, threads so fine as to be almost invisible.

'Evidence bag, please,' he said, and the technician obliged.

Once the samples were taken, Sandy picked up a measuring stick and checked the dimensions of the lesion.

'The murder weapon you're looking for has a nine-inch blade.'

'Any special features?' Julie asked.

'A filleting knife – single, smooth edge, tapering to a narrow point. Not your common or garden kitchen knife or switchblade. Thin and razor-sharp, the kind a professional chef or fisherman might use.'

'Any sign of a struggle?'

'No obvious defensive wounds, although the skin on the hands is too badly damaged to be sure. Let me deglove him.'

The door slammed and DC Gibson left before Sandy had removed the skin from the hands and inspected the flesh underneath.

'The man was right-handed. No defensive wounds.'

'Suggesting he knew his assailant?' Julie asked.

'Or was taken by surprise,' Sandy said. 'If I was to hazard a guess, I'd say there were two assailants. One clubbed him from behind with something large and heavy, like a cricket bat, then he fell forward onto the other assailant who stabbed him from the front.'

Sandy demonstrated with a sharp jabbing motion.

'Whoever wielded the knife knew exactly what they were doing. A single cut straight between the fourth and fifth ribs, severing the great coronary vein and anterior intraventricular artery of the heart. Our mystery man would have died almost instantly. This looks more like a calculated killing than a brawl that got out of hand.'

'Drug-related?' DC Gibson was back, a little green around the gills, but his voice was steady.

'We'll have to wait for toxicology, but he doesn't look like a user,' Sandy said. 'No track marks visible on the arms or legs. If he's a supplier, he's a cut above the norm.'

'Rosie, can you try some more pictures of the face?' Julie asked. 'Maybe we can use them for ID.'

A flash lit up the room as the photographer took pictures.

Julie walked over to her. 'Let me see.'

Together they looked at the photos in the viewfinder.

'We can't show those photos to the public.'

'The swelling will go down in a few days,' Sandy said. 'But he'll lose the muscle that defines the shape of his face. What about a reconstructive sketch?'

'Good idea,' Julie turned to DC Gibson. 'Can you arrange that, please?'

The pathologist completed his examination and signalled for the mortuary technician to take a set of dental X-rays. But Sandy was far from finished.

'Let's look at those clothes again,' he said.

The mortuary technician brought them back to a polished steel table. Each piece of clothing had been photographed, labelled and bagged ready for drying.

'What's interesting here,' Sandy said. 'Is what's missing.'

'No socks,' Adrian said.

'Odd for this time of year, don't you think?'

'We're all slaves to fashion,' interjected DC Gibson, stretching out his leg to show that he too wore no socks.

'Interesting,' Sandy said. 'But not conclusive.'

'No underpants either,' Adrian added.

Sandy looked over at DC Gibson. 'A common sartorial choice?'

DC Gibson blushed. 'I don't know what sartorial means, but if you're asking if I've got kecks on, you bet.'

Sandy smiled. 'And I don't know what kecks are, but I can guess you're fully dressed.'

He picked up the transparent plastic bag with the T-shirt inside and held it up to the light. Sandy was a good teacher, a man who knew that observation is not enough; curiosity is everything.

'What do you notice?' he addressed DC Gibson who frowned but said nothing.

'Let me give you a clue,' Sandy said. 'The man was stabbed.'

'No bloodstains,' the constable muttered. 'But they might have been washed away.'

'Where did the knife go in?'

'Here.' DC Gibson pointed to the top left. 'Oh, wait. I see it now. There's no tear.'

'Very good,' Sandy turned the bag with the T-shirt round to show a rip on the back collar. 'But there is one here. Now what do you think caused that?'

DC Gibson's hand shot up. 'I know, Doc.'

'Put your hand down. You're not in class,' Sandy said. 'Come on, then.'

'That's where the security tag was torn off,' DC Gibson said. 'He nicked his clothes.'

'Or perhaps someone else did,' Julie said. 'Let's look at the jacket.'

Together they inspected the tracksuit top.

'No tears in the fabric around the chest, no damage to the zip, but there's another rip at the collar,' Julie said.

Sandy turned to the photographer. 'Show me the crime scene photos again.'

Rosie obliged and Julie stopped the sequence at the frame that showed the tracksuit top zipped up high on the chest.

'So, these are not the clothes he was killed in,' DC Gibson said.

'Give me your reasoning.'

He chose his words carefully. 'Because there's no cut in the T-shirt or jacket where the knife went in.'

'Very good.' Sandy smiled. 'You are also quite right that the seawater would have washed most of the useful evidence away, but you'd still expect to see some trace of bloodstaining if he was wearing these clothes when he was stabbed, and you'd definitely see a short tear where the knife penetrated.'

'You think he was naked when he was killed?' DC Gibson asked. 'Possible sexual motive?'

Julie frowned. Why were her team obsessed with sex and drugs? Was Cleveland so very different from her old force in North Yorkshire?

Sandy shook his head. 'I don't think he was naked when he was stabbed – I found some fibres inside the heart that were pushed in with the knife. It's more likely that someone undressed him post-mortem and put him in brand-new clothes. It's the shoes that are the real giveaway.'

DC Gibson stared at the trainers in the evidence bag. 'What can you see that I can't?' he asked.

'Do you have children, Constable?'

'Six.' DC Gibson beamed.

'My, my,' Sandy said. 'Heroic.'

'One with my first girlfriend and two with my ex-wife, and she already had two of her own, and . . .'

Sandy held up a hand and Julie suppressed a smile.

'Do you ever help your children to tie their shoes?'

'Not in our house,' DC Gibson said. 'All the kids' shoes have Velcro these days.'

'These shoes are the wrong size. Far too small. A push fit. They would have been agony to walk in, but judging by the lack of damage to the feet, our victim took no steps in those trainers.'

'Interesting,' the constable said, 'but how does it help us?'

Sandy checked the labels on the clothes. 'George,' he said. 'Does that mean anything to you?'

'It's a supermarket own brand,' Julie said.

'Then my suggestion,' Sandy said, 'is that you contact this local George supermarket.'

'Asda,' DC Gibson said. 'George is the brand name for clothes from Asda.'

'I suggest you contact them and see if anyone stole a shell suit, T-shirt and trainers in these sizes, perhaps even between the hours of six o'clock and midnight on Wednesday.'

'You think they killed him then went to steal some clothes?'

'If they acquired the clothes in advance, it suggests an additional degree of premeditation, does it not?'

'Gotcha,' DC Gibson said. 'Shall I follow up, ma'am? Those places have wall-to-wall CCTV. Whoever nicked the clothes might be caught on camera.'

Julie shook her head. 'Pass it on to DS Wharton once we finish.'

'What about the detritus found with the body?' Sandy asked.

'The what?' DC Gibson asked.

'The flotsam and jetsam,' Sandy smiled. 'The rubbish.'

Rosie brought her camera to show the pathologist the photographs she'd taken.

'DC Gibson has the list,' Julie said. 'Difficult to say whether it travelled with him or washed up separately.'

'Anything of note?' Sandy asked.

Julie nodded at her constable, who recited from memory. 'One three hundred and thirty-millilitre bottle of Irn-Bru. Eleven beer cans. Seven Walkers crisp packets. Three plastic shopping bags. One spray bottle of Provanto . . .'

'Bug spray?' Sandy asked.

DC Gibson shrugged and continued. 'Assorted garden netting, pieces of wood from a broken pallet, gardening gloves.'

'Is there still a garden centre near the marina?' Julie asked.

DC Gibson nodded. 'There's a wholesaler on Mainsforth Terrace, near the railway line.'

'Check with the café at the naval museum and the garden wholesaler. See if they recognise the brands,' Julie said.

'Will do.' DC Gibson nodded. 'Why would someone undress and dress a corpse?'

'Several reasons,' Julie said. 'One.' She held up her index finger. 'To send us down the wrong track.'

DC Gibson scratched his head. 'You mean, someone dressed him to look like a drug dealer?'

'Exactly.' Julie's middle finger formed a V with the index finger. 'Two,' she said, 'to destroy any forensic evidence that might identify the murderer.'

'Wouldn't the water wash that away?'

'Not entirely,' Julie said. 'It's amazing how much information our forensic wizards can extract from the slightest trace.'

Adrian nodded in support.

'Three.' Julie held up her ring finger. 'Maybe the clothes the victim was wearing at the time of the murder would identify him, or his workplace, or his business.' She nodded towards the mortuary. 'Someone dumped the body of our mystery man into the water in the hope that he would be swept out to sea and never found. But they took extra precautions just in case he washed back up. Precautions meant to throw us off the scent. Someone, somewhere doesn't want us to identify this man.' Julie smiled. 'Which is exactly why we are going to move heaven and earth to find out who he is.'

Chapter 4

When Julie got home there was a failed delivery note halfway through the letterbox.

Darn it. What had happened to Arni? He'd said he was home. Had he gone out again? Julie removed her shoes and put on her slippers.

A pair of filthy trainers lay on the hall carpet, just under the stairs. The shoes were barely visible under mud and grass. A sopping wet anorak slung over the banister had dripped water onto the shoes, turning the mud liquid as it ran onto the once-cream carpet.

'Arni!' she called.

No response.

She picked up her son's trainers and carried them to the kitchen scullery, placing them on a plastic tray. The rest of his sports kit was already here, along with his hockey stick. Everything soaked through, wet and muddy.

She washed her hands and called the supermarket delivery line. They said it was too late to reschedule tonight; the food delivery would have to be tomorrow.

'Arni!' she called again.

Silence.

Irritation gave her weary legs new bounce. She ran up the stairs. Arni's door was shut. She knocked. No reply. She turned the doorknob.

Her son was sitting in his underwear in front of the double screen of a gaming computer, watching – or perhaps orchestrating – a battle where people in camouflage gear wrestled with zombies. Books, magazines, dirty mugs and plates, discarded snack wrappers lay strewn across the floor.

'ARNI!'

With his headphones on he was oblivious to the rest of the world. The blood gushing from a machine-gun assault paled in comparison with the full-blown red mist that descended on his mother.

She strode across the carpet and yanked the headphones from his head.

He jumped with surprise, then his face lit up with the sweetest of smiles.

'Oh. Hi, Mum!' he said. 'What's for tea? I'm famished.'

She took a deep breath.

'There will be no tea because we have no food. Do you know why? Because you didn't answer the doorbell.'

'I didn't hear anything.'

'Because of the bloody headphones.'

'They could have texted me.'

'I'll go out and get some food while you clean up the mess downstairs.'

'What mess?'

The urge to slap him was so strong, she had to hold onto the hem of her jacket to stop her hands flying out.

'Get dressed, come downstairs and I'll show you.'

'Bad day, was it?' He made a face. 'Me too. We lost three to two.'

Julie spoke through gritted teeth. 'You can tell me all about it after you've cleaned up.'

'Just let me finish this game, OK?'

She bent down to the wall socket and switched off the computer. The red gore of battle faded to black.

'Mum!' Arni yelled.

'See you downstairs.'

If Julie felt a little better, it didn't last long.

Arni appeared at the kitchen door. 'Don't bother with food for me,' he said. 'I'm going to Eve's.'

Before she could say anything, he was gone. The front door slammed behind him.

Julie's anger boiled over and left her empty. She collapsed onto a kitchen chair and put her head in her hands.

She'd avoided confrontation with DS Wharton, ignored his direct challenge to her authority, and now everyone thought her weak.

She'd overreacted to her teenage son and now he hated her.

Could she get nothing right today?

Chapter 5

ALF

South Bank – Thursday, 7 November 2024

Alf started his night shift by replacing the batteries in the torch – batteries purchased using his own money – and bagged the old ones up for recycling.

There used to be a landline and computer in the cabin. The day-shift men complained to the bosses when the connection went dead, right around the time of the incident. The other security men called it the cable kerfuffle.

Alf had asked about the cable kerfuffle, but he never got a straight answer. The only thing everyone agreed on was that it all kicked off after a huge roll of brand-new cable appeared on site.

Kids tried to pinch stuff from the scrapyard all the time, but the mysterious delivery baffled everyone. As the bosses looked deeper, puzzlement turned to alarm. Strange things had been going on for months. Every night, security cameras at key locations froze for several hours, returning to operation before dawn. It was the level of organisation that worried management most. Scrap is a competitive business, no shortage of players looking to muscle in.

The police got involved and they caught a trespasser, some foreign guy, but apparently no charges were ever brought. It wasn't like he'd been caught stealing. They couldn't even pin the damage to the computer and phone connections on him.

Management cancelled the contract with Tiger Industrial Security and hired Alf to work night shifts, but decided it would be too expensive to run a new network cable to the Portakabin. The computer was removed and the desk phone replaced with a satellite phone.

Alf didn't mind being without internet. He always brought in a couple of books, borrowed from the library and returned as soon as he'd finished. No point in cluttering up the house with things that collected dust. One book was always factual – natural history or travel writing – and one was made up. He liked crime fiction best, but he'd try anything with a good story. A ripping yarn helped to pass the time. Twelve hours confined to a dimly lit Portakabin on a dark site could seem like a very long time.

Sometimes his daughter would call on the cabin phone – he didn't own a mobile – and she'd tell him all about her shiny new life far from home.

It was Alf who'd encouraged his daughter to stay on at school, to look for opportunities beyond Teesside, although he'd meant Newcastle rather than Melbourne. He didn't begrudge her the adventure. At least his grandkids were growing up in a place with a future, not fighting over the scraps of decline.

The boys didn't come to the phone these days, too old to want to speak to their grandfather and, with the time difference, usually at school when she phoned. Or out with their friends at the weekend. He couldn't honestly blame them. Pity they were such a long way away. He'd have liked to take them fishing, get to know them.

Alf looked around the cabin and sighed. Best get on with his chores.

The dayshift men were slobs. They'd got used to Alf cleaning up after them, washing their dishes, emptying the bin, scrubbing the toilet, shower and sink. He even tidied their paperwork, filing the deliveries and dispatches.

Just before midnight, Alf put food and milk out for the fox cubs, locked the cabin and set off on his regular patrol.

Last night's storm had washed the Teesside air clean, and stars twinkled in an indigo sky. He followed the fence round the perimeter of the scrapyard, starting with the section beside the trunk road, then along the rail sidings and finally down to the river. The fence stopped here, the river forming a more effective security barrier than any chicken wire could. He turned right and walked along the revetment towards the container port. The river was in spate, peaty water roaring along beneath his feet. He paused to admire the lights of the Zagrovyl factory, which towered over the far bank. Nothing to look at during the day, it was quite spectacular at night.

A cylindrical concrete structure, about three feet in height and diameter, protruded a few feet above the no-man's land between container port and scrapyard. This was the place where Alf came to talk to his wife.

As he neared his destination, the beam from his torch indicated that something was wrong.

'Oh, Grace,' he whispered.

The shells were the first things he brought here. After the funeral he walked every day. From Redcar to Marske and then on to Saltburn, catching the train back – or, with the addition of a bus journey, on to the Cleveland Way footpath between Boulby and Ravenscar, Staithes and Runswick Bay, Whitby and Robin Hood's Bay, as far as Scarborough and Filey. Grace hadn't been able to get out much when she was ill, and Alf hadn't liked to leave her alone. Now that he was free to do what he wanted, the sea called to him. But the miles of beach represented the loneliest of liberations. He found himself howling into the North Sea. Now her suffering was over, and his caring responsibilities had ended, any sense of release was curdled by shame and regret at not having done enough coupled with an unbearable sense of loss.

One day, he picked up a pretty shell and the sun came out. He held it up to the heavens and told Grace how he felt, the first honest unburdening since she'd been taken ill.

By the time he was offered the nightwatchman job, Alf had amassed a collection of contrition: shells of crabs, scallops, mussels and razor clams. Pebbles, too, granite and marble and obsidian, sea glass worn to a soft lustre and sea coal so black it swallowed light. Grace disapproved of clutter, but he hadn't been able to bring himself to throw the found objects away, so he brought them to work and arranged them in a spiral on this concrete pedestal.

Now all his precious things were scattered.

It wasn't so much a shrine to his dead wife as a collection of conversation prompts. After forty years of marriage, you sometimes ran out of things to say, and – let's face it – their chats were pretty one-sided these days. He got down on his hands and knees and combed the ground to collect the numerals of his grief clock, a chronology of despair.

Had the storm blown them from the circular plinth? It was odd the way they'd fallen, all towards the river. Had someone opened the lid, accessed the ventilation shaft for the old tunnel? Unlikely. But he could think of no other explanation.

He spent time putting the treasures back in order as best he remembered. As he rearranged the little offerings, it saddened him to see that some were damaged.

Once order had been restored, he cleared his throat.

'Well, Grace,' he said. 'Guess what happened last night?'

He put his hand in his coat pocket and pulled out the metal object that he'd collected the night before. It fitted neatly in his palm, but now he examined it more closely in the torchlight, he saw that it was not a piece of jewellery, but a tool in the shape of a cross. It had six different heads, one on each leg and two in the centre: a hexagon, a triangle, a square, a circle, and two shapes he didn't have the words to describe. He cleaned and polished it with his handkerchief before adding it to the collection.

He told Grace all about the fire, slightly exaggerating his role in putting it out. She wouldn't mind, she'd always loved his stories.

After he'd finished, Alf felt much happier. His wife had always been a good listener, and talking to her helped him sort out how he felt.

Trudging back to his cabin, he checked his watch. Not long now. Tonight's shift had flown by. It was always better to keep busy.

Chapter 6

JULIE

Hartlepool – Friday, 8 November 2024

The sun was rising as Julie left the house.

Last night, she'd waited up for her son until she could no longer keep her eyes open. She woke briefly, just before midnight, to hear his key in the front door lock, but it was warm in bed, and she couldn't face another late-night confrontation. Her alarm went off as he was leaving for hockey practice.

'Morning,' she called from the top of the stairs.

The front door opened and closed.

She watched him from the bedroom window. His rucksack looked small on his broad back as he set off on his bicycle. He'd changed so much, just in the last few months. His school trousers looked a little short, his coat no longer closed. If he needed new clothes, all he had to do was ask. Money was tight, but they could still afford essentials.

Tonight, then. She'd talk to him tonight.

It was still early but she was wide awake, so she decided to swing by the marina and bring the CSI team up to speed with the information from the coastguard and post-mortem.

Julie's stomach rumbled as she turned off the A19. Last night she'd found a tin of sardines at the back of the cupboard, but it hadn't been the most satisfying of meals, and she'd managed to get fish oil on the book she was reading. Arni had only left enough milk for a cup of tea this morning, so she pulled into the services and ordered a latte and a breakfast roll.

Her husband had always been the organiser in their family. They took turns cooking, but Matt had controlled the online shopping. He hated waste and operated a just-in-time stock control system from a shared spreadsheet. Since he'd left, since she'd had to take this job to make ends meet, things had spiralled out of control. She couldn't do everything herself. Arni was seventeen. It was time he stepped up.

Julie let out a long, satisfying burp as she drove over the hill and began the descent into Hartlepool. She'd been born in the town, but never really appreciated it until after she left. There was a faded glory still visible in the nineteenth-century buildings bordering the natural harbour of the headland. Hartlepool flourished as a North Sea port exporting coal from the South Durham mines. The main town had moved west, embracing steel making and shipbuilding. In the 1970s, the construction of a nuclear power plant brought well-paid jobs, as did servicing the oil industry, refurbishing modules that were towed into the deepwater harbour from North Sea oil wells.

Julie grew up at a time of rapid deindustrialisation. Coal was long gone. North Sea oil and gas were in steep decline and the import trade had moved from the exposed north end of the Tees Estuary to a container port on the more sheltered south bank. Transport links to the town became slow, unreliable and expensive, a damning combination for the jobless. Throughout her teenage years, the whole town began to feel like an island adrift, cut off from the rest of Teesside.

All that was changing now. The power station's life had been extended again and there was talk of new investment in nuclear electricity. On the quay, the largest wind turbines ever made were waiting to be shipped out to Dogger Bank. Hartlepool was busy reinventing itself. It was good to see life returning to the town.

The Historic Quay sparkled in the sunshine, almost indecently beautiful for a crime scene. The museum with its period houses and maritime adventure centre remained closed to the public with a CSM in charge.

She found Adrian standing on the dockside, shouting instructions to the dive team, who were already in the water.

'Lovely morning!' he greeted her with his usual cheer. Perhaps it was to compensate for the work he did. You needed a strong stomach to scrape bodies out of crashed cars or search the clothing of the drowned.

'Any luck with ID?'

'Nope, and I don't think we'll find anything. Look –,' he pointed to the water, clear as glass – 'we had a good look before the dive team went in and the only lead that looked promising turned out to be a book.'

A waterlogged paperback encased in an evidence bag sat inside a crate on the quay. She could just make out the familiar cover and title: *Nested – An Embedded Story.*

'You think it belonged to our guy?' she asked.

'The dive team reckon not. They think it's been here a while.'

'Not that long, it only came out this year.'

'You've read it, then?'

'Who hasn't?'

'I don't really like books,' Adrian said. 'Don't see the point of them. I'm more of a podcast guy.'

Julie couldn't imagine a world without books. Each to their own.

'I think it's unlikely that this is your crime scene,' he continued.

'Why do you say that?'

'There's good coverage, all the cameras were working. After you left last night, I checked that the motion sensors trigger the security lights. Your guys are doing a full analysis – frame by frame – back at base, but I watched it with DS Wharton yesterday and there's absolutely no sign of our guy.'

'Any evidence of a break-in?' Julie asked.

'The security here is solid. I wish every organisation was as well run as this one.'

The museum only had one public entrance, but the linked buildings all opened out on to an enclosed courtyard. In the centre of the museum complex the last Royal Navy frigate built in India, HMS *Trincomalee*, floated in its own quay.

'If there was no break-in, can we check yesterday's visitors?' Julie asked. 'Any chance our mystery man visited the museum during the day, got locked in and died trying to get out?'

Adrian shook his head. 'We'll double-check, of course, but the staff said that it was a slow day, and they didn't remember anyone matching his description. Isn't it more likely that he blew in with the storm?'

'Coastguard says it's impossible to get through the lock gates.'

Adrian smiled. 'Come with me.'

They walked the length of the HMS *Trincomalee* and Julie marvelled that a wooden sailing vessel so small could have carried so many men between continents.

A vivid memory stopped her in her tracks. She could almost see Jamie sneaking up the rigging, smiling and waving down at her. They'd come to see the tall ships, not long after the museum first opened. A rare outing for the whole family. If she closed her eyes she could see them all: baby Arni in a sling, little Flora holding her dad's hand, Jamie left to his own devices as usual. A happy family. Tears formed in her eyes. Whatever hateful things Matt said before he left, they had been happy once.

She opened her eyes and Jamie was gone.

'You OK, boss?'

Adrian called to her from the lock gates, his face full of friendly concern.

'Fine, thanks.' She hurried to where he was waiting.

'See that?' He pointed to the gap in the lock gate, easily wide enough for a body to float through. 'Damaged in the storm. That's why the divers netted it out last night.'

She looked beyond the lock gate.

'Can we expand the search to the marina?' She shaded her eyes against the slanting sun. 'Including all the boats.'

'I'd need some more people.'

Julie checked her watch. 'I'll see what I can swing.' She smiled. 'Do whatever you can with what you've got.'

'Not a priority, then?'

'I didn't say that.'

Adrian nodded. 'I'll get on to the harbourmaster and let you know if we find anything.'

Julie was driving to her office when a call came through from the coastguard. She accepted it, then pulled over into a lay-by.

'DI Cadell, I'm glad I caught you.' Sienna Sutton launched into an apology. 'I may have given you the wrong information yesterday. I spoke to the marina harbourmaster this morning and . . .'

'The lock gates were damaged in the storm.'

'How did you know?'

'I went to look for myself this morning.'

'Local knowledge, eh?' Sienna said. 'My bad.'

Julie softened a little towards the coastguard. There was too much bluster in the world. It was good to talk to a professional willing to admit to an error.

'What do we know about the circumstances?'

'I can't say much except that the deceased is male and we're launching a murder investigation.'

'Could he have gone into the water at the marina? From the quayside or one of the boats?'

'Why not at sea?'

'It's unlikely that a drifting object would get past the piers at the mouth of the marina.'

'Is there a gate?'

'There's no physical barrier, but the two piers are designed to shelter the navigation channel. They're pretty effective at keeping everything out that isn't deliberately sailing in.'

'But it's possible, right?'

'Anything is possible. We can estimate drift using computer modelling if we know the time and place he entered the water.'

'We don't know that yet. Can you work backward from where he was found?'

'We can try and backtrack, but I must warn you, there is a large degree of error associated with any model. Wind and tide data is not very accurate close to shore.'

'But you'll give it a try?'

'Of course. I'm liaising with the harbourmaster, who's talking to the CSM on the scene. No boats can leave until the CSM authorises it.'

'Good,' Julie said. 'I appreciate your help.'

'What about the CCTV?'

'We're checking it now.' Julie said. 'So, you think it's most likely he went into the water at the marina?'

'DI Cadell, I called this wrong last time, so I'm not going to speculate. While you're focusing on the marina, I'll get the model set up. Can you come down to Bridlington? It's a big data file and runs better on the mainframe here.'

'When do you suggest?'

'I'll work on it over the weekend and call you when it's ready.'

Chapter 7

Stockton-on-Tees – Friday, 8 November 2024

Brian loved his bike. It was the one thing that never let him down. He'd lost his job – sacked on the flimsiest of excuses. His football team were about to be relegated. His girlfriend – if you could still call her that – wasn't speaking to him. Again.

The hours he spent in the garage tinkering with the mechanical marvel that was a Triumph/BSA ensured that Magnus remained well-groomed, widely admired and much loved, everything that Brian was not.

He roared into the garden centre car park, manoeuvred Magnus into the bike shed and locked the front wheel to the stand with a U bolt before heading inside.

Living in a flat without a garden, Brian had little interest in the traditional garden centre merchandise, still less in the seasonal offering – who bought their Christmas decorations this early? Some sadists had designed the customer experience to maximise exposure to tat. You had to run the gamut of trinkets, pass through the many circles of capitalist hell to get to the café.

The coffee shop was a large conservatory with glass on two walls and overhead. Double doors connected it to the outside display of potted fruit trees and ornamental shrubs, garden sheds and pallets of fertiliser. There was also a small playpark.

No sign of the man he was meeting. Even though they'd never met in person, he was pretty sure he'd recognise Dameer from the Teams calls. It wouldn't take great visual acuity. Just eliminate the two ends of the population curve – those who were too old to work but had a pension fat enough to pay for modest outings, and those too young to be at school but too annoying to be shut up with at home all day. Every sort of pram and mobility scooter was lined up in the queue ahead of him, and those tables already occupied held the very old – in singles and pairs – and the very young with their nubile slaves. A group of young women, and one lucky man, sat laughing at a big table next to a soft play net where their charges dribbled. Oh, and one more demographic clue to Dameer Ghosh's absence: every single person in the café, including Brian, was white.

Brian jumped the breakfast queue and went straight to the coffee station, where he bought a cappuccino and kept the receipt. Really his host should pay. He took his coffee to an empty table with a view of the entrance and waited.

The breakfast station of the café was in full swing. Trays of glossy fried eggs showed no sign of the brown lace edges that his frying pan always added. Pink bacon with brown fat was crisped just right. His own grill took things from flobby to incinerated in a few seconds. There were more varieties of plump sausages than he knew existed – pork, chicken, venison, vegetarian, vegan, gluten-free. The frying pan of assorted field mushrooms sizzled next to a pyramid of golden triangles of fried bread. A skillet of grilled tomatoes sat next to a vat of baked beans. Brian was suddenly hungry.

He finished his coffee and looked around. No sign of Dameer. Where was he? Had there been some miscommunication? Brian got out his phone and checked the address he'd sent in his text message. Couldn't be clearer. He tried calling Dameer, but it went to a standard voicemail message, which he didn't bother to listen to. Maybe Dameer had confused the time, what with the clocks changing recently. Which way was it? Spring forward; fall back. But who had mechanical clocks these days? Your phone did everything for you.

Brian didn't feel like sitting around any longer being tortured by hunger, so he got back up and ordered a full English and another coffee.

At the till, he spoke to the cashier.

'Did you see an Indian gent in here earlier?'

The cashier shook his head. 'Sorry, mate. Not that I noticed.'

Brian took his time over breakfast, checking his phone between bites. No messages. The man was over an hour late.

Brian called the mobile again, but this time he waited to the end and left a message.

'Hi, Brian here. I thought we had an appointment today.' Brian tried not to let his irritation show. He needed work, and Dameer had seemed so keen. 'I'm leaving now, but my number is . . .' He rattled off his contact details. 'Please call me back as soon as you get this.'

Brian picked up his helmet and jacket and headed back to his bike, the only thing in this world that he could trust.

Back in the flat, Brian noticed the smell for the first time.

He hadn't been out in a while, so he'd sort of got used to it. But after the floral notes of the garden centre, the stink was harder to ignore.

Brian wasn't a slob, contrary to what his girlfriend (ex-girlfriend?) claimed. He'd simply reached a sensible accommodation with household chores, based on years of experimentation on what happened if you did nothing. Take dusting, for example. You made a rod for your own back if you went down that route. First of all, you had to clear away all the unopened post and manuals and books and magazines and pizza boxes and beer cans. And then the newly exposed surfaces started gathering dust. However much you wiped and polished, however hard you tried, the moment the sun shone, everything looked dusty again. A self-defeating activity easily avoided by keeping surfaces covered – minimum effort for maximum happiness.

Clothes did a similar job of protecting the floor. He'd mapped the laundry process. A dirty clothes basket simply introduced two completely unnecessary steps – dirty clothes in and dirty clothes out. Instead, he operated on a just-in-time demand-driven algorithm. Once he was down to his last clean T-shirt or greyest pair of Y-fronts, he gathered all the clothes lying on the floor of his bedroom and bathroom and stuck them in the washer.

He kept the bathroom and kitchen clean; he wasn't an animal. It didn't take much to wipe down the tiles once a week while he was showering or add an extra squirt of shaving foam to make the sink sparkle. There was bleach for the toilet and the kitchen sink, with a super-strength gunge buster for the regular occasions when they blocked.

He walked around the flat, nose in the air. There was something rank under all the mess.

Time to take action.

He called Betty, his ex-girlfriend, but she still wasn't picking up.

He'd have to make his own battle plan.

Brian opened his assault on the kitchen. The fridge was the usual suspect for bad smells, but it was almost empty. He removed the milk that had gone off. He couldn't find a bin bag, so he tipped the contents down the sink, regretting the decision as the curdled milk solids blocked the plughole. He left the tap running to clear it.

Next was the bathroom. A couple of the towels were overdue a wash and the mould on the shower mat had grown back again, so he scooped them all up and stuck them in the washing machine with DEFCON ELEVEN powder on a hot cycle. He tipped some drain cleaner down the plughole and wiped the specks of stubble from the sink with a wad of loo paper and dropped it in the toilet, which was pretty clean, but he gave the bowl a squirt of bleach before flushing twice for good measure.

His bedroom was in reasonable shape. He'd washed the sheets before Betty came round to collect her stuff, hoping for a reconciliation tumble, or at least a farewell quickie for old time's sake. He spent as little time as possible in there now. Odd how you got used to the shape of someone in bed, even when you had your backs to one another. These days he usually fell asleep in the computer chair or on the sofa in front of the TV rather than confronting an empty bed. Was she gone for good? It was so hard to understand women, what with their hormones and everything. All that pointless crying.

Brian moved to the living room. He found an old pillowcase and started filling it with the rubbish surplus to dust protection duty. The smell was getting stronger. Aha – there it was. Under the sofa, a polystyrene container with the rotting remains of a chicken parmo and chips, now covered in green spores and stinking to high heaven. He added it to the pillowcase, stopped by the kitchen to turn off the tap, added the milk carton to his haul, and then took everything through the garage door to the bin outside.

When he got back to the flat, his phone was ringing.

Dameer. About time.

He answered without checking the number, hanging up once he realised it was another cold call purporting to be from the Inland Revenue.

It was beginning to worry him that Dameer hadn't called back to apologise for missing the meeting. They'd always had a good working relationship. The engineer was polite to a fault, a highly educated Indian man who spoke English with a cut-glass British accent and still used phrases from the 1950s. *Hop, skip and jump.* He didn't seem like the kind of guy who'd just fail to show without explanation.

Brian dialled Dameer's number and this time he listened to the voicemail in full.

'Hi, you've reached the voicemail of Dameer Ghosh at Zebra Safety Solutions. I can't answer the phone right now, but if you leave your name and number I'll get back to you right away. If your enquiry is urgent, please call the main office on . . .'

Brian wrote down the international number and then dialled it. A woman answered.

'Zebra Safety Solutions, how may I assist you?'

'Hi, I was due to meet with Dameer Ghosh today, but I can't get hold of him.'

'Can I take your name please?'

'Brian Burrow.'

'And the number you're calling from, is that the best one to reach you on?'

40

'Yes.'

'And you're in the UK, right?'

'Yes.'

'May I ask what this is in connection with?'

What indeed. Was the 'consulting opportunity' with Zebra itself? Or with one of Zebra's clients? Or was Dameer thinking of striking out on his own? Had Dameer discussed things with his bosses? Brian didn't want to get him into trouble. Best to stick to the work they'd already done together rather than the mystery work Dameer wanted to discuss.

'We worked together on a project for Zagrovyl International.'

'Please hold the line.'

She had a nice voice. Foreign. Sultry. He closed his eyes and imagined an almond-eyed, dark-haired beauty with an hourglass figure. What was he doing pining over Betty when there were more than three billion other women in the world to choose from?

After a pause, the receptionist came back on the line.

'He's not answering his mobile.'

Well, she might have a hot voice, but he sensed a room temperature IQ.

'I know.'

'Can someone else help you?'

'No, I really need to speak to Dameer.'

'Do you have his mobile number?'

You could say many bad things about Betty, but at least she was smart.

'I've been calling his mobile all day,' Brian said. 'No reply.'

'That's odd,' she said. 'Leave it with me. I'll track him down and get him to call you back.'

Brian ended the call and scratched his head. It was Dameer who'd contacted him, not the other way around. The Indian engineer had sounded so very purposeful when he called, polite as always, but unusually firm in his determination that they meet and talk about his mystery project. Brian had interpreted his insistence as excitement, but now he wondered if there had been anxiety too.

What on earth had happened to Dameer Ghosh?

Chapter 8

JULIE

Middlesbrough – Friday, 8 November 2024

Julie looked up in surprise when Superintendent Chalmers burst through her office door. Surprise turned to alarm when DS Iain Wharton followed and closed the door behind them. What were they doing together?

'I asked your detective sergeant for a case update, but it seems he wasn't at the post-mortem,' her boss said, disapproval written all over his face.

Julie remained silent. She wasn't going to defend her management decisions in front of the weakest member of her team.

'That's right,' she said.

The super stared at her. 'Then why don't you update us both on why you've escalated this to a murder investigation. Come on, what do we have?'

Julie took a deep breath. Stick to the facts.

'Male, height six foot two, eighty kilograms, South Asian descent, aged between thirty and forty and previously in good general health. Waiting for toxicology, but no track marks or evidence of drug use. Cause of death was a single stab wound to the heart. No defensive wounds, but a blow to the back of his head with a blunt object may have preceded the stabbing. He was murdered sometime in the late afternoon or evening of Wednesday 6 November and found floating in Hartlepool Historic Quay under the HMS

Trincomalee the following day. We're working on the assumption that there were at least two assailants, the stabber and a cudgel-wielding accomplice. Judging by the condition of the lungs, he was dead long before he entered the water.'

'Do we have an ID?'

'No, sir,' Julie said. 'No sign of a wallet or a phone. He was dressed in a tracksuit and trainers, but due to lack of cuts or bloodstains, we don't believe he was wearing those clothes when he died.'

'Any suspects?'

'We don't know the identity of the victim, place of death or motive for murder, so I'd say we are a long way from identifying the assailants.'

'We're talking about Hartlepool, right? Have we rounded up the usual suspects?'

To her surprise, DS Wharton came to her rescue.

'We can't be sure he was murdered in Hartlepool, sir.'

The super frowned. 'So, what exactly is each member of your team doing, Inspector?'

Julie bit her lip. Since when did her boss get involved in that level of detail? Since his pal DS Wharton had gone whining to him about being left out?

'I'm following up with the coastguard and harbourmaster,' Julie said. 'To work out how far the body could have travelled. We estimate the deceased was in the water for less than twenty-four hours post-mortem. I'm also checking on boat activity and movements in and around the marina over that time frame.' She stood up. 'CSM Prosser and his crime scene team have widened the search area to include the marina.' She walked to the other side of her desk and stood beside her sergeant. 'DS Wharton is reviewing the CCTV footage and following up on the provenance of the clothing the victim was wearing.' She nodded towards the cubicles outside. 'DC Gibson is investigating the source of the rubbish that was found with the victim and continuing to try and match the victim with known missing persons.'

'Have we put out a call for information?' Superintendent Chalmers asked.

'The photographs of the deceased are too distressing to use. We'll have a reconstructive sketch early next week, and we plan to put the appeal out as soon as we have it.'

'Anything else?'

'We could use more people, sir.'

He grunted. 'Sorry, no can do.'

'In that case I'd like the team to work the weekend. The first few days are vital.'

'Hmm.' The superintendent frowned. 'I'm authorising limited weekend overtime, but only for the CSI team and DS Wharton. No one else. Is that clear?'

DS Wharton was the very last person she would have chosen, but time was of the essence, so she'd have to make do with the resources given.

'Yes, sir.'

Superintendent Chalmers stood and left the room. DS Wharton made to follow him.

'Iain, wait,' Julie said. 'I need a word.'

She'd been delaying the intervention. Confrontation was the part of the job she hated most, but they couldn't go on like this. In the police force, rank was sacrosanct. Julie couldn't allow her sergeant to brief their boss behind her back.

His sullen expression was back. 'What is it?'

Julie took a deep breath. Stay calm. Avoid accusation. Let him be the first to admit what he's up to. She nodded for him to sit and then put both hands on the desk. 'What was all that about?' she asked.

'Superintendent Chalmers called me in. Asked me about the case.' DS Wharton cleared his throat. 'I told him to talk to you.'

Julie waited. However infuriating he was, this man had the ear of her boss and that made him dangerous. Play it nice. Let him feel seen and heard.

'I see,' Julie said. 'What else did you tell him?'

DS Wharton folded his arms over his chest. 'Nothing.'

'And yet Superintendent Chalmers implied that you were unhappy about the work I'd assigned to you.'

DS Wharton met her gaze, and the fire returned to his eyes.

'That's because he knows me,' Iain said. 'But I didn't complain to him.'

Did she believe him? Perhaps it was the superintendent who had made the first move rather than the other way round. Iain didn't need to have complained verbally; he was incapable of hiding his body language. Perhaps he was telling the truth. In the interests of resolving this, she'd give him the benefit of the doubt.

'So, let's talk about why you're unhappy,' Julie said.

He sat forward. 'Why am I reviewing CCTV and talking to Asda while DC Gibson attends the post-mortem?'

That was an easy question to answer.

'How many times have you been to a post-mortem, DS Wharton?' she asked.

'Hundreds.'

'And DC Gibson?'

'I have no idea.'

'None,' she said. 'He needed the experience.'

She saw something register, a flicker of understanding that her decisions might not be all about him, but about the team. Then she saw pride get the better of reason. His brow creased and his eyebrows met in the middle.

'Don't pretend you weren't trying to make a point,' he said.

Julie resisted the urge to smile. It was true her motives had not been entirely uncomplicated. But she had her reasons. She took a deep breath. 'And what point would that be?'

'Search me.' DS Wharton shrugged.

'I think you know.'

She held his angry stare. He looked away first.

'What I said at the marina. I was out of order, I know that.'

Julie wasn't letting him off the hook yet.

'In what way?'

'I challenged your authority,' he said. 'In public.'

'You did,' she said.

'I apologise,' he said between gritted teeth.

'Actions have consequences, DS Wharton,' she said. 'Remember that.' She waved a hand. 'You can go now.' She opened the folder on her desk.

'Wait,' he said.

She looked up.

'Before the super called me in, I spotted something on the marina CCTV,' he said. 'A trawler, the *Lainey Rose*, came in round about the time our man must have gone into the water. There was a lot of activity on deck. Hard to make out, but it might have been an argument.'

Julie nodded. 'Interesting.'

'When are you going to talk to the harbourmaster?'

'Why do you ask?'

'I'd like to come too.'

Julie hesitated. Had she been firm enough? Had he got the message? He'd admitted to breaking rank at the dockside, to challenging her authority in front of an audience. His apology had been grudging, but it was an apology nonetheless. They were a small team, and she needed everyone on board. And at a practical level, the super had only authorised overtime for a sergeant, not a constable.

'You'll finish the tasks already assigned? The CCTV review and tracing the clothes?'

'Yes, ma'am.'

Julie nodded.

'Tomorrow at ten, then. I'll meet you at Hartlepool Marina.'

Julie was packing up to go home when the pathologist, Sandy Armstrong, called on the desk phone.

'Do you have a moment?' he asked.

Julie checked the time. If she left in the next half an hour she'd be home in time for the rescheduled food delivery.

'Sure, what's on your mind?'

'I've been thinking about the dentistry,' he said.

'And what did you conclude?'

'If I had to make a guess,' Sandy said, 'I'd say our mystery man grew up in South Asia but spent time in America.'

'Because of his teeth?'

'I've contacted the team in Newcastle. I'll talk to them on Monday.'

This was not new information. Why the phone call?

'Up to anything this weekend?' Sandy asked.

'Working,' Julie said.

'Tonight, then?' he asked. 'Fancy a drink?'

Aha, so this call wasn't entirely work-related.

Part of her wanted to say yes, and part of her knew it would be a mistake. On the one hand, what could be nicer than spending a relaxing evening with Sandy? He was smart and funny and quite sexy for his age. And then she remembered the food delivery that needed to be put away.

'I'm sorry, something on.'

She felt sad after he said goodbye, but it was too soon, far too soon. And she didn't need a pity date.

The traffic on the A19 was at a complete standstill. She tried texting Arni, but there was no reply. She arrived home to find the house empty and a 'while you were out,' note from the supermarket delivery with details of her options. Too late to pick it up now . She decided to cancel it.

Where was Arni?

Julie checked the family calendar.

Shit, shit. The school sports committee meeting. She'd promised to get involved. Offered to chase up pledges for the auction at the hockey team fundraiser. *One ringside seat at a post-mortem.*

When she got to the school, the car park was empty. The meeting was over. She kept her eyes open for her son on the way home, but he'd probably gone to his girlfriend's again. She didn't know much about Eve other than that she was a star player, already captain of the female hockey team. Where did she live? What did her parents do? How much freedom did they give their daughter?

Arni was seventeen. Matt had had the birds and bees talk with his youngest son years ago. Was it her job to remind him about safe sex? And not just sex. About the emotional side of relationships, his responsibilities as a man? A far more complicated conversation now Matt had abandoned his family.

Arni's father wasn't much of a role model.

Julie stopped off at a late-night store to buy essentials – milk, bread, eggs and pizza.

Back home, she put the oven on and texted Arni.

Sorry I missed the meeting.

One tick. Two ticks. Pause. Blue ticks. Pause. Typing . . .

CNCLD

Cancelled? Because she'd failed to show? Or maybe she wasn't the only one with other commitments.

You want some pizza? Just about to put one in the oven.

One tick. Two ticks.

She put some washing in the machine. No detergent. Damn, she should have picked some up at the shop.

Blue ticks.

What else was low? She should do a proper shop tomorrow on her way back from Hartlepool. She opened the cupboards and started making a list.

Her screen lit up.

Typing . . .

RDY 8TN

He'd already eaten.

What time are you home?

One tick. Two ticks. Pause. Blue ticks. Pause. Typing . . .

L8

Julie sighed. She might as well have gone for that drink with Sandy. If she was going to mess up, why not get some pleasure from it? Better to feel happy and guilty than rotten and useless.

She put the smaller of the two pizzas in the oven and opened her book.

It stank of fish.

Chapter 9

The weekend dawned, cold and bright. Julie was up in time to make breakfast. Her son appeared at the kitchen door in his hockey kit.

'Good morning,' she said. 'You fancy scrambled eggs?'

'OK,' he said.

She waited until he'd finished eating.

'Arni, I think we need to talk.'

'What about?'

So many things. One at a time.

'About our argument.'

'It was hardly an argument,' Arni said. 'More like an assault.'

'Pardon?'

'First, you invade my personal space without asking.'

'I called out and I knocked on your door,' she said. 'You had your headphones turned up too loud.'

'Then you attack me.'

'I removed your headphones so we could talk.'

'Then you scream at me.'

Had she screamed? 'I don't think so.'

'You swore.'

Did *bloody* still count as swearing?

'I'm sorry for that, but you did provoke me.'

'How? I was just chilling after hockey.'

'You left your filthy trainers on the carpet with a sodden anorak dripping all over them.'

'I cleaned that up.'

Julie closed her eyes. It was true; he'd tried. He'd spread the mud, rubbing it in, creating a much wider stain on the carpet. Now it would need a professional clean. As if she didn't have enough to do.

'You missed the food delivery.'

'No, Mum. You were late.' He clenched his fists, and the words came out like machine-gun fire. 'You ordered the food. You knew when it was arriving. You didn't share that information with me.'

'I checked you were in.'

'At no point did you tell me you were expecting a delivery. And you didn't give the delivery firm my number.'

'You wouldn't have heard your phone either.'

He gnashed his teeth in exasperation. 'You don't need to hear your phone, Mum. When there's a message, it lights up and vibrates – like this, see?'

His sarcasm was almost harder to bear than his anger.

'Look, Arni. Things are tough at work right now.'

'You think I don't have my own problems?' he said. His face crumpled, and suddenly she saw the child again.

'I have to go to work now,' she said. 'Let's talk tonight?'

He shook his head.

'It's an away match today, remember. I'll be back very late. What about tomorrow?'

'I'm working Sunday too,' she said.

'Whatever.' He shrugged and got to his feet. 'Just whenever you can fit me in.'

'Wait . . .'

But he was gone.

Julie cleared the breakfast things away, rinsing traces of egg off the plates before stacking them in the dishwasher. She didn't remember parenting being this difficult when Flora and Jamie were Arni's age, but then there had been two parents, and she'd had a job that flexed. For all his faults, she had to admit that Matt had been a good father, setting clear rules and establishing boundaries. Her job had been unconditional love. She sensed that Arni needed something different from her right now.

But what exactly?

Julie listened to an audiobook as she drove to Hartlepool, the road as familiar as her own hands on the steering wheel. The traffic was lighter at the weekend, and she arrived early, in time to lend the CSI team a hand with a fingertip search. After an hour on the marina, her fingers were numb, and she was glad to have an appointment to go to.

In the harbourmaster's office, Julie sat beside a heater and wrapped her fingers around a mug of hot chocolate, letting the warmth restore her equilibrium. Nitrile gloves were important for preserving evidence, but they weren't a lot of use for keeping hands warm.

A few minutes after ten, the door flew open and DS Iain Wharton appeared in the doorway, a chilly blast of air blowing past him. He failed to spot his boss in the corner by the heater, marching over to the woman at the printer.

'Cleveland Police,' he announced. 'I have an appointment with the harbourmaster. Can you tell him I'm here?'

In the nook beside the heater, Julie cringed. Iain was a bull in a china shop. Was it self-importance that made him so loud? Or a deep sense of insecurity for which he was constantly compensating? Overcompensating. He wasn't the brightest light in the harbour, but she'd worked with dimmer ones. None quite as unreconstructed though.

The woman extended a hand. 'Vera Enright, Harbourmaster.'

DS Wharton did a double-take. 'You're the harbourmaster?'

'That's right,' she said.

He shook her hand, inspecting her carefully. 'Shouldn't you call yourself harbourmistress instead?'

'Heavens above.' Vera's eyes twinkled. 'You're the first person ever to suggest that!'

The sarcasm was lost on him.

'It would avoid confusion—' he began.

'I guess it's because the word *mistress*,' Vera raised her voice, talking over him, 'is more often associated with a kept woman, a woman who has an illicit extramarital sexual relationship with a man in return for financial support. I tend to avoid terms that can only be applied to women in a derogatory fashion. You know, like promiscuous, nymphomaniac, slut and whore.'

Iain's jaw dropped.

Vera smiled and continued. 'Whereas *master* suggests authority and control, and when you're dealing with something as unpredictable as the North Sea, I prefer the illusion of strength.'

Julie emerged from the corner.

'Sit down, Sergeant,' she said. 'You're late.'

DS Wharton slunk into a seat.

'Here's the list you asked for, DI Cadell.' The harbourmaster pulled a few sheets of paper from the printer and passed them over. 'There are five hundred berths, but only one hundred and twelve are occupied right now,' she said. 'Most are moored for the winter. I've marked up a map of the boats to show which ones have regular visitors – some people spend time on their boats even when they're not sailing.'

'What about vessel movements on Wednesday night?'

'We had five ships seek shelter before the storm. Three left early the following morning, the other two are still here to repair damage.'

'We'll start with the boats still here. What about those that left before the body was discovered? How do we get in touch with them?'

'Two headed south. I've tracked down the yacht *Aquamarine* – it's based in Scarborough marina. The fishing boat *Gallant* was heading back out to sea. I'll print out the owners' contact details.' Vera clicked some keys on her desktop and the printer whirred into action again. 'The third boat was going north. I'm just checking with the Aberdeen coastguard.'

'Aberdeen?'

'That's the HM Coastguard Centre for Scotland,' she said. 'They'll know where the *Lainey Rose* is now.'

At the mention of the *Lainey Rose*, DS Wharton sat forward.

Julie cut in before he could say anything.

'We'll want to speak to the skippers of each boat, and any crew members who might have witnessed something on Wednesday night.'

'Understood.'

Julie could feel the tension radiating from DS Wharton.

'My colleague has been checking the CCTV,' she said, and nodded at him to speak.

'Were there any reports of a fight aboard the Scottish fishing boat?'

'*Lainey Rose*?' Vera shook her head. 'Not that I know of. Were the police called?'

'No,' DS Wharton said.

Vera looked at the berth map. 'Talk to Mr Collins. He owns *Silver Spirit* on Berth Eighty Four. Not much gets past him and his wife, and I know they were carrying out maintenance on Wednesday.'

DS Wharton bounded out of the office. Julie hung back.

'Thank you,' she said.

'You really think your man fell off a boat in the marina?' Vera asked.

Fell, or was pushed? Murdered on a boat then dumped in the water? But why the delay after the stabbing? And why tip the corpse into the marina? If you were going to dispose of a body, why not sail out to sea? There had been plenty of time before the storm.

'Investigation is a process of elimination,' Julie said. 'We have to explore everything in order to rule it in or out.'

'Well, if there's anything I can help with,' Vera said, 'just let me know.'

Outside the harbourmaster's office, DS Wharton displayed a new energy. He moved from foot to foot, a coiled spring ready to jump into action.

'Shall I follow up on the *Lainey Rose*?'

He wanted this so badly, she was tempted to refuse.

HR had told her, in confidence, that DS Wharton's bias for action, his evident antipathy towards the painstaking trawl that made up most of modern police work, was one of the reasons he had repeatedly missed out on promotion. If she was to be a good boss to this difficult man, she should be coaching him through his weaknesses rather than pandering to his preferences.

What was it that made this man tick? He craved male company, especially the sort of company where his police badge made him top dog. He was desperate to escape the tedium of CCTV tapes and supermarket phone calls: to swap thoroughness for drama and conflict.

On the other hand, he displayed an experienced cop's sixth sense. Follow the trouble. If she went south to talk to the Humber coastguard, it made sense to send him north.

The chase after the *Lainey Rose* could serve as the reward for the hard graft of interviewing witnesses.

'Thank you, DS Wharton,' she said. 'But first things first. Speak to all the potential witnesses in the marina, including Mr Collins,' she said.

His face fell.

'I'll head back to the office, talk to the Scottish and Yorkshire police and see if they can spare someone to interview the crews of the boats local to them.'

'But what if . . .'

She held up a hand.

'Once we know where the *Lainey Rose* has docked, I'll decide how to follow up.'

Bridge Street HQ was quiet on a Saturday afternoon. Most of those working the weekend were keeping an eye on sporting events. She contacted the Yorkshire force first, then the Scottish and Borders Police. Neither could promise anything before a manning review on Monday, but nor did they have any objection to the Cleveland police following up by themselves. Territory was less important than budgets.

A message from the Humber coastguard informed her that the model was almost finished.

Julie called Sienna Sutton.

'Are you working tomorrow?' Julie asked.

'Can do.'

'Then I'll swing by early afternoon.'

As she was writing up her notes, a message came in from the harbour-master.

The Aberdeen coastguard reported that the *Lainey Rose* had docked at Eyemouth, but it was heading out tomorrow for a herring run which meant a week or more at sea.

She called DS Wharton and gave him the news.

'Once you've finished the interviews at the marina, I suggest you head up to Eyemouth.'

'Yes, ma'am.' He couldn't hide his glee.

Julie spent an hour and a small fortune in the supermarket on the way home. After unpacking the food, she cooked a shepherd's pie for Sunday and then threw together a quick stir fry with noodles for herself. She'd just sat down for a solitary TV dinner when Flora called.

'Mum, there's an emergency.'

Julie sat up so fast her plate tipped, the noodles slithering over the side and onto the carpet.

'Darling, are you OK?'

'Can't chat now. I just need to know how to make an apple pie.'

Julie looked down at her ruined dinner and sighed.

'And how is that an emergency?'

She went to the kitchen to get a cloth and some water.

'Look.'

The phone lit up with a picture of pastry, a lacy mess almost as bad as the one on her carpet.

'Did you make the pastry yourself?'

'I tried.'

'Is there any dough left?'

'Yes, but it's like breadcrumbs. It won't roll.'

'Add a bit of cold water – just a tiny bit.'

'Now it's all sticky.'

'Put lots of flour on a flat surface, roll the sticky stuff around in it until it's doughy. Then wrap it in cling film and stick it in the fridge for an hour.'

'I can't afford an hour. I've got someone coming round to dinner in ten minutes.'

Julie scraped her own spilt dinner from the floor back onto her plate.

'Someone nice?'

'Not like that. Should I have cooked the apples first?'

'Are they Bramleys? Proper cooking apples?'

'Just regular eating ones.'

'Then best if you peel and core and cut them up thin and simmer with a tiny bit of sugar and lemon.'

'I don't have any lemon. Will orange juice do?'

'No. Use water, but just a drop, OK? Enough to stop them burning.'

'How long for?'

'Until soft.'

'How long is that?'

'Five mins, max.'

'Thanks, Mum. Bye.'

As Julie scrubbed the soy sauce stain from the carpet it occurred to her that her daughter never asked – even in passing – how she was. Which was understandable. Good parenting ought to be taken for granted. A parent's job was to be supportive, helpful, invisible. But these days, Flora never even asked about Arni and that was unlike her – she adored her baby brother. Maybe they chatted on WhatsApp. Perhaps Flora knew exactly what was going on in Arni's teenage brain. Next time they spoke, Julie would ask her advice.

Julie chose a new book, one that didn't smell of fish, and went to bed.

Chapter 10

Arni was still asleep when Julie left on Sunday morning. She'd considered taking him a cup of tea, but it was grey and rainy outside, and she didn't think he'd be thrilled about missing his once-a-week opportunity for a lie-in.

The sun was low in the sky as she approached Whitby. The moors road would be packed with beachgoers on summer weekends, but on an early November day it was almost empty.

She wondered if Arni was up yet. At least he'd find the fridge full again and tonight's dinner already made. When she got back, they could go through his school clothes, see if there was any hem left to take down on his trousers. If not, they could order new ones.

She didn't pay much attention to the motorbike behind her until the driver started flashing his headlight at her. She indicated left and began braking, pulling into a woody lay-by where she rolled down her window. The reflection in the rear-view mirror showed the motorbike pulling in behind her car. She watched as the rider dismounted and rocked it onto the centre stand. He – through the leathers she could tell the rider was male: yes, most definitely a man – walked towards her car, removed his helmet.

'DI Cadell.' He smiled, his teeth even whiter than she remembered. 'Long time, no see.'

'DI Riley.' She frowned. 'Am I under arrest?'

He reached into a side pocket and withdrew a pair of handcuffs. 'It can be arranged.' He dangled them through the window.

'On what charge?'

'Driving while failing to admire the view.'

Now she grinned, opened the door, got out of the car and embraced him.

He put an arm round her shoulder and turned her so they could both see the autumn forest, the moors and the coastline below. The rain had become a fine mist and a double rainbow filled the sky.

'How have you been?' she asked.

'No one to fight with since you left.' He sighed.

She elbowed him in the ribs. They'd applied for the same promotion. DI Caron Riley had been successful, she had not. It had made the decision to transfer from the North Yorks force to Cleveland Police much easier. Julie had needed a fresh start in more ways than one.

'What brings you up to the moors?'

He let go of her.

'Just out for a ride.' He smiled. 'Chasing rainbows and pointing them out to those too lost in contemplation to notice.' He met her eyes. 'And you? What brings you out this way?'

'Murder inquiry. Following up potential witnesses.' She pointed south. 'On my way to Scarborough.'

He nodded. 'Let me know if you need any support.'

'I will,' she said. 'Thank you.'

'How's Flora?' he asked.

Caron had arranged work experience for her daughter with the family veterinary practice.

'Enjoying uni,' Julie said. 'Lots of friends.'

'And Arni?'

She grimaced and sighed. 'A moody teenager.'

'He'll grow out of it. Is he planning to follow his siblings . . .'

Just the tiniest of pauses and then he continued.

'To uni?'

'Right now, he's obsessed with hockey. Or at least, obsessed with the captain of the female team.'

Caron laughed.

'What about you?' Julie asked. 'How's . . .'

She struggled to remember his wife's name.

The sound of motorbikes roaring up the hill filled an awkward silence.

'Got to go.' Caron pulled on his helmet.

As he passed her on his bike, he raised a leather gauntlet in farewell.

Julie remained outside her car for a while, contemplating the view.

The heavens opened as Julie turned into Foreshore Road in Scarborough. She parked and ran through the rain to the the café overlooking West Pier. Dr Andy Gower, a local GP and owner of the yacht *Aquamarine*, and his friend Roland Trust, were waiting for her inside.

The interview took less time than their coffee. The two men had been heading down the east coast after a few days of holiday, exploring the Farne Islands from Amble. They'd hoped to make it back to Scarborough on the day before Storm Babel, but as the gale warnings became increasingly alarming, they'd elected to duck into Hartlepool Marina and spent the night in one of the quayside hotels. Neither of them had seen or heard a thing.

Dr Gower offered her a tour of the yacht, but Julie declined. It was a pocket-sized yacht compared to others in the marina. Julie had a hard time imagining two men fitting into the boat, let alone three.

Back in the car, she logged her report and checked for news from DS Wharton.

Nothing.

She texted him with a reminder that every interview should be logged.

It was still raining when she arrived in Bridlington. Julie drove straight to the Humber Maritime Rescue Coordination Centre, a large white building at the end of North Promenade with a panoramic view over the bay. Inside the operations room, Sienna Sutton was waiting for her in front of a bank of computer screens. Her hair was cut very short, dyed purple, and her ears had multiple piercings, the studs glittering under the control centre lights. The uniform of the HM Coastguard, a short-sleeved white shirt with black and gold epaulettes, revealed arms covered in tattoos.

She got to her feet and held out a hand. 'DI Cadell.'

'Call me Julie, please.'

'Sienna.' Her grip was warm and firm.

'The model is all set up and ready to go.' Sienna pulled a second chair up to her workstation. 'Any progress with the investigation?'

'We're speaking to everyone who was in the marina at the time the victim went into the water, but so far we have no eyewitnesses.'

'Did he drown?'

'No.' Julie shook her head. 'The pathologist reckons he was dead several hours before he entered the water.'

'Any idea how long he was in the water?'

'Less than a day.'

'And you want to know how far a body might have travelled in that time?'

'Exactly.'

'Time of interest is the night of the sixth of November, right?'

'Right.'

'I've just received real-time data from Storm Babel and loaded it up.' Sienna stood up. 'Let's get a cup of tea while the model's running.'

Julie followed her to a small kitchenette with a kettle and fridge and watched as her host measured out an exact amount of leaf tea and added boiling water to a ceramic teapot.

'Let me show you something while it's brewing.' Sienna opened the door to a large meeting room, the walls covered with maps and charts.

Julie followed the coastguard to a map of Britain.

'The coastal sea currents flow mainly north to south.' Sienna waved her hand down the east coast, from the Firth of Forth above Edinburgh to the Humber estuary below Hull.

'It would be hard to get a dead body into the sea from most of these beaches.' She tapped the mouth of the Tyne then ran her finger down the smooth coastline. 'Too shallow.' Her finger stopped just above Hartlepool, almost exactly halfway between the north coast of Scotland and the south coast of England where an outcrop of land stuck out into the sea. 'Anything travelling close to shore wouldn't make it round this headland.'

She stepped sideways to a more detailed map of the river, the Tees Estuary forming an open mouth under the headland's hooked nose.

'The River Tees discharges into the North Sea and flows south.' Sienna ran her hand down the coast from the Tees to the Humber.

'So, what you're saying is that there's no way a body could have floated into the marina from the sea, either from the north or the south,' Julie said.

'The first time I ran the model it gave a zero point zero zero one per cent probability,' Sienna said. 'Which was why I suggested you start with the marina.'

'Isn't there a river that runs in from the west? The Hart Beck?'

Sienna shook her head. 'It's more of a stream, and it runs underground through a series of grates before discharging to the north.' She tapped the map. 'Let's see if that tea is ready.'

They returned to the kitchen. Sienna put a splash of milk in each mug and then filled them up with strong, brown tea.

They returned to the workstation and Sienna tapped a few keys.

'Oh, now that's interesting,' she said.

Julie took a sip of tea. 'How so?'

'The data from Storm Babel changes everything.'

Julie stared at the swirling patterns on the screen, moving whorls of blue and red and green and yellow.

'Can you explain?'

'The night your guy was murdered, the rivers were in spate. When that happens, you get some unusual currents in the estuary.'

'Unusual how?'

'Spinning eddies,' she said. An anticlockwise swirl at the mouth of the Tees.'

Julie leant in, transfixed by the gyrating spirals.

'So, he could have come down the River Tees?'

'Contrary to everything I said before.' Sienna smiled. 'It's a definite possibility.'

She tapped some more keys, and a contoured map appeared on the screen.

'In twenty-four hours in storm conditions a body could have travelled almost twenty miles. The overflow channels at the Tees Barrage were opened before the storm – I checked – so the locus of possibility goes back almost as far upriver as Yarm.'

Julie sat back.

'What time was high tide on the night of November sixth?' she asked.

'Just after midnight.'

'The body was first spotted in the marina about twelve hours later. Can you run the model again for twelve hours instead of twenty-four?'

Sienna tapped some keys and then sat back, sipping her tea.

A new map flashed onto the screen. This time the contours stopped at the Riverside Stadium in Middlesbrough.

'A better option if you wanted to dispose of a body,' Sienna said. 'The river is channelled into a man-made canal downstream of the Transporter Bridge. The banks are steep, and the water is deep.'

Julie nodded. 'And there's plenty of industrial wasteland.'

'I've been using the model in reverse,' Sienna said. 'Starting from where you found the body and asking it to plot where it might have come from. Let me run it again, but this time going forward.'

'Not sure I understand.'

'Let's assume the body went in at midnight. I'll drop it in at half-mile intervals from the Transporter Bridge onwards and use the real-time weather data to see how likely it is to have ended up in the marina within twelve hours.'

'OK.'

'From all the data – forward and in reverse – I can build you a composite map which gives you the probabilities for each location. Might help you narrow your search.'

'How long will that take?'

Sienna glanced up at a clock on the wall. 'I'll set it to run overnight,' she said. 'You'll have the results in your inbox first thing tomorrow morning.'

Julie stood. 'Thank you.'

'Bear in mind that the model is an approximation. The output is expressed in probabilities,' Sienna said. 'You may have other, more useful clues as to where he came from. Can you tell anything from the clothing?'

Julie debated how much to say. 'The clothing isn't helpful.'

'Did any other stuff wash up with him?'

'Yes, we're following that up.'

Sienna nodded. 'Best of luck,' she said.

The sun had dropped below the clouds, illuminating the golden sands of Bridlington Bay as Julie filed her report. She pondered her discussion with the coastguard as she headed inland to pick up the fast road north. The coastal road might be beautiful, but it was slow, and darkness was already falling.

She listened to the radio until the opening synth chords of 'Talk' by Khalid filled the car with memories and a lump formed in her throat.

A sandy beach. A blue sky.

Don't go there. Not now. Stay in the moment. Focus on the job.

She turned off the radio and drove the rest of the way in silence, brain whirring, trying to link the new findings to those of the post-mortem. Why had the murderers delayed disposal of the body? Were they waiting for high tide? Hoping that the body would be swept out to sea and never found? If so, they reckoned without Storm Babel.

Someone had gone to a lot of trouble to disguise the man's identity. Removing all personal effects. Dressing him in new clothes. If his identity was so critical to his killers, then it must be key to solving this case. Until she found out who the victim was, where he was murdered, what he was doing before his murder, she had no idea why anyone would want to kill him. And without an identity, location or motive, how was she to find the culprits and bring them to justice?

When Julie got home, she was ravenous. She opened the fridge only to find that Arni had polished off the shepherd's pie. All of it. She could have wept.

He'd left a note.

Gone out with Eve. Back late.

She made herself an omelette and turned on the TV, channel-hopping as she ate, trying to find something immersive, but nothing grabbed her attention.

Trouser hems. That's what she could do.

Arni's room was tidier than usual. Probably Eve's influence. The bed was made, the cups and plates had been returned to the kitchen and the magazines and books were in a pile.

Her son's approach to tidying his clothes centred around hiding them away. She found two pairs of school trousers stuffed into the bottom of the wardrobe. Fishing them out, she inspected the hems. No more than an inch, was that enough? On one pair, the waist button was also missing. Probably time to bite the bullet and order new clothes.

Something fell out of a pocket. Square and silver. A condom packet.

Julie stared at it.

Well, what did she expect? At least he and Eve had the sense to take precautions.

At a noise behind her, she whirled round.

'What are you doing in my bedroom?'

Arni stood in the doorway.

'I was just . . .' She held up the trousers.

'Snooping,' he finished for her. He scooped up the silver packet, walked over to his desk, put it in a drawer and turned on his computer.

'Arni! I . . .'

He turned on her then, his face distorted with anger, advancing towards her.

She stood her ground.

'Look, it's OK,' she began.

'GET OUT!' he screamed, his face a rictus of rage.

She stood frozen in horror, unable to recognise her own son as he put his hands on her shoulders, propelled her from the room and locked the door.

Julie went to bed, defeated and troubled.

Chapter 11

The coastguard was true to her word. When Julie arrived in the office on Monday morning, an email was waiting for her with a link to the updated model output. Julie clicked to upload the new map of location probabilities and went to make a cup of tea.

DC Gibson intercepted her in the corridor. 'Morning, boss,' he said. 'Good weekend?'

Without waiting for a reply, he handed her a large envelope.

Inside was the police artist's reconstruction sketch. She studied it carefully. Without the bruising and the swelling, the deceased had once been a good-looking man. No single feature stood out, but in combination, his face was unique. Someone would be able to identify him.

'What do you think?' DC Gibson asked.

'Looks pretty good.'

'Comms want to know if you're OK for a press conference this afternoon.'

'Yes,' she said. 'No later than four o'clock, please.' She needed to talk to Arni, find out what on earth had prompted his outburst last night. and that meant getting away on time for once.

DC Gibson nodded. 'I'll let them know.'

When Julie got back to her computer, it was to find that the download had failed, referred to IT for cybersecurity checks. She called the IT helpdesk and

65

trudged through interminable automated options. As she progressed up the Monday-morning queue, she sipped her tea. It tasted insipid compared to the Yorkshire brew Sienna had served. Maybe she should stop using cheap teabags and invest in a pot. The tea was cold before she spoke to a person who promised to speed up the checks and release the file as soon as possible.

Julie opened the case file and tried to read between the lines of DS Iain Wharton's terse weekend report.

After speaking to the couple on Berth 84 – who confirmed that there had been an altercation aboard the *Lainey Rose* – he'd driven up to Eyemouth to interview Captain Curry and the crew before the trawler left on the Sunday tide. The argument had been about shore leave. It had been quickly resolved and no one was missing.

There was a bad-tempered brevity in DS Wharton's report. This had been his lead, and he'd craved the glory of solving the case single-handedly. It was now clear that the whole incident aboard the trawler was another red herring.

An activity log from this morning informed her that DS Wharton was back at the marina to finish taking witness statements.

Two things infuriated her about this. The first was that she'd told him to finish the interviews before going north, the second was that he clearly hadn't read the report she'd filed yesterday before leaving Bridlington. The new information from the coastguard, using the data from Storm Babel, showed that the body could have been washed down the River Tees, in which case he was probably wasting his time in the marina. She debated calling him and ordering him back to the office but decided against it. In the interests of thoroughness, he might as well finish what he'd started.

Now, what about the map?

A message from IT informed her that the attachment from HM Coastguard had passed its cybersecurity check and was ready to download. But when she tried to open it, she got an error message.

Cursing, she rang IT and went through the option dance. No, I have not forgotten my username or password. No, I'm not experiencing any printer problems. She keyed in **0 to cut to the 'speak to a real person' option.

'IT Helpdesk, here. Martin speaking. How may I help you?'

'I'm trying to open a document from HM Coastguard.'

'OK, let me take a look.'

He took her through the usual security questions – date of birth, mother's maiden name, postcode.

'I just need to jump onto your computer if that's OK.'

A dialogue box appeared on the new laptop.

'Can you click accept?' he asked.

Julie did as she was told and watched as the cursor started moving all by itself. Windows opened and closed and lines of incomprehensible code, white on black, started scrolling across the screen.

'What are you doing?' Julie asked.

'Loading the extra drivers you'll need for the file.'

'How long will that take?'

'Hmm. This is not straightforward. Who did you say the map was from?'

'HM Coastguard.'

'Can you get back in touch and ask if they can send the file in another format?'

'Like what?'

'A pdf?'

'It's an interactive map.'

'I'm afraid we don't support the software.'

'And yet it's OK for HM Coastguard? Aren't we both government agencies?'

'The IT support function comes from an external service provider. And HM Coastguard and Cleveland Police use different IT contractors.'

Julie sighed. 'I'm in the middle of an active investigation. I need this information.'

'If you get back to HM Coastguard, I'm sure they can send the file to you in a more acceptable format. Any problem, just get back to the helpdesk.'

'But—'

'Is there anything else I can help you with?'

'No thanks.'

'You'll be asked to rate the service you've received today.'

Julie cut the call with a bad-tempered growl.

DC Gibson knocked and poked his head round the open door.

'Comms are arranging the press conference for four p.m.'

'Good,' Julie said.

'I'm heading off to speak to the gardening wholesaler on Mainsforth Terrace.'

Julie nodded. 'OK.'

'And I thought you should know,' his voice dropped to a whisper. 'The super is on his way up.'

Superintendent Chalmers marched into her office and picked up the sketch.

'Does it look like him?' he asked.

'As far as I can tell.'

'What time are you briefing the press?'

'Four o'clock, sir.'

'I think I'll come along.'

Julie's heart sank. Her talk with Arni would have to wait. Maybe it was as well. Let him cool off first.

'I'll move it to six p.m. so it can go out live on the evening news.'

Julie bit her lip to stifle a protest. If that was the best time to gain the widest audience, then so be it. Her official working hours, after all, were the hours needed to get the job done. Patching things up with Arni would have to wait.

'Yes, sir.'

After her boss left, Julie found it hard to concentrate.

Why had Superintendent Chalmers insisted on attending the press conference? Didn't he trust her? Or was it because he liked to hog the limelight, to make everything about him? She sighed. His presence was going to interfere with the simple message she wanted to give.

Who is the man in the morgue?

Chapter 12

The audience chatter grew louder as the three representatives of Cleveland Police entered the press conference: first, Claire Darling from Corporate Communications, then DI Julie Cadell and Superintendent Graham Chalmers from Serious Crimes. As they settled on the podium, the screens behind them lit up with the logo for Cleveland Police and its brand-new animated strapline: Transparency, Impartiality, Public Service, Integrity.

The room was packed; even the press officer seemed a little taken aback at the numbers.

'I think we might have a problem,' Claire whispered. 'We have reporters from the *Yorkshire Post* and *Private Eye.*'

'Must be a slow day in the cesspit of journalism,' muttered the super. 'Just make sure we don't stray off topic.'

'Off topic?'

Julie raised an eyebrow in enquiry, but the press officer shook her head.

'Not now,' she mouthed.

Claire spoke first. She gave a brief introduction, set out the rules of engagement and then Superintendent Chalmers read out a statement.

'On Thursday morning, the body of a man was discovered in the water of Hartlepool Historic Quay. A murder inquiry has been launched. DI Julie Cadell is leading the investigation.'

Julie took over. 'We are appealing to the public to help us identify the victim, a man of South Asian ethnicity, aged between thirty and forty, height six foot two inches, weight around twelve stone.'

The screens showed the police artist's sketch of the dead man's face.

'Anyone who recognises this man and can tell us when he was last seen alive, who he was with and what might have happened to him can contact the police direct or anonymously through Crimestoppers.'

The Crimestoppers logo and number flashed onto the screen.

'The press briefing is up on the Cleveland Police website.'

Claire stood up and waved some folders. 'And I have hard copies here for anyone who wants one.' A handful of journalists raised their hands, and Claire distributed the printed packs. 'And now, any questions?'

There were a few questions. How did he die. No comment. What was he wearing. No comment.

Vikram from the *Yorkshire Post* stood up. 'Do the police have any leads?'

Julie nodded. 'We're following up several lines of enquiry.'

'We won't hold our breath, then,' he said. 'Only ten per cent of recorded crime in Cleveland is ever solved.'

A ripple of amusement ran round the room.

'But then, many crimes aren't even reported, are they?' Vikram said. 'Superintendent Chalmers, perhaps you'd like to tell us what happens to drunk drivers if they happen to be serving police officers.'

Claire intervened. 'We're here to talk about a murder inquiry, Vikram.'

'Where it matters even more that evidence is kept secure. If you can't even keep track of a blood test on your own—'

'Save your point-scoring for another occasion!' Claire interrupted. The press officer might be small, but she could bellow like an ox. Even the mighty Vikram seemed momentarily cowed.

'And when will that occasion be, Claire?' he said, softly. 'When will the fourth estate get to hold the police to account?'

'You're in the wrong place, mate,' Claire said. 'Take a wrong turn on the A19? Yorkshire's down that way.' She pointed south. 'Now, any questions from the Teesside press?'

'I like the new logo,' shouted someone from the back. 'Transparency, Impartiality, Public Service, Integrity. TIPSI? Or should that be TIPSY, which sort of sums up Cleveland Police.'

The room erupted with laughter.

The superintendent rose to his feet, face red with fury.

'This press conference is over.'

'What was all that about?' Julie asked Claire as Superintendent Chalmers hurried away.

'Haven't you heard? It's an old story. Apparently a man was reported driving erratically after leaving a North Yorkshire pub. Bit of a car chase. When they finally caught him, he was over the county border with Cleveland. Turned out he was a senior officer, off-duty. He refused to be breathalysed, so they took him to the nearest station for a blood test. Cleveland Police "lost" the sample. No evidence, no charge.'

'Ah . . . I see.'

'That acronym though.' Claire swore under her breath. 'TIPSI. How could I not have spotted that?'

Chapter 13

BRIAN

Stockton-on-Tees – Monday, 11 November 2024

When Brian got out of bed on Monday, the day was almost over. That was the trouble with weekend gaming tournaments – you could only pull so many all-nighters before your body gave in. The low afternoon sun cast a rosy light over the clean and tidy flat as he checked his phone.

Teesside was trending on social media. Not the usual factory closures and lay-offs, this was Cleveland Police again. They'd really made the big time with their new logo: *Transparency, Impartiality, Public Service, Integrity.* Forwards it spelt TIPSI – quite appropriate after a senior officer caught drunk driving was never charged because his blood sample was 'lost'. Backwards it spelt I SPIT – which was the public's general response to the rebranding. Brian clicked through to the clip of the press conference, then froze. A pencil portrait flashed onto the screen, a police artist's sketch of a bearded man. The victim of a murder in Hartlepool.

That couldn't be Dameer, could it? Surely not.

Brian opened his laptop and typed in the company name: Zebra Safety Solutions.

The website wasn't particularly informative, a business-to-business listing by a distributor based in Dubai. He clicked on 'Meet the Team'. It was just a small outfit, but one of those irritating companies that insisted on showing you a presentation rather than allowing you to cut to the chase. First came managing director, Uzain Bagra. The face of a bearded man filled the screen, but he was older than the man on the Crimestoppers sketch. The Europe representative, a fresh-faced, clean-shaven young man by the name of Hans Guttner, smiled back at him. Middle Eastern sales were handled by the MD himself. The Indian subcontinent was in the hands of a Singh Patel, who had a face as round and fat as a full moon. The US representative was a woman with big hair. Finally, the technical director appeared. And there he was, Dameer Ghosh.

Shit.

Brian clicked on the website for the local newspaper, cursing at the adverts, until he found the police drawing.

He brought up the two photographs on his gaming screen and positioned them side by side. No, the faces were different. It wasn't Dameer in the police sketch. Definitely not.

He put the lasagne in the oven and turned it up to full heat. Back at the computer, he opened a face-recognition program. Eighty-eight per cent match.

Shit. No way.

Should he call the police? After his last run-in with them, it was not such a good idea.

He'd been genuinely worried about Betty. Yes, they'd had a fight. Yes, she'd taken her things and left. But then she went completely silent. She stopped answering his calls, vanished from social media, didn't show up in person for the pub quiz – which he almost understood – or even their online Dungeons and Dragons – which mystified him.

He asked people if they'd seen her, heard from her, but got nothing back except embarrassed silence. They told him to move on. No one except him seemed at all concerned by her absence from her usual places.

He began to imagine things. Bad things. They'd met online, chatted for hours before they met in person. Which was just as well as he'd probably never have fancied her if he'd just met her in the street. She might be a big lass, but her aura was beautiful: soft and warm and more than a little spicy.

In that golden time, when they were first together and completely immersed in one another, she'd told him about some bad dating experiences she'd had. She made the stories sound funny, but he thought they were downright scary.

What if she'd gone back online, met a serial killer, gone to his place and all that was left of her was bits in a garage chest freezer? All her other friends were just like, don't be daft. Was he the only one who really cared?

In retrospect, it had been a bad idea to go to the police after the pub quiz. He should have gone before, when he was still sober. But it was losing the pub quiz, something that had never happened in all the time they'd played in a team together, that made her absence suddenly unbearable.

At the police station he tried to report Betty as a missing person. They didn't exactly laugh at him but the more he explained, the more foolish he felt. He saw himself reflected though their eyes: a balding, middle-aged, overweight biker without a bike (he never drove Magnus when drinking), without a job and without a girl. A loser who was out of touch with reality.

They reminded him that it wasn't the first time he'd wasted police time. Which was completely unfair, as the first time it had been his employer that had wasted their time. Everyone knew – including the site manager – that Tad the Pole had been stealing from the stores. It was HR that decided not to pursue criminal charges. Betty's disappearance was completely different.

Betty's sister had called him the next day and told him to stop pestering their family. That Betty was fine and taking a break to recover.

Recover? Recover from what? From him? What was he – a bad dose of flu?

He didn't leave the house for days after that. His expedition to the garden centre café, to talk to a man about a job, had been his first step on the road to his own recovery from humiliation.

He wasn't about to put himself through all that again.

If the dead body in Hartlepool really was Dameer Ghosh, someone else would identify him. Dameer had flown in from India. He must have passed though passport control, taken a taxi, booked into a hotel, arranged meetings at all the engineering companies who regularly procured electronic components.

Brian cracked open a can of beer and took a long sip. It wasn't up to him to provide the police with information. Plenty of fellow travellers would recognise Dameer.

The lasagne smelt ready. Serves two, it lied. He ate it in front of the TV, half watching a rerun of *Disasters Engineered*.

He'd chosen the programme because – as a control engineer – the first section on the Chernobyl accident fascinated him. When the topic moved on to a disaster in India, he grunted with irritation.

India. Dameer.

What was it with the universe today? Morphic resonance. Sending him signals he really didn't want to receive.

He took another sip of beer and flicked through the free channels, failing to find something distracting.

What if the others who'd seen Dameer didn't know his name? Was the police sketch good enough for anyone to make the connection? Were others as observant as he was? Did they have access to the sort of software he'd used?

What had happened to the dead man, whether he was Dameer or not? The police reported that they were treating his death as suspicious.

All the more reason not to get involved.

The dead man in Hartlepool could be anyone. Face recognition software was only as good as the information you fed it. Confirmation bias made it easy to draw the wrong conclusions.

He should know.

He didn't need to do anything.

He wasn't going to do anything.

Someone else would identify the dead man in Hartlepool.

It probably wasn't even Dameer Ghosh.

Chapter 14

JULIE

Middlesbrough – Tuesday, 12 November 2024

Julie arrived early at the office, ruminating on the car crash of a press conference. What could she have done differently? How could she have dissuaded Superintendent Chalmers from attending? It wasn't as if she could order her boss to stay away. Should she have enlisted Claire's help beforehand? The press officer might have held sway.

It was times like this that she missed her old boss in the North Yorkshire police service. Stuart supported his officers rather than getting in their way. But then in her old job she'd never had to lead a press conference. As a part-time police sergeant, she'd always been in the back room, making sure things ran smoothly for others, giving the inspectors all the information they needed. Doing the work that DS Wharton should be concentrating on.

Could she blame her boss and sergeant for the mess? Or did she have to admit the responsibility was hers?

In the police leadership course she'd attended, they'd had a workshop on the Peter Principle, the theory that people are promoted to their level of incompetence. What if she'd smashed through the glass ceiling, earned promotion from part-time DS to full-time DI only to discover she wasn't up to the job?

And it wasn't only work that was troubling her. She'd arrived home too tired to face another fight with her son and he'd left the house this morning while she was still in the shower. She couldn't let the personal interfere with the professional.

Julie opened the case file and stared at the sketch of the mystery man. The artist had caught something special, the spirit of the man, a quiet beauty.

Someone had to care more about the victim than their own careers. Someone had to go beyond the usual suspects to find his killers.

And stop them ever killing again.

Julie called her team into the office. The contrast between the eager face of DC Gibson and the thundering gloom of DS Wharton was almost comical. She turned first to her sergeant.

'Tell me what you found at the marina.'

DS Wharton ran through his interviews, all inconclusive.

'Just the other fishing boat left to track down,' he said. 'The *Gallant*.'

'Forget it,' she said.

'But—'

'We have progress,' she said, swinging the monitor round to show him a map open on her screen. It had taken three tries and several IT interventions to obtain the coastguard information in a form she could access - a series of screenshots.

'The night of Storm Babel the River Tees was in flood. The Tees Barrage overflow was opened, leading to some unusual currents in the estuary. The coastguard now believes our victim could have been swept down the river, from as far upstream as here.'

She pointed to the container port.

'Which ties in rather neatly with some real intelligence DC Gibson collected yesterday.'

The constable beamed and Julie gestured for him to share his news.

'I visited the gardening wholesaler off Mainsforth Terrace in Hartlepool,' he said. 'The rubbish we found with the body couldn't have come from there.' DC Gibson drew pointed to the map on the screen. 'There's a road and a railway line and no drainage between the warehouse and the sea. But the owner did recognise the bug spray. He said that sort of stuff isn't made in the UK anymore, it's all imported and comes in through the container port at South Bank.'

Julie had read the report that DC Gibson had filed last night after attempting – and failing – to have a civilised conversation with Arni. The report might have a few grammatical and spelling errors, but it was thorough. Unlike DS Wharton's brief postings.

'Excellent work, DC Gibson!'

Her constable flushed with pleasure.

'You want me to go and check it out?' DS Wharton asked.

Julie shook her head. 'Where are we with the Asda CCTV footage?'

'Nothing yet,' he began.

'Then that's your priority,' Julie said. 'I need something before we brief the super tomorrow.'

DS Wharton scowled.

'DC Gibson,' she said. 'Grab a pool car. You and I are going to visit South Bank.'

On the way to the container port, they took a detour via the new Greggs drive-through. Julie bought them both sausage rolls and coffee. Too early to celebrate, but she had a good feeling. Spreading the net wider gave them more chance of catching leads, something that would crack the case.

The gateman issued passes and directed them to the main office block. A receptionist took them up a curved stairway to a conference room with a view of the river and the Seal Sands industrial park beyond.

'Detective Inspector Cadell?' The man who came to meet them was dressed in the kind of suit that cost money. He shook her hand and then advanced towards Chris. 'And you must be . . .'

'DC Gibson.'

'Jorgen Trewick,' the sharp-suited man announced. 'Press and comms.'

Sounded like gym equipment, and when he took his jacket off, Julie could see that he was a man who worked out.

'So, officers.' He smiled to show perfectly white teeth. 'How may I help you?'

'We're investigating the murder of an unidentified man found in Hartlepool Historic Quay,' Julie said.

'A long way from here.'

'Along with the body, we found some gardening-related materials.'

Julie nodded at DC Gibson and he pulled out his list.

'A spray bottle of Provanto,' he said. 'Assorted garden netting, parts of a broken pallet, gardening gloves.'

'Did you take delivery of such items recently?' Julie asked.

Jorgen frowned. 'DI Cadell, how much do you know about container shipping?'

'Very little.' She shrugged. 'That's why we've come to talk to you.'

'We handle half a million containers every year – that's about ten thousand a week.' She could tell that gym bunny director was proud of his statistics. 'Each twenty-foot shipping container is a sealed steel box that could contain a single product – or be made up of literally thousands of individual items.' He smiled his most patronising smile yet. 'So, I'm afraid your question is not one that I can answer.'

'Do you open the containers here?'

'Most of our containers remain sealed. They are removed from the ship by crane and loaded straight onto a lorry or a train and leave the port intact.'

'Don't you inspect what's in them?' DC Gibson asked.

'You'd have to speak to HM Customs about that.' When Jorgen smiled, you practically needed sunglasses for that wattage. 'We receive, unload and load. But there are some containers which contain smaller deliveries for multiple customers. They go to our warehouse for de-stuffing.'

'Dee what?' DC Gibson asked.

'Apologies, it's a technical term.' Jorgen frowned with the effort of trying to find words simple enough for his audience. 'We unpack some containers here.'

'Perhaps,' Julie suggested, 'a tour of the riverfront would help us to understand the scale of your operation.'

'Indeed, I was going to suggest the very same.' The director got to his feet. 'I'll arrange a minibus.'

The port was busy. Seven cranes moved huge steel boxes in a rhythmic dance of lorries and trains, picking them up as if they were as light as Lego bricks. Julie had always thought of a port as a place where lots of thick-necked stevedores toiled. Apart from the crane operators in glass boxes high up above the quay, and the truck and train drivers in their cabs, the place was deserted.

'Can we see the warehouse?' she asked. 'Where you unpack the part shipments?'

'But of course,' Jorgen said. 'We have several, but let's start with the closest one.'

The first warehouse was clean and well organised. The containers were manoeuvred up to a freight door, and then a pallet truck removed the contents directly into the warehouse. Julie marvelled at the array of packages laid in neat rows on the concrete floor. Some sealed – cardboard or wooden boxes – and some wrapped in plastic, crates of onions and trays of beer bottles stacked side by side.

'All the warehouses are much the same.'

And he was right. After the third one, Julie thanked him and suggested they'd seen enough.

Back in the minibus they stopped at a crossroads to let a truck go past. It was transporting a metal container with a squashed corner.

'Do the containers often get damaged?'

'Mistakes happen,' Jorgen confessed. 'But we report and investigate and try to learn when things go wrong.'

'Can we follow that one?' Julie asked.

Jorgen looked at his watch and his mouth tightened.

'I'd like to see where the damaged containers go,' she said.

Jorgen instructed the driver, and they drove away from the cleanest part of the port to a fabrication shop, behind which was a graveyard of containers and beyond it a stretch of waste ground running right down to the river.

'We don't own the containers, but we can do small repairs for the owners or their insurance companies, or arrange a sale.' He smiled. 'They are surprisingly popular round here. Apparently they make excellent temporary kitchens or garden bars.'

'Stop the minibus, please,' Julie said.

'What is it?'

She pointed to a yellow skip.

The skip was overflowing with rubbish that must have been removed from the damaged containers or had blown down from the fabrication shop. There was a little bit of everything in there.

Julie followed the perimeter fence down to the river.

'Look!' she called to DC Gibson.

There it was, a green snake of garden netting, half in and half out of the water. Entangled in its web were two spray bottles with a familiar label – Provanto.

'Gotcha!' Chris punched the air.

'Call Adrian Prosser,' Julie ordered, then turned to her host while Chris made the call.

'Mr Trewick,' she said. 'I'd like to investigate further. Please can you arrange to cordon off this area.'

She waited until her constable had finished the call.

'DC Gibson,' she said. 'Go with Mr Trewick and wait for the search team at reception. I'll wait for you here.'

Julie stood alone beside the river and stared across at the far bank. Between here and Hartlepool lay the Seal Sands chemical complex and more than a century of industrial activity.

She looked down at the grey water. At low tide, the banks of the river channel were exposed, glossy red-brown mud. What secrets ley buried in that sludge? How deep would they have to go to find them?

Chapter 15

Middlesbrough – Tuesday, 12 November 2024

Dr Sandy Armstrong, the Home Office forensic pathologist, had a small office at James Cook University Hospital. Julie waited outside until he raised a hand and waved her in.

'Coffee?' he asked.

'Thank you.' The office might be tiny, but Sandy had his own coffee machine. Judging by the sleek Italian design it belonged to the doctor himself rather than the NHS. She selected a latte, and the machine whirred into action.

She'd been on her way back to HQ when she got Sandy's message and made a detour to the hospital.

'Good weekend?' he asked.

'Chasing boats,' she said. 'A weekend of red herrings.'

'No time for yourself?' He handed her the coffee.

She met his eyes. What was his game exactly? Was he interested in her as a colleague or was he pursuing some other agenda? Divorced men like Sandy – clever and rich, witty and attractive – couldn't have any difficulty finding new partners. Had her refusal to go out for a drink with him wounded his vanity? Piqued his interest? Did she present a challenge? She met his green eyes but could see nothing there except friendly concern. Don't flatter yourself, girl. He knows your history. He's just being kind.

'Do you have children, Sandy?' she asked.

'All grown up.'

'How were the teenage years?'

'Undoubtedly the toughest,' he said. 'The teenage brain is plastic, changing so fast it's hard to keep up. You still got one at home?'

'My youngest boy. We're not on speaking terms at the moment. Any advice?'

'Take time to listen.'

'What do you do when they won't engage?'

'Create the conditions – time, space and place – then wait. Let them control the timing, let them choose when to open up.'

Julie sighed. Time was the one thing they never seemed to have.

'Walks are good,' Sandy continued. 'Occasions where there's another purpose so that the conversation can come naturally. Just the two of you, side by side. Sometimes it's easier to talk when you're not face to face.'

It made sense. Of course it did.

'Thank you.' She finished her coffee and put the empty cup down. 'Any more thoughts on the case?'

'Yes.' Sandy opened his laptop. 'Let me show you something.'

He connected his computer to a wall screen and a black-and-white picture appeared in front of them.

'What am I looking at?' Julie asked. 'Giant teeth?'

'Exactly,' he said. 'See here – he pointed to the bright white pillow nestling between two greyer ones. 'This is an implant – an artificial tooth – between two original ones.'

'Why does the artificial one look brighter?'

'It's denser. The natural enamel of the tooth is a crystalline calcium phosphate – hydroxyapatite, the hardest substance in the body. The implant has a ceramic crown – lithium disilicate in this case. It shows up brighter in X-rays, but was colour-matched to blend in with the original teeth, which is why we didn't notice it during a visual examination.'

She nodded.

'This is the surface of the implanted tooth.' He pointed to the top of the white pillow. 'It's what your tongue feels inside the mouth.'

She ran her tongue round the inside of her own teeth. She was overdue a check-up. Arni too.

'And here,' Sandy pointed to the middle, a ghostly helter-skelter, 'is the titanium screw of the implant that goes right down, past the gum, through the former root of the tooth, into the jawbone.

'You can see there is extensive osseointegration, the fusing of the natural bone with the implant, so we can tell this is at least two years old.'

He clicked on his laptop and a close-up appeared on the wall screen.

'Notice anything?' he asked.

Julie peered at the image, then put her glasses on.

'Can't say I know what I'm looking for.'

'Let me rotate.'

Sandy used his mouse to show a different view.

'See anything now?'

'Enough of the guessing,' she said. 'Tell me what you see.'

'There's something etched into the implant,' he said.

Now that he pointed it out, she could just about make out a string of tiny letters and numbers.

'What is that?' she asked. 'Some sort of part number?'

'Or a unique label.'

'Something we can use to identify our man?'

He shrugged.

'It's worth a try.' He closed his laptop. 'I'm guessing that we're no closer to finding a name by other means?'

'Early days.'

'Would you authorise a request to extract the artificial tooth to get a better look at it?'

'What's the protocol?'

'It's fully covered as an identification option,' Sandy said. 'I'll deal with the paperwork.'

'But, once we find the family, if there's to be a viewing . . .'

'The bereaved don't usually look inside the mouths of their loved ones.'

'Then knock yourself out.' She stood up.

'Thank you, DI Cadell.' He stood to open the door for her, stepping back into the office to let her pass.

'You're most welcome, Dr Armstrong.'

Julie paused in the doorway and turned back.

'When you said there was something odd, was this it? The ID number on the tooth?'

'The rest is just gut feel,' he said. 'But the expert sensed it independently.'

'Explain.'

He leant against his desk. 'Healthy guy, excellent oral health. Almost no tooth decay and no other significant repair work. Implants are expensive. You usually see them after a lot of other things have been tried first. A hierarchy of repair in other teeth. This guy doesn't even have major fillings. It just feels odd.'

'Maybe it wasn't tooth decay that led to the tooth replacement. Maybe he knocked it out in an accident.'

'Possibly, although it's in the wrong place for that to be likely.'

He pointed to his own mouth to show the position of the tooth.

'And if a healthy tooth is damaged by external impact there are usually less invasive ways to repair it.'

'So, what are you saying?'

'I called an old friend last night,' Sandy said. 'Frank and I were at university together. He moved to the US not long after qualifying as a dentist.'

'What did he say about the dental implant?'

'He agreed that it was probably done in the US.'

'And the number on the artificial tooth? Does it give us a way to establish the victim's identity?'

'Possibly,' Sandy replied. 'The American Society of Forensic Odontology have been calling for unique identification markers ever since implants became more widespread. Looks like someone was listening.'

'Someone? Like who?'

'The military, maybe.'

Julie raised an eyebrow.

'So, what are you saying? Our victim might be an American soldier?'

'Frank suggested we try NamUs.'

'The US missing persons database?' Julie shook her head. 'We don't know for sure he's a US citizen, and why would he be listed as missing if he only died a few days ago?'

Sandy shrugged.

'Frank's going to ask around. Find out who manufactures implants with unique ID numbers. See if there's any way to trace them back to an identity.'

'We could certainly use a break.' Julie sighed.

'You OK?'

'You saw the press conference?'

'I heard about it.' Sandy chuckled. 'TIPSI. That's priceless.'

'More like incompetent.' Julie sighed.

'I guess Cleveland Police will be getting a new logo.'

'I should have—' Julie began.

'Stop right there.' Sandy held up a hand. 'Self-doubt is a luxury you can't afford in the Cleveland police force. There are people who'll seize on the smallest chink in your confidence and chisel it wide open.'

'But I feel bad.'

'Because you're a good person. But remember.' He joined her at the door. 'It's not what you feel that matters. It's what you do.' He took her hand and squeezed it. 'You're a great police officer, DI Cadell, analytical, thorough and honest. Unlike some in the force. Focus on what you can control, handle what you can't. If anyone can solve this case, you can.' He let go of her hand.

Julie thought about Sandy as she made her way out of the hospital. Where did confidence like that come from? Were you born with it, or could you develop it? She must ask him sometime. Maybe over a drink.

A message from Claire flashed up on her screen. The press conference had been watched online by over ten thousand people, the highest number yet.

Thanks to her buffoon of a boss, they'd gone viral. Perhaps Superintendent Chalmers had done her a favour. It was up to her to capitalise on that. What had Sandy said? Focus on what you can control. Perhaps she should start closer to home.

Julie got out her personal phone and texted Arni.

You fancy dinner out tonight? Caruso?

One tick. Two ticks. Blue ticks. Typing . . .

FLM NT

Film night. Fair enough. It was his regular evening with the boys. He had a nice group of friends, and they took turns selecting a movie to watch together.

What had Sandy advised? Try putting the ball in his court for once. Give him some control.

Another night, then? You tell me a good day.

The phone rang and she picked it up expecting to hear Arni's voice, but it was her friend Kim Simmons.

'Hello stranger, how are you?'

Julie sighed. 'I've been better.'

'I hear you bumped into an old colleague at the weekend.'

'News travels fast.'

'Caron's not married anymore, you know,' Kim said.

'And why do you think I'd be interested in that random piece of information?'

'He asked if you were.'

Julie grinned to herself. 'Did he indeed.'

'Don't tell anyone I told you,' Kim said. 'But seriously, Caron's a great guy.'

'Can't say I noticed,' she lied.

Kim changed tack. 'When are you coming over? I have a new horse you're going to love.'

'Things are a bit busy right now.'

'Work?'

'Murder investigation.'

'Weekends too?'

'Depends.'

'How about one evening?'

'I've got Arni to think of.'

'He's practically an adult,' Kim said. 'I'm beginning to think you're avoiding me.'

Kim had always been a good and faithful friend, taking care of her through her worst times. It was unfair to push her away.

'You're quite right,' Julie said. 'It's been far too long.'

'How about this Saturday?'

Julie opened her diary. Arni had a hockey tournament in Scotland and the team were staying at the host school overnight. Even if she had to work, she could have a late dinner with Kim, stay over and go riding early Sunday morning.

'Saturday it is.'

Julie ended the call to see a message from Arni.

Cn V cm?

Can Eve come. Come where? Julie had to scroll back to see what he was replying to. She'd suggested dinner at Caruso's, their local Italian. She'd left it up to Arni to choose the day.

What did his reply mean? She wanted to talk to him, mother to son, and he wanted his girlfriend to come along? What role was Eve to play? The referee in a battle? His union rep standing up to the evil boss of the house? His lawyer to protect the accused against DI Mum?

She started to type.

No, just you and . . .

She sighed and deleted the text. She'd presented an olive branch. Offered him some element of control. Now was not the time to negotiate conditions. Just accept his proposal. Unconditionally. If he didn't want to be alone with his mother, then she shouldn't force it. Eve seemed like a nice girl. Use this opportunity to get to know her better. Once things were smoothed over, they could find a time to be together, just her and Arni, and patch things up properly.

Sure

His message came much later. Just three letters.

Fri

At least Friday hadn't been completely disemvowelled.

Julie opened the case file and updated her notes. Things seemed to be diverging when they should be converging. Instead of eliminating things they were opening up new possibilities. She put her head in her hands, suddenly overwhelmed.

What had Sandy said?

It's not what you feel that matters. It's what you do.

What had she done? She'd chased down blind alleys. All that distraction with the boats, only to discover that the crime scene was probably far away from where the body was found.

If anyone can solve this case, you can.

And she would.

Just as soon as they identified the mystery man.

Chapter 16

BRIAN

Stockton-on-Tees – Tuesday, 12 November 2024

'DAMEER GHOSH.'

Brian woke from a dream and sat up in bed shouting the name. His body was bathed in sweat and his muscles ached, as if he'd run a marathon in his sleep.

He'd been standing on the shore. A stony beach like the one at Seaham. It was night-time but a full moon illuminated the water. A man was swimming, calling for others to join him. Brian knew it was too cold for swimming and tried to warn the man about the riptide. But the words wouldn't come. He couldn't speak, couldn't wave, couldn't move. Brian stood rooted to the spot.

He watched in horror as Betty appeared at the other end of the beach and began undressing. Her skin was glowing in the moonlight; she always looked better with her clothes off. What was she doing naked on a beach in winter? She waved to the man in the sea and then ran into the water to join him.

At first, Brian was consumed by jealous rage.

What was it about a bearded idiot who went skinny-dipping in winter that made him attractive to Betty? In his dream she didn't even look his way, neither noticed nor acknowledged the man she'd been living with for so many years he'd lost count. What made her run from him, Brian, into the arms of a stranger? Betty didn't even like swimming.

That's when he clocked that the man in the sea was in trouble. He looked familiar – dark hair, amber eyes – although the name wouldn't come to him at first.

Betty wasn't going to him as a lover, but as a rescuer.

He wanted to help; he really did. To show Betty that he wasn't lazy or selfish or cold or uncaring or all the other insults she'd hurled at him. He really wanted to save her. To save himself. He was screaming inside.

But he couldn't move a muscle.

Now he was awake, he had to do something. Tell someone about Dameer. Best to act now, while the nightmare lingered, before he was awake enough to talk himself out of it. While it still felt like he was doing this for Betty.

The Crimestoppers website claimed they didn't track caller ID or computer IP addresses, promising not to record calls or request any personal contact information, but he wasn't taking any chances.

He logged on to a VPN and created a fake profile. You don't get to be a cybersecurity expert without learning how to cover your tracks.

He didn't think much of the form: *arson, assault, fraud, theft, computer misuse* . . . oh, he could tell a tale or two about that . . . *drunk driving, drugs, illegal tobacco, terrorism, wildlife crime.* There was no missing persons option among the listed crimes. The only other possible category was *murder (including attempted/planned murder)*, but when he went down that route it wanted to know about the perpetrators, not the victim. In the end he selected *other.*

Where did the crime or incident take place?

Well, the police already knew that, didn't they? He typed in the address of the Hartlepool naval museum.

Do you know when it happened?

He keyed in the date from the news report.

Tell us more about the crime

He started typing. *Cleveland Police are looking for information about a body found in Hartlepool. He looks a bit like someone I know. I was due to meet him, but he didn't turn up.* He deleted the last two sentences.

Tell us about the person or people involved

The police sketch of the Hartlepool victim looks like a visiting engineer called Dameer Ghosh who works for Zebra Safety Solutions, he typed.

Do you know any contact details?

Brian filled in the contact number for Dameer's employer.

He skipped the next questions about weapons and vehicles.

If we need to clarify any of your information or you think there might be extra information you can give, are you prepared to create an anonymous login?

Ha – nice try. Brian ticked the box that said, *No, I have given all the information that I can.*

Brian went back to bed.

Chapter 17

JULIE

Middlesbrough – Wednesday, 13 November 2024

Julie hadn't even parked when DC Gibson waved her to stop outside the office. She rolled down the car window.

'I think we might have found something!' he said.

'I'm listening.'

'Near the skip but on the other side of the container port fence there's evidence of a recent bonfire.'

'Good work! Is the area secure?'

'Yes,' he said. 'And Adrian Prosser is on the line.'

Julie took the mobile phone he thrust through the window.

'Morning, Adrian.' She listened as the CSM explained his plan to split the crime scene team in two. 'Yes, I approve.' She handed the phone back to DC Gibson. His eyes shone, but there were dark circles under them.

'Have you been up all night?' she asked.

'It's OK—' he began.

Julie shook her head. 'It's not OK. I need you firing on all cylinders. The crime scene team can take over now. Go and get some rest.'

'Yes, boss.'

After filing the morning report, Julie drove to South Bank. Two white tents had been erected, one either side of a barbed-wire fence. She parked by the roadside and continued on foot.

Because the River Tees meandered as it approached the sea, the Zagrovyl factory on the north bank was due west from where she stood, directly across the river. The land reclaimed from the sea was so flat she could see the towers and columns, the spheres and flares all the way to Hartlepool.

Once she had updated her mental map, she turned towards the crime scene team and made a beeline for CSM Adrian Prosser.

'So, what do we have here?' she asked.

He pointed to the far tent. 'That's where the bonfire was. Judging by the ash, it was mainly clothing. Not much left intact, but we'll get some good information all the same.' He pointed to the fence which was festooned with fluttering tags. 'Looks like the clothes were thrown into the scrapyard from here before being doused with petrol. Some scraps got caught on the barbed wire in between. We're getting some good samples.'

'You think this might be our murder scene?'

'Come and see,' Adrian said. He lifted the flap of the larger tent. A white-suited technician stood back from an area that had been cleared of grass and weeds. Behind the mask, Julie recognised Val Hesslewood, Adrian's star forensic technician. Adrian shone a laser torch onto the ground. At the centre of the cleared area was a jet-black stain. He screwed a yellow filter onto the torch and the patch began to fluoresce with a pale blue glow.

'What d'you reckon?' Adrian asked the forensic expert.

'It's definitely blood,' Val replied. 'And given how far it has spread, a hell of a lot of it. I've sent samples off for rapid DNA testing.' She pointed to a digital clock hanging from a canvas strap. 'We should know in a few hours if this blood is human and whether it came from our mystery man in the morgue.'

'Good work,' Julie said. 'Any sign of a murder weapon?'

Val pointed to a pair of technicians pegging out the search area. 'If it's on dry land, we'll find it.'

Chapter 18

'Case number 021284.' Julie unmuted the microphone and opened the meeting. 'The Hartlepool murder. First week update.'

She clicked a button on her laptop and the large screen at the end of the meeting room lit up.

'We probably all know one another, but please introduce yourselves for the record. First, our colleagues joining us remotely.'

The little boxes with names changed to video thumbnails, each expanding to full screen when the attendee spoke.

'Superintendent Chalmers,' said a gruff voice. 'And if you lot don't know who I am we're in bigger trouble than I thought.'

Everyone laughed. It looked like her boss was calling from his car on his mobile phone. At least he wasn't driving.

'Document Controller, Karen Potter.'

Karen was in her office. It was only a mile across town, but it was raining outside, and she didn't drive.

DI Cadell turned from the screen.

'And in the HQ conference room we have . . .'

'CSM Adrian Prosser.'

They went round the table introducing themselves.

'Detective Constable Chris Gibson.'

'And finally, chairing this meeting, I am Detective Inspector Julie Cadell.' Julie flashed the agenda onto the screen.

'Where is DS Wharton?' The super barked.

Where indeed?

'He should be here,' the super insisted.

This bromance between her boss and her sergeant was becoming annoying.

'He'll join us as soon as he can,' Julie said and shared her screen to display the meeting agenda. 'I suggest we take the items in the order they appear,' she said.

'I'd rather jump to the new forensics.' The gruff voice of her boss grated on Julie's nerves. He couldn't miss a chance to remind everyone who was top dog. 'I may have to leave for another meeting.'

'Of course, sir.' She kept the irritation out of her voice. 'Over to you, Adrian.'

Adrian Prosser took control of the screen.

'The crime scene was established on the south bank of the River Tees at map location 54°36'12.6'N 1°09'22.1'W and extended for approximately twenty-five square metres over two contiguous properties, one belonging to the container port, one to a scrapyard . . .'

'CSM – start with a summary, please,' the superintendent interrupted. 'Why did you go there and what hard evidence did you find?'

Julie knew how Adrian liked to present things. A methodical scientist, he'd want the facts to speak for themselves and be robust enough to stand up in court. Condensing all that work into a few bullet points was not his forte. His mouth opened and closed but no sound came out.

Julie came to his rescue.

'I'll answer the first question, sir,' she said. 'DC Gibson identified the crime scene location after interviewing local businesses and then working with a search team.'

'And what took you away from Hartlepool in the first place?' The super sounded annoyed.

'Some materials found with the body matched waste at the container port on the south of the river. The coastguard confirmed that, in the time between death and discovery, it was possible that Storm Babel could have carried the victim that far.'

She looked over at Adrian and raised an enquiring eyebrow.

Adrian nodded, swallowed hard and continued.

'And in the remains of the bonfire, sir, we found scraps of clothing.'

'What links the clothing to the victim?'

'There are several strong correlations . . .'

'His size, for example?'

'We only found charred remnants. An accelerant had been added to assist in combustion.'

'A what?' asked DC Gibson.

'Petrol,' Adrian said and flicked to the pictures in the appendix.

Sample AP122 – charred piece of silver-grey wool and cashmere fabric. Probably from the gusset of a pair of trousers.

'The clothes were thrown over the perimeter fence, doused in petrol and set alight,' he continued. 'Fortunately for us, the bundle of clothes snagged on some barbed wire and the CSM team extracted unburnt silk.'

Sample AP147 – torn piece of pale pink silk with pearl button still attached.

'Do you have a match with the fibres found in the stab wound?' Julie asked.

'We're still working on that,' Adrian said. 'Visually, yes. At twenty times magnification under the microscope the fibre samples look similar to those from the post-mortem, but we have some more tests to run to get a conclusive result.'

'Any ID?' barked the super.

'The CSI team are sifting through the ash,' Julie said. 'But it doesn't look like it.'

'And news just in.' Adrian looked up from his phone and smiled. 'The blood we found in the soil on the edge of the container port is a better than ninety-eight per cent DNA match to the victim.'

'Good work, team,' Superintendent Chalmers growled. 'Someone has gone to great lengths to try and hide the identity of our victim. But they reckoned without Cleveland Police, eh?'

'And Storm Babel,' added Julie. 'For once, the weather was on our side.'

'Now, what about suspects?' the super asked.

'DS Wharton is working on that,' Julie said. Throw the boss a bone. Praise his golden boy to keep him sweet. 'He's busy tracing the clothes the victim was wearing. They were likely stolen.'

'Security tags torn off,' DC Gibson explained. 'With any luck the thieves were caught on the supermarket CCTV.'

'But we still don't know who our dead guy is?'

'No,' Julie said. 'DC Gibson, try Crimestoppers again, see if they've managed to sift any genuine information from all the nonsense.'

The super glared at her. They both knew that the car crash of a press conference had led to thousands of hoax calls.

'Toxicology?'

'Results are back and clear. No trace of drugs or alcohol.'

'Missing persons?' the super asked.

DC Gibson shook his head. 'No matches.'

'And no witnesses to the crime itself?'

'Not so far,' Julie said. 'But we're widening the net.'

There was no sign of Arni when she got home. Was he avoiding her? Julie decided to enlist her daughter's help.

'Hi, Flora.'

'Oh, hi, Mum.' She sounded sleepy.

'How was the apple pie?'

'A disaster, but it didn't matter. We had a good laugh about it.'

A rustle of sheets and a male voice. She couldn't be sure, but it sounded like *Come back to bed, Flo.* Was that apple pie man?

'Can't talk now, Mum.'

'OK, darling, give me a call when you're free. We'd love to . . .'

The phone went dead.

Chapter 19

Julie arrived at HQ and called her team into the office. DC Gibson bounced from foot to foot like an excited puppy until she pointed at the meeting area where DS Wharton had already taken a seat.

'Any luck with the supermarket CCTV?' she asked.

DS Wharton sat up, his back ramrod straight.

'No,' he said.

'The super noted your absence yesterday.'

'You told me not to come to the briefing until I had something,' he said. 'I don't have anything yet.'

Had she said that? Or had he just interpreted it literally?

'What's the hold-up?'

'They have several stores each with multiple cameras.' He shrugged. 'That means a lot of footage.'

DI Cadell turned to DC Gibson. 'What about Crimestoppers?'

He beamed. 'We have a possible ID.'

'Great,' she said. 'Tell me more.'

'They've been swamped with calls since the appeal, members of the public claiming to recognise our man, but most were obvious prank calls or turned out to be dead ends. I got them to send me all the others, the ones not yet eliminated, and I went through them one by one last night.' He opened a file and extracted a form which he pushed towards Julie. 'This one, which came in online, looks most promising.'

Her face broke into a smile, and she passed the printout to DS Wharton.

'Dameer Ghosh,' he read out loud and sniffed. 'Bit vague, isn't it? What do we know about the informant?'

DC Gibson frowned. 'Nothing,' he said.

Julie gave DS Wharton a hard stare. 'You know as well as I do that Crimestoppers is anonymous,' she said. 'Let's keep it that way.'

'It's hardly compelling . . .' DS Wharton began.

'I know, so I googled him,' DC Gibson opened the file again and laid a screenshot from a company website on the table. 'This is a photo of Dameer Ghosh. Can you see the likeness?'

'Not really,' DS Wharton said.

'Possibly,' Julie said. She pointed to the contact numbers on the form. A personal mobile and an employer landline. 'Can you call these international numbers? See if anyone answers.'

DC Gibson frowned. 'I would have done it already, but I'm not authorised to make calls outside the UK.'

Julie picked up her phone and tapped a few keys. 'Consider yourself duly authorised.'

The wattage of DC Gibson's smile threw DS Wharton into thunderous brooding shadow.

The kitchenette wasn't big enough for two. Julie waited in the corridor while DC Gibson made his lunch. He whistled as he worked.

Her detective constable was always smiling. His unflappable good humour made up for his apparent naivety. People mocked the lad, but she now knew he wasn't nearly as simple as he made out. He wore his inexperience as a sort of protective armour. He asked questions instead of pretending he already knew everything. And he was helpful. And proactive. Eagerness went a long way in this jaded department.

'I called the mobile number,' he said. 'It went straight to voicemail.'

'And the landline?'

'A company called Zebra Safety Solutions in Dubai. I left a message asking Dameer Ghosh's boss to contact you.'

'Thanks.'

'Here.' He handed out the first mug. 'Dash of milk, right?'

It looked the right colour. She sipped at it and gave him a thumbs up.

'Perfect, thanks.'

'Are you horse riding this weekend?' he asked.

It struck her that he was also more observant than his fellow officers.

'If the weather holds,' she said. 'What about you? Any plans?'

'Might take the kids to the garden centre,' he said. 'Unless there's any overtime going?'

Nice try. 'You'll have to speak to Sarge about that,' she said. 'How old are your kids?'

He was still reeling off names and ages when her phone beeped. She ended the water cooler chat with an apology and hurried back to her office to answer.

'Uzain Bagra from Zebra Safety Solutions is on the line.'

'Put him through.'

She closed the door and picked up her desk phone.

'Thank you for calling back, Mr Bagra.' She pulled out her notepad. 'My name is Julie Cadell and I'm a detective inspector with Cleveland Police. We're making enquiries about a man named Dameer Ghosh. Do you know him personally?'

'Yes, yes – I know Dameer well. We've worked together for many years.'

'He's an employee?'

'A sales support agent. He works on commission.'

'What does he sell?'

'Solutions.'

The managing director of Zebra Safety Solutions in Dubai spoke better English than she did. His voice was silky smooth. She adjusted her chair, wondering if she was a reverse snob. The confidence of privilege always aroused her suspicion.

'I'm not a customer, Mr Bagra. I don't need a sales pitch.'

'Sorry, Detective.' He coughed. 'We're a distributor for suppliers of gas sensors.'

'Like the carbon monoxide alarm in my boiler cupboard?'

'Exactly, although we sell business to business rather than direct to the public. Chlorine dosage for swimming pool treatment rooms. Emissions measurement for power stations. Toxic alarms for chemical factories.'

She jotted the information down. Unlikely to be relevant, more detail than she'd probably ever need, but experience had taught her to document everything before ruling things out.

'Do you know his current location?'

'He's on a business trip in Europe.'

'Where exactly?'

'I'd have to check.'

'When did you last hear from him?'

'We met in person last month.'

'Where?'

'Dubai airport.'

'Has anyone from your office spoken to him more recently?'

'My office has been trying to contact him since yesterday. But he's not answering his phone or replying to emails.' He coughed. 'Detective Inspector, forgive me but it would help if you could tell me what this is about. Is there some sort of visa problem?'

'We're investigating the murder of a man in Hartlepool.'

'And you think Dameer might be involved?' He laughed. 'No, no, that's impossible!'

'We're concerned that Dameer Ghosh might be the victim.'

'Victim? Of a murder?' Uzain let out a gasp. 'You mean, Dameer's dead?'

'We don't have any positive identification yet,' she said. 'So you'll understand how important it is for me to get back to the questions.'

'Of course. Please proceed.'

'You met in Dubai. May I ask what the meeting was about?'

'Our quarterly sales meeting. Dameer is our technical expert. He flies in from India whenever he can.'

'Where was he heading after the meeting?'

'My secretary booked his flights and accommodation. I'll ask her to share his itinerary with you.'

'Do you have contact details for his next of kin?'

'I'll check with HR.'

'As soon as possible, please, Mr Bagra.' Julie read out the direct email address. 'Please mark it for my attention.'

Julie ended the call and remained seated, trying to gauge her disquiet. Was it just the posh voice and exaggerated, almost theatrical, reactions that made her distrust Mr Bagra? She didn't think she was that shallow. It was his apathy that disturbed her. Most people are curious about murder. They usually want more details than the police can share. If the victim was known to them they ask how the victim died. Whether or not he suffered.

She made a note to follow up on Zebra if the dead man's identity was confirmed.

Her tea was cold now. On her return from the kitchenette with a fresh cup, the itinerary arrived. Dameer Ghosh had flown from Mumbai to Dubai, then Dubai to Frankfurt, followed by a series of trips, by plane and train inside mainland Europe. She was beginning to think this was another dead end when she turned the page to find confirmation that he'd visited England: an Amsterdam to Teesside hop early on Wednesday, 6 November. He was due to fly home today, Teesside-Amsterdam-Mumbai.

The itinerary also contained details of the accommodation booked in mainland Europe – mid-range business hotels, together with taxi transfers from the airport – but for his trip to England last week there was nothing under local accommodation or travel, just the unhelpful phrase 'personal arrangements'.

Had Dameer stayed with friends or relatives? If he'd been in a hotel, surely someone would have noticed his absence after a week? Unless it was a place where his room wasn't cleaned every day, a self-catering apartment or a lodging house. Not all were listed. Local knowledge was required.

She picked up the phone.

'DC Gibson,' she said. 'Check if Dameer Ghosh passed through Teesside airport last week, and if so, whether he caught his return flight this morning.' She read out the flight details.

'Will do.'

'And where do engineering contractors stay when they're in Teesside?'

'Depends,' he said. 'Haverton Hill, Seaton Carew, Redcar . . .'

'See if you can find out where Dameer Ghosh was staying,' she said. 'If he's our victim, someone will have noticed a missing guest by now.'

Chapter 20

BRIAN

Stockton-on-Tees – Thursday, 14 November 2024

Brian couldn't sleep, so he opened his laptop and watched the rest of the *Disasters Engineered* episode that he'd paused.

What a strange old world. Brian prided himself on keeping up to date with the world of industrial safety. After all, it was – had been – a key part of his job as a control engineer. He knew all about Chernobyl, the subject of the first section of the TV documentary. He'd played *S.T.A.L.K.E.R.*, running around in the exclusion zone dodging mutants. He'd forked out good money to watch the Craig Mazin five-part dramatisation on HBO. Ask Brian about Deepwater Horizon, Fukushima, Milford Haven, and he'd be able to tell you what part control systems had played in each accident.

And yet he knew next to nothing about a 1984 accident that the TV programme claimed was the worst in the world. The Indian gas tragedy happened almost forty years ago and yet the factory was still standing, the equipment abandoned and the land fenced off.

That's when Brian had his brilliant idea. He'd been dabbling with game design ever since he was a teenager, built many prototypes but never found a concept original enough to attract any backers.

What about a new computer game based on the accident in India?

The game *S.T.A.L.K.E.R.* had made its inventor, Sergiy Constantinovych Grygorovych, a fortune. The company, GSC Game World – named with the founder's initials – had just this year raised four billion dollars in funding. Players loved the idea of a dangerous area locked away from daily life. The idea of a vast contaminated zone in the middle of a busy city made the project even more exciting.

Graphics would be no problem; he still had the software package he'd used at Zagrovyl for routing network cables among the pipes and tanks and towers. With so many chemical factories on his doorstep in Teesside, it would be easy to take photos and videos and then superimpose some jungle flora and exotic fauna.

For the first time in several months, Brian felt a surge of excitement and a sense of purpose.

He cracked his knuckles and went searching for information about Bhopal.

Chapter 21

JULIE

Eaglescliffe – Thursday, 14 November 2024

As soon as she got the call, Julie called in the crime scene team then drove straight to The Locomotion, a pub named in honour of the first locomotive to carry passengers on a public railway, the Stockton and Darlington Railway. DC Gibson had confirmed that Dameer Ghosh had arrived in Teesside on 6 November but failed to catch today's flight home. The detective constable had also found the missing man's lodgings.

The red-brick Victorian pub in Eaglescliffe had two bars and a restaurant on the ground floor, and rooms above. A CSI van was already outside. Julie parked at the end of Station Road and walked back.

Adrian Prosser met her at reception.

'So, what do you think?'

'It's the absence that's most interesting,' Adrian said. 'The visitors' book has disappeared. Fortunately, the landlord and bar staff have excellent memories. Dameer Ghosh checked in on Wednesday 6 November and was shown straight to his room.'

Julie followed him up the stairs. In the corridor outside room number 4 she put on a white suit, nitrile gloves and shoe protectors.

Adrian opened the door.

The small room was clean and tidy. The bed hadn't been slept in and there was no sign of any personal possessions.

'Do we conclude that he never came to his room? Just checked in early, left his suitcase downstairs and went off for his first meeting?'

Adrian shook his head. 'The landlord, Jim, confirmed that his room was ready when he arrived. Molly from the bar took him upstairs and showed him how to work the shower.' He pointed to the Do Not Disturb sign hanging from the door handle, now protected by an evidence bag. 'Some guys work night shift and don't want to be disturbed in the morning. Molly assures us she hasn't been in or cleaned the room since he arrived, although she was planning to go in today.'

Julie looked around. 'Let me guess. No ID, no wallet, no laptop, no phone?'

'Worse than that,' he said. 'It's as if he was never here.'

'Maybe he didn't like the room, decided to leave and find somewhere else?'

'And wiped everything down to remove his fingerprints? Shook everything out and filtered out any stray hair or skin cells?'

Julie sighed. 'So, what do you think?'

'I think that whoever murdered him, the same people who burnt his clothes and dressed him in new ones, found his room key and came here to remove all traces of him.'

'Did they leave any traces themselves?'

'Spotless,' Adrian said. 'We're dealing with professionals here.'

'If anyone can find something,' Julie said, 'you can.'

'I shall try my best, but don't hold your breath.'

As Julie left The Locomotion, her phone pinged a reminder. Damn. It was the hockey team fundraiser tonight. It had completely slipped her mind. She drove straight to Arni's school, but there was no sign of him or Eve in the sports hall.

'Mrs Cadell, how nice to see you.'

Arni's coach was one of nature's enthusiasts. No wonder the players worked so hard; he was the kind of adult figure that inspired teenagers.

Ridiculously handsome, with a winning smile, Martin was a gifted athlete who'd missed selection for the Olympic team by a hair's breadth due to injury. He was known as the toughest coach in the school, but also the fairest. He made the players work, but he helped them win.

'I was hoping to catch you,' Martin said.

Julie smiled, looking forward to hearing about her son's latest successes.

'Is Arni OK?' he asked.

'What do you mean?'

'He's missed morning practice four days in a row.'

'Really?' He'd left at the usual time, out of the house shortly after 7 a.m. every day this week. She'd heard him. So where did he go if not to hockey practice?

'I've had to drop him from the team next Saturday.'

Was that why Arni was so volatile? Hockey meant a lot to him. He was hoping to make captain before the end of the year.

'He didn't say.'

'Look, he's one of our most talented players. But it's one rule for all. No practice, no match.' He met her eyes. 'Unless there's something going on that I should know about. Make allowances for.'

Julie looked away. She'd changed job to escape that sort of look. The knowing glances, the intrusive curiosity, the unwanted advice, the awkward sympathy. It wasn't fair to expect Arni to change schools or hobbies, so the coach probably knew all about the accident that had robbed him of his brother. Given his father's absence from Saturday matches, Martin would have realised that the family had split up, too. But that was all history now. Was there something new on Arni's mind? Did Arni confide in Coach Martin? Clearly not.

'Let me talk to Arni,' she said.

But what she meant was, let me find a way to get Arni to talk to me.

Chapter 22

When Julie got home, Arni's shoes and schoolbag were in the hall, but his light was off and his door was closed. She listened outside for a while and then knocked but there was no reply. She cracked the door open. Arni was asleep, his breathing slow and regular, his back to her. He'd thrown off the covers and curled into a ball, his long legs pulled up tight to his stomach. Julie backed out of the room, closed the door and went to the kitchen to grab something to eat.

When had it all gone so badly wrong? she wondered. When had Arni changed from being a sunny, happy child to a taciturn, angry stranger?

It wasn't just puberty or all the other events that life had thrown at their family. Or at least, none of those events individually. Arni had been the one who kept things together after Jamie's accident, kept the whole family united for a while. He'd been so young, only thirteen years old when his brother died, and his grief had been raw and pure. He'd tried to look after her when Matt left, refusing to even see his father for a while, taking responsibility around the house. So, what had changed?

Arni was in love and sexually active. Big deal. It was his body and his life. He was seventeen after all, and his girlfriend was eighteen. Right now, Julie was more worried about getting him school trousers that fitted properly.

Was it Arni who'd changed, or was it her? Since moving jobs for the promotion, she was working long hours. Even if she got home in time to make tea, they didn't talk much. They ate in front of the TV. Sometimes she even fell asleep on the sofa, waking to find the dishes cleared away and Arni already in his room. He got up at the crack of dawn, ostensibly for hockey practice, and yet the coach revealed that he hadn't been turning up.

What was going on with her youngest boy, her once-sunny, good-natured, even-tempered, beautiful son? Of her three children, he'd been the easiest child to raise. Was that because he had two older siblings? Both Jamie and Flora had adored their baby brother, found him endlessly entertaining, and he'd flourished in the sunshine of their love.

Did Arni still confide in Flora? Maybe things would get easier when she was home for the holidays. Term wouldn't end until mid-December. Too far away. Maybe Flora could make a flying visit next weekend? Or Arni could go and visit his sister. Julie dialled her daughter's number, but it went straight to voicemail.

'Hi, darling,' she said. 'Call me back.' She debated saying more, then decided against it.

She toyed with the idea of calling Matt, but he'd made it clear that she was not to call him at his new partner's house unless it was an emergency. Perhaps she'd try him at work tomorrow. Or was that just abdicating responsibility? What could Matt do?

Julie set her alarm for 6.30 a.m., dragging herself out of bed when it buzzed her awake. Arni's schoolbag and sports kit was still in the hall. She defrosted sausages and bacon while the grill was heating up. At 7 a.m. there was no sound from Arni's room, so she made a cup of tea and took it upstairs.

She knocked on the door. 'Arni?'

No reply.

She knocked again, louder this time. 'You want a cup of tea?'

She put the mug down and called him from her work phone, so he wouldn't recognise the number.

'Yes?' His sleepy voice reached her from the phone and from behind the door.

'Cup of tea?' she asked.

Not waiting for his reply, she opened the door.

He sat up in bed to take it from her.

'Thanks,' he said, without meeting her eyes.

'No practice this morning?'

He shook his head.

'Then you'll have time for breakfast.' She made it a statement, not a question. 'Full English waiting downstairs.'

Julie waited until her son appeared, showered and dressed, before making scrambled eggs, tipping it onto hot plates and adding the grilled tomatoes, crispy bacon and fat sausages.

She refilled their mugs from the teapot but waited until he'd finished eating before making her apology.

'I'm sorry I was late last night,' she said.

'Late?' he asked.

'To the hockey fundraiser.'

'But you went?'

'Yes. I got there about eight o'clock.'

'I'd already left.'

'I know.'

He took a sip of tea, avoiding her eyes.

'Did you speak to Coach?'

'Yes.'

'Then you know I'm dropped from the team.'

'Martin said you hadn't been to practice.'

'He's right.'

'But you still left early . . .'

'Yes.' He stood up and slammed his mug down on the table. 'To avoid exactly this sort of inquisition.'

'Arni, wait!'

'No, Mum. You don't get to totally ignore me and then suddenly go all stern parent on me.'

'I wasn't . . .'

'There's lots going on. Hockey is the least of my troubles.'

'Tell me.' She opened her arms wide. 'I'm here. I'm listening.'

Her phone rang. She flicked it to silent, but the damage was done.

'Wasn't that your work phone?' he asked.

'It was.'

'Aren't you obliged to answer it?'

'I'll call back. Nothing is more important than you.'

'That makes a change.' He sighed. 'We can't talk now.'

'When, then?'

'Tonight.'

'With Eve?'

'Yes, Mum.' His voice was hard. 'With Eve.'

Julie swallowed. 'OK, then.'

Julie waited until Arni had set off for school before checking her work phone. She didn't recognise the number, but she called it back.

'This is Detective Inspector Julie Cadell from Cleveland Police. I missed a call from you.'

'My name is Alvi Zaidi.' The accent was Geordie. 'My brother's employer contacted me.'

'Your brother's name is?'

'Dameer. Dameer Ghosh.'

'And his employer?'

'Uzain Bagra at Zebra Safety Solutions.'

Julie closed the kitchen door.

'Did Mr Bagra tell you why we want to speak to you?'

'He said,' the voice of the woman on the other end of the phone cracked with emotion, 'he said that . . . that something bad happened to Dameer. I can't believe it. There must be some mistake.'

'Alvi, I am very sorry to tell you this, but we fear that your brother is dead.'

'That's not possible.'

'We know he arrived in Teesside by plane but failed to board his scheduled return flight. He didn't sleep in the room he booked or attend the meetings he arranged.'

'There could be other explanations,' Alvi said. 'Maybe he changed his plans.'

'Maybe so. But I'm sorry to say that we have a body in the morgue matching his description. That's why we need someone who knew him well. To help us with the identification.'

'I'm on my way,' Alvi said. 'I'll be with you by noon.'

'I'll meet you at James Cook Hospital in Middlesbrough – you know where it is?'

'I know.'

'If you have any recent photos of your brother, can you bring them with you?'

'I will, but I still don't believe there's any connection.' Alvi's voice dropped to a whisper. 'What happened to the man in the morgue?'

'We can try to answer your questions when you arrive, but I'm afraid there's a lot we don't yet know,' Julie said. 'We're hoping that you can help us.'

Chapter 23

Middlesbrough – Friday, 15 November 2024

Julie marched through the entrance to James Cook University Hospital and made a beeline for the main lift.

The doors opened and several people got out: a doctor in blue scrubs with a stethoscope around her neck; a couple of nurses; an old woman in dressing gown, pyjamas and slippers clutching a packet of cigarettes; a teenage boy, so skinny he looked almost skeletal; a man with two small children, a boy holding his leg, a girl in his arms, her eyes wide with fear and wonder.

Once the lift had emptied, Julie stepped inside and pressed the button for the basement. The doors closed but the lift didn't move. Alone in a confined space, a featureless box, a metal coffin, her thoughts turned to death.

There'd been no need to identify her son's body. They were all with Jamie, the whole family, when the machines were finally turned off and he slipped from life to death. There was no post-mortem either – rules were different outside Europe. The hospital staff were so kind to them, so respectful. The police, too.

Even before Jamie's accident, meeting the bereaved had always been the hardest part of her job. Attending a post-mortem was easier than talking with relatives. Especially when she had no answers. As the lift descended into the bowels of the hospital she wished she'd taken the stairs, just to delay the meeting a little longer.

A security guard met her at the entrance to the morgue. She flashed her identification and stepped through the double doors.

The Family Liaison Officer came out to meet her. Donna was one of those people born to comfort others. An active listener, calm and practical, she could find hooks of hope in another's despair, tugging on the right threads to help the grieving come to terms with a future without the person they'd loved.

'Donna, good to see you. Has the sister arrived?'

'Yes.'

'How's she doing?'

'Anxious,' Donna said. 'It's only to be expected.'

They walked down the corridor to a small room, furnished with a settee and two chairs. One wall was curtained off. A petite young woman stood as they entered. Dressed in trainers, jeans and a white blouse, she pushed back her long dark hair to reveal a strikingly beautiful face.

'Alvi,' Donna said. 'This is DI Julie Cadell, the officer in charge of the investigation.'

'Thank you for coming so quickly.' Julie held out a hand.

'I'm sure this is a case of mistaken identity,' Alvi said.

Perhaps she was right. The strikingly beautiful young woman looked nothing like the murder victim. Yes, they were both of South Asian origin, but Alvi's round face, full lips and button nose were completely different from the square jaw, high cheekbones and aquiline nose of the man in the morgue.

'Then hopefully you can help us clear this up,' Julie said.

Donna filled three glasses of water from the dispenser and placed them on the table.

Julie took a seat opposite Alvi.

'Has Donna explained to you what's going to happen?' she asked.

Alvi nodded. 'But I'm not sure I took it all in.'

'When you are ready, we open the curtain.' Julie pointed at the wall curtain that hid a window and door. 'The deceased will be on the other side.'

'Can I go through?'

'If you wish,' Julie said. 'You'll need to put these on.' She pointed to the box of plastic aprons, shoe protectors and gloves before leaning forward. 'I need to warn you that there is significant bruising.'

Alvi took a sip of water and closed her eyes. Her lips moved in silent prayer. The she stood up. 'Let's get this over with.'

The curtain slid away to reveal a trolley on the other side of the glass.

Alvi closed her eyes.

'Tell me when you're ready,' Donna said.

'I'm ready.'

Donna nodded at the mortuary technician who pulled back a white sheet to reveal the head and shoulders of the corpse. Both arms lay under a tarpaulin which was tight against the body and pulled up to his chest.

Julie took a deep breath. However much she'd seen, however many atrocities she'd witnessed, the stillness of death still had the power to unnerve.

'No,' Alvi whispered. 'No, it's not him. It can't be.'

'Are you sure?' Donna asked.

'I need to get closer,' Alvi said.

They put on the protective clothing and stepped through into a small, windowless room.

A cry escaped Alvi as she approached the body.

'I'm afraid he was in the water for several hours,' Julie said.

'Dameer, my . . . brother . . . has a birthmark under his left ear.' Alvi's voice was hesitant.

With a gloved hand the mortuary technician turned the head to the right, away from them. In profile it was easier to imagine the man this had once been. And the birthmark under his ear left no room for doubt.

'Can you recognise him now?'

'Yes,' Alvi whispered.

'I need you to formally identify him.'

'This is Dameer Ghosh.'

'I'm so sorry for your loss,' Julie said.

'Do you want some time with your brother?' Donna asked.

Alvi nodded.

Donna brought her a chair.

'May I touch him?'

Donna nodded. 'Just don't disturb the tarpaulin.'

Julie stepped outside to give the sister some privacy and switched her personal phone on. A missed call from Flora. She left the morgue and called back.

'Hi, Mum.'

'Hi darling, how are you?'

'Is Arni OK?'

'Arni? Why do you ask?'

'He's been sending me odd texts.'

'Like what?'

'Oh, just sibling stuff. But at odd times of day and night.'

'He'd love to see you. Any chance you could pop home for a weekend?'

'Can't right now. Too much on.'

'Maybe he could come and see you?'

'I'm not a babysitter.'

'He's seventeen.'

'But is he OK?'

'Your guess is as good as mine. He's hardly home.'

'Not OK then.'

'Why don't you call him.'

'He's not answering. Tell him to ring me, OK?'

'Flora, wait—'

But her daughter had already cut the call.

Chapter 24

Julie took a little time to gather her thoughts before starting the interview. Alvi had been reluctant to come to the police station directly from the morgue, claiming that she needed to travel home. She was given the option of an interview now or returning on Monday, and eventually agreed to 'get it over with'.

'I am so very sorry for your loss.'

Julie stretched out a hand and touched Alvi's arm as they entered the interview room. It was intended to comfort, but Alvi flinched as if she'd been tasered. DS Iain Wharton was already inside. He stood up and introduced himself before starting the recording device.

'For the record, could you state your name, please?' he asked.

'Alvi Zaidi.'

'And your current address?'

Alvi gave a London address.

'Also present, DS Iain Wharton and Senior Investigating Officer, DI Julie Cadell.'

'Thank you for agreeing to talk with us today,' Julie said. 'We want to find out who did this terrible thing to your brother and bring them to justice.'

Alvi bowed her head.

'We're hoping you can help us with some background,' Julie continued.

'What can you tell us about Dameer?'

'What do you want to know?' Alvi sounded almost sullen.

'Let's start at the beginning,' Julie suggested. 'Where was he born?'

'India.'

'Where exactly?'

'Madhya Pradesh.' Alvi shifted in her seat. 'Bhopal.'

Why was that name familiar? Some TV programme Arni had been watching during dinner.

'My brother became an engineer and then got a job with Zebra Safety Solutions.'

'Where did he study?'

'First at IIT in Kanpur, then he got a scholarship to do a master's in the US.'

Which explained the dentistry.

'You were born in India too?'

Alvi shook her head. 'My father and his first wife divorced. He moved to England and remarried. I was born near here, in Bishop Auckland.'

'Any other brothers or sisters?'

'Not that I know of.'

'And your father?'

'My father passed away last year.'

'I'm sorry.'

'At least he didn't live to see this.' Alvi sighed.

'What about Dameer's mother? Is she alive?'

Alvi shook her head. 'His mother died long ago.'

'Was your brother married?'

'No.'

'In a civil partnership?'

Something passed over Alvi's face. A wave of strong emotion. Grief? It looked more like rage. She asked for water and then sipped it slowly for a while.

'Dameer was a very private man. If he was in a current relationship, he never mentioned it or introduced me to anyone.'

'Do you have any more up-to-date pictures of your brother?'

Julie expected Alvi to show them on her phone, but Alvi reached into her bag and pulled out some prints.

The first was a passport photo. His hair was shorter, and he was unsmiling, but he was still striking. The second looked like a graduation snap; not one of the posed portraits that parents hang on their walls, this was taken by a friend rather than a professional. Dameer was looking straight into the camera. He looked alive, happy, handsome. It was a look full of love.

'Who took this photo?' Julie asked.

'I did,' Alvi said.

The last photo was of Dameer and Alvi together. They were very different, Dameer much bigger and darker than his elfin sister, but both were strikingly beautiful people.

'May we keep these?' Julie asked.

Alvi hesitated. 'Will I get them back?'

'Of course,' DS Wharton said. 'We'll make copies and post the originals back to you. Shall we send them to your home address?'

Alvi nodded.

'What was your brother's job at Zebra Safety Solutions?'

Alvi shrugged. 'You'd have to ask them.'

'When was the last time you saw your brother?'

'Eighteen months ago.' Alvi's eyes filled with tears. 'At our father's funeral.'

'You've not seen him since then?'

'I've had no contact with him.'

'No phone calls, texts, chats?'

'Nothing.'

'You weren't close?'

'We were close once. But we argued at the funeral.'

Alvi dropped her eyes.

'And that's the last contact you had with him?'

'That's right.'

'Did he have close friends?'

'Probably, but he was several years older than me. We moved in different worlds.'

'Was he a religious man?'

'A practising Muslim.'

'With relatives back in India?'

'Possibly.' Alvi shrugged. 'My father broke all family ties when he moved to England.'

'What about maternal relatives?'

'I know nothing about my father's first wife. My mother wouldn't allow it. The first time I was aware that she even existed was after she died.'

'Do you have any idea what Dameer was doing in Teesside?'

Alvi shrugged. 'I assume he was here for his work. Ask his boss.'

'Were you planning to meet?'

'Not like this.' Alvi began to cry.

It is painful to witness the grief of another. DS Wharton made eye contact with Julie, his body language suggesting that they interrupt the meeting.

DI Cadell gave an imperceptible shake of her head. Alvi Zaidi had more to tell them, and the loss of control might help break down the barriers. There was grief and pain but something else.

'Are you angry with Dameer?' Julie asked.

Alvi looked up, startled into silence.

'What makes you say that?'

'Just answer the question.'

'Yes.' Alvi nodded. 'I am angry. I'm angry that he didn't tell me he was in England. I'm angry that he made no attempt to come and see me. I'm angry that he died before we had a chance to reconcile.'

Alvi laid her head on the table and wept.

DS Wharton wrote something on his notepad and pushed it towards Julie. *Terminate?*

Julie shook her head and put a finger to her lips.

They waited in silence until Alvi's sobs abated.

'Are you OK to continue?' DS Wharton asked.

She shot him a grateful look. 'Do I have to?'

'Is there anything else you'd like to tell us about your brother?' Julie asked.

'No, but I have some questions.'

'Fire away.'

'How did he die?'

'A single stab wound to the heart. If it's any consolation, it would have been a quick death.'

'The papers say he was found in the water. He didn't drown?'

'No. He was already dead when he entered the water.'

'Was he beaten?'

'Possibly a blow to the back of the head, but most of the bruising is post-mortem.'

Alvi bowed her head.

'When can you release . . . my brother's body?'

'Not yet, I'm afraid.'

'He should be buried according to his traditions.'

'I understand that, but this is a murder inquiry.'

'He's dead. What else can his body tell you?'

'We're going to find out who did this terrible thing. When it comes to court, the defence have the right to perform a second post-mortem.'

'So, whoever murdered him can mutilate his body all over again?'

'Everyone has the right to a fair trial.'

'And my brother has the right to a burial.' Alvi's eyes blazed.

'I'll speak to the coroner,' DS Wharton said.

'Thank you.'

'Help us find out who killed him, Alvi,' Julie said.

A tremor passed over the young woman's body. What was she afraid of? The voice that emerged was deep and strong.

'I will,' Alvi said. 'He deserves nothing less.'

'Interview terminated at,' DS Wharton looked up at the clock, 'our forty-seven p.m.'

Julie waved DS Wharton away and walked the witness to the building exit.

'How are you travelling back to London?'

'Train.'

'I'll show you the shortcut to the station.'

'There's no need—'

'I could use a breath of fresh air.'

They walked along Bridge Street, side by side.

'Alvi, is there something you're not telling me?' Julie asked.

The younger woman continued walking, staring straight ahead.

'I know this is hard,' Julie continued. 'But anything you remember, no matter how small, no matter how personal, might help us to unlock this case and catch your brother's killer.'

Alvi stopped.

'Goodbye, DI Cadell,' Alvi said. 'I can find my way from here.'

Julie pressed a card into her hand.

'This is my direct number. Call me any time, day or night.'

Alvi walked away. At the entrance to the tunnel under the railway line she stopped in front of a wastebin. Without looking back, she dropped the white card in, then continued walking.

Julie shook her head and turned back. Grief affected people in so many different ways.

After all, she should know.

Chapter 25

Stockton-on-Tees – Friday, 15 November 2024

Brian pushed his chair back from the computer as the printer whirred. He'd used his Zagrovyl redundancy settlement to buy the best home office equipment that money could buy. His gaming equipment was state-of-the-art: a super-fast laptop, a 55-inch high-definition curved screen, ergonomic mouse and keyboard and top-of-the-range audio. He'd spared no expense on the workstation either: a desk with motor and telescopic legs that became a standing desk at the touch of a button. Not that he often stood up when using the computer. It had sounded like a good idea, but in reality being on his feet made him dizzy. And the chair was so comfy – everything was adjustable, from armrests to lumbar support. He could lie right back or tip the seat forward, and the castors whizzed smoothly over the laminate floor as he gathered the proposal from the printer.

BB Games Galaxy – he liked the sound of his new company name, proud to use his own initials and declare his billionaire ambitions. The company logo was a stylised representation of the kinetic train sculpture that rose above Stockton High Street every day at 1.06 p.m – the Stockton Flyer gave a sense of place and had a fine retro steampunk vibe.

His first game trilogy would be called *B.H.O.P.A.L.*

Brian's research into the 1984 accident had shocked him. The number of victims was staggering. Thousands killed overnight, and hundreds of thousands injured when a cocktail of toxic gases escaped from the chimney of a pesticide factory. The horribly contaminated factory site still hadn't been cleaned up and the equipment remained standing, frozen in time, forty years on.

Shocking but inspirational; the story concept was coming along nicely.

In *B.H.O.P.A.L.* 1, a group of rebels, banished from society, take refuge inside the fenced-off land surrounding the old factory. They adapt to survive on whatever they can hunt and forage within the contaminated zone, plus the occasional night raid out into the hostile city.

Plenty of conflict: the enemies outside – politicians, police, army, religious fanatics; the wildlife inside – tigers, wild boar, snakes, spiders, vultures and the mutant crocodiles emerging from the sludge of the hazardous waste ponds with ghostly, luminescent spirit birds on their backs.

No shortage of challenges and puzzles either – building shelter, finding fuel, purifying water, identifying medicinal plants to treat illnesses; and of course - as in any fight for survival with constrained resources - many battles between the rebels themselves as they form alliances and fight over what sort of society they want to create inside the zone.

Brian cracked his knuckles.

Now for the fun bit.

Time to write some code.

Chapter 26

JULIE

Middlesbrough – Friday, 15 November 2024

'Well done!' The super was in a tremendous mood. He slapped DS Iain Wharton on the back and advanced towards Julie. She slid behind her desk in case he tried to hug her; he was well known among the female staff for his wandering hands.

'All we have is a positive identification,' she said.

'And the scene of crime,' the super said. 'With the A-Team on the case, you'll have this crime solved in no time.' He nodded at the clock. 'Knocking-off time. You two have been burning too much midnight oil. C'mon, let me buy you a drink.'

'I have a couple of things to wrap up, sir,' Julie said. 'I need to inform the victim's employer. I'll be along as soon as I can.'

'You need this guy?' The super pointed to her sergeant.

'Not at the moment.'

'C'mon, Iain my lad, let's get out of here and wet our whistles.'

The expression on DS Wharton's face was priceless. Even though she didn't always see eye to eye with her sergeant, he was a dedicated policeman. He would sip a soft drink while the super got drunk. The flash of sympathy vanished. Serve him right for dancing with the devil.

'See you in The Applegarth, DI Cadell.' He threw an arm round DS Wharton. 'That's an order.'

Julie called the dead man's employer in Dubai, but her call went straight to voicemail. What time was it there? She checked. Three hours ahead. She composed a careful message, thanking Uzain Bagra for his help, informing him of the positive identification of Dameer Ghosh by Alvi Zaidi, his half-sister, and requesting further information to assist with the investigation into his death, including full details of Dameer's meeting schedule in Teesside.

She tidied up a couple of reports, updated the database, and when she was out of excuses for further delay, packed up and headed out.

Julie hesitated outside the pub. The smell of stale beer and the raucous laughter reminded her that The Applegarth was the last place she wanted to be on a Friday night. If she'd fancied a little downtime with her team, she wouldn't have chosen this location. The pub was too crowded, too noisy, too male. Even if she'd suggested a calmer venue, the super's presence would ruin it. Anyway, she never drank when she had the car. Especially after so little sleep. The super's idea of a reward was her idea of a punishment. Best get it over and done with.

As she pushed the door open, she caught sight of Caron. He was standing at the bar, looking away from her, but she recognised his broad back immediately. What was he doing here? This wasn't his patch. North Yorks Police were headquartered in Northallerton and Caron lived deep in the countryside. Was he here on joint-force business? Or hoping to bump into his former colleague?

Julie took a step back, letting the door close again.

It would be lovely to see Caron. But not here. Not where you had to shout to be heard. Not with half of Cleveland Police watching and listening and wondering and gossiping.

Her phone buzzed. Arni.

Oh, shit.

Julie arrived at the restaurant to find Arni and Eve already installed in a private booth. They sat close, their heads together, blonde and dark hair mingling. She drew back and took a moment to observe them.

'Mum?' Arni seemed surprised. 'You made it!'

'So little faith.' Julie smiled. 'I promised, didn't I?'

Eve looked paler than normal.

'Hi, Eve,' Julie greeted her. 'Everything OK?'

'Not really,' Eve said, and her eyes filled with tears.

Arni put an arm round her shoulders. 'Let's order,' he said. 'Then we can talk.'

Whatever was troubling her son, it was clear that it involved his girlfriend as well.

At first, they ate in silence.

'Mum, there's no easy way to say this,' Arni said.

Julie put down her cutlery and met his eyes.

'I'm pregnant,' Eve said.

Ah, so there it was.

If they'd already decided on a termination, they probably wouldn't have invited her to this meeting. Julie took a gamble.

'Congratulations,' she said. She smiled at Eve and then at her son. His face broke into the most radiant expression she'd seen in a long time. He looked so young that the lump to her throat threatened to choke her.

Julie took a sip of water and turned back to Eve. 'How do you feel?' she asked, as gently as she could.

'Apart from sick?'

'Apart from sick.'

'It's kind of . . . um . . . mixed,' Eve said, her eyes darting to Arni.

'Have you told your mum and dad?'

'Not yet,' Eve said. 'Mum'll have hysterics, and Dad will march me to the nearest abortion clinic.'

She started to cry again.

Julie swallowed hard, then reached out to take Eve's pale, cool hand in her warmer one.

'It's your body, Eve. No one else gets to tell you what to do with it.'

Julie stretched out her other hand towards Arni's. He took it.

'Look, guys, I'm so glad you told me. I'll support you with whatever you decide, but this is a big decision that will affect the rest of your lives.' She brought their hands together. 'You need some quiet time to think it through.'

Eve raised her head. Her eyes were full of gratitude.

'Do you have plans for the weekend?'

Arni shook his head.

'We both got dropped from hockey. Eve's dad doesn't know yet.'

'This might be a daft idea,' Julie said, 'but if there's no tournament, how about you come away with me Saturday to Sunday? I'm heading to the moors where it's remote and peaceful.'

Eve sighed. 'That would be so lovely.'

Arni nodded.

'Give me a minute, then,' Julie said.

She walked to the bar, pulled out her phone and dialled her friend.

'Don't tell me you're going to cancel,' Kim said.

'That depends,' Julie said. 'Have you got any cottages free?' Her oldest and dearest friend had inherited a large farm with stables. She rented out the empty cottages as holiday lets.

'I've always got room for you,' Kim said.

'It's for my son and his girlfriend, if they come too.'

'The more the merrier,' Kim said. 'Do they share a bed?'

'Oh yes.' Julie laughed bitterly.

Kim laughed. 'Like that, is it? Well, I have a one-bedroom cottage free on Saturday night. You can stay with us in the main house.'

'Perfect,' Julie said. 'We'll take it.'

Julie paused a moment to compose herself before returning to the table. The question she wanted to ask, *how far along are you?* was shorthand for how much time do you have left to make a sensible decision? Eve obviously thought her parents would demand she end the pregnancy. Julie wanted to support the couple by remaining as neutral as possible. Arni's expression of pride and love almost broke her heart. Did these poor children really have the faintest idea of what was involved in bringing up a child?

Chapter 27

It was the perfect autumn morning. Julie and Arni met Eve at the school and then turned the car south. They drove up into the moors under a bright blue cloudless sky, descending into a hidden valley with tumbling streams filled by the recent rainfall. The low sun shone through the ancient woodland; a light breeze caressed the tops of the trees, the dry leaves glowing in shades of copper and gold. As the car came to a halt outside the farmhouse, Kim was there to meet them dressed in riding gear: knee-length black boots, beige jodhpurs, a high-necked white blouse and a short blue hunt jacket.

'So good to see you!' She enveloped Julie in a hug, before recoiling in mock surprise as a young man got out of the front passenger seat.

'Arni! Is that you? When did you get so tall and handsome?'

He blushed and turned to open the rear door for Eve.

'But you're punching above your weight with this beautiful lady.' She winked at Arni and moved forward to gather Eve into a big hug. 'You must be Eve.'

'Pleased to meet you,' Eve said a little stiffly.

'Catch!' Kim tossed a set of keys overarm and Arni dived to catch them. 'You and Eve are in lovebird cottage on the other side of the paddock. Make yourselves at home while I borrow your mum. She's staying right here with me.'

Julie followed her oldest friend into the kitchen.

They'd met at kindergarten and were inseparable throughout primary and secondary school. It was Julie who'd first introduced Kim to Stuart Simmons, a fellow trainee in the police service. It wasn't exactly love at first sight – Kim was in an anti-establishment phase at art school – but the two were married not long after Julie and Matt.

Even though Julie and Stuart had started their police careers together, Stuart quickly moved onto a different track. While Julie was having babies, taking advantage of a civilised amount of maternity leave, Stuart rose through the ranks to become her boss and ultimately Chief Constable.

Julie was catching up on Kim's news over a cup of tea when Arni appeared at the farmhouse window.

'Quick word, Mum?'

Julie left her mug and stepped out into the garden.

'Everything OK?'

'Cottage is lovely. Just one thing.' He nodded towards the kitchen. 'You won't say anything to Kim, will you? You know, about Eve?'

Poor children. How they wore their hearts on their sleeves at that age. Had they not realised that pregnancy wasn't something you could hide for very long?

'No, darling. Of course not.'

'Thanks.'

'You fancy a walk, later?' Julie asked.

'Sure.' He smiled. 'I'll meet you back here in an hour.'

They walked through the wood, beside a stream, emerging onto the high moor just as the sun broke through the clouds.

'I'm sorry, Mum,' Arni said.

'These things happen.'

'We were being careful, but . . .'

She held up a hand. 'No need to explain.' Should she tell him that his elder brother was completely unplanned? Perhaps now was not the time.

'What do you think we should do?'

'I'd rather hear what you're thinking.'

He took a deep breath.

'It's all a bit of a jumble.'

'Eve took a test?'

'Three tests. All positive.'

'Any idea how far along?'

'Seven weeks.'

They still had time for non-surgical intervention.

'Has she seen her GP yet?'

'She's got an appointment on Tuesday.'

'Good,' Julie said. 'The doctor will be able to explain the options . . .'

'Eve thinks abortion is murder.'

'Is she religious?'

'Not really. But she reads a lot.'

'And you, what do you think?'

'You really want to know?'

'I do.'

He sighed. 'Feels like the first ray of hope since Jamie died.'

'Oh, Arni!' Julie turned away to hide the tears in her eyes.

'I'm sorry, Mum.' He was crying openly now. 'I know how hard it has been on you. And now I'm just adding to your problems.'

Julie gathered him into her arms.

'You're both so young. You have your whole lives ahead of you. Having a baby at seventeen—'

'Eighteen,' he interrupted. 'Eve's already eighteen and I will be by the time she's born.'

'She?'

'That's what Eve calls her.'

'How will you support a family?'

'I'll get a job.'

'What about A levels? What about uni?'

'Lots of people don't go to uni. There are other options.'

'And Eve's parents? How do you think they'll react?'

'Badly.' He grimaced. 'She's dreading telling them.'

'They might surprise her.'

He shook his head. 'I don't think so. She's an only child and they have very fixed ideas about her future. She thinks they'll kick her out if she refuses to terminate.'

'You know she's always welcome to stay with us,' Julie said. 'While you figure things out.'

'Thanks, Mum.'

Should she mention the perilous state of the family finances? The fact that, without Matt, she could barely cover the mortgage payments? They'd agreed that she'd move out as soon as Arni went to university, sell the house and release some equity. They hadn't told the children yet.

She couldn't give Arni the impression that Eve could move in permanently. That they could bring up their baby in his family home. How would Matt react? Wait. I'm not the bad guy in this mess. Matt is the one who abandoned us. He can give Arni the lesson in hard financial reality.

'How would you feel about talking to your dad?'

Arni grimaced. 'Do I have to?'

'Look, darling,' she said. 'You know I'll stand by you and Eve, whatever you decide, but I have to be honest and tell you that there are . . . practical limits. Your dad can explain.'

They walked as far as the viewpoint. The rolling hills stretched out before them, the wooded valleys a riot of late-autumn colour.

'What do you want to do tonight?' Julie asked. 'Kim has invited us all to dinner.'

Arni shook his head. 'Would you mind if Eve and I don't join you?'

'Not at all. This is your weekend escape. Use it any way you wish.'

'We're going to walk to the farm shop, then I'm going to cook.'

Julie smiled. 'I'm impressed.'

Emerging from the wood, they parted ways. Julie watched her son stride away and felt a rush of love that threatened to engulf her.

'You on call tonight?' Kim asked Julie.

'No.'

'Good.'

The sound of a cork popping made her smile.

'Stu's at a work thing, back late. He sends his apologies, but you'll see him tomorrow.'

'Just us, then.'

'Good. I haven't had you to myself for ages.' Kim filled two large glasses. 'Tell me the truth. How are you doing?'

It was late by the time they decided to call it a night. Kim brought Julie an extra blanket and hovered in the doorway of the guest room.

'I had planned to invite Caron over,' she said. 'But he thought he might not be welcome.'

'Not welcome? Why?'

'Apparently you avoided him at the pub last night.'

So, Caron had seen her change her mind at the doorway of The Applegarth.

'I'd promised to take Arni and Eve out to dinner.'

'You're OK if Caron comes riding with us tomorrow?'

Julie looked away to hide a smile. 'Of course,' she said to the window.

'I've a horse that needs attention.'

'I thought it was his mum who was the vet.'

'Caron's good with the behavioural stuff. I guess it helps if you grow up with a lot of animals.' She blew a kiss. 'Night-night – sweet dreams.'

Julie's dreams were surprisingly sweet, and she wasn't entirely sure she was fully awake when she spotted Caron in the paddock the next morning, mounted on a magnificent jet-black stallion.

She showered, dressed and went downstairs to find everyone sitting around the kitchen table.

'Afternoon, Detective Inspector.' Stuart saluted her. 'Late night, was it?'

'Evening, Chief Constable!' she replied. 'You're one to talk.'

He laughed. 'You remember DI Riley?'

'Of course!' Julie waved at Caron, and he grinned back, before resuming his discussion with Arni.

Julie filled her plate from the breakfast bar and took the empty chair beside her son's girlfriend. Eve looked much better today. There was colour in her cheeks and the worry lines had almost disappeared.

'Did you sleep well?' Julie asked.

Eve nodded. 'Twelve hours,' she said.

'You must have needed it.'

'So then, what's everyone up to today?' Kim asked. 'I have horses that need exercising. Anyone fancy a trot over the moors?'

'Eve and I are going for a walk,' Arni said quickly.

So protective, Julie thought. She stuck up a hand. 'I'd love to brush off the cobwebs.'

'You can have Matilda. Caron's on Blackstar. I'll take Sherry.'

'Earth to Stuart – you still with us?'

He put down his phone. A chief constable's work was never done.

'Coming riding?' Kim asked. 'Like you promised?'

He leant over and kissed her. 'I'll take Whisky.'

It was interesting to see how people changed as they rose up the ranks. Most people left their old colleagues behind, used their position to justify a cooling of former friendships. Stuart Simmons, newly appointed Chief Constable of North Yorkshire Police, was quite the opposite. With every promotion he'd become a more intense version of his best self. He used his rank to get things done. He once told her that the job of a boss was to remove obstacles for others and then get out of their way. Stuart was always willing to help. Of course, it had a lot to do with the person he'd married. Kim and Stuart were very different. She was an artist from a family rich enough to own horses, and he was a working-class boy with a fierce passion for public service. Chalk and cheese, yin and yang, they were good for each other.

The riding party set out over the moors. They overtook Arni and Eve on the bridleway, the teenagers hand in hand, laughing at some shared joke. They were sweet together, those two. How best to warn them what was in store if they chose to go ahead with the pregnancy? Having a child, while children themselves, would change their lives. Could they make it work? Times had changed. These days, there was no stigma attached. Maybe they could make a go of it if they really wanted to. Was she ready to be a grandmother? As if life wasn't complicated enough.

Matilda was a sweet-natured horse who needed very little guidance. Julie had been riding these trails ever since she was a child, and she drifted into autopilot.

'Penny for them?'

Caron rode up beside her.

'They grow up so fast,' Julie said.

A flicker of pain passed over his face. Julie could have kicked herself. She remembered now that Caron and his wife had tried many rounds of IVF before giving up hope of ever having children. She quickly changed the subject.

'Catch any more rainbows lately?'

He smiled. 'I was in your neck of the woods on Friday. I dropped into The Applegarth hoping to see you.'

She damped down the little surge of pleasure.

'Sorry,' she said, and jerked her head back at the distant walking figures. 'Family stuff.'

'He's grown up well, your Arni,' Caron said. 'I gather he's thinking about joining the force.'

News to her, but it might not be such a daft option if he was serious about getting a job.

'I told him he'd be better off going to uni first,' Caron said. 'He can always join later via the graduate programme.'

'He's exploring options.'

Caron nodded.

'What about you?' he asked.

'Me?'

'How are you?'

'Fine,' she said.

'You fancy a drink sometime?'

Hell, yes.

'Maybe when this murder investigation is over?' She tried to make it sound nonchalant.

Blackstar began to fidget, bucking his head and kicking his heels.

'I need to give this animal a proper run,' Caron said. 'I'll call you, OK?'

And then he was gone, a dark tornado galloping over the brow of the hill and into the mist.

Kim rode over and winked.

'You can stop drooling now,' she said.

Julie composed her features.

'Did you put him up to that?'

'Up to what?'

'Are you matchmaking again?'

'Me?' Kim opened her eyes wide in feigned innocence. 'Of course not.' She smiled. 'Although you do make a very handsome pair.' Her face became serious. 'He's had a rough time since he split up with his wife. You could be good for one another.'

Julie shook her head. It takes more than two broken people to make a whole. 'Caron is a friend. But that's all he is and all he'll ever be.'

She almost convinced herself.

Chapter 28

When Julie arrived at work on Monday morning, her boss was already outside her office. Prowling.

'Good morning, Superintendent Chalmers,' she said.

'Morning, DI Cadell. What news do you have for me?'

Her boss was a night owl, not renowned for his early starts. He already knew that they had a positive ID on the victim. What had happened over the weekend to bring him here so early?

'Nothing new since Friday, sir.'

'Didn't see you at The Applegarth.' He growled his displeasure.

'No, sir.'

'Make more of an effort to fit in, Cadell,' he said. 'Let your hair down from time to time. Socialise with your fellow officers. Does wonders for team motivation.'

Those with an alcohol problem liked to see it as the solution. She doubted very much that DS Iain Wharton would have particularly welcomed her presence in the pub on Friday, and he was the only member of her team who'd have been there. DC Chris Gibson had knocked off early to spend time with his new baby and however many of his other five children he was caring for at the weekend. Sandy and Adrian were always good company, but the pathologist never went to The Applegarth, and last Friday night the CSM had been working overtime, combing through a suspiciously clean bedroom at The Locomotion.

Hey-ho. Never allow facts to get in the way of the current bee in the boss's bonnet.

'Yes, sir,' she said.

'So, what is your team working on?'

'CSM Prosser is coordinating the search at the deceased man's lodgings. DS Wharton is reviewing CCTV. DC Gibson is . . .'

'Witnesses? Suspects?'

'Once we have the itinerary from the victim's employer, we'll be working through that to see if—'

'Give DS Wharton something meaningful to do, will you?'

'CCTV is meaningful.'

'But not his forte.' The super sighed. 'Iain came to the police force from the army. He's an athlete, built for action. You'll find him a good man if you use him right.'

'And you don't think I'm using him right?'

'He'll be more value to you away from a desk.'

'In that case,' DI Cadell used her coolest voice, 'I need some extra support.'

'God loves a trier.' The super laughed. 'I'll see what I can do.'

The appointment schedule for the Zebra technical sales manager, Dameer Ghosh, was waiting in her inbox. The first page was a list of company names. Details of previous orders and values had been redacted – a thick black pen drawn through the numbers – but there were notes on potential upcoming investments.

The second page had what looked like a list of firm meetings. Friday was blocked out, and there were no entries for the weekend or for the first days of the following week. Only the return flight was detailed – Teesside to Amsterdam to Mumbai, India.

Julie read through the document line by line, then stared up at the ceiling.

An email arrived from HR. A civilian investigation officer had been assigned to work with her team. CIO Nadia Latif would report at 11 a.m.

Julie picked up the phone.

'DS Wharton, can you come in here?'

He took his time, slouching in the door frame, a picture of hulking menace.

'How are you getting along with the CCTV review?'

'Making progress.'

'I've arranged some assistance.'

He bristled. 'You think I can't handle it?'

'I need your help elsewhere.'

He glanced at her from under hooded brows as if expecting some trick. 'With what?'

'Dameer Ghosh's itinerary has arrived,' Julie said. 'Let's go out and talk to the people he was meant to meet. We could split the interviews between us.'

He brightened visibly.

'I'll take Wednesday's appointments. Can you take Thursday's? There are three – a gas terminal, a tank farm and a fine chemicals site.'

She printed off the page with the contact details.

'What's the angle?'

'We're looking for anything that might explain what he was doing here, what sort of man he was, what sort of business he was involved in, why anyone would want to kill him.'

He turned the page. 'I wonder what he was planning to do at the weekend. You'd think he'd want to visit that lovely sister of his. Seems odd, coming all this way and not making contact.'

Julie shrugged. 'She claimed to be unaware of his trip.'

'You don't believe her?'

'Open mind, Sergeant. I'm keeping an open mind,' Julie said. 'And the super has found a civilian investigator to join our team. CIO Nadia Latif is on her way over. Show her the ropes, OK?'

'Yes, boss.'

Julie could see that DS Wharton left the office a much happier man.

If she had been a good boss, she would have been happy too. But Julie couldn't quite shake her annoyance at Superintendent Chalmers for his interference. She'd trust her boss as far as she could throw him, which – given his girth – was not very far at all.

Julie had just finished a call with the Indian High Commission in London when there was a light knock on the window. She looked up from her desk but couldn't see anyone through the glazed panel. The knock came again, and this time she saw a small hand through the glass. A child? She got up and opened the door. The civilian investigator waited patiently outside in her wheelchair. Eleven o'clock sharp.

'Come in,' Julie said.

CIO Nadia Latif, her hair hidden by a neat hijab, beamed as she entered.

'Morning, DI Cadell. I hear you have some real work for me.'

'Morning, Nadia, and welcome to the team.'

Julie reached into her desk drawer for the photos supplied by Alvi Zaidi. She selected the portrait of the murder victim at his master's graduation in the US, looking straight into the camera with such intensity it was as if he was present in the room. She handed it to the civilian investigator.

'Take a good look at this man,' she said. 'His name is Dameer Ghosh. A visitor from India. He was murdered in Teesside and we're going to catch his killers.'

The young woman's eyes sparkled.

'How can I help?'

'Report to DS Iain Wharton. He has some CCTV that needs your eagle eyes.'

The CIO's mouth and shoulders dropped a little.

'I need you to be careful and thorough.' Everything that DS Wharton was not. 'An investigation like this stands or falls on attention to the smallest details.'

The CIO sat up straight and smiled.

'Yes, boss.'

Julie grabbed her car keys and followed the wheelchair out of the office.

'Great to have you on board.'

Chapter 29

Middlesbrough – Monday, 18 November 2024

The fastest route from police HQ to Seal Sands was over the Transporter Bridge, the bright blue structure that defined the skyline of Middlesbrough. Built in 1910, the double-cantilevered zigzag framework held a gondola, a suspended platform to ferry vehicles back and forth over the steel river, while permitting the tall ships to sail up and down the River Tees unimpeded. But the tall ships had long gone and the Transporter Bridge had been closed since 2019. The red and silver Newport Bridge, a vertical-lift bridge that no longer moved, was closed for maintenance, so she took the concrete A19 flyover and came off at the first exit, joining the queue of contractor traffic snaking through Haverton Hill.

Ahead of her, a jumble of man-made geometric shapes emerged from the mist. Plumes of steam rose from cooling towers to join an already cloudy sky. A gas flare shot up to singe the clouds, turning them from grey to orange and pink.

On Wednesday, 6 November, the murder victim had arrived from Amsterdam, checked into his lodgings at The Locomotion in Eaglescliffe and then set off for his two scheduled meetings in Seal Sands.

The land reclaimed from the estuary was full of life, in the form of hundreds of cigar-shaped seals. Brown adults wallowed while little white pups played. The animals took advantage of the tidal mudflats and waste heat from industry.

Julie took a right at the fire station and continued along the road until she saw a signpost for Zagrovyl International, turning into the visitors' car park as the heavens opened. She parked as close as possible to the gatehouse, pulled her jacket over her head and made a dash for the entrance.

'I'd like to speak to Sue Bell, please,' Julie said through the hatch.

The gateman turned to a colleague. 'Is Sue in today?'

The other man shook his head. 'She's on maternity leave.'

'Since when?' Julie asked.

'We can't give out personal information.'

'Then I'll speak with the site manager.'

'Mr Cosby?' The gateman looked doubtful. 'He's very busy . . .'

Julie flashed her badge.

'DI Cadell from Cleveland Police.'

Julie was issued with a site pass and directed to reception where Alan Cosby came to meet her. It took a bit of persuasion, but once she'd reminded him of the special provision in the Data Protection Act of 2018 permitting disclosure of personal data to the police, he softened his stance and called for assistance in the form of a stern-faced woman who introduced herself as Marcia Chipchase, Head of Human Resources at Zagrovyl Seal Sands.

Julie shook her hand and got straight to the point. 'When was Sue Bell last on site?'

'Wednesday the sixth of November,' Marcia said. 'She started her maternity leave the following day.'

'Did she receive a visitor that day? From a company called Zebra?'

'Just a second.' Alan Cosby snapped his fingers at the receptionist and repeated the request. Marcia got up and went to the counter, returning with a printout.

'Yes. A Mr Dameer Ghosh came on site to see Sue.'

'What time did he arrive?'

Marcia ran a finger down the report. 'Thirteen forty-nine.'

In good time for his 2 p.m. appointment.

'What time did he leave?'

The report provided no answers. Marcia returned to the reception desk and was joined by Alan. There was a long discussion, raised voices, and Alan returned alone shaking his head.

'We'll have to look into that.'

'Did Dameer Ghosh meet with anyone else?'

'Only Sue would be able to tell us that.'

'Then it's vital that I speak to her.'

'Given her condition, I'm not sure . . .'

'Why don't you call her now and find out if she's available?'

Alan bristled, but then snapped his fingers again.

'Call Sue,' he shouted over to the receptionist. 'Ask if she's willing to speak to the police.'

'Thank you.' Julie stood up and approached the woman behind the desk. 'Please tell her it's urgent,' she said. 'And ask her to phone me back on this number.' She slid a card across the counter.

Julie had just reached the car when her phone rang.

'Mrs Bell, thanks so much for getting in touch.' Julie opened the car door and ducked inside to get out of the rain. 'You're on maternity leave, right?'

'Sort of.' The voice was vaguely familiar, but Julie couldn't quite place it. 'I have another month before the due date, but I'm the size of a bloody house and I've been forbidden from waddling around the site.'

The rain was coming down hard now. Julie pressed the ignition, and the windscreen wipers swooshed into life.

'I guess they want you to be safe.'

'Pregnancy isn't an illness. My brain is still working,' Sue said. 'Anyway, I was glad to hear from you. We met once, but you might not remember.'

'Did we? I'm very sorry, I don't remember.'

The windscreen wipers sped up as the intensity of the rain increased.

'You did some emergency response coordination training for us a while back.'

'Susan Strong?'

'That's me!'

It all fell into place. 'Now I remember. A couple of years ago, right? That was a very well-organised exercise. Is Bell your married name?'

'That's right. I took my wife's surname.'

'Double congratulations.'

'So how can I help you?' Sue asked.

'It might be better if we met in person,' Julie said.

'Fantastic. I'm going stir-crazy alone in the house.'

'I can come to you.'

'No. The house is a tip, and I need a break. How about we meet at the Saltholme café? I'm in Greatham and it won't take me long to get there.'

The Saltholme nature reserve provided a wildlife oasis in the middle of an industrial desert. Julie drove to the visitor centre and parked her car facing east, away from the towers and flares of the chemical complex, looking out over reed beds instead. The shallow pools were alive with wading birds who didn't seem to mind the rain.

Another car drew up beside her, and a heavily pregnant woman struggled out.

Julie straightened her shoulders, grabbed an umbrella from the boot and stepped out to shelter her witness.

They took the lift to the first floor. Julie ordered at the counter while Sue settled at a table beside a window with a panoramic view.

'It's good to see you again,' Julie said, transferring the teapot, mugs and scones from the tray to the table. 'You look well.'

'Actually, I feel great,' Sue said. 'Which is why it's so annoying that HR insisted I start my maternity leave early. I'd rather have the time off after the baby is born.'

'How long do you get?'

'Six months in total, plus accrued holidays. I've been saving those up.'

Sue swirled the pot then poured some tea into a mug.

'Strong enough for you?' she asked.

'Looks fine.'

Sue continued to pour the tea and handed a mug to Julie.

Julie blew on it before taking a sip.

Sue added milk to her empty mug and then filled it with tea. 'So come on, what's all this about?' she asked.

'I believe you met with a Mr Ghosh last week. From Zebra Safety Solutions.'

'Dameer? Yes, I saw him briefly, on my way to an antenatal check-up. I left him with my maternity cover,' she said.

'Who is your maternity cover?'

'A guy called Simon Sharp.' Sue sighed. 'Nickname Sharpie, though he's more blunt than sharp. In reality, there's not much of my job he can cover, but he'll keep routine IT stuff ticking over. It's hard to find experienced control systems engineers who don't cost the earth.'

'How did Dameer seem to you?'

'Apart from charming?' she laughed. 'I don't know how to answer that. He's always charming.'

'You'd met him before?'

'Yes. In India. At the Zagrovyl site in Panki,' she said. 'A genuinely nice guy, and super smart.'

'What was the most recent meeting about?'

'A routine sales call,' she said. 'He brought me a gift, too. A book for the baby.'

'That was thoughtful,' Julie said.

She refilled their teacups and waited while Sue ate her fruit scone.

'I'm afraid I have some bad news. I'm sorry to be the one to tell you.' Julie took a deep breath. 'Dameer Ghosh is dead.'

Sue's eyes opened wide. 'No!'

'His body was found in Hartlepool Marina on the morning after you met with him.'

Sue gave out a strangled cry.

'Are you OK?'

'Yes.' Sue dabbed her eyes with a paper tissue. 'It's just a shock, that's all.'

'Let me get you some water.'

Julie filled a glass from a jug on the counter. She waited until Sue had dried her eyes and taken a sip.

'Are you OK to continue?' Julie asked. 'We can take a break. Reschedule?'

Sue shook her head. 'What happened?'

'That's what we're trying to find out.'

'But how did he die?'

'He was found in the water at the Hartlepool Historic Quay.'

'Did he drown?'

'It's a murder investigation,' Julie said. 'That's as much as I can say.'

'The mystery man on the news? That was Dameer?' Sue shook her head and reached for her phone. 'No, there must be some mistake.' She clicked through to a news website with the police sketch. 'That could be anyone. How can you be sure it's Dameer?'

'His sister, Alvi, identified him. She lives in the UK.'

'I didn't know he had a sister here.'

'Half-sister. Seems they were estranged.'

'I can't believe he's dead.' Sue shook her head from side to side. 'Poor, poor man.' She turned to the window and stared out at the rain pelting the reeds.

Julie waited.

Eventually Sue looked back at her. There was a new energy, a controlled anger in her voice. 'How can I help?'

'We need to know who else he spoke to, what time he left and where he went after your meeting.'

'I left before him,' Sue said. 'I have no idea what his plans were. He suggested meeting up one evening but I never heard from him.' Her eyes filled with tears again. 'And now I know why.'

'Can you think of any reason why someone would want to harm him? Anything at all?'

Sue shook her head.

'What about the rest of your team? Who else did he speak to at Zagrovyl?'

'Just Sharpie, as far as I know.'

'I can contact Simon Sharp at Zagrovyl, I assume?'

Sue nodded.

'If there's anything else,' Julie stood up, 'anything at all that comes to mind, please get in touch with me.'

'Trust me,' Sue said. 'I will.'

Back in the car, Julie phoned the Zagrovyl reception and asked to speak with Simon Sharp.

The receptionist put her through to his extension, but after three rings it went to voicemail.

'This is DI Julie Cadell from Cleveland Police. I need to speak with Simon Sharp urgently. Simon, please ring me back as soon as you get this.' She left her direct number and then called reception again with the same message.

Chapter 30

BRIAN

Stockton-on-Tees – Monday, 18 November 2024

Brian had barely slept over the weekend. He'd been too busy creating the game that was going to make his fortune. *B.H.O.P.A.L.* was going to be bigger than *S.T.A.L.K.E.R.* Bigger and better. BB Games Galaxy was going to go multinational, and Brian, founder and CTO, was going to become a millionaire.

If he was honest, the sections of code that had felt elegant, even beautiful as he was writing them, chugged once compiled – all janky frame drops and bugs. Disappointing – so much effort for so little impact. Story of his life, really. Some optimisation was required. Of course, he didn't yet have access to all the fancy tools and plug-ins that professional game development companies took for granted. Teesside University had one of the best animation labs in Europe; he'd hire a couple of graduate students to tidy things up and create a good-looking demo before going to market. Once he'd brought a few investors on board, he could really get going.

As the weak dawn light crept around the blinds, he decided to give the flow charts a rest and focus on the creative angle. This was the sort of thing that he'd left up to Betty in the past. When they'd discussed creating games together, she'd been the one who'd come up with the story arc, the hero's journey. She loved to get lost in the worldbuilding and character development. Well, Betty wasn't here to interfere any longer, so he'd just have to do it himself.

But first he needed to sleep.

It was dark when Brian woke up, but his mind was crystal clear, brimming with ideas. He got out of bed, made a mug of tea and got back under the covers with a pad of paper and a pencil. Old school. Analogue.

B.H.O.P.A.L. 2 – Mutant Revenge. The mosquitoes emerging from the toxic waste ponds are evolving. A bite from a mutant insect makes the human male rebels lethargic, while giving superpowers to the human females. Should they drain the swamps or breed spiders to control the mosquitoes? Men versus women. Arachnids versus insects.

Brian experienced a surge of pride as he completed his outline. It was his best work. Even Betty couldn't help but be impressed.

When Brian's phone lit up with his girlfriend's picture, his heart did a double somersault.

'Brian, what are you playing at?'

Betty's voice was sweet and husky. He'd missed her musical voice so much.

'You like the game outline?' he asked.

'No,' she said. 'I don't like it. I don't like it one little bit. Come on, Brian, you can't turn an ongoing tragedy into a silly game.'

Silly game? That stung. But she hadn't finished throwing poisoned darts at him.

'What's next?' she asked. 'Darfur? Gaza?'

The same old Betty. Always taking the moral high ground, forever fighting the good fight. He attempted to defend himself.

'Chernobyl is an ongoing tragedy, and it doesn't stop you playing *S.T.A.L.K.E.R.*'

'The two situations are completely different,' she said.

'Why?' he asked. 'Because the Russians invaded Ukraine?'

'Because it was a Ukrainian who developed *S.T.A.L.K.E.R.* He knew what he was talking about. It was his people, his country, his story to tell.'

'You're accusing me of cultural appropriation? Telling me to stay in my lane?'

This was an argument they'd had many times before. Could a stale pale male get nothing right these days?

'It's more than that,' she said. 'It's in bad taste to profit from the pain of others.'

'It was almost forty years ago,' he protested.

'The Ukrainians owned their problem. With international help they contained it. Before the Russian invasion, the exclusion zone was a major tourist attraction. The people of Bhopal have been abandoned and ignored.'

'Well, to be fair, the Chernobyl nuclear accident threatened the whole of Europe and the only people who suffered from the gas tragedy were the very poorest Indians.'

'And that makes it OK?'

There was no point arguing with Betty.

'No, of course not.'

'Anyway, it's not just something that happened in the past, Brian. The pollution from the abandoned chemical plant in Bhopal is still ruining lives today.'

'How come you know so much about all this?'

'I read, Brian.'

It had always been a bone of contention that while Betty curled up with a book, Brian relaxed with computer games, sometimes playing, but when he was feeling creative, writing his own code. The past results never quite matched the ambition, but he'd put a lot more work and done a lot more research for this game than for any of his previous projects.

'So do I.'

He'd read all the US reports. One from the US company who owned the site at the time of the accident and one from a US consultant.

'You've swallowed the conspiracy theory hook, line and sinker.' She quoted from his detailed character list. 'You've invented a saboteur, a single worker responsible for the tragedy, and the fight for truth and justice is reduced to tracking down one rogue individual.'

'I thought all that was pretty clear-cut,' he protested.

Her laugh was loaded with derision. 'Have you read the Greenpeace report on Bhopal? Or the one from Amnesty International? Or *The Atlantic*?'

'No, but . . .'

Betty had always been more left wing than him. It was a bit of a stumbling block at first. They saw the world differently. He gradually came to realise that they were working with different information, and once they shared – and debated – their sources they often came to broadly similar conclusions, both prepared to change their minds or agree to differ.

'What triggered this sudden interest in India, Brian?'

'I know someone who was born in Bhopal.'

'Then talk to them about it.'

'He was murdered.'

That shut her up.

'You might have seen him in the news,' he added. 'Dameer Ghosh.'

'The Hartlepool murder victim? You knew him?'

'We'd worked on a few projects together. He called me to say he was in the UK and asked if we could meet up. He was murdered the same night.'

Brian was suddenly aware of how sad it made him feel.

'I'm sorry,' she said. 'That's rough.'

The old Betty was back. He preferred the loving, caring Betty to the cross, shouty Betty.

'Are you OK?' she asked.

'Not really,' he said. And he wasn't. He really wasn't.

'OK, Brian,' she sighed. 'I think I understand now. With this game, you're working through your grief, and that's important.'

Grief? Was he grieving? He didn't think so. He was sad about Dameer, of course he was, but theirs had been a strictly professional relationship. Yes, there'd been a meeting of minds when it came to control networks and cybersecurity, but he'd never even met the guy in person. When Dameer disappeared, Brian had been mainly irritated. One – he'd wasted time preparing for and attending a meeting that never happened, and two – the first real prospect of a new job had vanished. When the idea of the *B.H.O.P.A.L.* game had come to him it seemed like a consolation prize. But if he said all that to Betty, it would make him appear unfeeling and shallow. He bit his lip. Perhaps he really was unfeeling and shallow. But then anyone would appear cold compared to someone as warm as Betty. Best to say nothing and let her draw her own emotionally charged conclusions.

'You still there?' she asked.

Why did he feel like crying all of a sudden?

'Yes,' he said.

'This is important,' she said. 'If you're going ahead with this game, at least make sure you have the right background information. If I send you some links on Bhopal, do you promise to look at them?'

His mouth went dry with hope. 'If I read them, can we meet to talk about things?'

Her voice changed, from soft to hard. 'What things?'

Damn. He'd gone too far, too fast.

'Bhopal, I mean.'

She sucked air through her teeth.

'Maybe.'

Chapter 31

JULIE

Hartlepool - Monday, 18 November 2024

Julie passed through the security barrier and entered the long drive towards the nuclear power station, a massive concrete fortress at the very north of the Tees Estuary. She parked opposite the visitor centre and stood aside as a crocodile of primary school children, chattering excitedly, followed the tour guides towards the generator hall. Forty years old and – according to the posters – still generating enough carbon-free electricity for all the houses in the north-east of England, this was a poster child for clean energy, safe enough to bring schoolchildren to site. At least when everything was running smoothly.

Inside, she came face to face with a cardboard cut-out of an armed police officer. A life-sized photo of a member of the Civil Nuclear Constabulary, the police force entrusted with maintaining security on and between nuclear facilities. Behind him was a scale model of the nuclear core and several hands-on interactive exhibits explaining atomic energy without the mathematics.

A young woman came forward to greet her and Julie flashed her badge.

'Officer, how may I help you?'

'I called earlier. I'm making enquiries about an engineer who was due to visit the site on Wednesday the sixth of November.'

The woman nodded. 'It was me you spoke to.' She introduced herself as Sylvia Rossi before leading the way to a meeting room.

'Tea? Coffee?'

'Just some water.'

Sylvia went to the water cooler and filled a paper cup. She sat opposite Julie and opened a laptop.

'Dameer Ghosh from Zebra Safety Solutions . . . Hmm, yes, he was booked in for four p.m. but then it was cancelled,' she said. 'Rescheduled for Thursday the seventh at ten a.m., but he didn't show.'

'Was a reason given for cancelling the meeting?' Julie asked.

'Not that I know of.'

'Did Dameer cancel the meeting himself?'

'I'm not sure. I didn't take the call.'

'Do you know what the meeting was to be about?'

'A routine sales call.'

'With you?'

'Yes, I'm a nuclear physicist working in engineering procurement.'

'Can you be more specific about the purpose of the meeting?'

'Zebra supplies us with parts for some of the safety sensors on the plant.'

'Had you met Dameer before?'

'No,' Sylvia said. 'But we often speak on the phone. He's always extremely helpful and technically very knowledgeable.'

'I'm very sorry to inform you that he's dead.'

Sylvia's jaw dropped. She closed the laptop and brought both hands to her mouth. 'Oh, that's terrible,' she said. 'What happened?'

Julie slid the untouched cup of water across the table and waited as Sylvia drank it.

'We're conducting a murder investigation,' Julie said. 'Is there anything you can tell me that might assist us in our investigation?'

Sylvia shook her head. Julie stood and refilled the paper cup from the water cooler.

'Anything at all?'

'It might be nothing . . .' Sylvia paused. 'But we did have a lot of trouble with his security clearance.'

'Oh?'

'As an Indian national he had to pass some extra checks. First time round there were all sorts of warning flags against his name.'

'Can you be more explicit?'

'We have to screen for potential terrorists.'

'And he flagged up as high-risk?'

'Yes. When we dug deeper the problem disappeared. Possibly a case of mistaken identity – it might be a common name in India.'

If Julie had arrived unsettled, her unease was ten times worse when she left.

She drove back via Zagrovyl International, only to find that Simon Sharp had not been seen at work that day. Both Marcia Chipchase from HR, the person with access to personal contact details, and site manager Alan Cosby, the only one who could authorise their release, had already gone home for the day. She left a message and headed home at a civilised time for once, buying vegetables and fruit on the way so she could cook a healthy dinner.

A Tesla was parked directly outside her house. It wasn't a reserved space, but most of the neighbours respected the natural boundaries and she was annoyed to have to drive to the end of the road to find somewhere to park. She collected the brown paper bags of carrots, onions and potatoes from the boot, along with the apples and oranges, and wished she'd paid five pence for a plastic bag.

The man in the Tesla got out as she reached her house. His face was vaguely familiar. Police work meant contact with a wide cross-section of the local population, and Julie sometimes struggled to place a face out of context.

'How dare you?' he shouted, slamming his car door closed.

The man was not happy, that much was clear. What was more, his unhappiness appeared to be directed specifically at her. Was he dangerous? Julie made a dash for the front door, but he was faster. Onions and oranges spilt from their bags. He stood in her path, blocking her way.

'This is my home,' she said. 'Please let me past.'

'Not until you've explained what the hell you are up to.'

Julie hit the panic button on her phone. 'The police are on their way.'

'Good,' he said. 'Then they can arrest you for kidnapping.'

It dawned on her then who he was. Mr Evans. Eve's father. She'd seen him last at the hockey social.

'Kidnapping?'

'Haven't you and your son done enough? Now you're trying to twist Eve's mind,' he shouted. 'She's my daughter, not yours.'

Julie took a deep breath. His daughter must have told her parents about her pregnancy. No wonder he was upset.

'Why don't we go somewhere where we can talk . . .'

'I don't want to talk. I don't want to see you or your filthy son ever again. All I want is my little girl back.'

He raised his head and bellowed. 'EVE! I know you're in there. I'm coming to get you.'

There was no point trying to stop him. He was a big man. A big, angry man. She watched him hammering at the door, hoping that Arni and Eve were not inside. Or if they were, that they'd have the sense not to open the door.

Julie stepped back into the street and texted her son.

You OK?

Her phone pinged.

FRGT KYS

This was a man contemplating fatherhood and he couldn't even remember his house keys? Although maybe the two were connected; he had much to be distracted about. The phone pinged again.

U HM?

She typed a reply, complete with vowels *and* punctuation.

I'm not home yet.

It was half true – there was a furious father between her and home, his knuckles bloody from the assault on her reinforced front door. He wouldn't get very far. She'd beefed up security after Matt left, on the advice of a police colleague.

She texted Arni.

Is Eve with you?

A thumbs up.

Wait there. Send me your location? I'll come and get you both.

Mr Evans turned and advanced on her. 'Give me your keys,' he yelled.

Now that she knew her son was safe, the fear descended. Dry mouth, cold sweat, heavy limbs that refused to move, the black taste in her mouth and ringing in her ears.

The squad car arrived just in time, lights and siren blazing. A constable got out.

'What seems to be the problem here?'

Mr Evans puffed out his chest.

'The problem is that this woman,' he made a dismissive gesture towards her, 'this woman has kidnapped my daughter.'

DI Cadell dragged her badge from her pocket and flashed it at the constable. She took a deep breath and formed her words carefully, her tongue fat and disobedient.

'My s-s . . . s-s . . . son,' she stammered. Stop. Breathe. You can do this. She closed her eyes to block out the aggressive, hulking man looming over her and tried again. 'My son and Mr Evans's daughter are in a relationship,' she explained. 'One that Mr Evans seems to be unhappy about.'

Mr Evans stamped his feet.

'Do you deny that you lured Eve away on Saturday when she should have been playing hockey?'

Julie opened her eyes to see little drops of spittle flying from his mouth. Disgust gave her new strength.

'They were both dropped from their teams,' Julie said. 'I was due to stay with friends and invited them along. Your daughter is an adult who can make her own decisions.'

The constable raised an eyebrow. 'How old is your daughter, Mr Evans?'

'Eighteen,' he said. 'But that's not the point.'

'Mr Evans,' Julie said. 'Your daughter Eve is welcome in our house any time she wants. She is free to come and go as she pleases. You, however, are not welcome. If you want to talk with me and my son in a public place, we will meet you. But for now,' she made every syllable count, 'GET. OFF. MY. PROPERTY.'

His chest sank, his shoulders dropped, his head tilted forward, his limbs started to tremble. As the anger evaporated he was left visibly deflated.

'You want to file a report, Inspector?' the constable asked.

She addressed Mr Evans. 'Do I need to apply for a restraining order?'

He didn't say a word, walked past her, got into his car and drove off.

Chapter 32

Judging by the sideways glances, word about last night's altercation had already spread around the station. DC Chris Gibson was the first to give voice to the curiosity.

'You OK, ma'am?'

'I'm quite well, thank you, Constable. Why do you ask?'

'Heard you had a run-in with a certain Mr Ethan Evans last night.'

'And how did you hear that?'

He had the grace to look slightly embarrassed.

'Oh, jungle drums,' he said. 'You know.'

'No, Constable, I don't know. Police work is confidential. If we break the trust with those we serve, then . . .'

He listened to the lecture, waiting until she was running out of steam.

'I know, ma'am. I'm sorry, ma'am, but you need to know something. That man is trouble.'

Julie stopped and stared at him.

'What do you mean?'

'One of the biggest crooks on Teesside. He runs security, waste and building services firms, hires out people and skips and forklifts and dumpers and cranes to building sites. He's gone bankrupt more times than you've had hot dinners. Every time, he just starts up a new company. He's regularly in court, but nothing ever sticks. Witnesses withdraw testimony the moment his lawyers get involved. Too rich and slippery to catch.'

This was Eve's father? The Tesla-driving businessman?

Oh Arni.

Last night she'd collected the fruit and vegetables littering her path and unlocked her door with trembling hands. Once inside, she hadn't dared to sit down, needing to surf the wave of adrenaline until Arni and Eve were safe.

She'd found the two of them by the river, laughing at something on Eve's phone, lost to the outside world. She bought everyone pizza on the way home, and they ate from the boxes at the kitchen table while Eve recounted the disastrous meeting with her parents. Julie cleaned the family bathroom and put fresh sheets on the double bed in the guest room. She collapsed into her own bed and was asleep before her head touched the pillow.

In the morning, Julie offered to accompany Eve to her GP appointment, but Eve declined. They all left the house together. Arni looked terrified, but there was a steely glint in Eve's eyes.

Time to focus on work. Julie opened her laptop and fired off an official request to the Office for Nuclear Regulation. What were Dameer Ghosh's security clearance problems? Why was he initially flagged as a security risk? What information did the intelligence authorities hold on him? Would it help them understand why a man so universally liked and respected should have become the victim of a brutal murder?

She failed to focus on the budget spreadsheet that was next on the list, so she went for a walk through the open-plan office and stopped at the desk of the newest recruit to the team.

'DI Cadell.' The young woman almost saluted.

'CIO Latif.' Julie nodded at the array of pot plants on the window ledge. 'I see you're settling in.'

'South-facing,' she said. 'Nice and sunny here.'

'I was wondering if you could help me.'

'That's my job.'

DS Wharton was still interviewing people at the factories and businesses the murder victim had been due to visit. It was a good opportunity for Julie to take the CIO through the CCTV priorities. Top of the list was the main crime scenes – the port and scrapyard and the no-man's land in between. Next was persuading Asda to release CCTV that might identify who had stolen or purchased the clothing found on the murder victim. Then there was Teesside airport – immigration and arrivals to see if the victim had been travelling with anyone, or if someone had met him at the airport. And Station Road, the street outside The Locomotion from the time he'd checked in and then afterwards to try and spot who had emptied his room.

Back in her office, Julie checked her personal phone. There was a missed call from the school informing her that her son was absent, and a text message from Arni.

Eve says GP was great. She's been referred to a counsellor.

That probably meant she was keeping her options open.

Julie sent a blue heart.

Arni began typing.

Can you ring the school? Make up some excuse for why we're not coming in.

Could she? Yes. Would she? No. Even if she'd been willing to make up an excuse for Arni, she could certainly not lie on behalf of someone else's child. Even before the run-in with Ethan Evans, that was a step too far.

It was great having communicative, loving Arni back, great being friends again, but she was still a parent. It was up to her to do the hard stuff too.

You shouldn't be missing school. Isn't there a teacher you can talk to?

Arni had to step up and take responsibility.

She waited for a reply, but her phone screen was still dark when she pulled out of Middlesbrough Police Station car park and onto Bridge Street.

She drove to Zagrovyl. Simon Sharp had not appeared for work. Alan Cosby and Marcia were on a business trip. After a painful series of interviews with their underlings, she obtained Simon Sharp's telephone number and home address.

She dialled the mobile. It went straight to voicemail.

'This is Detective Inspector Julie Cadell from Cleveland Police. I need to speak with you urgently. Please return my call as soon as you get this.'

When Julie got home, the house was empty. A message was scrawled on the back of an envelope on the kitchen table.

Meeting Dad for dinner – I may stay over.

If Arni expected his dad to be sympathetic, then he might be in for a nasty surprise. But then it was hard to tell how Matt would react. Back when they were first married, he'd been furious when Julie had told him she was pregnant, worried about how they'd afford a family on top of the mortgage and car loan. She had pointed out that he'd played a significant role in their predicament – after all, it took two to tango. He'd come round quickly and had been a good, if rather stern, father. Her role had always been that of peacemaker.

The note said I, not we. Had Eve gone home? Poor lass, Julie didn't envy her facing up to her furious dad, Ethan Evans. But perhaps his anger was born from concern. Parents can show love in confusing ways.

Julie investigated the rescued fruit shop haul. The apples had come out in bruises, huge brown welts from being dropped when Ethan Evans confronted her, so she threw them away, along with some of the oranges whose bruising felt internal. The potatoes, onions and carrots looked OK, and she had a sudden urge to make lentil soup. She climbed up on a chair to get the pressure cooker down, put some music on and poured herself a glass of wine.

The phone rang. Her old friend.

'Stuart, hi.'

'Police charity shindig this weekend. Spare ticket. Fancy coming along as my guest?'

Julie thought about Arni and Eve. They might need her.

'I don't think I can.'

'Kim will be disappointed.'

'I'm sorry.'

'Caron too.'

Despite herself, Julie smiled. Kim must have put him up to this. 'I never took you for a matchmaker.'

'You've had a tough few years, Julie. Cut yourself a little slack.'

'When is it?'

'Saturday the twenty-third at Gisborough Hall. Seven p.m. cocktails, eight p.m. dinner. Black tie.'

'What, I'm expected to wear a ballgown? I'm definitely not coming.'

'Kim says a cocktail dress is fine.'

'Oh, you mean select one from among my extensive collection?'

He laughed. 'You don't need to decide now. Let me know on Friday, OK?'

'Assume I can't come,' she said. 'I'll call if anything changes.'

Julie got to work in the kitchen. There was something soothing about chopping the onions, washing the lentils, peeling the carrots and potatoes, tasting and adjusting the stock.

Maybe the wine helped.

Or maybe it was thinking about a date with Caron.

The fact that it wouldn't, couldn't happen made the fantasy all the sweeter.

Chapter 33

'Case number 021284.' Julie said. 'The Hartlepool murder. Second week update.'

'First of all, let's welcome CIO Nadia Latif to the team. She'll be working with DS Iain Wharton.'

'Nice to have you on board,' DC Chris Gibson said.

'As you all know, we have a positive identification,' Julie said. 'Thanks to a Crimestoppers tip-off, we were able to name the victim.'

The super nodded. 'Well done.'

'Dameer Ghosh was an Indian national,' Julie continued. 'He was visiting Teesside on behalf of a company based in Dubai. We made contact with his employer, who contacted his next of kin. His half-sister, Alvi Zaidi, a UK national, came forward and made the positive identification.'

'Good work, everyone.'

'We also know exactly where the murder took place.' Julie nodded at CSM Adrian Prosser.

'The crime scene team were called to a patch of waste ground between the container port and a scrapyard on the south side of the river. We found blood in the soil which matches that of the victim and residues of burnt clothing nearby.'

'Did you find the murder weapon?'

'No, sir.' The CSM shook his head. 'From the post-mortem we know that it was probably a nine-inch filleting knife, but it has not been found so far. We're still checking the waste ground and riverbank. If it went into the river along with the victim, at high tide before the storm, it's most likely at the bottom of the North Sea by now.'

'Do we have any suspects?'

'Not yet, sir,' Julie said.

'Nothing on CCTV?'

'The waste ground is a blind spot between the security systems of both the port and the scrapyard,' DS Wharton said.

'How about cameras on the access roads?' the super asked.

'The CIO is checking,' DS Wharton said. 'Unfortunately the recent bad weather took out the key cameras.'

'Which suggests the murderer chose that spot deliberately, that they knew what they were doing,' the super said.

'Or that the victim chose the spot for a clandestine meeting,' DS Wharton added.

Julie felt a prickle of irritation.

'DC Gibson tracked down where the victim was staying,' she said. 'No trace of him left behind.'

'No personal possessions?'

'Not a single fingerprint,' CSM Adrian Prosser added.

'How do we know the victim was ever in the room?'

'Molly from the pub opened the room and explained how the shower operated,' DC Gibson said.

'We don't know exactly when the room was wiped clean,' Julie added.

'We're checking the security cameras on Station Road,' DS Wharton added. 'But it's a popular area and it could have been any time.'

'Focus on the night of the murder,' Julie said and earned herself a scowl from her sergeant.

'It was a professional job,' Adrian added. 'Someone knew what they were doing. They took the visitors' book, too.'

'No one saw these cleaners?'

'It seems not.'

'Perhaps the victim cleared the room himself?' DS Wharton said.

Julie ignored the comment. 'Any progress with the victim's clothes?'

DS Wharton shook his head. 'I'm still waiting for the CCTV footage.'

'Get CIO Latif to chase that up,' Julie said.

The sergeant glared at her.

'Was our man a person of interest to the Indian authorities?' the super asked.

'No, sir,' Julie said. 'The nuclear power station mentioned they had some initial difficulty getting security clearance for him. I'm following that up.' She took a sip of water. 'I also informed the Indian consulate of his death, but as his registered next of kin lives in the UK, they won't have any further involvement.'

'A wealthy man?'

'We don't believe so, but by all accounts he dressed well, so maybe he gave the appearance of being wealthy.'

'Could it be robbery? Laptop, phone, all personal items are missing, I take it?'

'At this stage, we're not ruling anything out.'

'Possible sexual motive,' DS Wharton said.

Julie appraised him with an icy stare.

'Why do you say that?' she asked.

'Well-dressed, well-groomed, unmarried man in his thirties. Travels a lot. Described by his sister as a very "private man".' DS Wharton made exaggerated quotation marks in the air. 'I guess homosexual behaviour is still frowned upon in some circles.'

'Illegal in many Muslim countries,' the super added.

'But not in India,' Julie insisted. 'Nor in the UK.'

'What if he arranged to meet someone by the river,' DS Wharton continued. 'Someone else sees the two of them getting it on and decides to teach him a lesson.'

'Why just him?'

'Colour of his skin? The way he dresses? Maybe the other one ran away.'

'Or the other one was in on the plan and led him into a trap,' added the super. 'Suggested a ride to his place, but it turned into a one-way trip.'

'We're not ruling anything out.' Julie attempted to close the conversation down. 'But let's work with facts, not speculation.'

'His clothes had been removed. Fact,' DS Wharton said.

'After he was murdered,' Adrian interrupted. 'The fibres in the wound to the heart recovered at post-mortem match the fibres found on barbed wire near the bonfire, suggesting he was stabbed through his old clothes, which were then removed, thrown over a barbed wire fence and set alight. Luckily some of the shirt material snagged on the fence.'

'Did we recover anything else of note from the bonfire?' the super asked.

'The residue of clothing recovered from the fire was heavily charred,' the CSM said. 'The forensics lab are doing some further tests to see if we can identify any blood or knife tears in the fabric, but I'm not confident. It's hard to see why anyone would go to so much trouble to burn his clothes if he'd removed them voluntarily.'

'Maybe things got out of hand,' DS Wharton said.

'It looks more like a calculated killing than a crime of passion,' Julie insisted.

'What about witnesses?' the super asked. 'Who else did our victim come into contact with?'

'We received a list of appointments from his employer,' Julie said. 'DS Wharton and I are interviewing each contact on his list.'

'I completed the last of my four factory visits,' DS Wharton said. 'The story was the same everywhere. Nobody had ever met Dameer in person. No one had a bad word to say about him. Meetings were at his request and expected to be routine sales calls.' He frowned. 'I now know more about toxic gas sensors than I ever wished to know.'

'Dameer Ghosh was murdered before he could attend most of his scheduled meetings,' Julie added. 'I interviewed Sue Bell, the only person we know to have met him before he died, and she's identified one other person, Simon Sharp, who I hope to speak with today. Those are the only two known work contacts who he met with before he died.'

'What about the Crimestoppers tip-off?' DS Wharton asked.

'Obviously it was anonymous,' Julie said.

'Obviously.' The super frowned.

'Did the informant ask for a reward code?' DS Wharton asked.

'No.'

'Then what was their motivation?' DS Wharton asked. 'It's a lead we should follow.'

Julie clenched her jaw. 'Perhaps we should start with real evidence, like the bloody supermarket CCTV, before we start . . .'

The super banged his fist on the table. 'Enough. You've had two weeks and unlimited resources. Stop fighting among yourselves and get me results.'

He stormed out of the room.

Julie felt the blood boiling in her veins. She stood and pointed at DS Wharton.

'You,' she said. 'In my office.'

He remained seated.

'NOW!'

Julie unlocked the door to her office and let DS Iain Wharton enter first. She closed the door behind her and pulled the blind down over the glass.

'I refuse to sit through another meeting with the super where it looks like we aren't working as a team.'

DS Wharton gave her a hard stare. 'Well, we're not.'

'And whose fault is that?'

'You give us tasks, but you don't share what's really going on. You don't tell us what you're thinking.'

'You think I know something I'm not sharing with you?'

'Well, I bloody well hope so. Otherwise this scattergun approach is going to get us nowhere.'

Julie took a deep breath.

'In that case, let's get the team together and sort this out.'

CIO Nadia Latif, DC Chris Gibson and DS Iain Wharton gathered in the incident room.

'I need to make sure that everyone understands what we're doing and why,' she said.

No one met her eyes.

'Let's start with a timeline.' Julie stood at the board and drew a horizontal line. She marked a cross at the right. 'Time of discovery – Thursday the seventh of November at eleven a.m.' She put a second cross to the left. 'Time of death approximately six p.m. on the previous day, Wednesday the sixth of November.' She moved further left and made several crosses at 2 p.m., 11 a.m. and 10 a.m. 'Multiple confirmed sightings up to three p.m. on Wednesday the sixth of November.'

She handed the pen to DS Wharton.

'Do you want to add the locations?'

DS Wharton took the pen and worked in the other direction, from the immigration record of arrival at Teesside airport, to the arrival at The Locomotion in Eaglescliffe, to the electronic clocking-in at the Seal Sands factory.

'Now let's talk about transport,' Julie said. 'We know that Dameer arrived on the early flight from Amsterdam to Teesside airport, and we have a record of the time he passed through immigration.' She put a question mark on the timeline. 'How did he get from the airport to his lodgings?'

'It's unlikely he took the train,' CIO Latif said. Everyone laughed. A local train went right past Teesside airport every half an hour but only stopped there once a week.

'No record of a hire car,' DC Gibson said.

'Most people have someone meet them or they get a taxi,' CIO Latif said.

'There's no taxi rank at the airport now, so it must have been prebooked,' DC Gibson added.

'We've checked all the cab companies,' DS Wharton said. 'And no one has a booking in his name or the name of his company.'

'So, someone met him at the airport.'

'Or he arrived with someone,' Julie said. 'DS Wharton, can you . . .'

DS Wharton threw down his notebook and glared at her. The room went quiet.

'Can I trawl through the airport CCTV?'

'Already on it,' CIO Latif said, so quietly Julie asked her to repeat it.

'Thanks,' Julie said. 'We know he then checked in to his Eaglescliffe lodgings,' she continued. 'What time was that?'

'Jim thinks it was eleven a.m.,' DC Gibson said, 'and that ties in with the flight time, immigration record and witness statements. Molly says they'd just finished cleaning the room when Dameer Ghosh arrived.'

'Do we know where he had lunch?' Julie asked

'The Locomotion serves food, doesn't it?' DC Gibson said.

'And there's the Waiting Room,' the CIO suggested.

'For vegans,' muttered DS Wharton.

'And Serino's,' added DC Gibson. 'Or One Stop.'

'Let me guess,' grumbled DS Wharton. 'You'll be wanting the CCTV on Station Road checked?'

'Already on it,' said the CIO, more confidently this time.

'See if he was alone or in company,' DS Wharton said.

'The next confirmed sighting is when he arrives for his appointment at Zagrovyl,' Julie pointed to the timeline. 'The factory gatehouse record is one forty-seven. Nice and sharp for his two o'clock meeting.'

'No way to get to Seal Sands without wheels,' DS Wharton said.

Julie nodded. 'So again, either a taxi or he has a local host.'

'Who hasn't come forward,' DS Wharton said.

'Which suggests that either they're unaware of our appeal for information,' Julie began.

'Or they have something to hide,' DS Wharton finished for her.

'This is where it gets strange,' Julie said. 'He arrived at the Seal Sands site before two p.m. but there's no record of what time he left.'

'What do you mean?' DS Wharton asked.

'The security guard didn't seem very concerned. He said all visitors must sign in, they can't get a security pass otherwise, but lots of them forget to sign out or return the pass.' Julie explained. 'His appointment was from two to three.'

'So we don't know for sure that he left Zagrovyl at three p.m.' DS Wharton said.

Julie nodded. 'Or how he got from Zagrovyl to the other side of the river.'

'Maybe he never left Zagrovyl,' DS Wharton said. 'Maybe he was murdered there.'

Julie shook her head. 'No – the blood found at the wasteland next to the container port is definitely his. And the CSM reported that there was a lot of it, enough to confirm that he was murdered on the south side of the river.'

'So, we have no idea where he was between three o'clock when his visit to Zagrovyl was due to finish, and around six p.m. when he was murdered,' DC Gibson said.

'Any chance he went back to his lodgings?' Julie asked.

'I'll talk with traffic,' DS Wharton offered. 'See if ANPR picked up the same registration at Teesside airport, Eaglescliffe, Seal Sands and South Bank between ten a.m. and six p.m.'

'Good,' Julie said. 'We also need to consider the hours after the murder.' She went back to the board and drew a cross between death and discovery. 'The post-mortem showed he was dead for a few hours before he went into the water. The coastguard's model suggests that the body was thrown into the water at high tide, around midnight.'

'So, his murderers, or their accomplices, came back before midnight, changed the dead man's clothes, threw him in the river and burnt the evidence.'

'Were there any witnesses to the bonfire?' CIO Latif asked.

'Good question,' Julie said.

'I spoke to security at the container port.' DC Gibson opened his notebook. 'Nobody noticed anything.'

'What about at the scrapyard?' DS Wharton asked.

'There was a note in the logbook which mentions a bonfire on the night of the murder. I've got the name of the nightwatchman, but I haven't managed to interview him yet,' DC Gibson said. 'He sleeps during the day.'

'Leave that interview to me.' DS Wharton looked up at Julie, a direct challenge in his eyes.

He was still spoiling for a fight, but she wasn't prepared to give him the satisfaction. There was too much at stake. And a fresh pair of eyes was always welcome.

'Fine.' Julie nodded her agreement. 'You speak to traffic first and then interview the witness.' She looked around the room. 'Now does everyone know what they're doing and why?'

There was a murmur of assent.

'Any questions?'

DS Wharton remained tight-lipped but said nothing.

'Then let's get to work,' Julie said. 'We have an approximately three-hour period before the victim was murdered in which we don't know what he was doing, where he was or who he was with.'

Julie stood up.

'Let's focus on this window. The one thing we do know is that at some point before six p.m. on the day he died, Dameer Ghosh met his killer.'

Chapter 34

ALF

Redcar - Wednesday, 20 November 2024

The doorbell rang again. Alf pulled the covers over his ears and tried to go back to sleep. Most decent people knew not to disturb a night-shift worker before mid-afternoon. He finished work at 6 a.m., and by the time he'd cycled home and washed and had breakfast, it was after 8 a.m. before he got to bed. He slept for six hours and then dealt with the house and garden before leaving at 5 p.m. to cycle back to work.

When the knocking started, loud, persistent, aggressive, he gave in and got up.

He grabbed his dressing gown, wrapping it over his pyjamas, and searched for his hearing aids. He barely recognised himself as he passed the mirror by the door. When had he become so old and decrepit?

Alf opened the door on the security chain. A thick-set man stood on the steps, fist raised to knock again.

'Mr Pearce?'

'I work night shift,' he said.

'And I work serious crime.' The man flashed a police badge. 'Detective Sergeant Wharton.'

Alf closed the door to release the chain and opened it wide.

'I need a word with you,' the policeman said, and stepped forward. 'Inside.'

Alf peered past the policeman to the street outside. 'That your car?' he asked. 'You might want to keep an eye on it.'

'Why?'

Alf looked up and down the street. 'Wild kids around here.'

'This won't take long.'

Alf led the way into the sitting room with the photos of Naomi and the boys on the mantelpiece. He rarely used the room these days, but kept it spick and span like Grace would have expected.

'You want a cuppa?' he asked.

DS Wharton shook his head. 'Not for me.'

The policeman sat down in Grace's chair. *Not there!* It was all Alf could do not to shout at him to move, so he turned his back and looked out of the window. The twitch of curtains opposite told him his visitor had been noted. The jungle drums would be beating. Alf sat on the sofa where guests were supposed to go.

'What's this about?'

'You work at South Bank Scrap, right?'

Strictly speaking Alf was employed by a security company that contracted out services to SBSS, but it was his place of work, so he nodded.

'Yes.'

'And you were at work on the night of Wednesday the sixth of November?'

'Yes.'

'Anything unusual that night?'

Alf cast his mind back. 'It would be in the logbook.'

DS Wharton nodded. DC Gibson had taken a picture of the logbook entry for that night and added it to the case file.

'According to the log, you found a bonfire and dealt with it.'

'That's right.'

'Did you see anyone?'

'Just a couple of kids running away.'

'Can you describe them?'

'It was too dark to see.'

'How did you know they were kids?'

'It's usually kids up to no good around there, but to be honest I just saw a couple of dark shapes through the smoke.'

'Any vehicles?'

'There was a taxi.'

'Which taxi company?' DS Wharton asked.

Alf closed his eyes and summoned the smell of petrol and charred feathers. A car slid out of the dark and passed under a streetlight.

'The car had a picture of a bird on the side.'

'Eagle Taxis?' DS Wharton tapped his phone and showed him a picture.

'Possibly. They're often in the dock,' Alf added. 'Whenever a ship comes in.'

'Are they now?' DS Wharton smiled. 'Did you see who was driving?'

'No.'

'Number plate?'

Alf shook his head. 'It was dark.'

'Make, model?'

'I don't know much about cars,' Alf said. 'I ride a bicycle.'

'Pity,' said DS Wharton. 'Is there anything else you can think of?'

Should he mention the raid on his bin by the foxes and the ferocity of Storm Babel? He sensed that the police officer wouldn't be interested.

'Nothing else,' Alf said. 'Did you find anything useful at the scene?'

'The crime scene team are still there.'

Alf had seen the white tents go up and obeyed the instruction to keep away.

'Anything else you can think of?' DS Wharton asked again.

Alf cast his mind back. The calm before the storm. The wind building. The flash of silver in the torchlight.

'Just one thing—' Alf began.

He was interrupted by a crash and the wail of a car alarm.

Alf went to the window.

'Oh, dear.' He sighed.

'What the fuck?' DS Wharton jumped up, took in the state of his car – slashed tyres and broken windscreen – and raced outside.

Alf watched DS Wharton through the window. At a click of a key fob, the alarm stopped. The police officer circled the car, kicking the deflated tyres with a foot, rage visible by the effort he put into it. His head shot up at a catcall, and then he was off, running down the street.

DS Wharton returned to the car, red-faced and empty-handed. Whoever he'd been chasing had outrun him.

Alf came out into the street. 'I'm very sorry about your car,' he said.

DS Wharton ignored him, busy on his phone arranging a tow truck.

'Do you want a cup of tea while you wait?'

DS Wharton glared at him with such contempt it hurt.

'Do you need anything else from me?'

'All I want,' the police officer growled, 'is to get out of this shithole you live in.'

'It used to be a nice street.' Alf felt the need to defend his home of forty years. 'But all the jobs have gone, and kids around here have nothing to do, no money, no prospects and nothing to look forward to.'

'They'll have even less to look forward to once I get hold of them.'

DS Wharton turned his back to Alf and walked away.

Chapter 35

JULIE

Middlesbrough – Wednesday, 20 November 2024

Julie took the call from DS Wharton before walking over to CIO Nadia Latif's desk in the incident room.

'Sarge ran into a bit of trouble in Redcar,' she said. 'He's waiting for a tow truck.'

'Is he OK?'

'Furious about his car. Tyres slashed, windscreen smashed. But at least he's not hurt,' Julie said. 'How are you getting on?'

'I've been on to the supermarket again.'

'Any idea why they haven't released the tapes?'

'Many stores, multiple cameras.' CIO Latif looked down and cleared her throat. 'Also, I think DS Wharton asked them to review the footage first, narrow it down.'

He did, did he? Hoping someone else would do the grunt work for him. Julie raised an eyebrow. 'Well, it's taking too long.'

CIO Latif nodded. 'They've agreed to send me everything. I'll go through the recordings myself.'

'Good,' Julie said. 'Identifying who stole the clothes would give us a lead we badly need.'

As Julie drove out towards Wynyard, she kicked herself for not having investigated the delay earlier. The thing about DS Wharton, the thing that annoyed her most, was not his barely repressed contempt, but the shallowness of his approach, how easily he gave up.

You instructed someone to go and look *into* something, and they looked *at* it instead.

If you open the fridge and can't immediately see the cheese, it doesn't mean it's not there. Anyone interested in finding something knows that it's necessary to take some action. To move the Tupperware box of leftover pasta and the half a grapefruit upside down in a bowl. Once they are out of the way, you have a clearer view, although it may still take the touch of a hand to lift the out-of-date bag of ready-to-eat salad to find a foil-wrapped hunk of cheddar underneath.

DS Wharton was not a team player. If he didn't make a discovery himself, if it wasn't his own lead, he had little interest in following it up. He was desperate for promotion, and that meant putting his own interests, his own search for recognition and glory, ahead of the interests of the team. Iain wasn't going to change overnight, so it was up to her to find a way to use him productively until the super agreed to move him off her team. Let him become someone else's problem.

Everything was taking too long. The trail was going cold. And she still hadn't managed to speak with Simon Sharp.

Julie arrived at the security barrier guarding the entry to the gated compound of Wynyard: tree-lined boulevards, lawns and mansions. This area was favoured by footballers and self-made entrepreneurs and – it seemed – contract control engineers. My, how the other half live.

The security guard raised the barrier. Julie followed the satnav, parking the car in front of a group of newly built houses, shaking her head as she took in the fake timbers and stable doors. Who in their right mind designed a new home to look like a wonky barn conversion? Or maybe the question was, who would hand over good money for such a thing? Someone with more money than sense. Including Simon Sharp, by the look of things.

No lights on. No car in the drive, but then there was a large garage. Julie got out of the car, double-checked the address and rang the front doorbell. The synth chords brought a smile to her face: the opening bars of the theme tune for the TV Series *The IT Crowd*. At least this Sharpie chap had a sense of humour.

No reply, so she rang again, then walked around the property, looking in the windows. No sign of life, but no sign of anything amiss either.

A security van pulled up next to her car and a man in uniform got out.

Julie flashed her badge.

'Can I help you, officer?'

'I was hoping to speak to Simon Sharp.'

'Haven't seen him for a few days.'

A neighbour opened the door and joined them on the common lawn, baby in arms.

'You looking for Sharpie?' she asked. 'You'll need a helicopter. He's working offshore.'

'I thought he had a local contract.'

'He packed that in.'

'Any idea when?' Julie asked.

'When something better came up,' she said.

The baby started mewling and the mother took it back inside.

Julie returned to the incident room to find that DS Wharton was in a foul mood.

'And after all that,' he fulminated to CIO Latif, 'he's lying!'

Julie walked in. 'Who's lying?' she asked.

'The bloody nightwatchman from the scrapyard.'

'And why do you think he's lying?'

'He claims he saw an Eagle taxi in the container port.' DS Wharton shook a piece of paper at her. 'I've checked the Automatic Number Plate Recognition records and none of their cars were anywhere near the scrapyard that night.'

'Write up his statement,' Julie said. 'It's worth digging a little deeper.'

DS Wharton grunted.

'Simon Sharp has disappeared,' Julie added. 'Can you make finding him your next priority?'

DS Wharton scowled. 'Maybe we'd better start with your friend Sue Bell.'

Julie was reluctant to disturb Sue Bell again; the woman had a right to a peaceful maternity leave, but better a call from her than from DS Wharton. She texted first and Sue rang back.

'How are you?' Julie asked.

'I wish people would stop asking me that,' Sue said. 'No one is really interested in how I am. All they want to know is when they'll get to see a cute baby instead of a cross woman who looks like a hippopotamus.'

Julie couldn't help the laugh that escaped. 'That bad, eh?' She remembered the feeling. 'I promise not to ask again – if you promise to tell me if it's a bad time to disturb you.'

Sue's tone softened a little. 'You're not disturbing me.'

'I can't get hold of Simon Sharp. He's not returning my calls.'

'Bit of a Scarlet Pimpernel, that one,' Sue said. 'He prefers to work from home even though he's contracted to be on site.'

'He's not at home either,' Julie said. 'His next-door neighbour seems to think he's accepted a job offshore.'

'I wouldn't put it past him to do both without informing either employer.'

Julie walked to the window and looked out at the grey sky.

'We'll keep looking,' she said. 'But if you have any ideas where I might find him, let me know.'

'I'm glad you called, actually,' Sue said. 'It may be nothing, but . . .'

She paused and Julie heard a groan as she shifted position.

'Everything, no matter how insignificant it seems, helps us build up a picture,' Julie said.

'Some of my control systems colleagues were made redundant recently. Head office decision to centralise the function. I didn't support it, but I had to implement it. Dameer seemed upset when I told him.'

'Go on.'

'He was concerned about one individual in particular. Said he'd hoped to meet up with him.'

'Name?'

'Brian Burrow.'

Why did that name sound familiar? Julie typed the name into the database.

'Were you able to put them in touch?'

'I shared Brian's personal phone number,' Sue said. 'I probably shouldn't have, but Dameer was very insistent.'

'You did right to mention it,' Julie said. 'I'll follow that up.'

'Do you need Brian Burrow's number?'

Julie stared at the information on the screen.

'No need,' she said. 'I already have it.'

Chapter 36

BRIAN

Middlesbrough – Wednesday, 20 November 2024

The only way Brian could describe Detective Inspector Julie Cadell was through her aura. It shimmered with gravitas. In his Dungeons and Dragons group, she'd have been a Paladin.

Everything about her was considered and deliberate: the way she dressed, the way she moved, the way she spoke, even the way she smelt, which was both floral and flinty.

She was older than him, but not, he guessed, by much. One of those women who'd never have stood out in a teenage beauty pageant – did they still have those? – but had aged well. She was slimmer and fitter than he was, which probably put her out of his league, but also taller, which might mean he stood a chance. Lots of men hated dating women taller than them, but it had never bothered him. Not that he'd ever succeeded. He wondered if she was single. He wasn't keen on the idea of competing against an angry cop partner.

'Thank you for coming in.' DI Cadell made eye contact.

Brian looked away first. 'It's no problem.'

The other cop in the room, DS Iain Wharton, looked like a right bruiser. More Barbarian than Fighter, Wharton relied on brute strength and raw fury to complement the honed skill of his boss. Or so Brian guessed. A winning combination, except their body language suggested they were anything but a team. The man looked like he'd chewed glass then swallowed a lemon.

The DI opened a file and took out the police sketch from the Crimestoppers news flash.

'Do you recognise this man?'

Brian's mouth dropped open and colour rushed to his face, turning it puce with rage before a chill seized his body. The bastards. So much for privacy.

'It was meant to be anonymous!' The chair legs screeched against the laminate as he pushed himself away from the table and rose to his feet.

'Pardon?'

'The Crimestoppers website guarantees that any information given remains anonymous.'

'This has nothing to do with Crimestoppers.'

'Then why am I here?'

'Sit down, please, Mr Burrow.'

She opened a folder and took out a piece of paper with the Zebra logo titled *Travel Itinerary – Dameer Ghosh.*

Brian sank back into his chair.

'You met with Dameer Ghosh on Wednesday the sixth of November.'

Brian shook his head. 'No, that's not correct,' he said.

'You didn't meet him on the day he visited Zagrovyl?'

'I don't work for Zagrovyl anymore,' he said.

'But you met him afterwards?'

'No. He called me. Said he was sorry to hear that I'd moved on. Asked if we could meet up.'

'When was this?'

'The meeting or the phone call?'

'Both.'

'He called – let me think – a couple of weeks ago. We arranged to meet on Friday the eighth.'

The Barbarian raised an eyebrow.

Brian ploughed on.

'When he didn't show up, I called his mobile and left voice messages, then I called his HQ.'

'And what did they say?'

'They promised to pass on a message.'

The searchlight of her green-eyed gaze made him wonder if the police had a file on him. *Brian Burrow – attention-seeking loser.* Had he been marked as a serial time waster? First his employer lets him down, then his girlfriend leaves him, and now even business contacts stand him up. He looked at her for telltale signs of derision, but she remained hard to read: silent and motionless.

The Barbarian, on the other hand, was sneering his face off.

Brian looked down at the sketch of the murdered man. 'Is Dameer dead?' he asked.

'Yes,' she said. 'I'm afraid so.'

'What happened?'

'This is a murder inquiry. An ongoing investigation. There's a limit to how much I can share at the moment. I'm sure you understand.'

'Poor sod.' Brian closed his eyes.

'I need to know the exact time he called to arrange a meeting.'

Brian pulled out his phone and opened the call record. Most of the calls under Dameer's name were outgoing. *Where are you? Call me.* He scrolled through until he found the first log, an incoming call.

'Wednesday November sixth at fifteen sixteen.'

DS Wharton stuck out a hand for the phone.

The Barbarian was quick, but Brian was faster. He jerked back and held his phone close.

'I'll answer your questions, but you're not getting my phone.'

DI Cadell nodded. 'How long did the call last?'

Brian checked. 'Nine minutes and thirteen seconds,' he said.

'Could you tell where he was calling from? Any traffic noise? Trains? Boats?'

Brian thought back.

'Not that I remember.'

'What did you talk about?'

'He asked how I was. We talked a bit about an old project, old colleagues, then he asked if we could meet up.'

'And you agreed?'

'I said no at first.'

'What changed your mind?'

'He asked if I was looking for work. Said he might have something for me.'

'Something?'

'I asked him, but he said we needed to discuss it face to face.'

'What did you think it was about?'

Brian shrugged. 'I don't know.'

'But you must have made a guess.'

'I figured that Zebra might be looking for some local technical support. They've installed a lot of equipment in Teesside.'

'What sort of equipment?'

'Mainly toxic gas sensors,' he said. 'Early warning devices.'

'And that's your area of expertise?'

'They all connect into bespoke control systems,' Brian said. 'Which *is* my area of expertise.'

'How well did you know Dameer?' DI Cadell asked. 'On a personal level?'

'Not well. We had a few business calls, talked on the phone and met on video conferences.'

'You never met him in person?'

'No.'

'Why was he in Teesside?'

Brian nodded at the itinerary. 'Zebra business.'

'Tell us about the meeting.'

'It never happened.'

'Remind us when it was meant to be?'

'Friday November eighth at ten a.m.'

'Where?'

'The garden centre on Yarm Road.'

'A garden centre?'

'It has a large café.'

'Did you go?'

'Of course.'

'What time?'

'I got there just before ten. I waited until after eleven.'

'Did you try to contact him?'

Brian checked his phone. 'Three ways,' he said.

'Explain?'

'His mobile, his email and finally via his HQ.'

'What can you tell us about Dameer?'

'I keep telling you. I never met him in person.'

'But you spoke to him on the phone, observed him through conference calls.' DI Cadell said. 'Sum him up for me.'

'Well-educated, well-spoken, well-dressed,' Brian said.

'Can you think of any reason that anyone would wish to harm him?'

'No. Everyone loved Dameer Ghosh.'

The two police officers exchanged a look.

'Thank you for coming in, Brian.' DI Cadell stood to indicate that the interview was over. 'Any holidays planned?'

He was wise to her now. 'Why do you ask?'

'We may have some follow-up questions.'

Brian left the station like a bat out of hell. The detective inspector might be cute, but she was too sharp for comfort.

Chapter 37

JULIE

Middlesbrough – Wednesday, 20 November 2024

After Brian Burrow had left, Julie turned to DS Iain Wharton.

So,' she said, 'what do you think?'

'He's hiding something,' Wharton announced.

'You reckon?'

'I'd like to see that phone of his.'

'I wonder why he didn't want to show us.'

'At least we know who supplied the tip-off to Crimestoppers.' DS Wharton grinned. 'Brian Burrow is a man who should never play poker.'

'He obviously doesn't trust the police if he thought we'd tracked him down through the anonymous call.'

DS Wharton picked up the itinerary with the Zebra logo and looked through the list of meetings. 'Why did you show him this? It doesn't have his name on.'

'Diversionary tactic.'

'It seemed to work.'

'Sometimes you have to move sideways to get ahead,' Julie said. 'Go round obstacles rather than bludgeon through them.'

'The obstacle being?'

'His lack of trust. So long as he thought he'd been lied to – about Crimestoppers being anonymous – he wasn't going to give any information voluntarily.'

'So, you presented an alternative lie?'

'You do have a way with words.' Julie twisted her mouth. 'It was preferable to telling him where his name came up.'

'Which was where?'

'Sue Bell. His former boss. Dameer Ghosh specifically asked her about Brian Burrow, requested – and obtained – Brian's personal phone number. She wanted to keep that quiet. I gather there's no love lost between the two of them since she made him redundant.'

'His defensiveness over his phone is a giveaway,' DS Wharton said.

'What are you thinking?'

'I'm thinking we might have a suspect.'

'Why Brian?'

'I think he took the call from Dameer on the afternoon of his death, arranged to meet him and then murdered him.'

'Post-mortem suggested there were two assailants.'

'Him and a mate, then.'

'What possible motive could they have?'

'Lovers' tryst?'

'You back on the sex thing?' Julie shook her head.

'He said he loved him.'

'Brain said that everyone loved Dameer, but he didn't mean romantic love.'

'How can you be so sure?'

'Whoever killed Dameer went to great lengths to hide his identity. Why would they then give an anonymous tip-off to Crimestoppers?'

'Assuming it was Brian – we only have his word for that, of course.'

'You think that was a double bluff?' Julie shook her head. 'Brian didn't strike me as that good an actor. More a man who wears his heart on his sleeve.'

'I'd still like to see that phone.'

'We'd have to have reasonable grounds. We don't have nearly enough to go on.'

'He's known to us,' DS Wharton insisted. 'For wasting police time.'

'He was prosecuted?'

DS Wharton shook his head. 'He received a warning.'

'In what circumstances?'

DS Wharton chuckled. 'Latest one was when his girlfriend moved out and he reported her as missing.'

'Was she found?'

''Course she was. She just didn't want to see him again.'

'You said latest one – were there other missing girlfriends?'

DS Wharton shook his head. 'He called the police in to his work to arrest a contractor thieving from the stores.'

'At Zagrovyl?'

'Yes.'

'What happened?'

'His boss intervened. Said they'd deal with the matter internally.'

And now Brian didn't work for Zagrovyl anymore. Julie stared at her sergeant. She couldn't quite square his obvious antipathy. His dislike of the man felt out of all proportion. What was she missing?

'I'd like to see those two reports,' she said.

'I'll get the civvy to print them out for you,' he said. Clearly he viewed the CIO as more of an administrator than a fellow investigator. But one battle at a time.

'Brian doesn't strike me as a hardened criminal,' she said. 'I don't see him as a cold-blooded murderer.'

'The quiet ones are deceptive.' DS Wharton tapped his nose. 'I reckon I could break him.'

'I reckon you could too,' Julie said. 'Which is why it's a bad idea.'

'Why?'

'Because we don't work like that, Iain. We don't bring people in on a hunch and browbeat them into a confession. That went out with the inquisition.'

'More's the pity.'

'Apart from anything else, the courts don't like it. It's no way to get a conviction. Focus on getting some real evidence and then we can bring him in again.'

When Julie got home, Arni was slumped in front of the TV.

'How was your dad?'

'About as useful as a chocolate fireguard.'

She suppressed a smile.

'Oh?'

'We got hammered.'

'Ah.'

Thank you, Matt. Just when some firm parenting was needed, you revert to adolescence. Well, maybe it was what Arni needed. To let his hair down.

'Is Eve OK?'

'I think so. She's back at home. She wants a couple of days to talk her parents round.' He bit his lip and looked so hung-over and miserable, Julie wanted to hug him better.

'You hungry?' she asked.

He nodded.

'I made some lentil soup last night.'

He followed her into the kitchen.

'Why didn't you tell me that you're planning to sell the house?' he asked.

Julie opened the fridge and took out the pan of soup, setting it on the hob at a low heat.

'Not until you've finished school.'

'But why?'

She shrugged. 'The mortgage is too big for my salary alone.'

'I could get a job . . .'

She smiled.

'You could, but you'll want a place of your own someday. Better to save up for that.'

Chapter 38

It was still dark when Julie woke, but her mind was crystal clear and making connections. She left a message for Arni and drove straight to Zagrovyl, asking to speak with either Alan Cosby or Marcia Chipchase. The security guard issued her with a pass, and she swiped through the turnstile.

The man who waited for her in reception appeared young at first. His bright blue eyes were set wide apart under a floppy blond fringe. It was only as she approached that she noticed the hair thinning at the temples, the wrinkles across his forehead and the way the ends of his thin mouth were dragged down by sagging cheeks. If this was youth, it was prematurely world-weary.

'DI Cadell?' He stepped forward and offered a hand to shake.

His skin was rough, cold and dry.

'I'm afraid Marcia isn't available,' he continued. 'She asked me to liaise with the police in her absence.'

His slight accent was hard to place. East European? Nordic? Despite his perfect English, he hadn't been born here.

'And you are?'

'Kris.' He smiled to show a jewelled tooth.

'Full name.'

'Kristoph Ingerson,' he said.

'What do you do here, Kristoph?'

'I work for Marcia in HR,' he said.

'And what's your role?' she asked.

'Admin mainly.'

'Then you may be able to help me. I need to talk with Simon Sharp.'

'Follow me.'

He led her to a small meeting room and logged on to a computer.

As he tapped the keys she noticed the cuts on his hands. Perhaps he had a night life as a tradesman or a major DIY project at home.

'Simon Sharp has resigned,' he said.

'When?'

He tapped some more keys.

'His letter is dated yesterday,' he said.

Before or after she visited his home in Wynyard? Before or after she asked for Sue's help to trace him?

'Kris, do you have access to gatehouse records?'

'I do, but . . .'

'Can you bring up Simon's attendance record for me?'

'I need authorisation.'

She flashed her badge. 'Hopefully this will suffice.'

He hesitated, then nodded, bringing the data up on the screen.

Simon Sharp had clocked in at 8.27 on the day of Dameer's murder. He'd clocked out at 5.03 p.m. The record showed similar starting and finishing times every working day up until Friday, 15 November and then nothing since.

'And Sue Bell?'

The record showed that Sue often started work early and finished late. However, on the day of the murder, her last day of work before starting maternity leave, she left the site at 2.26 p.m. Exactly as she claimed.

'What about visitors?' Julie asked. 'Can you show me the record for the same day?'

Kris obliged.

On 6 November 2024 Dameer Ghosh clocked in at 1.47 p.m. and clocked out at 3.05 p.m.

'Can you print out all the records for sixth November, please?'

The printer whirred into action.

When Julie got back to the office, it was to find a note from DS Wharton to say that the fishing boat *Gallant* had arrived into port, and he was going to Whitby to meet with the captain. Julie let out a shout of irritation. Hadn't he been paying attention to anything that had developed over the past two weeks? Didn't he understand that it was a pointless waste of time? But worse than that, when had she expressly countermanded her instruction to complete the Hartlepool Marina witness interviews? Was this her fault, yet again? She ground her teeth in frustration.

DS Wharton had also left a folder with three sheets of paper. The first two were brief logs of Brian Burrow's previous interactions with the police. The third was the report from traffic. There were no registration number hits. There was no sign of the same vehicle registration appearing at more than one of the places and times of interest on the day of the murder.

Julie entered the incident room. She pulled up a chair and laid the traffic report on the desk of the civilian investigator.

'How much do you know about ANPR?' Julie asked.

'When a vehicle passes an Automatic Number Plate Recognition or ANPR camera, the picture of a passing car is converted into a tag with number plate, time and location.' The CIO sounded as if she'd learned the training manual off by heart. 'Among other things, it can be used to calculate the speed between two points and issue a fine to the registered owner of the car if they exceed the limit.'

'Very good,' Julie said. 'Now, does it ever happen that the camera can't identify the number plate?'

The CIO nodded. 'Yes. Temporary plates that are not yet registered with the DVLA, or where a duplication is flagged – sometimes the same number plate miraculously appears simultaneously hundreds of miles apart.' She looked up. 'And of course if the plate is obscured, accidentally or deliberately.'

'Can we look at any unidentified tags between ten a.m. and midnight?'

'Which cameras?'

'Anything between these four points.' Julie brought up a map on her phone and highlighted the road that led from the airport, along the A66 to Eaglescliffe, across the Tees on the A19, east to the Seal Sands factory, then back over the Tees and south to the container port.

'I'll look through the download that DS Wharton obtained, and if I can't find anything, I'll request the full data again.'

Julie looked past the pot plants, out of the window. 'Tell you what,' she said. 'Why don't you skip the first step. Just go straight to the source data for me, OK?'

DS Wharton was too slapdash, he could have easily missed something, but she didn't want to come right out and criticise him in front of a team member.

CIO Latif frowned.

'When you give me a report, a summary is useful, but I always want the full data as an appendix.'

CIO Latif nodded. 'That makes sense.'

'No need to mention this to the sergeant,' Julie said. 'He has other things to focus on.'

Julie was not long back in her office when she heard the squeal of rubber and a hand tapped on the window. 'Ma'am?'

'Come in.'

The young woman opened the door.

'I've been thinking about what you asked me to do,' she said. 'Thing is, ma'am, the chain of command is there for a reason.'

'You're quite right,' Julie said. 'I apologise, I didn't mean to make you uncomfortable.'

The young woman held up a hand. 'Hear me out, OK?' She manoeuvred her wheelchair through the door and closed it.

'Nothing the older blokes hate more than women talking across rank. If Sarge catches me doing work directly for you, he'll think he's being bypassed.'

Which is exactly my intention.

'Send DS Wharton an email with this message.' CIO Latif passed a slip of paper over the desk. 'Let him pass it on to me.'

Julie studied the paper.

Please obtain a detailed weather report for 06 NOV 2024 between latitude: longitude 54.50920: -1.42941. . . a series of equally incomprehensible numbers followed . . . *together with* a 23-190465-DMOV-UN *report.*

'What's this?'

'Exactly what you asked me, with a little innocent weather data thrown in.'

'And how does this help?'

'This way, he asks me for what you want, and I send it straight to you.'

Julie frowned.

'How long will it take?'

The CIO pushed a folder over the desk.

'What's this?'

'The information you're about to ask for.'

Julie reached out to take the folder, but the CIO kept her hand on it.

'Send him the request first,' she said.

Julie took the slip of paper and typed it into an email.

The CIO let go of the folder.

'Just let me know if you need anything else,' she said. 'And I'll let you know how to ask for it.'

'This is absurd.'

'Trust me.' CIO Latif's voice dropped to a whisper. 'You can't be too careful around DS Wharton.'

Julie watched open-mouthed as the young woman spun the wheelchair round, opened the door and manoeuvred through it.

A slow smile spread across her face as Julie opened the folder that CIO Latif had delivered to her desk. She discarded the first page, a detailed weather report. The next pages listed all the unregistered vehicles that had passed ANPR cameras in the areas of interest from 6 November to the early hours of 7 November.

There were too many unidentified vehicles travelling over the A19 flyover in both directions to search through every line, and a fair few on the busy A66, but the traffic in and out of Teesside airport was sparse. One unidentified vehicle at 10.37 a.m. was around the right time for a pick-up from the Amsterdam flight.

The cameras on Station Road hadn't been operational, and a malfunction at the Seal Sands roundabout meant that most HGVs had been flagged as unidentified.

Finally, she reached the camera at the trunk road leading to the container port. There were two unidentified vehicles recorded on 6 November. One entered at 4.54 p.m. and left again 6.17 p.m. The other entered at 11.30 p.m. and left again at a quarter past midnight on 7 November.

She circled the entries of interest.

Back at her computer, Julie saw that DS Iain Wharton had already read her request. He responded to say that he'd passed the request on to the civilian investigator.

Julie picked up the phone and dialled the CIO.

'Can you access any photos?'

'I've already requested them for the following . . .'

She read out a list. She had identified the same data points, plus two more. Julie queried those.

'That's the Middlesbrough Asda superstore,' Nadia said. 'A car with an unidentified number plate entered the car park at nine forty-one p.m. and left at ten thirteen p.m.'

'Between the murder and the disposal of the body,' Julie said. 'Good. How long before we get the photos?'

'Traffic are swamped, so it will probably be tomorrow now,' Nadia said.

'I'll send them on as soon as they arrive.'

Julie turned on her personal phone as she walked to her car to drive home. There was a voice message from a number she didn't recognise. She closed the car door before pressing play.

Julie, it's Ethan

Ethan Evans. Since when were they on first-name terms? Come to think of it, how the hell did he know her number?

I just wanted to apologise for Monday night.

Bloody nerve of the man. She was owed more than an apology. Much more. And at least two bags of fruit.

The shock of Eve's news . . . upset me.

Well, she had to allow him that. The golden girl with her supermodel good looks, athletic and academic brilliance was the last person anyone would expect to get pregnant accidentally. Her family had been talking about Oxford, St Andrews, even Harvard.

Julie had been shaken, too, worried for both Arni and Eve. Shock was one thing; trying to break into someone's house was quite another. How would Ethan have felt if the tables had been turned?

But I think Eve's seen sense now.

What did he mean by sense? Maybe the GP and counsellor had been able to help her see that a future planned pregnancy would be better for everyone. That she could take a couple of pills and all this would be over. That Eve and Arni could concentrate on exams and their future. She hoped it was the GP and counsellor who had prevailed, not her bully of a father.

It's best if you keep your son away from my daughter.

Best for who? Was that a veiled threat? What did he think Arni was, anyway? A dog to be kept on a short leash? And his daughter? Was she a bitch to be locked up in a cage? Eve was the older of the pair, already an adult in the eyes of the law.

He's done enough harm.

How dare he. How fucking dare he.

When Julie got home, Arni was in the kitchen, his head on the table.

'Hi, darling.'

She leant over and kissed the nape of his neck.

He shot up angrily. 'Don't do that.'

She saw that he'd been crying.

'Arni, what's wrong?'

'Eve won't talk to me,' he said.

'She's at home, with her parents?'

He nodded.

'You think she's OK?'

He shrugged. 'You met her dad. He's a brute.'

'And her mum?'

'Medicated up to the eyeballs again,' Arni said. 'Apparently the stress of her only daughter needing some support is too much for her frayed nerves.' His voice was bitter.

Julie filled the kettle from the sink and put it on to boil.

'Is Eve going to school?'

'Yes,' he said. 'But she's avoiding me.'

'I guess she's just trying to figure things out.'

'And am I not involved in that decision?'

Julie sat down and took his hand.

'I can't imagine how hard this is for you, love. But it's her body.'

'And our baby.'

Oh Arni. You're just a baby yourself.

'It's not a baby yet,' Julie said. 'If Eve's parents want her to have a termination, and she knows that's not what you want, she's bound to be confused. Give her some time and space to think it through.'

'Her dad will pressure her.'

'All the more reason why you mustn't.'

He looked up at her, eyes soft and wide.

'You want her to have an abortion too, don't you?'

'I want what's best for her.'

'What about me? What about what's best for me?'

His eyes were big with betrayal. The hurt shining from them pierced her heart with a thousand tiny needles. She looked away and sighed. Time to grow up, Arni. Tough love.

'Arni, get real,' Julie said. 'You're not the one who has to go through pregnancy and childbirth.'

'So, men have no rights at all?'

Julie sighed. Where to start?

Chapter 39

Middlesbrough – Friday, 22 November 2024

When Julie arrived in the office the following morning, the images from traffic were waiting in her inbox.

Julie opened the file of photos and worked backward in time. The pictures at the container port junction were very grainy; it was impossible to make out much other than the partial number plate. The numbers 610 were visible in both photos, so probably the same vehicle. The times tied in perfectly with both the murder and the disposal of the body at high tide. The latter sighting also matched the time the scrapyard nightwatchman, Alf, saw a taxi leaving the container port.

The earliest photos were taken by the cameras at Teesside airport. This time, the images of the vehicle number plate were crystal clear. A black saloon car, registration MIC 610E, arrived at 9.52 and left at 10.37 a.m.. An upmarket taxi with a bird logo on the side. The number plates must be fake if ANPR didn't recognise them. Did Eagle Taxis run other, unregistered vehicles? Or was the logo a decoy – someone trying to deceive? Rivalry among local taxi companies in Teesside was fierce.

How was it that CIO Latif had achieved in a few hours what DS Wharton had failed to complete in two weeks?

Was he simply incompetent? Or was he covering something up?

Keep your friends close, and your enemies closer.

Julie called DS Wharton into her office. He greeted her with unusual enthusiasm.

'Morning, Boss.'

'How did you get on yesterday?'

'The skipper of the *Gallant* confirmed the *Lainey Rose* story. They put into port and left at similar times.'

She nodded and steepled her hands.

'Given that we now know the murder scene was elsewhere, do you think a day trip to meet a Hartlepool Marina witness was a good use of your time?'

The jovial mask slipped. He stared at her with such pure hatred, it took all her energy not to recoil.

Breathe. Breathe. You're just doing your job.

'I had other reasons,' he muttered.

Julie opened the case file to buy herself some time – just as she expected, there was no report filed, not even the dead-end interview with the *Gallant* crew.

'Since you haven't updated the case file, perhaps you'd like to share yesterday's developments with me?'

'Brian Burrow,' he said. 'There's something not right there. I wanted to track down his ex-girlfriend, the one he reported missing.'

'And?'

'She wouldn't talk to me, but I spoke with some of their goth and biker associates.'

The distaste with which he used the words *goth* and *biker* told her most of what she needed to know.

'And?'

'We need to speak to Brian Burrow again.'

She had the same thought, for different reasons. She wanted to know more about his first brush with the Cleveland police. The contractor accused of theft who was never charged.

'I agree,' she said. 'Bring him in.'

'Under caution?'

She nodded.

The cheerful demeanour returned.

'Oh, and ma'am.'

Of course, he would have to have the last word.

'Yes, DS Wharton?'

'I appreciate you keeping me in the loop and all, but it's OK to go direct to the civilian investigator if you want . . .' he made a dismissive gesture with his hand '. . . routine stuff.'

'Thank you, DS Wharton.' Julie kept her mouth in a straight line, fighting to suppress a smile.

Julie waited until she saw DS Wharton heading out onto Bridge Street before seeking out CIO Latif.

'What did you make of the pictures from traffic?' Nadia asked. She opened a file with prints of the photos and spread them out on her desk.

'We need to find out who owns and drives our ghost taxi,' Julie said.

'Already on the case, ma'am.'

'Do you think we can improve the resolution enough to see who's inside?'

CIO Latif shook her head. 'I can try,' she said. 'But judging by the angles, it's unlikely that even the best experts will be able to do much.'

'Hmmm,' Julie said. 'Pity.'

'I might have something better,' CIO Latif added. 'The Asda CCTV tapes have come in. I'm focusing on the Middlesbrough superstore in the time interval the ghost taxi was in the car park.'

'Excellent,' Julie said.

'And even if the mix of ANPR and CCTV isn't good enough to get a positive ID on the driver, we can still track every movement of the ghost taxi from before the sixth of November until right this minute.'

Julie nodded. 'The moment you know who drove the vehicle, let's bring them in for questioning.'

Chapter 40

BRIAN

Middlesbrough – Friday, 22 November 2024

DI Julie Cadell entered the room first. 'Brian, thank you for coming in again.' The green-eyed Paladin leant over the table to shake his hand.

'What's this about?' Brian asked.

DS Iain Wharton followed her. 'We just need to clarify a few things.' His grip was like a vice and Brian had to bite his lip not to yelp.

'I already told you everything I know,' Brian said. He hated the sound of his voice, shrill and whiny. He dropped his chin, inflated his chest and made a concerted effort to deepen the register. 'Which is precisely,' he ran a finger across his lips, 'zilch.'

'Then this won't take very long.' DS Wharton smiled like a snake. 'It's a PACE interview.'

'What's that?' Brian looked to the female officer.

'A legal term.' She frowned at the Barbarian. 'PACE stands for Police and Criminal Evidence Act 1984. It means we are interviewing you under caution and we have to read you your rights first.'

'You do not have to say anything,' DS Wharton said. 'But it may harm your defence if you do not mention when questioned something which you later rely on in court. Anything you do say may be given in evidence.'

Brian frowned. 'Am I under arrest?'

'No.' DS Wharton's smile was more lizard than snake now. 'You're attending this interview voluntarily – right?'

'Do I need a lawyer?' Brian asked.

'That's entirely your right,' DI Cadell said.

'You have a solicitor in mind?' DS Wharton asked.

'I don't know any.'

'We can arrange for the duty solicitor to attend,' DI Cadell said.

'Although it may take some time,' DS Wharton said. 'Is there anything you want to tell us in the meantime? Get off your chest?'

Brian mimed zipping his lips shut.

A solicitor by the name of Ruth Gaddas was found, a bird-like woman whose eyes darted backwards and forwards and side to side in a way that Brian found most disconcerting.

'Mr Burrow.'

'You can call me Brian, everyone does.' Which was not entirely true. They also called him goblin and dwarf, which he'd learned to be proud of, or loser or tosser which, while accurate, actually hurt.

'Brian, then. Are you clear as to what's going on here?'

'Clear as mud,' he said.

'I spoke with DI Cadell and requested full disclosure.'

'Disclosure?'

'An outline of the case under investigation and any evidence against you.'

'They don't have any evidence,' Brian said.

'DI Cadell is not revealing much, so you're probably right,' Ruth Gaddas agreed. 'They've provided me with the barest outline of the case, plus a police log on the previous two occasions you had contact with them which don't seem at all relevant.' The solicitor leant forward, and her eyes focused on his. 'This is your chance, in complete confidence, to set out your version of events. That way, I can give you advice about the law and inform you of your options.'

Brian sighed. How many times did he have to explain that he had never met the murdered man? Several times, as it transpired. Yes, Dameer Ghosh called me. Yes, we arranged a meeting. No, he didn't turn up to said meeting. He was fed up repeating himself.

'The police allege that you met him on the afternoon of Wednesday the sixth of November.'

'I did not.'

'What were you doing on that afternoon?'

'I was at home.'

'With anyone?'

'Alone.'

'Do you have an alibi?'

'I do not.'

'The police seem keen to see your phone.'

'They're not getting it.'

'I agree, but maybe you can tell me why?'

'It's got personal stuff on it.'

Pictures of Betty. She always looked better with her clothes off. She'd demanded he delete all the images when she came to collect her stuff. He'd wiped them and shown her. But then he'd recovered them because he could, and they were all he had left of her now.

'Personal stuff that might cause you trouble with the police?'

He shook his head. They were consenting adults. 'Pictures of my ex.'

'Would that be the ex who you reported to the police as missing?'

'I was worried about her,' Brian said. As it turned out, she was avoiding him, didn't want to see him. Betty said she still loved him but didn't like him any longer. That hurt more than anything else; he didn't much like himself either.

'Talk me through your day on Wednesday, November sixth.'

'There's not much to tell,' he said. 'I got up late.'

'What time?' she asked.

'Dameer's call woke me,' he admitted.

The solicitor failed to hide her astonishment. Beady eyes darted to her notes. 'At three sixteen p.m.?' she asked.

'I was up all night.'

She raised an eyebrow.

'Playing a Netz tournament,' he explained.

'Where?'

'In my flat.'

'Who with?'

'Online. It's a multiplayer computer game.'

'Ah,' she said. 'So, there would be a record, right? Did you also play later in the day?'

'No.'

'May I ask why?'

'I lost by a whisker in the very last round. I was pissed off.'

'I see.' She nodded. 'You went to bed when?'

'It was already light, so maybe nine a.m.'

'And you slept for six or seven hours until your phone rang.'

'Yes.'

'So, what did Dameer say to you?'

'He was a nice guy,' Brian said. 'I'm sorry he's dead.'

The solicitor rapped the table with her pen. 'Whatever you do, don't make comments like that in front of the police.'

'Why?'

'They have a way of twisting things.'

And how. He'd seen enough of the Barbarian in action to know the solicitor was right.

'Let's stick to the facts of your conversation,' she said.

'Look, I was still sleepy. I didn't really want to talk to Dameer at first.'

'Just tell me whatever you remember.'

'He wanted to know how I was, what I was up to and whether we could meet up.'

'And you agreed?'

'Not at first.'

'Why not?'

'Dameer wasn't a friend.' Brian paused and bit his lip. 'Just a work colleague from my old life.'

The old life where he got up early, washed and shaved, put on clean clothes, went to work, had colleagues who respected him, a girlfriend, a life.

'What changed your mind?'

'He asked me how I felt about Zagrovyl's new IT arrangements. I told him they were a recipe for disaster. He agreed, said I was one of the few smart enough to recognise the risks and that he'd always liked working with me. Asked if I'd consider helping him with something.'

'Something?'

'I tried to find out more, but he said we needed to meet in person.'

'Who suggested the date?'

'I did,' Brian sighed. 'I didn't want to sound too desperate.'

And he needed time to get a haircut and buy some clothes that fitted and brush up on the sort of protocols and code that Zebra might be interested in. A year is a long time to be out of touch with new developments.

'Who chose the venue?' She checked her notes. 'A garden centre, right?'

'I did.'

'Did he suggest meeting the same afternoon he called?'

'No.'

'You're sure about that?'

'Absolutely. He was on his way to a meeting.'

'Do you know who he was meeting, or where?'

'No.'

'What did you do after the call?'

'I went back to bed.'

'So, you didn't see anyone, talk to anyone, order a takeaway, use your phone or computer – anything that might confirm your whereabouts?'

'No.'

'You saw no one that day? Surely there's someone who can confirm that you were home at the time the police allege you met him.'

On and on. This one didn't know when to stop.

Brian had had enough.

'You know what Dameer was really worried about?' he asked.

The solicitor looked up. 'No, what?'

'A cyberattack.'

'Wait, I thought he was a salesman?'

'One of the smartest I ever met. He knew more about control systems and cybersecurity than most of the engineers he was selling to. I was the only one on the same wavelength.'

She pursed her lips and narrowed her eyes. 'You think that's what he wanted to talk to you about?'

'Maybe he wanted my help to stop a cyberattack.'

'I see.'

'Maybe someone murdered him to stop him talking to me.'

'I thought you were unemployed?' she said, voice laden with contempt. 'How could you help to stop anything?'

Harsh, he thought. There was no need to rub it in. He looked down at his shoes.

'Brian, would you say you were depressed?'

He shrugged.

'You lost your job, your girlfriend.'

'The pub quiz, my D and D mates, the Netz tournament,' he added.

'Have you thought about going to see your GP?'

He shook his head, frightened that his voice might betray him.

'Don't you think that would be a good idea?'

'You can't get appointments these days.' His voice remained steady.

'Have you tried?' she asked.

'No.'

'Then I suggest you call as soon as we're finished.'

'We're done?'

'Far from it. I'm going to put what you told me into a written statement, OK?'

Ruth Gaddas took out an old-fashioned fountain pen and started scratching the nib over a piece of lined yellow paper.

'Do you know why I lost my job?' Brian asked.

The lawyer made no attempt to hide an exasperated sigh. She stopped writing and looked up at her client.

'No, Brian, why did you lose your job?'

'Because I warned them that the risk of "outsourcing",' he made air quotation marks with his index fingers, 'control systems support far outweighed any benefit.'

'Brian, let me level with you. You're an unhappy man and I understand why you want to get all this off your chest. But if you go down this route with the police, it's going to go right over their heads. Look, don't get me wrong, the serious crime division do a great job in difficult circumstances, but they're not experts in cybercrime or terrorism. Other units look after those things. If you're not careful, there's a real danger of things snowballing out of control.'

Brian bunched up his fists and pressed them into his eyes.

'You don't understand,' he said between gritted teeth. 'Maybe there is a real risk. Maybe something terrible is going to happen.'

'I admire your spirit of public service, Brian,' she said. 'I really do.'

Whenever people used that tone of voice, they meant the opposite. The way her eyes kept darting to her phone told him she wished she was somewhere else.

'But as your solicitor, I must warn you that good intentions can be misconstrued. What if they think you're inventing a cock-and-bull story to hide something?'

'But I have nothing to hide!'

'Then stick to saying nothing,' she said. 'Apart from this.'

She handed him the paper with three lines. He read it quickly then nodded.

'You agree?'

'It's what I told you.'

'You say this and nothing else.'

Before he could protest, she was out of the door, holding it open for him.

Ruth Gaddas was just an Illusionist, a speciality wizard, skilled in the arcane arts of deception and trickery. She was a lot better at talking than listening.

'It doesn't feel right,' he said as they took their seats back in the interview room. 'Saying nothing.'

'Think of it as a tactic,' she said. 'To see if they actually have any evidence.'

'Won't that make me look guilty?'

'Innocent until proven guilty, Brian.' She smiled. 'That's the law.'

'My client would like to read out a statement,' Ruth Gaddas announced and handed him a piece of paper.

Brian cleared his throat. 'I have never met Dameer Ghosh in person. He contacted me on the sixth of November 2024 and requested a meeting. We agreed to meet on Friday the eighth of November 2024. He didn't turn up to said meeting.'

The Barbarian went over all the old questions.

'No comment,' Brian responded.

'May I ask you about something different?' DI Cadell said in her wisest Paladin voice. 'Last September, you called the police to your workplace to arrest a contractor named Tadeusz Makowski. You accused him of stealing from the stores. Can you tell me more?'

Brian glanced at his lawyer.

'How is this relevant to the case under investigation?' Ruth Gaddas asked.

'That's what I'm trying to understand,' DI Cadell said.

The solicitor shrugged and nodded at Brian.

'Some spares went missing from the stores. I checked the records and found that the same IT contractor, Tad the Pole, was on site out of hours every time it happened,' Brian said. 'I broke into his locker, found the evidence and called the police.'

'When you say spares?'

'Control system stuff – power supplies, I/O modules, switches, cable.' Brian could see that this meant nothing to the police. 'Specialist control stuff.'

'And when the police arrived?'

'The site manager sent them away.' Alan Cosby, that pathetic lickspittle, had a rubber band in place of a spine. 'He wanted an internal investigation first.'

'I see.' The green-eyed interrogator wrote something down. 'And did they investigate?'

'Yes.' Brian shrugged. 'They claimed they couldn't prove Tad the Pole had been stealing. The bastard claimed I'd planted the stuff in his locker.' He smiled. 'I did prove that there were irregularities in his attendance record, so they sacked him for that.'

'Irregularities?'

'He'd been accessing the gatehouse records database and making manual entries, pretending not to be on site when he was.'

'Wait a minute, why would he do that? Wouldn't he want to get paid for his hours?'

Brian shrugged. 'I guess the stuff he was stealing was worth more than his hours.'

'Stuff easily sold?'

'Definitely not.' Brian shook his head. 'It must have been stolen to order.'

'Who would want such specialised equipment?'

'Search me,' Brian said.

The green eyes flashed, and she wrote something down.

'If you had to make a guess?'

Brian glanced over at his legal representative. She shook her head.

'No comment,' Brian said.

'Thank you.' DI Cadell turned to DS Wharton. 'Over to you, Detective Sergeant.'

The Barbarian had been restless throughout the exchange, and now he leant forward with clenched fists and narrowed eyes.

'Let's cut the crap, OK?' The Barbarian had a rough voice. 'Why don't you tell us what really happened when you met Dameer Ghosh.'

Ruth Gaddas leant forward. 'I refer you to my client's statement. There was no meeting.'

The policeman ignored her and continued glaring at Brian.

'What happened on the afternoon of 6 November? You took his call and agreed to hook up.'

'My client has already—'

'Why don't you tell us what really happened, Brian?'

Brian hated the fact that his legs had turned to jelly in the face of Barbarian aggression. He tried to control the trembling by speaking calmly.

'No comment.'

'Tell us the truth,' the policeman growled.

Brian read out his statement for the second time.

'Are you married, Brian?'

'No.'

'Girlfriend?'

'Why are you asking?'

'Just curious.'

'Well, it's none of your business.'

'No one since Betty, eh? Must be lonely.'

'You have no idea,' Brian said sadly. 'I miss her so much. I never realised what love was until I was stupid enough to throw it away.'

'Enough,' Ruth Gaddas whispered. 'Stick to no comment.'

'So you were looking to make a new,' the policeman made air quotes with his fingers, '"special friend". I gather that Dameer Ghosh was an attractive man.'

'How dare you . . .'

The solicitor nudged him so hard he flinched.

'No comment,' he said.

'Officer, where is this line of questioning going?' Ruth Gaddas asked.

The brute ignored her.

'Brian, are you or have you ever been a drug user?'

'How is this relevant?'

'Just let your client answer the question.'

'No comment,' Brian said.

'Have you ever paid for sex or offered sex for money?'

'No comment.'

'How would you describe your relationship with Dameer?'

'No comment.'

The questions went on and on until eventually the policewoman held up a hand for the Barbarian to stop.

'I'm disappointed,' DI Cadell said in her sweetest Paladin voice. 'I thought you wanted to help us find out what happened to your colleague.'

'I do,' he blurted out before he could stop himself.

'Then do you think it's a good idea to say nothing, Brian?'

He looked from one police officer to the other and something snapped.

'Do you think it's a good idea to allow people in India to take remote control of a high-hazard chemical factory in Teesside?' Brian asked.

His lawyer laid a warning hand on his arm, but he shook it off.

DI Cadell gave him a hard stare. 'That sounds inadvisable.'

He knew she'd understand him.

'My point exactly,' he said.

'There must be safeguards,' she said.

'You would have thought so, wouldn't you?' Brian was on a roll now. 'The control and safety systems, the OT – operations technology – is meant to be ring-fenced, kept separate from the office IT – information technology. So why did Zagrovyl outsource and centralise everything to a single team based in Delhi?'

'A good question,' she said, leaning forward.

'Anyone see *Mr Bates versus The Post Office* on the TV? No one can make changes to the sub-postmasters' records, they said. Except it turned out that the software engineers sitting in HQ could do just that without leaving a trace. What if someone could do worse than just changing the accounts? What if someone could roam around inside an IT computer for weeks, months, years, until they found – or created – a weak link from IT to OT? Now it's not just the accounts they can mess with, they can take control of a high-hazard factory. With the right credentials – username, password and encryption key – the sleeping tiger wakes, a dangerous beast that can access anything from anywhere.'

'Did you share these concerns with your former employer?'

He was almost shouting now. 'That's what got me sacked.'

'DI Cadell.' The solicitor got to her feet. 'I think we've all heard enough.

My client is upset. He is here voluntarily and would like to leave now.'

DS Wharton squared up to her. 'You want us to arrest him?'

'If you have real evidence linking him to a crime, I'd like to hear it,' Ruth Gaddas said. 'But you don't have anything, do you?'

DI Cadell stood up. 'Interview terminated at five seventeen p.m.,' she said. 'Brian, you are free to go.'

DS Wharton left the room first, looking as if he was about to explode.

Chapter 41

JULIE

Middlesbrough – Friday, 22 November 2024

Back in her office, Julie switched her personal phone from silent. Two missed calls from the school and a third one incoming.

'Mrs Cadell?'

'Speaking.'

'It's Stuart Leslie from the school, Arni's form tutor.'

She took a deep breath.

'I know that Arni's attendance has been poor recently, Mr Leslie. I'm really sorry, but he's got some . . . issues to work through.'

'It's OK, Mrs Cadell. Arni came to see me. I'm glad he did. I think we can help.'

'How?'

'The school nurse has a lot of experience in these cases. It's more common than you might think.' The teacher sighed. 'Whatever they decide,' the form tutor continued, 'we can support them.'

'That's good to hear,' Julie said. 'But what does that mean in practice?'

'You'll understand that I can only speak with you about your son, Mrs Cadell?'

Of course. Eve was not her daughter. Mr Evans had made that quite clear.

'Yes.'

'I understand that Arni was also dropped from the hockey team.'

'He hasn't been attending practice.' Actions have consequences. Inaction even more so. 'I don't blame the coach,' Julie said.

'There's a youth sports event this weekend. It's residential, an outreach for the inner-city primary schools who don't have much in the way of sports facilities. Arni would be a real asset. A lot of work, but it's paid, and it might be good for him to have something immersive outside the usual routine. What do you think?'

'I think it's a great idea,' Julie said. And a weekend with little kids might dispel some of his romantic notions about fatherhood.

'Great. I wanted to check with you first. If we're good, then Coach Martin will approach him now.'

'Do you think he'll get another chance to return to the team?'

'Absolutely. They lost four nil without him on Saturday. This is just the first step.'

'Thank you, Mr Leslie.'

'You've got a great lad, you know, Mrs Cadell. I wish all the boys his age were as caring. Yes, the situation is far from ideal, but Arni is stepping up. He does you proud.'

When Julie got home, Arni bounded down the stairs with a spring in his step that had been missing for weeks.

'Hey, Mum,' he said. 'Guess what?'

She smiled to see the colour back in his cheeks. 'What?'

'Coach has offered me a job for the weekend. Helping kids try out different sports.'

'Wow, that sounds great.'

'You were right, you know.'

'About what?'

'About talking to the school. Mr Leslie's been amazing. Eve's seen a special counsellor. The nurse arranged it the same day.'

He gave her a big hug.

It was only as she was getting ready for bed that a sudden thought struck her. If Arni was busy this weekend, there was nothing to stop her going to the police charity ball. An opportunity to let her hair down, something to look forward to.

As she messaged Stuart with her change of heart, she felt a warm glow on her skin at the prospect of an evening with Stuart and Kim.

And Caron.

Chapter 42

North Yorkshire – Saturday, 23 November 2024

Julie didn't own an evening dress, much less anything suitable for a black-tie event, so she'd spent Saturday morning going around the Stokesley charity shops, finding a velvet sheath dress, calf-length with three-quarter sleeves, a scoop neck and low back. It fitted like a glove. She unearthed a pair of glossy heels from the back of the wardrobe – an impulse purchase and only worn once – and selected her flashiest earrings. Hair up or down? Maybe loose for a change. It made her feel less exposed.

At the sound of a car pulling up onto the street outside, she went to the window. Caron got out and she drew back, mouth suddenly dry, heart beating like a machine gun. What the fuck was she doing? This was all a terrible mistake.

She switched off the light and returned to the window, looking down on him as he opened the garden gate and walked up to the front door. He looked good in his dinner jacket and dress shirt, the bow tie slightly askew giving him a debonair charm. She relaxed a little. He was so far out of her league that she needn't worry. Caron had no interest in her. He was only carrying out the orders of her friend and his chief constable. Just relax and enjoy the occasion.

Julie was halfway down the stairs when the doorbell rang. She pulled on an old coat, buttoning it up so it covered her dress, and grabbed her bag and

221

scarf before opening the front door.

'Good evening,' Caron said.

'Hi.'

'Your carriage awaits . . .'

He stood aside to let her go first, the garden path too narrow for two to walk side by side. She noticed a rotting onion and nudged it into the undergrowth with the point of her shoe. If Caron noticed, he said nothing.

He opened the passenger door.

'Thank you.'

Caron walked round to the other side and got in.

'New car?' she asked.

'I borrowed it from a friend,' he said. 'The alternatives were a motorbike or a horse.'

Julie imagined trying to straddle a motorbike, or even worse, a horse in her ridiculous dress. Even side-saddle would be a stretch too far for the fabric. But Caron would look magnificent. She hid the grin that tugged at her lips. 'How's Blackstar?' she asked.

'A bit of a handful,' Caron said. 'Some people buy horses for their looks and only discover temperament later.'

'The owners pay for his upkeep, and you get to ride him?'

'Whenever I get the chance.'

'You don't have your own horse?'

'Alas, my salary doesn't stretch to that,' he said. 'Does yours?'

Julie laughed and shook her head. 'I rely on Kim.'

'Did you learn to ride together?'

She nodded. 'And you? You grew up in Zimbabwe, right?'

'Mum was forever taking on hopeless cases, animals with owners who couldn't afford the upkeep or treatment as they aged. We lived in the countryside, far from the nearest town, with a veritable menagerie.'

Julie laughed. 'I bet you have some stories.'

Caron shifted in the driver's seat, as if not all the stories he could tell were idyllic.

The grand gates of Gisborough Hall appeared in the car headlights, and they passed into parkland.

'Have you been to one of these charity balls before?' Caron asked.

'No,' Julie said. 'And you?'

'Never,' he said. 'I confess to being a little nervous.'

It struck her suddenly that he was genuinely terrified.

She smiled and relaxed a little. 'Don't worry,' she said. 'I'll look after you.'

When she stretched out a hand to reassure him, skin on skin, something electric passed into her body. Had he felt it too?

Julie escaped to the cloakroom to hand in her coat and check her make-up. When she came out, Stuart and Kim had already found Caron and were waiting for her with a glass of fizz.

'My word!' Kim looked at Julie admiringly. 'You certainly brush up well. Give us a twirl.'

Julie obliged.

'I think we all look rather splendid,' said Stuart. 'Here's to another successful collaboration between the police forces either side of the River Tees. Cheers!'

'No more shop talk, please?' Kim begged.

'What's young Arni up to this weekend?' Stuart asked.

She told them about the primary school sports camp.

'That means you can go wild tonight,' Kim whispered, and winked.

Julie knew almost no one else at the event; most of the tables had been sponsored by local businesses. She recognised the names of the older companies, local transport and haulage firms, former ICI ventures that had been bought up by outfits like Zagrovyl International. Newer business focused on renewables: wind, solar and tidal energy. The biggest sponsor was a hydrogen marketing outfit that had provided a silver balloon shaped like an airship above every table.

Caron pointed to it as they sat down.

'Do you think it's full of hydrogen?' he asked.

'I hope not.' Julie shuddered. 'We don't want a repeat of the Hindenburg disaster.'

The first course was served, a game terrine with toast and a glass of rosé wine. Caron took the vegetarian option and water.

'Maybe it's helium,' Caron said. 'After dinner I shall inhale it and serenade you in a squeaky voice.'

Julie laughed. 'You certainly know how to charm.'

The main course was served. Roast beef served in a giant Yorkshire pudding with gravy and all the trimmings and a silky red wine.

Caron wasn't drinking, a good thing if he was driving her home, and he'd ordered a celeriac steak instead. Had he become a puritan in all things?

'I didn't remember you being vegetarian,' Julie remarked.

'The more time I spend with my mum's animal friends, the less I want to eat them.'

'You're back on the farm?'

'After Cynthia left, it made sense.'

Cynthia. That was his ex-wife's name. What to say? I'm sorry.

But she wasn't.

Julie had met Cynthia, Caron's wife, only once, at a works event. They hadn't taken to one another. Julie and Caron had been in competition for a promotion at the time, and she'd assumed that the frosty reception had been a wife protecting her husband. Julie had learned the real reason much later. Cynthia and Caron had just found out that their final shot at IVF had failed. It was rough on both of them, but Cynthia took it hardest.

'How is your mum?' Julie asked to change the subject.

'Firing on all cylinders,' Caron replied. 'Showing no sign of retiring. In fact, she's taken on two new vets to grow the practice.'

'She certainly inspired my daughter,' Julie said.

'I think it was mutual. She was made up to hear that Flora got in to vet school. You know they're still in contact?'

Julie felt a pang of jealousy. 'Recently?'

'I believe so.' Scrutinising her face, he backtracked. 'Just some vet stuff.'

When her plate was clean, Julie excused herself and reached the bathroom before burping, to the amusement of the women touching up make-up.

Julie shrugged. 'Can't help it.'

'Better out than in,' said a large lady covered in pink frills.

As Julie was making her way back to the table, a man rose from the Zagrovyl table.

'DI Cadell?'

'That's me,' she said. She recognised him immediately but allowed him to introduce himself.

'Alan Cosby.' He extended a hand.

'Site Manager at Seal Sands, right?'

'For my sins.' He frowned. 'Did you manage to speak to Sue Bell?'

'I did.'

'How is she?'

'Blooming,' Julie said. 'If a little bored.'

'That won't last long,' he said. 'Once the baby is born.'

'How are you managing?'

His brows met in puzzlement.

'What do you mean?'

'Who looks after your control systems without Sue?'

'I don't worry about the control systems,' he said. 'All the support comes from India these days.'

'What about cybersecurity?'

'Sue has a deputy.'

'Not since head office made him redundant.'

A flash of irritation crossed his eyes.

'She has maternity cover.'

For a site manager, he didn't seem to have much of a grasp.

'You mean Simon Sharp?' Julie said. 'He's resigned.'

He regarded her with a cool gaze.

'And why are my internal company arrangements any business of the police?'

'Sharp was the last known person to see the victim of a murder.'

'The man who drowned in Hartlepool Marina?'

She didn't correct him.

'His name was Dameer Ghosh.'

'But there can't be any connection between his murder and Zagrovyl.' He sounded almost peevish.

'We don't know that yet,' she said. 'How well do you know Brian Burrow?'

He frowned. 'I worked alongside him for many years.'

'How would you describe him?'

'A bit of an oddball, but he was good at his job.'

'Fantasist?'

'Only in the sense that he ran the company Dungeons and Dragons club, but that was in his own time.'

'Conspiracy theorist?'

'Brian was pretty down-to-earth. I was sorry to see him go.' He shrugged. 'But times change, and businesses must stay competitive. Our partners in India are . . .'

'Brian's been helping us with some enquiries,' she said. 'He has concerns about your cybersecurity arrangements. You might want to hear him out.'

He glared at her.

Caron waved at her to indicate the final course had arrived.

'Excuse me.'

'Have a good evening, DI Cadell,' Alan Cosby said, although his expression clearly wished her otherwise.

Dessert was a hot apple crumble.

'I didn't know if you wanted custard or ice cream, so I got one of each.' Caron gestured towards the two bowls, one covered with a smooth layer of yellow sauce, the other with a white peak that was starting to melt at the base. 'You choose.'

'You don't have a preference?'

He shook his head.

Julie took the crumble with custard and dipped her spoon in.

'Was that Alan Cosby you were talking to?' Caron asked.

'Yes, do you know him?'

'Unfortunately, yes.'

'Oh.' She stopped eating, although the pudding was delicious. 'Not a fan?'

'He used to live next door to the farm,' Caron said. 'My mum wasn't sorry when he moved.'

'Tell me more?'

'He kept his dogs outside in a cage and didn't seem to have any routine for them. Their distress bothered everyone except him.'

'He's about as interested in his employees as his dogs,' Julie said.

'Is he connected to your mystery man case?'

'It's no longer a mystery who the victim is. His sister identified him.' She pushed away her pudding, no longer hungry. 'Dameer Ghosh was an Indian engineer working for a company who supplied specialist components to industry. No one we've spoken to had a bad word to say about him. It remains a mystery why he was murdered.'

'How did he die?'

'Stabbed.'

'You have the murder weapon?'

'Not yet.'

'What's Alan Cosby's connection?'

'Dameer Ghosh was last seen in the factory where Alan is site manager. He was murdered on the other side of the river, directly opposite the Zagrovyl site. The contractor he was with has disappeared.'

'No leads?'

'Just a disgruntled engineer who was fired from the Zagrovyl site and claims there is some cybersecurity conspiracy afoot.'

'Chewy.'

Julie sighed. 'Impossible.'

'Not for you,' Caron said. 'You've always been great at puzzles.'

Her heart missed a beat. It was a small compliment, but it sounded genuine. 'You reckon?'

'I know.' He smiled. 'I miss you, Julie,' he said.

Her heart made up for lost time, beating faster and sending a new warmth

227

round her body.

She sighed. 'Sometimes I wonder why I moved to Cleveland Police.'

'You moved because of me,' he said. 'Because I got the job that you deserved.'

It was the first time they'd spoken about his promotion. Yes, it had hurt at the time. But then it had been a bad time for Julie; everything hurt back then. Had she behaved to Caron as badly as DS Iain Wharton was behaving to her? Had she displayed her seething resentment for all to see? She didn't think so. But then, Caron had handled things well. Which meant he was probably the right choice for the job. God, managing people was so hard. Why had she ever craved something she was so bad at?

'I'm beginning to think I'm not really leadership material,' she said.

'Bollocks,' said Caron, his dark eyes twinkling. 'I'd follow you anywhere.'

The tingle was a full-on dance band now, the beat in her heart gaining intensity, the music pulsating through her veins.

Julie looked up to see Kim watching them.

'D'you think we could get out of here?' Julie whispered.

Caron sprang to his feet. 'I thought you'd never ask.'

Julie led the way through the French doors and down the stairs from the ballroom into the garden below. The sky was clear, peppered with stars, the moon not yet risen.

Beech trees lined the old avenue leading up to the grand house. Julie and Caron made it as far as the first row of trees. Impossible to say who initiated the kiss. The moment they were out of sight of the grand, brightly lit entrance, Julie looked up at Caron and he looked down at her and their lips connected. His kiss was gentle, enquiring. She kissed him back, answering. He put his arms around her, and she pushed him back against the smooth bark of a tree, pressing her body into his.

Julie shivered with desire.

'Are you cold?' Caron had the most beautiful voice. Always had. Deep, rich and melodic. He opened his dinner jacket, wrapping it around her and pulling her close to his chest, his skin warm through the fine cotton of his dress shirt. He bent his head to nibble her earlobe before whispering. 'Shall

I take you home?'

They collected their coats and drove away from the bright lights of the grand old house into the blackness of unlit country roads. Julie glanced at Caron's profile, stern and still. They didn't touch, but every time his hand slid around the steering wheel, or his fingers grasped the gear stick, little shivers of anticipation surged through her core.

Caron parked outside her house, switched off the engine, took her face in his hands and kissed her.

'Thank you for tonight,' he said.

'It needn't end yet,' Julie said. 'Why don't you come in?'

'What about Arni?' Caron asked.

'Back tomorrow afternoon.'

She started to open the car door.

'Wait,' Caron said. 'There's something I should tell you.'

Chapter 43

BRIAN

Stockton-on-Tees – Saturday, 23 November 2024

In between reading, writing and coding, Brian got his weights out again and tried to run through the exercise programme he used to do daily. Shocked at how much strength he'd lost in just a few months of couch potato idleness, he looked around for gentler exercise, offering to take his elderly neighbour's dog for a walk. He also carried out the second flat clean in a month – the house had never look tidier and his clothes smelt fresh.

He felt good, too. He'd completed the outline of the trilogy, and he was proudest of the final game.

B.H.O.P.A.L. 3 – Legends of the Zone would be the search for the truth. The thousands of white wading birds contain the souls and wisdom of those who died in the accident. Condemned to survive by living symbiotically with the crocodiles, the spirit birds use their beaks to floss between the teeth of the mutant reptiles, their memories fading with every interaction. The truth-seeker is in a battle against time to prove what really happened to cause the accident, to punish those responsible, to make reparation and clean up the mess.

Brian composed a message to Betty, thanking her for sending all the information over and for changing his thinking. He didn't ask if they could meet. He understood now that he had to let her go.

I've been thinking, he wrote, *how sad I am that I never got to talk to Dameer Ghosh, the man who was murdered. There are so many things I could have asked him. I wanted you to know that you were right, about many things, but about this in particular. The police haven't got a clue. They're so far out of their depth it's laughable. I'm going to try to find out what really happened to him. Just thought you should know.*

He pressed send, and ten minutes later his phone lit up. Betty. His hands were damp and shaky as he picked up.

'*Legends of the Zone*,' she said. 'Now that's more like it.'

He beamed.

'You approve?'

'I think it has potential,' she said.

High praise indeed.

'So what do you think happened to your friend, the Indian guy who was murdered?'

'I have a theory,' he said.

'One you're willing to share?'

'Not on the phone,' he said.

She laughed, that lovely, full-bodied, full-throated foghorn of a laugh that he'd grown to love. Everything Betty did, she did with gusto.

'OK then,' she said. 'I get it. Why don't you come over to Whitby for breakfast tomorrow and tell me all your conspiracy theories?'

Brian smiled, and felt a great weight lift from his shoulders.

'I do still think you should talk to people in India,' she said. 'You had lots of colleagues there. Dameer wasn't the only one. Why don't you reach out?'

After he finished the call, he opened up LinkedIn – a platform he'd been avoiding for months as people congratulated each other on new jobs while completely ignoring his 'open to work' status. Betty was right, there were other Indian engineers he'd enjoyed working with at Zagrovyl International. It wasn't their fault that he'd lost his job when the control systems support had been centralised. At least he knew there were a few good engineers involved. He clicked on Ajay's profile, but he'd moved jobs a few months ago and wasn't accepting direct messages. Same with Ravi. Finally he tried Suranjan's profile. Brian froze.

Under the smiling photo was a black banner, 'In Remembrance'.

Suranjan was dead? How was that even possible? There was no information on what or where or when. Poor guy, he was only young. Brian began searching for more information. What he discovered horrified him so much he couldn't sleep.

As dawn broke he got Magnus out of the garage and set off for the coast.

If there was one person who would know what to do, it was Betty.

Chapter 44

North Yorkshire – Sunday, 24 November 2024

When Julie woke on Sunday morning, Caron was already dressed.

'I'm sorry,' he said. 'I have to go.'

Julie sat up. 'Work?'

'A motorbike accident near Whitby. Traffic wants a second opinion.'

'I can make you breakfast.' She sat up.

'It's fine,' he said. 'Go back to sleep.'

Julie felt a sudden rush of embarrassment and slithered back down into the bed, pulling the duvet up to her chin.

He bent down and kissed her. 'Thank you, Julie.'

For what? she wondered as she watched him leave. For letting him stay last night after what he told her?

Or for letting him go?

Arni was buzzing after his sports camp, recounting stories of sweet, funny, sad and naughty kids, full of indignation at the scale of deprivation and scarcity of opportunity just a few miles from the leafy village where they lived. If the weekend had been designed to make him more realistic about

233

parenthood, it seemed to have had the opposite effect.

Julie switched her personal phone to silent and diverted her work phone to DS Wharton, who was on weekend duty. She gave Arni her full attention. They ate at the kitchen table, without the TV for once. If Arni noticed that his mother was unusually quiet, he didn't say anything.

Chapter 45

Monday morning dawned, cloudless and breezy, a beautiful sunrise colouring the sky as she drove Arni to hockey practice before continuing on to work.

'Morning.' She overtook CIO Latif in the Bridge Street car park and walked beside the wheelchair until they reached the police station. 'Good weekend?'

'Not so bad,' Nadia replied. 'And yourself?'

What Julie didn't say was, I went to a black-tie dinner and tried to seduce my once-greatest rival in the North Yorks police force, but he's having some issues since his wife left and has taken a temporary vow of celibacy, so we just cuddled and in the morning he vanished, which makes me think it was all a big mistake and I'm sad because I really like him. But that's the least of my worries, as my son's girlfriend is pregnant and he thinks he wants a baby, and she isn't sure, and her father – who is probably a crook – is absolutely furious.

What she did say was, 'Fine, just fine.'

She'd had two missed calls from Caron on her personal phone last night. One she'd ignored because Arni was in full flow. The other had been after she'd gone to bed, and she didn't want him to catch her crying.

In the safety of her office, she checked to see if Caron had left any messages. Nothing. Flora had sent a new picture. A winter coat she'd seen. A thinly disguised request for money.

Nice, Julie typed. *When are you coming home?*

One tick. Two ticks. Blue ticks. Typing . . .

Maybe next weekend?

Arni would be pleased.

Julie distracted herself with numbers. She was finalising her presentation for the budget meeting when DC Gibson appeared in the doorway.

'Yes, Constable, what is it?'

'Have you seen the TV news?'

Julie looked up from her spreadsheet.

'Do I look as if I'm sitting here watching TV?'

'He's in the *Northern Echo* too.'

Give me strength. 'Who is?'

'Our friend Brian Burrow.'

'What about him?'

'Motorbike accident.'

'Where?'

'North York Moors, near Whitby.'

Julie picked up the phone and dialled Caron's direct number.

'Julie?' He picked up immediately. 'I'm in the middle of something. Unless it's quick, can I call you back?'

'It's quick,' she said. 'The motorbike accident on your patch, did it involve a Brian Burrow?'

'Yes.'

'He's a person of interest to us.'

'Are you at HQ?'

'Yes.'

'I'll be with you shortly.'

DS Iain Wharton knocked at the door. 'DI Riley, North Yorkshire Police is here to see you.'

Julie's head snapped up to see Caron in the doorway. He held his helmet in one hand and wore his motorbike leathers so well it was almost painful to watch him move. She looked away only to notice that DS Wharton appeared even more fascinated. Was her sergeant a man in denial? It would explain a great deal.

'I was in the area so I thought it would be easier to drop by,' Caron said.

DS Wharton followed him into the room.

'That was good of you,' she said, holding out a hand. He took it lightly. A message? But of what? A reminder that – whatever had or hadn't transpired between them – they were colleagues. As if she needed to be reminded of that. A man in a relationship with a female colleague was to be congratulated. Women were not judged so leniently. But Caron knew that. So perhaps it was just sensitive discretion. Don't worry, I won't embarrass you in front of your team.

And nor would she.

'Please.' Julie indicated the small table. 'Have a seat,' she said.

DS Wharton hovered. She debated whether to send him away, but on balance decided that would just arouse his suspicions as well as his ire. Her sergeant was the last person she wanted to suspect . . . suspect what? You couldn't even call it a one-night stand.

She pressed her fingernails into her palm to stay focused on the matter in hand.

'I understand you're interested in Brian Burrow,' Caron said.

'That's right,' DS Wharton answered before she had a chance to gather her wits. 'We're very interested.'

'What can you tell us about his accident?' Julie asked.

'His motorbike went off the road yesterday morning. On the A171 just before the descent into Whitby from the Moors.'

Julie frowned. Not far from where Caron had shown her the rainbow.

'That road is a death trap for bikers,' DS Wharton said.

'Tell me about it,' Caron agreed. 'I was with the traffic experts on the scene yesterday. The air ambulance took Mr Burrow to James Cook, but he was in a bad way.' Caron shook his head. 'I've just come from intensive care. They're not sure he'll pull through.'

'Any witnesses to the accident?' DS Wharton asked. 'Any CCTV?'

'None.'

'Any other vehicles involved?'

'If there were, they didn't stick around,' Caron said.

'Where has the bike gone?' DS Wharton asked.

'A garage in Whitby. It was badly smashed up,' Caron said. 'May I ask the reason for your interest?'

'You know about the case at Hartlepool Historic Quay?' DS Wharton said.

'Of course,' Caron said, then glancing at Julie, 'I read about it.'

'Brian Burrow was due to meet with the victim, Dameer Ghosh, on the day the body floated into the quay,' DS Wharton continued.

'You think he was responsible for the murder?'

Julie held up a hand to interrupt her sergeant.

'We released Brian Burrow on Friday,' she said. 'All the evidence against him was circumstantial – we didn't have enough to charge him.' She laid both hands on the table. 'He denied ever having met the victim or having any idea what happened.'

'Any previous?' Caron asked.

'Speeding offences,' DS Wharton said. 'Cautioned for wasting police time. Nothing major.'

'Chances are this is a straightforward traffic accident,' Caron said.

'I get that,' Julie said. 'But can you make sure it gets thoroughly investigated?'

Caron's eyes flashed. 'Are you implying that the North Yorkshire police service would be anything but thorough?'

'I'm sorry, I didn't mean to suggest . . .'

'It's OK.' He stood to leave, stopping by the door to make eye contact with Julie. 'I'll keep you updated.'

'Could you keep me in the loop?' DS Wharton asked and held out a card.

Caron took it and turned on his most charming smile. 'But of course.'

DS Wharton actually blushed.

This was ridiculous. She and Caron needed to talk like adults, clear the air. 'I'll walk you out,' Julie said.

Just at that moment a tall, thin man with a shock of red hair appeared in the corridor. What on earth was Dr Sandy Armstrong doing in Middlesbrough Police Station?

'Can I have a word?' he asked.

'I can take care of DI Riley,' said her sergeant, a little too eagerly.

I bet you bloody could, given half a chance, she thought sourly.

Could she ask Sandy to wait in her office? What was it that she wanted to say to Caron? Should she reassure him? Tell him that it didn't matter about Saturday night? That – however well-meaning Kim and Stuart had been – the weight of expectation had been too great? That she still fancied the pants off him and if he wanted, she was willing to give things another try? Or wait until he was ready? Or not. Maybe Caron had realised his mistake, that he wasn't really interested in her? Perhaps, for him, there was a missing spark? Did she really want to have such a personal conversation at work?

Sandy was a busy man, not someone used to being kept hanging around. She said goodbye to Caron and turned to the pathologist.

'What brings you to Bridge Street?' she asked.

'Remember I said I'd talk to Frank, my dentist friend in the US?'

Julie watched Caron stride down the corridor, side by side with DS Wharton.

'Mmm-hmm,' she said.

Julie craved reassurance. That it wasn't her fault they hadn't had sex. That he didn't find her unattractive, even though she was clearly too old, too ugly, too fat and too forward.

Sandy was still talking at her. Something about a company who worked for the US government. She tried to focus on what he was saying.

'I have a name,' he said, 'Purchew Medical.'

Caron reached the end of the corridor without a backward glance. Julie turned her attention to Sandy.

'Thanks for following up, Sandy,' Julie said. 'It's not really important now we've identified our mystery man.'

'I'm not so sure,' Sandy said and scratched his head. 'You mind if I call them?'

'Knock yourself out,' she said.

239

Julie returned to her desk, but he remained in the doorway, hovering.

'Who was your visitor?' he asked.

'DI Riley. North Yorks Police.'

'A former colleague?'

'We didn't overlap much.' Painfully true. In so many ways.

Sandy raised an eyebrow. 'I'm sure he'll make DS Wharton very happy.'

Had Sandy sensed something she'd missed? Perhaps Iain had the sort of spark that Caron was looking for.

'What are you up to next Monday?' Sandy asked.

Before she had a chance to answer, he continued.

'I've got a spare ticket for a comedy night at Middlesbrough Town Hall next Monday – you fancy coming along?'

She felt suddenly reckless. 'Why not?'

Julie got home in time to cook an evening meal.

'Dinner in ten minutes!' she shouted into the hall.

No reply.

Her personal phone rang. Caron. She'd call him back after dinner.

She turned down the gas and climbed the stairs.

Arni's door was partly open and through the gap she could see him, intent on some shooting game.

She laid a hand on his shoulder, and he jumped.

'Mum!'

'What are you playing?'

'*Final Mission – Undercover.*'

'Shouldn't you be revising?'

'All work and no play makes Arni a dull boy.' He sounded more cheerful this evening. 'Bit of relaxation is important for my mental health.'

Kerching.

The screen lit up as a metal tag burst into light and a score counter at the top right went into triple figures.

'What are you collecting?'

'Dog tags. Each soldier has one.'

'And each one is unique?'

'In real life, I guess. In the game I get ten points for a regular enemy soldier and up to one hundred for an officer.'

Another metal tag lit up, but this time it turned blood red, and the numbers went down.

'What happened there?'

'Friendly fire. Unintended consequence of modern warfare, I'm afraid.' He grimaced. 'Worst is if your mum walks in without knocking and distracts you, causing the death of one of your own spies.'

'A spy?'

'One of the good guys. A soldier who's infiltrated the enemy and works undercover.'

'How do you know who's who? He's hardly likely to have I AM A SPY engraved on his dog tag.'

Arni clicked a switch, and the screen turned a shimmering blue.

'Special goggles,' he announced. 'The spy wears their true ID under the skin. It shows up under low-wavelength, high-frequency light.'

'Like X-rays.'

'Longer-range and less damaging.'

'So, before you shoot, you check to see if there are any spies.'

'Sometimes you don't have time,' Arni sighed. 'Sometimes it's kill or be killed. Now, can I get back to my game?'

'Dinner's in . . .' She checked her watch. 'Dinner's ready now.'

'Danny,' Arni said into his earphones. 'Got to go. Can you take over?'

She stood in the doorway, watching him press some keys. The cursor changed colour, and the game continued on screen as he took off his headphones.

It was an alien world to her, gaming. Growing up beside a farm, all her activities had been outdoor. She and Matt had fretted about Jamie's screen time, but their son still got the grades he needed for the university course of his choice. Flora had been even more addicted to her phone, but by then Matt was always travelling and Julie had stopped trying to regulate what she didn't understand. Perhaps she should make more of an effort to keep up with the changing times.

In the kitchen, Julie took the baking tray out of the oven and stuck it on a wooden chopping board while Arni set the table.

'I saw Eve at school today,' he said.

'How is she?'

'Much happier now she's been back to the counsellor.'

Julie wanted to ask if she'd made a decision but bit her tongue while she served squares of lasagne and added salad. Arni would tell her in his own time. She passed him his plate and waited.

Arni tucked into his food and helped himself to seconds.

'All our options are still open,' he said. 'We're going to talk about it properly tomorrow night.'

She waited until he'd finished eating.

'How do you feel about everything?' she asked.

He looked up at her with his big eyes. 'Would it be OK if we talk about this after tomorrow?'

'Of course,' she said and fetched the fruit bowl. 'Can I ask you about something completely different?'

Arni took a banana and peeled it. 'Sure.'

'Just now, before you came down for dinner, what did you mean when you asked Danny to take over?'

'Danny doesn't have the latest subscription, so I let him play as me sometimes.'

'You give him your login?'

'No, I let him play from mine.'

'Remotely?'

'Duh!' he mocked. 'He's not the invisible man in my room.'

'How does it work?'

'What is this, Mum? The inquisition?'

'It's for a case I'm working on,' she said.

He raised an eyebrow.

'The murder case? The one in Hartlepool?'

So, he did take an interest in her work.

'Another case,' she lied. 'What do you know about cybercrime?'

'Not a lot,' he said.

'If Danny can access your computer, could he do anything else apart from playing . . . what's it called?'

'*Final Mission – Undercover.*' Arni laid the banana skin on the table. 'I don't think so, but I've never really thought about it.'

'What if Danny was in another country?'

'Makes no difference,' Danny said. 'So long as he's got fast internet.'

'How do you know it's really Danny?'

''Cos he's my friend.'

'I know, but just for the sake of argument, what if one of his brothers pretended to be Danny?'

She knew Danny was one of several boys.

Arni shook his head. 'How do you know it's Kim when you're chatting on Facebook?'

'I guess I just assume it's her.'

He shook his head. 'Remember when her account was hacked, and you started getting odd messages – even you guessed right away.'

She let the *even you* pass.

'OK, so we recognise people by more than their faces and voices – but what if Danny tried to take over the game when you didn't want him to?'

'Danny wouldn't do that.'

'Someone doing a really good job of pretending to be him?'

'I'd still know.'

'Someone holding him at gunpoint?'

'It would still be my choice whether to let him in. And if I didn't want to, I could just flick a switch.' He frowned. 'Like a certain police officer forgetting she was a mother did in this very house not long ago.'

Not long ago. The time he'd ignored the food delivery and she'd been mad and unplugged his computer. More than two weeks ago, and it felt like an eternity.

A man had been murdered and she was no nearer finding out why.

Chapter 46

DC Gibson hopped from foot to foot outside the budget meeting.

Julie waited until the last slide of the super's introductory presentation before going to the door. 'What is it now?'

'Chief Constable on the phone for you.'

'Which one?'

'Which phone?'

'Which chief constable?'

'There's more than one?'

'Yes, Chris. Is it Paul from Cleveland or Jane from Northumbria or Stuart from North Yorkshire?'

'Stuart Simmons.'

'North Yorkshire. Put him through.'

Julie made her apologies to the meeting chair and slipped into the office next door.

'Bad time?' Stuart asked.

'Oh, you know. Budgets.'

'I might have something more interesting for you.'

'I'm listening.'

'Caron tried to call.'

Shit. She'd forgotten to call him back last night.

'He tried again this morning, but your over-efficient constable wouldn't put him through.'

'So, you pulled rank? How despicable.'

'I know, I know.' His voice turned serious. 'I think you might want to hear this. First, I have a question for you.'

'Fire away.'

'How did your Hartlepool guy die?'

'Stabbed.'

'Did you find the murder weapon?'

'No.'

'Any idea what you're looking for?'

'A nine-inch filleting knife.'

'Brian Burrow had a bundle of rags in his motorcycle pannier. Wrapped around a knife that meets exactly that description.'

She leant forward. 'Interesting.'

'I'm guessing you'll want to recover it yourselves?'

'We most certainly do.'

'I'll start the chain of custody paperwork. Should Caron liaise with your terrier of a constable?'

'No, he can talk direct to me. I'll chew the terrier's ear, so he doesn't make the same mistake twice.' Julie stood up. 'Where's the evidence now?'

'Caron will know,' Stuart said. 'I'm happy for Cleveland Police to take the lead on this one, Julie. Anything you need, just work with Caron.'

'Thanks, Stuart.'

He cleared his throat. 'That won't be a problem, will it, Julie?'

'No problem at all.'

Julie walked to her own office and closed the door before calling Caron.

'Caron, I'm so sorry . . .' She was about to launch into her apology when he interrupted her.

'DI Cadell,' he said. 'I'm in the car with DS Wharton.'

What the hell?

'I gather you've heard the news?'

She flicked her internal switch. Personal to professional.

'I just spoke to your chief constable,' she said.

'We're leaving Northallerton now and should be in Whitby in about an hour.'

'Can I speak to DS Wharton?'

'Wait, I'll put you on speakerphone.'

The background noise turned to a roar.

'DS Wharton, have you arranged CSM support?'

'Not yet.'

'I'll get someone to meet you there,' she said. 'Where exactly?'

Caron interrupted. 'Texting you the address now.'

The super appeared at her office window.

'We're about to restart the meeting, Julie.'

'Sir, I have to—'

'Budget meeting takes priority. DS Wharton can handle the Whitby trip.'

So, everyone knew apart from her?

'I'll just call the CSM, sir.'

'The North Yorks crime scene team can handle the transfer.'

She bit her tongue and followed him out.

As they passed the ladies' toilet, she cleared her throat. 'See you down there, sir.'

'I'll wait for you,' he said.

Inside the cubicle Julie made the call.

'Adrian, I need you to stop whatever you're doing and get someone to Whitby before DS Wharton gets there.' She kept her voice as quiet as possible. 'Texting you the address. It looks like we've found the murder weapon.'

Julie struggled to focus on the budget presentation. Assistant Chief Constable Bruma was presenting on behalf of the Minimax team, the group that focused on counter-terrorism – labouring the increased threat from South Asia to justify an increase in budget and staffing while all other departments were facing significant cuts.

Julie knew she shouldn't be here in an office in Middlesbrough. She should be in Whitby, making sure everyone kept an open mind.

How did DS Wharton know about the discovery of a possible murder weapon in Brian Burrow's motorbike pannier before she did? Caron told him, of course. Or rather DI Caron Riley. She'd confused the personal and professional when she'd ignored his calls. All she'd been thinking about was the inevitable brush-off – still be friends, blah blah – and how much it was going to hurt.

Face it. Why would such a beautiful man be interested in her? How could she be such an idiot as to invite him home in the first place?

She thought back to the moment they'd shared under the rainbow. Was that a coincidence? Did Caron know she'd be driving on that road?

Julie chewed a strand of hair as she tried to line up the sequence of events. She'd informed Stuart Simmons that she was interviewing a potential witness in Scarborough, just as she'd informed DCI Rose Irving in the Scottish police that DS Wharton was on his way to Eyemouth. It was common politeness when an officer from one police force strayed into the territory of another. Occasionally, the local force had useful intelligence to add or even sent one of their own along, too.

Stuart had invited her over for lunch, and she'd explained the exact timing of her journey when she refused. Could Stuart have told Caron?

Not that she suspected Stuart of doing anything wrong, other than matchmaking – and that was probably Kim's initiative anyway. Stuart and Kim were her friends, on her side. If Stuart hadn't called her direct, she wouldn't even have known about the discovery of the murder weapon – the potential murder weapon – until it was too late.

Was Caron really just out for a ride that day, or had he been waiting for her? And if so, why? What possible motive could he have? Had he been checking roadside cameras? Identifying locations without coverage?

On the day of Brian's accident, why had Caron been called away? He had no role in traffic. Yes, he was ex-traffic in another force and a motorcycle rider himself. Did the traffic investigator want a second opinion? Did that mean there was more to the accident than met the eye? Or had he just needed an excuse to escape from her bed?

Caron and DS Wharton appeared as thick as thieves. Had they met before? In The Applegarth the night she chickened out? Or was this an older friendship?

And what about Superintendent Chalmers? Why was he being so obstructive? What part did he play in all this?

Her brain was whirling.

Who could she trust?

The room went quiet. It was as if the nine men around the table could hear her private thoughts. When she looked up she saw Superintendent Chalmers staring at her.

'DI Cadell?'

The super drummed his fingers on the table.

She looked around a table of expectant faces.

'Can you take us through your budget pack?'

Julie stood up.

She had always been on top of her numbers and the presentation went reasonably well, she thought. Until the questions.

'DI Cadell, you are the only department head who hasn't asked for more staff.'

'I've assumed we keep at least one trainee DC post. That's included in the budget numbers that I've shown you. CIO Nadia Latif is doing a great job.'

'You don't want another DI?'

'I prefer to bring people in as and when the workload warrants.'

The super bowed his head, shaking it from side to side, and Julie wondered what she'd missed.

'Wait!' Julie caught Assistant Chief Constable Bruma on his way out. 'Could I have a quick word?'

He smiled. 'Sure.'

'Who's our expert on industrial cybersecurity?'

'One of our vacant posts at the moment,' he said. 'The police don't pay enough, so we struggle to retain the good IT professionals. There's a huge demand in the private sector. We do all the training and then,' he pursed his lips, 'whoosh! Away they go.'

'I see.'

'By the way,' he said. 'I admire your courage.'

'My courage?'

'The CFO likes to see us fight. Before the budget reviews, he encourages us to overstate our requirements and then watches us tear each other to shreds. You were the only one who didn't play.'

No one told me the rules of the game. 'That was my first budget review.'

'I guessed. Why are you looking for a cyber expert?'

'A case I'm working on.'

'It's my background, so you could always try me.' He looked at his phone. 'But first, I have yet another meeting to go to.'

After the budget meeting, Julie found CSM Adrian Prosser waiting outside her office.

'Did you get my message?' she asked.

'I did.'

'Who did you send?'

'No one.'

'What?'

'I was given strict instructions by Superintendent Chalmers to leave the evidence transfer in the hands of DS Wharton and the North Yorks police.'

Julie felt the anger rising.

'It's already arrived,' he added.

'The whole motorbike, or just the pannier?'

He shook his head. 'Just the weapon and the fabric it was wrapped in.'

She shook her head in disbelief.

'Your sergeant DS Iain Wharton brought it back.'

Julie put her head in her hands. Evidence-handling protocols were among the strictest in the service and she couldn't begin to count the number of rules that Iain must have broken. 'No court is going to like that,' she said.

'Exactly,' he said. 'Although, from what I hear, your suspect is unlikely to live long enough for it to come to court.'

Julie felt no sense of triumph, no excitement at how close they were coming to wrapping up the case. The klaxon of corruption was deafening. The impossibly convenient accident, the presence of the murder weapon, the shortcuts in evidence transfer could only be designed to draw attention away from something else. But away from what? Some inconvenient truth that was worse than framing an innocent man? DS Wharton had been convinced that Brian Burrow was the murderer, and Superintendent Chalmers had backed him all the way. On Friday, they didn't have enough hard evidence to arrest him, yet suddenly . . .

The fault rested with her – she had no other credible suspects.

Or did she?

Julie called her contact in the Scottish police.

'DCI Irving.'

'Hi, Rose, it's Julie from Cleveland Police.'

'You must be telepathic,' she said. 'I was just about to call you.'

Julie felt a little flutter of hope.

'You've found Simon Sharp?'

'I'm afraid not,' Rose said. 'There's no record of him offshore.'

'That's odd.'

'All helicopter transfers require a training certificate and photo ID,' Rose continued. 'No room for stowaways.'

'So maybe he's supporting an offshore rig remotely. Working onshore.'

In which case, why wasn't he at home in Wynyard?

She'd left a message at his house asking him to phone urgently, and the security guard had promised to inform them the moment he returned.

'The plot thickens, I'm afraid,' Rose said.

'In what way?'

'I put an alert on his name to see if anything came up. And bingo. This morning, his parents registered a missing person report.'

Julie whistled through her teeth.

'I gave them a call, just in case it related to a different person, but he matches your profile.'

'When did they last see him?'

'Not for a while. They live in Fife. But he phones home regularly. He hasn't been in touch since the fifth of November.'

The day before he met Dameer Ghosh.

'And they waited until now to report it?'

'No, they tried to report it earlier, but I'm afraid the initial assessment didn't identify him as being at any risk from harm. The local police assumed he was just another contract worker who forgot to tell his family what he was up to.'

'And now?'

'His parents collected evidence. They went to his house. Checked his computer. He used to be very active on social media – there's been nothing since the sixth of November.'

The day that Dameer Ghosh was murdered.

'I'd like to talk to them.'

'I guessed you would. They're on the train heading south, back to his house. They won't get in till late, but they can be reached there tomorrow after ten.'

'Thank you.'

'How's the investigation going?'

'No comment.'

Rose laughed. 'Well, if you ever need a shoulder to cry on, you know where to find me.'

Julie put down her phone and sat at her desk, staring into space. Another missing control engineer. Just what they needed.

Had Simon Sharp been involved in the crime? Had he disappeared to avoid being caught? Or was Simon Sharp another victim?

She called Sue Bell.

'Could we meet?'

'Of course.'

'Tomorrow? Saltholme. First thing?'

'I'll be there.'

A small hand tapped on the window.

'Enter!'

CIO Nadia Latif rolled in.

'You want the good news?'

'I'm listening.'

'I found the ghost taxi.'

'Excellent!'

'A Mercedes saloon registered to Osprey Executive Cars in 2011.'

'Do we have the driver details?'

'Not yet. The company secretary reported it stolen in October this year.'

'That old excuse?'

''Fraid it might be genuine. There are no additional ANPR records for the number plate MIC 610E apart from those on the sixth of November, and no hits on any unidentified car of the same model either side of that date.'

'Damn,' Julie said. 'Where's our ghost taxi now?'

'That's the other piece of bad news,' Nadia said. 'A car matching the exact description was found on Aislaby Road on the morning of the seventh November. It had been set alight.'

She handed Julie a photo. The logo was just visible under the charred and blistered paintwork if you knew what you were looking for.

'So, the bird logo was an osprey, not an eagle,' Julie said.

'Traffic says they get a lot of joyriders in stolen cars. They take off the real number plates to avoid being caught on camera, stick on something that would pass a casual glance, but is usually a duplication or non-existent.'

'Where's the wreck now? Adrian might be able to find something . . .'

CIO Latif shook her head. 'The case was closed yesterday. The wreck was released and scrapped the same day.'

Outside, a door slammed closed.

Julie banged her fist on the desk.

To be this close only to find that the evidence had been destroyed. Could that be a coincidence? Or was someone else trying to stop her? As soon as she found a new lead, something closed it down. Something or someone? Someone on the inside?

Patience. The closer she got the more reckless they became. It was only a matter of time before reckless became careless.

And she'd be watching and waiting.

Arni was meeting Eve tonight, so Julie waited up for him. By the slam of the door, she could tell that all was not well.

She hovered outside the kitchen.

'Before you ask, Eve didn't turn up,' he said.

Julie made a sympathetic noise.

'Her parents have imposed a curfew. Taken away her phone. Cut off the internet. They're even talking about moving her to a new school.'

'She's eighteen, Arni. An adult in the eyes of the law.'

'But not,' Arni said, 'in the eyes of her parents.'

'You fancy some cocoa?'

'And you're just as bad!'

He raced upstairs and slammed his bedroom door.

Chapter 47

North Yorkshire and Teesside – Wednesday, 27 November 2024

Julie woke to the sound of Arni leaving the house. It was still dark outside, too early for hockey. Perhaps he'd arranged to meet Eve before practice.

She showered and started assembling her professional armour. Something told her this was going to be a tough day.

Julie arrived at Saltholme before the visitor centre opened. She parked on a verge and crossed the road on foot to study a huge sign with a map of the Seal Sands chemical complex.

She started walking along the road towards the Zagrovyl factory. High in the sky, raptors circled. Peregrine falcons were known to use the tall structures to hunt from.

A police car pulled up beside her.

'Morning, madam.' The driver rolled down his window and showed her his warrant card. DS Vaziri from the new Minimax team. 'May I ask where you're going?'

'Morning, Sergeant.' She flashed her badge.

'Jump in, DI Cadell,' he said, unlocking the passenger door. 'It's not safe to walk on this road. Where to?'

'I'm early for an appointment at Saltholme. Thought I'd take a stroll,' she said. 'To get a feel for the area.'

'I'll give you a guided tour.'

'Let's start with Zagrovyl International.'

He drove down the road and stopped the car outside the sprawling manufacturing plant.

'What do they make here?' she asked.

'Agricultural chemicals,' he said. 'Fertilisers and pesticides.'

'I should know this,' she said, 'but is there a permanent police patrol in this area?'

'No,' he said. 'We work closely with the Civil Nuclear Constabulary,' he said. 'But we're not armed like the CNC.'

'And you just happened to be passing?'

'No, ma'am,' he said. 'Someone called you in. Thought you looked mighty suspicious.' He smiled. 'We're on high alert right now.'

'What's the concern?'

'Terrorist attack.'

Julie turned to look at him.

'What sort of terrorist attack?'

'Teesside has the highest concentration of high-hazard manufacturing sites in England,' he said.

'You mean like the nuclear power station?'

'Yes, and gas pipelines and chemical factories that handle all manner of flammable and toxic materials.'

'But they all operate safely,' she said. 'Don't they?'

'So long as they keep the nasty stuff inside in the vessels and the pipes,' he replied. 'Our job is to make sure no one interferes with that.'

Julie nodded. 'I think I'd better get back to Saltholme and leave you to do your job.'

By the time Julie returned to her car, the Saltholme café was open, and Sue Bell was sitting at a window cradling a mug of cocoa.

'I won't get up, if you don't mind,' Sue said. 'It takes a crane to move me these days.' She winced as she moved. 'It's not quite clear to me how this giant baby is going to get out.'

Julie laughed. 'It's not an ideal design, I grant you that.'

'You have children?'

'Yes.'

Julie never knew how to answer when asked how many children she had. How many children she gave birth to, or how many still lived? Fortunately, Sue was still focused on the mechanics of separation.

'Any advice?'

'On childbirth?' Julie blanched. If women shared their honest experiences of childbirth, the human race would die out.

'It's top of my to-do list right now,' Sue said.

'My youngest is a teenager. I can barely remember his birth.' No point in scaring Sue. After all, every woman has a different experience, a different pain threshold. And however bad it felt at the time, it eased once the baby was born. No one had told her the real agony came later.

Sue changed the subject.

'I heard about Brian Burrow's motorcycle accident,' she said. 'Any more news?'

Julie shook her head. 'He's still in intensive care.'

'Do you know what happened?' Sue asked.

'His motorbike crashed on a quiet road. If other vehicles were involved, they didn't hang around. Another motorcyclist found him by chance. Apparently there were no working cameras in the area.'

'Do you think it was an accident?'

'As opposed to?'

'Suicide?' Sue sighed. 'I always felt bad about making him redundant. He was good at his job, but he used to rub senior management up the wrong way, never knew when to keep his trap shut. The diktat to centralise came from Global HQ. It wasn't like I was given a choice. I was . . .'

'Just following orders?' Julie finished her sentence for her.

Sue grimaced. 'Brian went downhill fast after he left Zagrovyl. I met with him a couple of times, took him out to lunch, tried to help him get a new job, but after Betty, his girlfriend, left him he just couldn't control his bitterness and anger.'

Julie put down her coffee mug.

'I'm afraid it gets worse,' she said.

'How can it be worse than attempted suicide?'

'Can I speak in confidence?'

Sue put her hands on her swollen belly. 'Can't guarantee the Shrimp's discretion, but it'll be a while before she's talking.' She leant forward. 'I absolutely promise not to tell another soul.'

'It'll all be out this afternoon anyway,' Julie said. 'Brian is about to be arrested on suspicion of Dameer's murder.'

'No! I don't believe it.' Sue pushed back her chair. 'I worked with him for ten years. He might be a nerd, but he's a gentle soul. I could just about imagine him attempting to end his own life in a state of extreme depression, but no way would he be physically violent.'

That chimed with Julie's assessment, but she couldn't give voice to it here. 'May I ask you about something else?'

'What now?' Sue looked and sounded thoroughly rattled.

'Simon Sharp.'

'You've found him?'

Julie shook her head.

'He's now officially registered as a missing person.'

'Oh.'

'I'm on my way to speak to his parents, but according to the missing person report, they haven't heard from him since the night before he met Dameer.'

'You think there's a connection?'

'What can you tell me about Sharpie?'

'Are you asking if he could have murdered someone?' Sue thought about it for a while. 'I don't know him as well as I know Brian, but Sharpie struck me as pretty low wattage when it came to planning. I couldn't trust him with anything complex.'

'I thought control engineers were practically rocket scientists.'

'There are harder things than launching rockets, you know.' Sue laughed. 'Sharpie earned his stripes with the millennium bug, 1999 and all that, remember?'

'When airplanes were about to fall from the sky and all electronic devices were going to go bananas?'

'Exactly. Exaggerating cyberthreats and making people scared is a great way to drum up work.' She sighed. 'He had a good CV, but we soon found out he had limited imagination. Brian was a whiz at everything – he loved problem-solving. Sharpie was only interested in making money.'

'One thing I don't understand,' Julie said. 'His parents are adamant that he went missing between the fifth and seventh of November. But the site records show he clocked in and out up to the day we started looking for him. Did anyone actually see Simon Sharp after Dameer was murdered?'

'You'd have to ask the people on site.'

'I intend to,' Julie said, 'but I wanted to check something with you first. If someone had his pass, how easy would it be to make it look as if he'd clocked in and out?'

'You mean if he gave the pass to someone else and asked them to clock in and out for him?' She shook her head. 'Used to be very common until we fixed the turnstile. These days gatehouse security is wise to that sort of fraud.'

'So, it's impossible?'

'There is another way. You tamper with the electronic record. We fired a guy in IT last year for doing exactly that.'

'What was his name?'

'Everyone called him Tadpole.'

Tadpole. Tad the Pole. Julie checked her notes.

'Tadeusz Makowski?'

'That sounds about right.'

'The contractor Brian Burrow accused of stealing stuff from the stores?'

'God, that was embarrassing.' Sue grimaced. 'Final nail in the coffin for Brian as far as senior management was concerned.'

'Was there any substance to his allegation?'

'We never got to the bottom of it. Brian was the engineer responsible for control system spares and he could be a bit obsessive. Now all that is controlled centrally.'

'From India?'

'That's right.'

'Brian didn't seem very happy about that.'

'It cost him his job.'

'You're OK with it?'

'There's a really good team in Delhi. They employ super-smart engineers, the kind we struggle to retain in the UK.'

'But from a cybersecurity perspective?'

'That's kept in-house and local.'

Except, Julie thought to herself, when the expert is on maternity leave and her back-up has vanished.

After a bright sunrise, clouds had gathered. A fine drizzle pit-pattered onto the trees lining the approach road to Wynyard. Rain-washed autumn leaves glowed russet and gold against a leaden sky.

Swish-swipe, chatter-squeak. Inside her car, Inspector Julie Cadell adjusted the speed of the windscreen wipers. Too slow, and a film of water formed between passes, blurring her view of the road ahead; too fast and the rubber blades juddered against the glass for want of lubrication. She stopped at the security gate, got out of her car and flashed her badge at the window. The guard who controlled access to the gated community came out with a large umbrella, emblazoned with the logo of Wynyard Hall.

'Can I help you, officer?'

She stepped under the portable shelter. 'Do you know this man?'

The clearest photo of the control engineer had been attached to the missing person report. She pulled it out of her briefcase and showed it to the guard.

'That's Simon Sharp, isn't it?'

'Yes. When did you last see him?'

'Oh, a while ago. He's working offshore now.'

'Did Simon tell you that?'

'No, it was his neighbour at number seven.'

Julie made a mental note to interview the woman with the baby.

'When did you last speak to him?'

Rain drummed on the nylon as the man checked his logbook.

'Bonfire Night, November fifth.'

The night before the murder.

'And what did you talk to him about?'

'He was complaining about the noise of fireworks,' the man said. 'I promised to take a look.'

'And what did you find?'

'A party outside the estate. Nothing I could do.'

'And did you see him after that?'

The security guard shook his head.

Julie thanked him and drove on.

Mr and Mrs Sharp were waiting for her. As she turned into the cul-de-sac, Mr Sharp was outside his son's house, dressed in yellow oilskins, raking the front lawn. Mrs Sharp darted from the bay window, opening the front door as Julie turned into the drive and pulled up behind a battered old Volkswagen Polo. An elderly couple, one tall, one small, both so frail they looked as if a sharp gust of wind might blow them away like autumn leaves.

Julie introduced herself and followed the couple to the kitchen where Mr Sharp took off his rain gear while his wife made tea.

'Any news?' Mrs Sharp asked.

'I'm afraid not,' Julie said.

'It's so unlike Simon,' Mr Sharp said, running a bony hand over his bald head. 'He phones us every Sunday, come rain, come shine.'

'He's a good son,' Mrs Sharp added. 'Always looking out for his old mum. Flowers on Mother's Day, chocolates at Easter, home for birthdays and Christmas.'

'He's been all over the world, my lad has,' Mr Sharp said. 'He can name his price, you know.'

'Tell me about the last time he called,' Julie asked.

'Tuesday night, fifth of November,' Mrs Sharp said without hesitation. 'He knew I had chemo that day and he always phones to check on me.'

'He wanted advice on the garden, too. Whether to plant spring bulbs before the frost sets in.' Mr Sharp smiled indulgently. 'Truth be told, he's not much of a gardener. I always put things right when we come and stay.'

'Did he talk about his work?' Julie asked. 'Did he mention plans to change job?'

'Oh, no. He likes his work and living down south,' Mrs Sharp said. 'We're always trying to persuade him to come back to Scotland, aren't we, Sid? But he has a good life here in Teesside – as you can see.'

She waved a hand, indicating the modern kitchen and house beyond.

'Does he live alone?' Julie asked.

'I know what you're thinking, but you'd be wrong,' Mrs Sharp said. 'He has lots of lady friends. He's just not ready to settle down yet.'

'Playing the field, my lad,' added Mr Sharp. 'Good on him.'

'Has he ever done this before?' Julie asked. 'Broken off contact for a few days or weeks?'

'Never,' they said in unison.

'Not even when he was working in Nigeria,' his mother added. 'Even with all the trouble, he still found a way to let us know he was OK.'

'And remember when he was in Saudi and all the phones were down?' his father added. 'He sent us a telegram – I didn't even know such things still existed until the doorbell rang, and there it was! Hand-delivered!'

'Does he have any siblings?'

'He's an only child,' Mr Sharp said.

'Any close friends who might . . .'

'We've been in touch with everyone who might know where he is. No one has heard anything from him since the seventh of November.'

'Is his car here?'

'Yes, in the garage.'

'May I see?'

Simon Sharp drove a top-end electric Mercedes-Benz, model EQS with 2024 number plates. Not only brand new, but sparkling clean, inside and out. A water hose lay on the garage floor beside a bucket with a sponge.

'Does Simon have a cleaner?'

'I don't think so.'

'Did you clean your son's car?' Julie asked.

Mr Sharp shook his head.

'I like gardening, but I'm not much interested in cars.'

'When he travels, does he usually drive?'

'Yes, unless he's going offshore, in which case they send a taxi to bring him to the airport.'

As they left the garage, Julie noticed a curtain move in the window next door.

'Do you know his neighbour?' Julie asked, nodding in that direction.

'Christine?' Mr Sharp cleared his throat. 'Not really,' he said.

'I think I'll go and have a word with her.'

The neighbour was less forthcoming than last time. She didn't invite Julie in, stepping into the porch and pulling the door behind her.

'Baby's sleeping,' she whispered. 'Don't want to wake him.'

'You mentioned that Simon Sharp had gone offshore,' Julie said. 'How did you know?'

'A man delivered his car,' she said. 'When I asked him where Simon was, he told me he'd got a new job offshore and wouldn't be around for a while.'

'When was this?'

'Just before you came round the first time.'

'Did you get his name?'

'No.' She smiled. 'More's the pity.'

Julie was beginning to understand why Mr Sharp was less than keen on his son's neighbour.

'Can you describe the man?'

'Nice-looking bloke. Great cheekbones,' she said.

'Hair colour?'

'Very blond, almost white and cut really short.'

'Anything else?'

'Blue eyes,' she said. 'And did I mention the cheekbones?'

'You did,' Julie said. 'Was he local?'

She shook her head. 'Sexy foreign accent,' she said.

'Thank you Mrs . . .'

'Bracegirdle.' She made a face. 'Well, that's my partner's surname. He works offshore. It's no life for me, stuck here all on my own while he's away.'

As if to remind her of his existence, the baby wailed.

Julie handed Christine Bracegirdle a card. 'We're very concerned about Simon Sharp. His parents have reported him as a missing person. If you think of anything else that might help us find him, or about the man you spoke to, please give me a call.'

Julie returned to the house where Simon's parents were watching from the kitchen window. She shook her head to let them know that the neighbour had been of little help.

'Mrs Bracegirdle spoke to someone who returned Simon's car to the garage.'

The colour drained from his mother's face.

'Simon doesn't lend his car to anyone.'

Julie repeated the neighbour's description, but the elderly couple just shook their heads.

'I'm so worried,' Mrs Sharp said. 'I just know that something bad has happened.' She shivered. 'I can feel it in my bones.'

'I'm sure we'll find him, Mr and Mrs Sharp,' Julie said.

As she drove away she reflected that she had not been completely honest with the Sharps. Who had driven his car and why? The ultra-clean house and car bothered her. Both had all the marks of a professional job. Julie was sure she would find their son, but she couldn't guarantee that he'd be found alive.

Chapter 48

Middlesbrough – Wednesday, 27 November 2024

'Case number 021284. The Hartlepool murder. Third week update.'

Julie paused and looked around the room, noting the absences. Adrian Prosser, the CSM, had sent apologies, having been called away to other cases. DS Wharton was missing again, without apology or explanation. The biggest gap was the absence of her boss. Superintendent Graham Chalmers didn't attend every case review, but she'd have expected him at this one. She checked the remote attendees – even thinner on the ground.

On the other hand, she had people she could trust: DC Gibson, CIO Latif and – by video link – Val Hesslewood, an expert forensic technician from the CSI team and the ever-dependable Karen Potter from records.

'Let me summarise the developments since last week,' Julie said. Everyone sat forward expectantly. 'You all know that a man has been arrested in connection with this case, but if you can be patient, I'd like to cover that last, so we don't let it overshadow the other developments made.'

With a collective sigh, everyone sat back again.

'DC Gibson – can you speak for DS Wharton?'

The constable nodded. 'DS Wharton interviewed the nightwatchman, Alf Pearce, who put out the bonfire at the scrapyard on the night of the murder. Mr Pearce also reported seeing a taxi leave the area. Over to you, CIO Latif.'

Nadia smiled. 'I checked the ANPR records again. This time I looked at unrecognised numbers and found the same vehicle in several places of interest at key times: at Teesside airport when the victim's flight arrived from Amsterdam, at The Locomotion in Eaglescliffe when he checked in, at Zagrovyl International in Seal Sands just before his meeting, at the road leading to the container port just before and after the murder, and again either side of high tide. The car had a bird logo – as the witness described – but a false number plate. I identified the vehicle as stolen from Osprey Executive Cars earlier this year. It was abandoned and set alight.'

'Great work,' Julie said. 'I've logged a request for CSI support. What are the chances of forensics taking a look at the scene of the burnt-out car?'

'And the car itself?' Val asked.

'Already removed and scrapped.'

'I'll talk to Adrian as soon as the meeting finishes.' Val nodded. 'I gather we have another priority—'

Julie held up a hand. 'We'll come to that. But first, any luck with the victim's lodgings?'

'We found absolutely nothing.' She shook her head. 'I've never seen anything quite like it.'

'Interesting,' Julie said. 'In other developments, Simon Sharp, the last person to see the victim when he visited Zagrovyl, is now officially missing. I spoke to his parents, and they believe he vanished at the same time as our victim.'

DC Gibson scratched his head. 'Didn't someone say Mr Sharp was still working up until last week?'

'According to company records. But I can't find a single eyewitness.'

'Maybe he works remotely.'

'He does part of the time, but he's also not been home since the night of the murder.'

'Staying with a friend, but still working?'

'Possible, but his car is in the garage at his house.' She turned to Val. 'Another vehicle I'd like you to have a look at.'

Val nodded. 'I'll add it to the list.'

'And let's see if there are any CCTV or ANPR sightings after the sixth of

November.' Julie wrote down the registration number of Simon Sharp's car and pushed it over the table to CIO Latif.

'You think he's falsifying his work record?'

'It wouldn't be the first time. An IT contractor,' Julie checked her notes, 'Tadeusz Makowski, was sacked from Zagrovyl last year for exactly that infraction.'

Karen Potter unmuted herself. 'That name rings a bell.'

'Same guy was accused of theft by Brian Burrow,' Julie said.

'Yes, but I've seen his name in connection with something else,' Karen said. 'Leave it with me.'

'Thanks,' Julie said. 'And finally, we interviewed Brian Burrow under caution. Brian admits to arranging a meeting with the victim, but claims it never took place. Last weekend Mr Burrow suffered a serious motorcycle accident and is now in hospital in intensive care. North Yorks Police found a knife in his saddlebag which matches the description of the murder weapon. Over to you, Val.'

'As you say, it matches the description, but we haven't been able to find any evidence linking it to either Brian Burrow or Dameer Ghosh.'

'Other than the fact that it was in Mr Burrow's saddlebag?'

'I'm afraid there were some–' Val coughed– 'irregularities with the evidence transfer, so it would be better if we could find some independent evidence. We haven't given up yet.'

'Keep working on that,' Julie said.

'DS Wharton is searching Mr Burrow's flat,' DC Gibson added.

So that's where he was. Julie had requested the search warrant but hadn't been notified that it had come through.

'With CSI support?' Julie asked.

Val shrugged. 'Not that I am aware of. No request logged.'

Julie bit her lip. 'Then I'm making an official request as soon as this meeting is over – can you give it top priority.'

'I'll send someone right away.'

'Let's wrap this up, then. Anyone else got anything to add to the case review?'

Chapter 49

'Well done!' The superintendent strode into Julie's office, grinning from ear to ear. 'Crime solved in record time!'

Julie stood up. 'If you're referring to the murder of Dameer Ghosh,' she said, 'I'm not convinced that Brian Burrow is our murderer.'

'Caught red-handed, what more do you want?' the super said.

'Have forensics confirmed that the knife in his saddlebag is the murder weapon?'

'Not yet, but it's just a matter of time.'

'He's not exactly in a position to defend himself, is he?'

'Unfortunate, most unfortunate.'

Hypocrite. Julie could tell her boss thought exactly the opposite. Whatever platitudes he mouthed, he clearly considered it a stroke of luck that the accused was in a coma and very likely to die before the case ever came to trial. Julie felt a surge of sympathy for the injured man.

'What was Brian's motive?' she asked.

'I gather he's a bit of a loner.'

'That's not a motive.'

'Into weird fantasy games.'

'Dungeons and Dragons is pretty mainstream, even old-fashioned,' she said. 'And even my son plays *Fallout*.'

'Brian Burrow reported the victim missing. Murderers often want police attention.'

'Crimestoppers is strictly anonymous, so we can't use that information against him.'

'I thought he told you himself?'

'Not exactly.'

Just what had DS Wharton told the super?

'The suspect knew the victim,' Superintendent Chalmers continued. 'The murder weapon was found in his possession.'

'We don't yet know for sure that it's the murder weapon.'

The super grinned. 'Bit of a coincidence if it's not.'

Or a plant? Could DS Wharton have planted the evidence? Julie didn't trust DS Wharton not to take shortcuts, but she had never considered that he might deliberately distort an investigation. As for the super, she knew he was more interested in quick results than the truth, but would he really go so far as to frame an innocent man? Worse, could the Cleveland police have been involved in causing the accident? In league with Caron from North Yorks? Julie felt physically sick. Was her judgement so poor?

'I'd like the crime scene team to look at a house and car in Wynyard. Simon Sharp, the last person known to have contact with the victim, has vanished.'

'Don't go there, Julie.'

'What do you mean?'

'We've already arrested the culprit.'

'Whatever happened to innocent until proved guilty?' Julie protested.

'If Mr Burrow survives and wakes up, he can defend himself. If he dies, case closed.'

'And his missing colleague?'

'Let the mispers unit handle that.'

Julie looked down at her polished shoes.

'Cheer up, Julie. It's time to celebrate. Look on the bright side. Your team did an excellent job.'

'They are doing the job they're paid to do, sir, the job that society expects them to do. There are still a lot of loose ends to tie up in this case.'

'Let's leave all that to Iain, shall we?'

'DS Wharton?'

'Soon to be DI Wharton.'

Julie's chin dropped.

'I'm not sure he's ready, sir.'

'I've known him a lot longer than you have, Inspector.'

Those two were too alike to spot each other's flaws. Which is exactly why promotions were handled by independent boards.

'Granted, but—'

'His promotion will be confirmed this week,' the super said. 'Celebration at The Applegarth on Friday. I trust you'll be there to add your vote of support?'

Julie decided that silence was the best response.

'Iain can wrap the case up,' Superintendent Chalmers said. 'Free you to move on to something else.'

Julie shook her head. 'I don't think that's wise, sir.'

'The mystery is solved.' The super smiled. 'We have more important things for you to be working on.'

'Like what?' she said.

'The Minimax team need some support. They have a new terrorism alert, moving to amber.' He smiled again. 'Wasn't it you who said we should move resources as and when the workload warrants?'

'I want to finish this investigation . . .'

'This investigation is finished.' His jovial demeanour switched to a cold, hard stare, and his raised voice cut like a knife. 'Hand over any outstanding actions to Iain, thank your team and report to ACC Bruma on Monday.'

'But . . .'

'That's an order, DI Cadell.'

'Yes, sir.'

Julie held it together until she was out of the building. Her car key was in the office, but she couldn't face walking back past her team to get it. Instead, she walked down to the river, fuming, channelling her fury into activity.

When her anger ran out, she collapsed onto a bench and put her head in her hands.

Failure. She was a failure. A total and abject failure. She'd let everyone down: her family, her team, Dameer Ghosh – the victim of a murder, and Brian Burrow – a man almost certainly wrongly accused.

And because of her incompetence the real murderers were still out there. And – if Brian was to be believed – there was worse to come.

Julie got home to find Arni in the kitchen.

'I'm making dinner,' he announced proudly.

It wasn't the first time he'd cooked; all her children could follow a recipe, but he rarely did.

'Smells lovely,' she said.

'Shakshuka.'

'My favourite.'

'I know.' He looked up sheepishly. 'Sorry about last night.'

'That's OK.'

She waited for him to elaborate, but he was intent on checking the recipe on his phone. It lit his face, and she noticed a little splash of tomato on his nose. Julie had to pin her arms to her sides to resist the urge to wipe it off. Boundaries had to be respected.

'Do I have time for a shower?' she asked.

'Bad day?'

She nodded. 'What about you?'

'I'll tell you later.'

She managed to hold it together during dinner. Arni had enough to cope with without finding out that his mum was a total failure.

But when Kim called, she could no longer hold back her misery.

Chapter 50

Seal Sands – Thursday, 28 November 2024

Julie sat in her kitchen nursing a cup of tea that had long gone cold. She stared out of the window at her ragged garden and wished that she had parents like Simon Sharp's who came to help rather than to cause chaos.

Her mother and father had separated when she was sixteen and divorced just before she met Matt. Both parents remarried, new partners who were themselves divorcees with children. Her father lived in Sussex and never remembered his grandchildren's birthdays – he'd always relied on a partner for that, and his second wife had other priorities. Her mother had divorced again and lived alone in Spain. She'd always been forgetful, but with age it looked like her memory lapses might be an early indication of something more serious.

Julie gave Arni a run to hockey then returned home, unable to face going into work. She sent a request to HR for a short-notice holiday, texted her boss and was staring into her teacup when the doorbell rang.

Stuart Simmons, Chief Constable of North Yorks Police, and her former boss, stood in the doorway.

'Can I come in?' he asked.

'Is everything OK?' Julie asked. 'Kim . . .'

'Kim's fine, but there's something I need to say to you.'

'I'll put the kettle on.'

He shook his head. 'Sit down, Julie. This isn't easy for me so all I ask is that you hear me out.'

She sat at the kitchen table, but he remained standing.

'I told them not to hire you,' he said.

Julie looked up at him, smiling, waiting for the punchline, but Stuart looked away.

She felt the ground slipping beneath her feet. Stuart had been her first friend at police academy. He was the one person in the force she'd always been completely honest with, expressing every doubt or fear. She could debate anything with him. They might not always agree but he would always listen, could always see both sides of any argument, sometimes even changed his mind.

'Why?' The question came out of her mouth before she could stop it.

'I told them you weren't leadership material.'

Her stomach twisted and the sudden pain brought tears to her eyes.

As a leader, Stuart was a man whose judgement she trusted. She'd never doubted his ability as he rose to stratospheric ranks. And yet he had doubted hers?

She glanced up at him through welling tears, and a sudden fierce anger took hold of her. She blinked hard until she could see him clearly again, the friend and colleague who'd betrayed her, lied to her. He must have felt the heat from her burning eyes because he collapsed onto a seat, staring at his shoes.

'In what way am I not leadership material?' she asked, her voice ice cold.

'I told them the truth – you're a great team player,' he said. 'Quiet, thoughtful, analytical.'

'Aren't those good things?'

He sighed. 'A leader can't be too nice.'

Semantics. He meant nice as in *soft*. A weak leader could certainly be too soft. But what if by nice you meant empathetic? Could a leader have too much empathy? Didn't it depend on how you used it? There was a difference between understanding other people and giving in to them. You could be nice and still tough. Couldn't you? Wasn't she?

What were the words they used for leaders: decisive, brave, powerful, authoritative . . .

'I tried to dissuade you,' he said.

And it was true. She'd welcomed his concern for her well-being, was flattered by his desire to keep her on his own team. Julie had been sure she'd have made DI in North Yorkshire if the promotion boards hadn't always come up at the wrong time: maternity leave, bereavement, divorce. She'd tried hard not to resent the colleagues promoted over her, or brought in from the outside, men like DI Caron Riley. Now she saw, with horrible clarity, that Stuart didn't rate her.

Why hadn't he been honest with her? Stuart had been a colleague she'd trusted absolutely.

'Why are you telling me this now?'

'Two reasons,' he said. 'One, because it tells you something about the force you're working with.'

Julie frowned. 'In what way?'

'If I was recruiting externally, and a senior officer from another force expressed reservations, I would pause, explore the concerns openly at interview. But after I spoke to them, Cleveland Police seemed even keener to hire you. Which suggested to me that they didn't actually want a "high-flyer". Stuart made air quotation marks with his fingers. 'My suspicion was that they'd been forced to hire a female DI and were happy to set you up to fail.'

Julie shivered at the casual cruelty of his words. Was her mental image of Stuart completely out of date? She still saw him as a twenty-one-year-old graduate on their first day of police academy. How had she failed to notice the change? This wasn't the charming man she'd introduced to her best friend. When had he become so cold and callous? Had Kim seen the change in him too? Or had it been so gradual that neither of them had noticed?

'So, you don't rate Cleveland Police, and you don't rate me?' It was impossible to keep the bitterness out of her voice. 'A marriage made in heaven?'

'I was wrong.'

His voice was so quiet that she wasn't sure she'd heard him.

'Pardon?'

'I said there were two reasons for telling you this now. I was right about the force. I don't trust Superintendent Chalmers.' He let out a long breath. 'But I was wrong about you.'

Julie wasn't sure she wanted to hear what was coming next. How much more could he hurt her?

'I'd never seen you as a leader, because you were never given the opportunity to lead. You're adaptable, you slot into any team and pick up the things that need doing without complaint. You're self-effacing, you bolster the roles that need support without any grandstanding about paygrades. I confused your flexibility with a lack of drive and ambition. None of us appreciated how much you did behind the scenes until after you left.'

Julie let out the breath she'd been holding in.

'You're authentic and empathetic, curious and creative, analytical and resilient. I was a fool not to see that before, an idiot to let you go to another force. I sincerely hope you'll come back to us as a senior leader one of these days.'

Julie didn't know what to say. She bit her lip.

'You've got this, Julie. Don't let the bastards win. Go back and show them what you're made of.'

After he'd gone Julie continued to sit at the kitchen table. Her head was spinning. He'd told her to go back. Go back where?

Wait. She hadn't been sacked. She hadn't been demoted. In his incompetence, her boss was moving her to the one outfit that might take the threat of terrorism seriously.

And she still had the weekend to gather the evidence she needed.

Her phone rang.

'I need to talk to you.' Sue Bell sounded upset.

'Usual place?' Julie asked. 'I can be there in thirty minutes.'

The Saltholme café was almost empty. Julie ordered a coffee and joined Sue at the window.

'Maybe it's the hormones,' Sue said. 'Maybe I'm channelling my fear of childbirth into fanciful conspiracy theories.' The foam from her hot chocolate made a milk moustache. 'But when I heard the news about Suranjan, I desperately needed to get out of the house.'

She ran her tongue over her upper lip and then wiped the foam she couldn't reach with a napkin.

'Who's Suranjan?' Julie asked.

'One of the Indian control engineers. I got to know him quite well when I visited the factory near Kanpur,' Sue continued. 'He invited me to his home, and I met his family. He used to work in Panki, but he moved to Delhi as part of the centralisation of the control group.'

Julie waited.

'This morning I found out that he was killed in a car accident two weeks ago.'

Julie sat up straight. 'What?'

Sue passed her phone over the table. The screen showed a death notice. A black-bordered picture of a young man.

'He was only thirty.'

Julie stared at the photo as if willing the man to talk to her.

'Did Suranjan know Dameer?'

Sue nodded. 'They worked together on several projects.'

Julie ran her hands through her hair.

'Do you know anything about the circumstances?'

Sue shook her head. 'When Suranjan moved to Delhi, his wife stayed in Kanpur to look after the kids and his parents. They couldn't afford to move to the capital. He travelled between cities. The traffic in that part of the world is terrible.'

'But it was . . .' Julie emphasised the word *was* as if to reassure herself. 'It *was* an accident?'

'I guess.' Sue bowed her head. 'But doesn't it seem a strange coincidence?'

'I don't like coincidences,' Julie said.

'Can you investigate?'

'A traffic accident involving an Indian national in India?' Julie shook her head. 'Even if I was still on the case, I doubt I'd get anywhere.'

'You're no longer investigating Dameer's murder?'

'My boss thinks it's solved.'

'By blaming Brian?' Sue shook her head in disbelief.

'When we interviewed Brian he seemed concerned about cybersecurity.'

'Yes, and he was right to be,' Sue sighed. 'We discussed his concerns about HQ plans to centralise IT and OT support,' Sue said.

'Remind me what OT stands for.'

'Operations technology. The control systems. As distinct from IT, the information technology.'

'And they're completely different?'

'They used to be – 3-15psi pneumatic tubes and 4-20mA cables, but now it's all "intelligent" programmable software with Wi-Fi connections. That's part of the problem – the old distinction isn't as clear-cut anymore.'

'Which was exactly Brian's concern.'

'He was almost resigned to losing his job, but he wanted everyone to understand what additional safeguards they needed to put in place if they were determined to go ahead.'

'And did you act on his concerns?'

'I followed his recommendations to the letter,' Sue said. 'Brian knew what he was talking about when it came to cybersecurity.' She sighed. 'I alerted senior management to the things that were out of my control. Like the reorganisation.'

'But it still went ahead?'

'Yes. HQ ignored him.'

'Although I gather he insisted on addressing them direct?'

'Yes. I was barred from the meeting as it was an HR appeal and had to be independent of me as the line manager who made him redundant.'

'Who was there?'

'The chair of the appeal panel was the site manager, Alan Cosby.'

'Does he know about Suranjan?'

Sue nodded. 'It was on LinkedIn.'

'Maybe I'll drop by for a little chat.'

It was a short distance from Saltholme to Zagrovyl International, from low reeds full of wading birds to a tall chemical plant full of huge geometric shapes all connected by miles of cabling and piping.

'Detective Inspector Cadell for Alan Cosby,' she announced herself at the gatehouse, flashing her badge.

'Is he expecting you, Inspector?'

'No.'

'Just a minute and I'll make a pass for you.'

The site manager appeared rattled by another visit from the police, however hard he tried to hide it.

'DI Cadell,' Alan said. 'To what do I owe this unexpected pleasure?'

'I wondered if you could throw some light on something for me.'

'I shall do my best.'

'Have you had any recent contact with Simon Sharp?'

'Who?'

'A control system contractor.'

He sniffed. 'Not really my area of focus. Let me check with HR.'

He left the room and returned with Marcia from HR.

'You were asking about one of our contractors?' she said.

'That's right. Simon Sharp,' Julie said. 'I understood that he was employed as maternity cover for Sue Bell.' She handed Marcia the photo from the missing person report. 'Is this him?'

'Yes, that's Simon. He worked alongside Sue for a few weeks, then resigned shortly after she left.'

'Did he give a reason?' Julie asked.

'No,' she said.

'I've asked this before, and I'll ask it again.' Alan couldn't hide his irritation. 'Why are the police obsessed with contractor attendance?'

'Because Simon Sharp's parents have now reported him missing,' Julie said. 'And because he was the last person to be seen with murder victim

Dameer Ghosh.'

'You think there's a connection?' Marcia asked.

Julie didn't answer, instead she said, 'You'll have heard about Brian Burrow?'

'Brian hasn't worked here for almost a year . . .' Alan began.

'But you know he had a motorcycle accident last weekend.'

'I heard,' Marcia said. 'Terrible. How is he?'

Julie ignored the question and ploughed on. 'Did you also hear about Suranjan Singh?'

The site manager looked baffled.

'One of our control engineers in India,' Marcia said. 'I saw the sad news on LinkedIn.'

Alan shrugged. 'So?'

'I hadn't even heard the term control engineer before I started investigating this case, and now – suddenly – they're an endangered species,' Julie said. 'Dameer Ghosh was murdered, Simon Sharp has vanished, Suranjan Singh is dead, and Brian Burrow is in intensive care. Am I alone in wondering what the link is?'

'How could there be a link?'

'I believe that Brian warned you of potential risks when you decided to centralise IT and OT services in India.'

'That was a head office decision.'

'And yet you, Mr Cosby, are presumably responsible for the safety of the Seal Sands site and, as the most senior representative of Zagrovyl, in the best position to challenge head office if you deem a decision unwise?'

Marcia came to her boss's rescue. 'Brian Burrow appealed the redundancy decision, and we brought in a senior safety adviser from HQ to review his concerns. The upshot was that his appeal failed, and he was made redundant.'

'May I see the letter he sent in support of his appeal?'

Marcia and Alan exchanged glances. The site manager gave a brief nod, and she left the room.

'I'm not sure I follow where you are going with this, DI Cadell,' he said.

'I don't believe in coincidences.'

'What coincidence?' Alan huffed. 'None of the people you just mentioned are Zagrovyl Seal Sands employees. Dameer was a travelling salesman.' The way he said it was laced with contempt. 'Suranjan worked for HQ in India.' He leant forward. 'Simon is a contractor with an attendance problem, and Brian is an ex-employee who rode his motorbike too fast.'

Marcia returned empty-handed.

'Any luck?' Alan asked.

She shook her head. 'Brian Burrow's HR file was sent to an archive, a normal procedure for leavers.'

'Then please retrieve it urgently and deliver it to me at Cleveland Police HQ.' Julie handed her a card.

Julie drove to James Cook University Hospital. A uniformed policeman stood outside the room where Brian Burrow lay. Julie flashed her badge at him and pushed the door handle, opening the door a few inches.

Beep . . . beep . . . beep

The man on the bed was unrecognisable under the swathes of bandages, surrounded by a spaghetti of tubes and wires. Brian Burrow had been a sturdy man; he looked so frail now.

A woman in a vintage floral dress sat by his side, holding his hand and reading aloud from *The Hobbit*. Too young to be his mother. A sister perhaps? Or a friend?

Julie took a step back and motioned for the police guard to show her the visitor log. Betty McAlister. Aha, the missing girlfriend had returned.

Julie slipped quietly into the room and waited until the woman paused for breath.

'Hi,' she said. 'I'm Detective Inspector Julie Cadell.'

'Betty.'

'Nice to meet you, Betty. How's he doing?'

'Not well.'

'It's good that you're here.'

Betty rounded on her angrily. 'And it's your fault that he's here.'

Julie shook her head. 'I'm sorry you feel that way.'

'You hounded him.'

'He missed you,' Julie said.

Betty paused. 'Did he talk about me?'

'Yes.' Julie nodded. She looked down at the dying man.

I never realised what love was until I was stupid enough to throw it away.

Poor Brian. He'd worn his heart on his sleeve, even in a police station under caution. How could anyone believe that he was a master of deception and a cold-blooded murderer? But how was she to prove otherwise?

'I'm glad I caught you. I wanted to ask you something.'

'What if I don't feel like talking to the pigs?'

'That would be perfectly understandable,' Julie said. 'But hear me out – you might be able to help me get to the truth.'

'The truth, ha!' she mocked. 'When have the Cleveland police ever been interested in the truth?'

'Were you and Brian together when he was being made redundant?'

'Yes.'

'Did he ever show you the letter appealing against his redundancy?'

She shook her head. 'I told him to move on. He was obsessed.' She lowered her eyes. 'We fell out about it.'

'Do you know if there's a copy of that letter anywhere?'

'His boss should have it.'

'I'm following that up with Zagrovyl,' she said. 'Anywhere else?'

'On his home computer, maybe?'

DS Wharton had obtained a search warrant for Brian Burrow's flat immediately after the arrest. Forensics probably already had the computer.

'You should look at the video, too,' Betty added.

'What video?'

'He went into work to hand over the letter and the meeting was recorded.'

'Did Brian know?'

'It was Brian who recorded it on his phone. Wait,' Betty said and opened a large handbag. 'He sent it to me.' She took out her phone and scrolled. 'Sorry, looks like I deleted it.'

As Julie was leaving the hospital, she called Adrian Prosser.

'Who's looking at Brian Burrow's personal computer?'

'Whoever it is, it's not my team.'

What were her chances in persuading DS Wharton to look for tangential evidence? He would only be interested in evidence that would confirm Brian as their principal suspect.

'What about his phone?' Julie asked.

'A little bird told me it hasn't been found so far. Neither at the scene of the accident nor at his home.'

'Don't you think that's odd?'

'Julie,' he said, and it sounded strange, being called by her first name, 'everything about this accident is odd. I suggest you steer well clear.'

Exactly what she wasn't going to do.

When Julie got home, Arni was on his way out.

'Don't wait up for me,' he said. 'I'll be late.'

'Where are you going?'

'Meeting Eve,' he said. 'Her parents want to see me tomorrow, so we're going to talk things through tonight.'

'I'll be out tomorrow night too. I'm changing department, so it's a leaving do.'

Arni stopped and scrutinised her face. 'You OK with that?'

Julie shrugged. 'So long as they still pay me.'

Her son paused at the front door.

'You know what you were asking about? The cybercrime thing?'

'Oh, that.'

'I was asking around—'

'You didn't tell anyone it was something I was working on, did you?'

Arni groaned in disgust. ''Course not, Mum!'

'Good,' Julie said and then, 'Sorry, love. It's been a difficult week for both of us.'

'Anyway, there was this guy, some German working in California for Microsoft, who discovered that hackers had been tampering with the SSH protocols in part of the Linux operating system.'

'You've lost me already.'

'What matters is this hacker had effectively created a "back door".'

'A back door?'

'A secret way in. Like if I'd let Danny play a game on my computer and he'd written some extra lines of code to my operating system so that he could come and go whenever he wanted without invitation.'

'Like cutting an extra key? Leaving the door on the latch?'

'Even cleverer. Like creating a brand-new door that no one can see and then remodelling the house from the inside.'

'But you can always flick a switch, right? Turn everything off.'

'The clever ones put in a new data highway. So, if you try to disconnect them, they just carry on through a different route.'

'How is that possible?'

'Look, Mum, there are cybersecurity experts in the police force, aren't there?'

'Of course.'

'I'll send you the article,' he said. 'You can pass it on.'

She felt a surge of pride as she watched him go. Her child had grown up. She kept forgetting how much he knew, how mature he'd become. For the first time she imagined him as a colleague and smiled. There was no need to worry about Arni. Whatever life threw at him, he'd always land on his feet.

Chapter 51

Middlesbrough – Friday, 29 November 2024

Julie took a last look around her office. All she had to show for her time in Serious Crimes was waste: twelve bin bags full of paper for shredding, and a wastebin overflowing with quotidian rubbish. Her computer files were tidy now, any confidential information – the cases she'd closed – moved to central document control. So much hidden work for each result.

She took in the slightly scuffed standard office furniture. Would Iain Wharton move in here? She couldn't bring herself to give him his new title. Struggling to accept his promotion from sergeant to inspector, she'd been avoiding him.

'DI Cadell.' The super entered her office without knocking, a female administrative assistant in tow. 'I have some paperwork for you to sign.'

The young woman passed her a clipboard with a thick document.

Julie stared at it.

'Standard confidentiality agreement,' the super said.

'I already—' she began.

'Routine admin stuff,' he said. 'Update to the National Security Act.'

If it was routine admin stuff, then why was he here?

The super pointed to the document. 'I'll need your signature before I approve your transfer to the Minimax team.'

He made it sound like she was the one who'd asked for the transfer.

Julie skim-read the document and shook her head. 'This goes further than the contractual confidentiality agreement. I'd have to check this with the union lawyer.'

'In that case, I need your computer and phone while you consider your position.'

Consider your position. That sounded ominous.

'Please unplug your laptop for me,' he said.

His female assistant advanced towards her desk.

'Wait, what's going on? What are you doing?'

'And hand over your phone.'

'My phone?'

He came forward so his big red face was inches from her own.

'We can do this nice and calmly . . .'

Superintendent Chalmers snapped his fingers, and a pair of PCs entered.

'Or we can make a fuss for all to see.'

Julie couldn't afford to lose this job. She moved aside so they could get on with her humiliation. What choice did she have?

The constables took away the bags of paper while the administrator picked up the laptop and phone with a scowl.

The superintendent was the last to leave.

'Celebration tonight at The Applegarth,' he said cheerfully. 'See you there. Five o'clock sharp.'

Julie closed the door behind the raiding party and sat at her empty desk, her head in her hands.

She ignored the first few rings of her desk phone, but when her personal mobile started ringing, she checked the caller ID. Dr Sandy Armstrong probably wanted to talk about teeth again.

She answered the call.

'Congratulations,' he said.

'On what?'

'On your assignment to Minimax.'

Julie twisted her mouth.

'And on closing the Hartlepool Marina case,' he said.

Julie said nothing.

'Mystery solved, eh?' Sandy said.

'Not really,' Julie said.

'Oh? I was told that the murderer was in custody?'

'We still don't have a motive.'

'Your suspect isn't talking?'

'Brian Burrow is in a coma.'

'Ah, well, here's something that might interest you.'

Julie moved her hands over the empty desk, searching for a laptop that was no longer there.

'I followed up with Purchew Medical,' Sandy said.

'With who?'

'The people who make dental implants.'

'Funny,' she replied. 'I was just thinking about that before my boss took my computer away.'

'He did what?'

'And my phone,' she said. 'So petty.'

'Take it as a compliment,' Sandy said. 'If he's scared of you, it means you're more powerful than you realise.'

Julie let out a snort of laughter. 'Doesn't feel like that today.'

DC Gibson knocked on the window, miming the sinking of a pint. Julie checked her watch. Ten to five. She gave him a thumbs up, then held up ten fingers.

'You coming to The Applegarth tonight?' Julie asked.

''Fraid not,' said Sandy. 'Anyway, it's not as if you and I are saying goodbye. I work across all the departments in all the police forces. Anywhere there's a dead body, I'm your guy.' She heard him take a deep breath. 'This move will be good for you, Julie. Get away from Chalmers. You'll like Bruma and the team at Minimax.'

'Wait,' Julie said. 'What did Purchew Medical say?'

'Absolutely nothing. Claimed we'd found a standard part number. But my friend got curious. He's now convinced that the US military, the CIA and other agencies probably add unique identifiers to dental implants of those in service, but it's all very hush-hush.'

'For identification post-mortem?'

'Exactly. A sort of back-up dog tag. A unique ID number that can't easily be removed from the corpse or destroyed.'

Julie thought back to the game Arni had been playing. *Final Mission – Undercover.*

Did they really know the first thing about Dameer Ghosh?

A soldier?

A spy?

A terrorist?

A double agent?

'You still OK for Monday?' Sandy asked.

Julie's mind raced. What was she doing on Monday apart from starting a new job?

'The comedy club at MTH,' he added.

'Looking forward to it,' she lied.

Julie was about to switch off the light when her desk phone rang.

'DI Cadell.'

'DS Vaziri here from Minimax. A little bird tells me you're transferring to us on Monday.'

'So I'm told.'

'And that you're temporarily disconnected?'

'My laptop and phone are staying here, apparently.'

'I'll arrange new ones,' he said. 'Will you be at home,' he read out her address, 'tomorrow morning at ten?'

'Yes.'

'We'll set up overnight and deliver the new equipment to you at home. Log on with your old credentials, but please change them immediately.'

'Thank you.'

'Looking forward to having you on the team.'

And for the first time she thought that maybe she could look forward to it as well. The transfer had felt like a slap in the face when Superintendent Chalmers had announced it. But perhaps Sandy was right. It could be a positive move.

The Applegarth was packed when she arrived. DC Chris Gibson was already in the queue for the bar, so she pushed her way through the throng to intercept the transaction.

'My shout,' she said.

'Big round,' he warned.

'You give the orders,' she said. 'I'll pay.'

He smiled. 'It used to be the other way around.'

She thought about that as she waited. *I gave the orders, and the team paid the price.* Was that how they saw her? Someone detached? From her point of view, the reality was the complete opposite. She got far more involved in cases than was wise. But did they see that? Had she shared enough with them? Or too much?

She added a lime and soda to the order, paid, and helped him carry the drinks over to the table where DS Iain Wharton was holding court.

'I hear congratulations are in order,' she said, handing him a pint of beer and a whisky chaser.

'Finally!' Iain said.

Was he referring to the arrival of his drinks, or news of his promotion? He took the glasses and turned away.

Julie handed out the other drinks from her tray and took her lime and soda to the table next to CIO Nadia Latif.

The wheelchair stuck out from the table, and Nadia had to move every time someone wanted to access the back yard for a smoke.

'You OK there?' Julie asked, pulling up a stool to sit next to her. 'Don't you want a drink?'

'I can't stay long,' Nadia said. 'My dad's coming to pick me up.'

'You live at home?'

She nodded. 'Couldn't survive without my mum's cooking.'

Superintendent Chalmers stood up and banged a fork against his pint. By the way he swayed, she suspected it was not his first drink of the evening.

'A toast!' he announced. 'Please raise your glasses to soon-to-be Detective Inspector Iain Wharton!'

Everyone stood, except Nadia, but she cheered loudly enough to make up for it.

The super beamed. 'Nice ring to the title, don't you think?'

'Music to my ears,' Iain said.

When the men started singing, Julie sat down again.

'Are the rumours true?' Nadia asked, leaning over to be heard above the noise.

'What rumours?'

'That you're leaving us?'

'Temporary assignment to the Minimax team.'

'When?'

'Monday.'

Nadia whistled.

'How temporary?'

Julie shrugged.

'Can I come with you?' Nadia asked.

Julie smiled. 'I think Serious Crimes will need you more than ever.'

'I know the Hartlepool Marina case is closed and all that,' Nadia said.

Julie met her eyes. 'But?'

'You remember Karen Potter thought she'd heard the name Tadeusz Makowski before?'

'Yes.'

'He was arrested for trespassing in the scrapyard.'

'South Bank Scrap Services?' Julie's eyes opened wide. 'Our crime scene?'

'Yup.'

'When?'

'Not long after he was sacked from Zagrovyl.'

'Interesting,' Julie said. 'Can you send me the report?'

Nadia nodded. 'And another thing,' she said. 'I got some new pictures of the ghost taxi from the Seal Sands roundabout.'

'I didn't think we got any ANPR hits there.'

'Your new friends in Minimax have some better technology.'

Nadia placed her phone on the table and flicked through some photos. The taxi with the bird logo. A close-up through the passenger window: Dameer Ghosh, very much alive. Another photo through the windscreen: a young man with pale hair and high cheekbones.

'Who is he?'

'Definitely not the owner,' Nadia said. 'I finally tracked him down. Omar Matar is sixty-four years old. He ran Osprey Executive Cars until heart problems forced him to stop driving. The car hasn't been licensed or taxed for a year. His wife reported a break-in to their garage in Hutton Rudby on 31 October this year, and that's the last anyone saw of his car until we picked it up on CCTV with false plates, before finding it burnt out near the airport.'

'Did you tell DS Wharton about this?'

'He wasn't interested.'

'Send me everything,' Julie said.

'Come on, girls!' The super was very drunk. 'What are you two gossiping about?'

Julie cringed inwardly and wondered how soon she could get away. And how far.

Chapter 52

North Yorkshire – Saturday, 30 November 2024

At ten o'clock on the dot, the doorbell rang.

Julie opened the front door. DS Vaziri stood on her doorstep.

'ACC Bruma asked me to deliver this.'

He handed her a black bag with the new laptop and phone.

'Instructions are inside,' he said. 'Don't forget to change your password.' He turned and left.

Julie took the bag inside and closed the door.

'Who was that?' Arni appeared at the top of the stairs, hair dishevelled.

'Just work stuff,' Julie said.

'How was your leaving party?'

'I survived,' Julie said. 'How were Eve's parents?'

He shuddered. 'Weird.'

'You want a cup of tea?'

'No thanks.' He yawned. 'I'm going back to bed.'

Julie took the new laptop to the kitchen and worked through the set-up instructions, but when she tried to log back in with her new password, a message popped up onscreen asking her to contact IT.

Her call was answered almost immediately.

'IT Helpdesk.'

'Hi, it's DI Julie Cadell. I'm having some password trouble.'

The call handler took her through the usual security questions – date of birth, mother's maiden name, postcode.

'Is this a new computer?' the call handler asked.

'Yes.'

'Minimax?'

'Yes.'

'OK, I'm going to have to pass you over to advanced security.'

Julie put the phone on loudspeaker while she made tea for herself. The canned music was an instrumental version of a song that had been playing as she left the pub last night.

'DI Cadell?'

A disembodied female voice jerked her out of a reverie.

'Yes.'

'My name is Anika. I work with advanced security. I just need to jump onto your computer, if that's OK.'

A dialogue box appeared on the new laptop.

'Can you click accept?' Anika asked.

Julie did as she was told and watched as the cursor started moving all by itself. Windows opened and closed and lines of incomprehensible code, white on black, started scrolling across the screen.

'What are you doing?' Julie asked.

'Checking for malware.'

'The computer is brand new, it was only delivered five minutes ago.'

'We can't be too careful,' Anika said. 'You have three new messages with large attachments. One is external, from Betty McAlister, and two internal, one from CIO Nadia Latif and one from Karen Potter. Were you expecting them?'

Julie felt a tingle of anticipation.

'Yes.'

'Running an antivirus scan,' Anika said. 'OK, I've sent them to our file transfer and download site for a full check and replaced the attachment with a link.'

'How long will that take?'

'A few seconds, if they're legit. Longer if any clean-up is required. Can you try to log on again?'

The sign-in screen reappeared. Julie entered her old username and new password, and the computer sprang to life.

'Is there anything else I can help you with?'

'No thanks.'

'You'll be asked to rate the service you've received today. It would really help me if you could give me a good review.'

'Of course,' Julie said.

'Thank you for calling,' Anika said. 'Have a great day.'

Julie opened Betty's email first. She'd managed to retrieve the deleted video from her hard drive. She sent a brief message to accompany it. Without understanding all the technical jargon, Julie gathered that some information had been lost, but there should be enough left to get the gist of things.

She topped up her mug of tea and clicked the link.

The video was surprisingly good quality. Brian was visible close up as he pretended to arrange his coat over a chair at the end of the room. His face zoomed in and out until all the chairs around the table were clearly visible. There must be a wireless camera on the coat collar or top pocket because he alternated between checking his phone and adjusting the coat. As he moved back to his seat, she was shocked at how different he looked: so much younger, fitter and healthier.

She checked the date of the file. It was just over a year old.

Alan Cosby and Marcia from HR entered the room followed by a tall man in a three-piece suit.

'Brian.' The woman opened the meeting. 'You asked to speak to us in the presence of a representative from corporate safety.' She extended her arms. 'This is Simon de Vaal, who has flown over from the Netherlands. Simon has global responsibility for Health, Safety, Environment, Corporate Social Responsibility and Community Engagement.'

'That's quite a portfolio,' Brian said. 'What do you know about major accident hazards?'

'We try to avoid them.'

Alan and Marcia laughed.

Brian remained stony-faced. 'And yet,' he said, 'you plan to centralise support for key safety systems, the critical line of defence against major accidents. You plan to make me redundant, along with seven other control engineers in Europe and North America and rely on expertise remote from the operating sites?'

'To optimise and improve the service,' Marcia interjected.

Brian ignored her and directed his question to Simon. 'I'd like to know what cybersecurity risk assessment you have carried out.'

'Our IT department . . .' Simon began.

'I'm not talking IT,' Brian interrupted. 'I'm talking about OT. This is not about keeping information secure. This is about making sure the operations technology works properly – the factory automation, the basic process control and critical safety-instrumented systems.'

'IT and OT are kept quite separate,' Simon said.

'Until someone connects them,' Brian said. 'All it takes is an ethernet cable. You plug in a new printer that has a wireless capability, a sensor that's Bluetooth enabled. Just an operator charging their phone through a USB port on an OT workstation is enough to compromise the separation.'

'Impossible. We have procedures and protocols—'

'Not worth the paper they're written on without local enforcement,' Brian interrupted. 'Those examples are all things I have seen on site – and stopped – in the last few years.'

'Even if what you say happened, there are many more layers of defence, including hard-wired safety trips,' Alan said.

'Are you some sort of dinosaur?' Brian almost exploded. 'Hard-wiring went out with the Stone Age. Even the safety-instrumented system has a programmable logic controller.'

'But the systems remain totally independent,' Alan shouted and banged his fist on the table.

'It depends on who maintains them,' Brian said.

Simon held up a hand, attempting to calm the site manager.

'Let me see if I have understood,' he said. 'Brian, you're concerned that someone external could take remote control of the critical site safety systems?'

'I do it every Sunday from home. I run a routine maintenance health check and upload any patches.'

'Because you have the right access.'

'So, who will do it when I'm no longer here?'

'It will be restricted to a few trusted individuals with the right security clearance.'

'Where?'

'On site.'

'What if there is no one available on site? You're making seven people redundant. How do you expect those who remain to cope with the increased workload?'

'The support from India will lighten their workload in other areas so they can focus on safety-critical systems.'

'Back to my question then. Will there or won't there be technicians in India accessing the control system in the UK?'

'They'll only have access to the most basic areas. The safety-critical components will remain locked away.'

'Not if you have the right password.'

'Don't worry, Brian. Those passwords will continue to be site controlled.'

'Do you know where I manage critical passwords for this site?'

Simon sighed. 'I'm sure you're about to enlighten us.'

'I use a specially encrypted program on my laptop,' Brian said. 'If someone gains remote access to my IT laptop, they could potentially change all the OT passwords for safety-critical systems, lock me out and start making changes from India.'

'That's impossible.'

'Tell that to the Saudis. Triton attack 2017 in Petro Rabigh,' Brian said. 'Look it up.'

Marcia broke the stunned silence.

'What exactly are you saying, Brian?' she asked.

'Beware of unwanted guests,' Brian said. 'You open your front door and before you blink they've occupied the whole house and dug a secret tunnel.'

'Nonsense,' Simon said. 'We're constantly monitoring for breaches of security.'

'These attackers are patient, good at hiding, masters of disguise.' Brian wagged a finger. 'Centralising the control systems support is like bringing in the Trojan horse.'

'What have horses got to do with anything?' Simon looked puzzled.

'Battle of Troy. Greeks retreated from the battlefield leaving the gift of a huge wooden horse outside the citadel. Trojans brought it in. At night, the Greek soldiers hidden inside crept out and opened the gates, allowing their army back in. Victory.'

Alan made an irritated tutting noise. 'We're not playing *Troy Total War* or some other computer game. We're manufacturing chemicals. What has this example got to do with your appeal?'

Brian sighed and started muttering under his breath. The last phrase was clearly audible on the phone recording before the video dissolved into static. 'How a numpty like you got put in charge of a site like this is beyond me.'

Julie smiled. Having met Alan Cosby, it was hard not to agree.

And, for all his faults, it was hard not to admire Brian Burrow. Dead or alive, she wasn't ready to let him be thrown to the wolves.

'New computer?' Arni appeared at the kitchen door.

'You're very observant,' she said.

'What are you watching?'

She closed the laptop lid. 'Work stuff.'

'I heard the case was closed.'

'New stuff,' she lied. 'You fancy some breakfast?'

Over a breakfast of French toast, Arni gave her a summary of his dinner with the Evanses. They'd been civil enough, but it had quickly turned into an interview.

'All they wanted to know about were my prospects. What my plans were.

What university I'll apply to. How much I'm expected to earn. I should have prepared a fucking business plan.'

Julie winced at the profanity. Matt had always tried to avoid swearing at home and censured their children if they transgressed. But Matt wasn't here now, was he? She let it go.

'I guess the Evanses think these things are important.'

'But I don't. And I didn't think Eve did either. But now I'm not so sure.'

He looked different this morning, drawn and serious.

'You think she's having second thoughts?'

She regretted the words the moment they were out of her mouth. Arni's anguish was too much to bear.

'I don't know what she thinks. She wants time apart so she can figure things out.' He looked away to hide the tears in his eyes. She gripped her chair with both hands. She so very badly wanted to reach out and hug him, but he had to make the first move.

'What are you doing today?' Julie spoke gently.

'I said I'd go and watch the team. We're playing at home.'

'Maybe they'll need a sub.'

He smiled, the worry lines vanished, and the Arni she recognised was back.

'Here's hoping!'

'You want a lift?'

'If you're going that way.'

'I think I am.'

Julie sat in the car and read the email from Karen Potter. Tadeusz Makowski had been arrested while trespassing on the South Bank Scrap Services site but then released without charge. The report was frustratingly brief. No photos and no real details. Finally she opened the email from CIO Latif. It contained the Osprey theft report, a rather cursory investigation into the disappearance of an unlicensed taxi from the owner's garage, all the ANPR photos.

The owner of Osprey Cars, Omar Matar, lived in Hutton Rudby, not far from her son's school playing fields. She drove round twice and then parked in the street in front of what had once been a Georgian cottage. The stables had been adapted to make a garage.

She pressed the doorbell and waited. No answer. No one home.

Next stop was the location of the burnt-out car. It was a beautiful day, so after queuing to cross the bridge over the River Tees at Yarm, she turned left onto the back roads and followed the river through Aislaby until she spotted the turn-off just before Middleton One Row.

St George's Church seemed like an odd place to wreck a car. Judging by the report it hadn't crashed, just been driven here and set alight. How did the driver get away? Either there was an accomplice in another vehicle, or he'd walked somewhere.

She entered the churchyard. This area had been an important air force base in the Second World War and there were Commonwealth war graves here. Young men who died in action.

The sun caught the lettering on the headstone of Sergeant R. J. McInnes, a pilot in the Royal Canadian Air Force. Died 13 August 1941 at the age of twenty-one. The same age Jamie had been when he died.

She and Matt had argued over the memorial. She'd wanted to bring her son's body home and bury it somewhere beautiful. Matt was more interested in the practicalities. They didn't belong to any church, and graveyards were already bursting with the faithful who got first dibs on places. In the end, she agreed to a local cremation, and they brought the ashes home, scattering them, with friends and family, in the places Jamie loved. It had been the right decision, but she still missed having a place to go where she could grieve.

Somewhere in Canada, the McInnes family had been informed of their son's death. Perhaps they'd come here after the war, to see the base their son had flown out of, to find out what had happened to him, to see where he was buried. She knelt and began tidying the grave, removing the withered autumn leaves that had blown up against the stone. Before long she found herself weeping. For the young pilot. For his siblings. For his sweetheart. For the children he never had. For his parents.

And for herself.

Startled by the noise of a plane taking off, she dried her eyes and walked to the edge of a graveyard. The church appeared to be in the middle of nowhere, but in fact it bordered the back of Teesside airport. It would be easy to walk from here to the airport boundary road, only a couple of hundred metres away over a field. In the middle of nowhere and yet right next to the airport. Could that be a coincidence, or had the driver chosen this location deliberately?

Julie drove on to Middleton One Row and parked outside The Devonport. She found a table in the snug next to an open fire. She ordered a roast beef sandwich with a side of roast potatoes.

Arni texted to say that he'd played in the second half of the school hockey match and scored the winning goal. He was going to celebrate being back in the team tonight and would eat out and stay over at Danny's.

Julie looked at the map on her phone. She wasn't far from the place where Flora had done her work experience. It was Caron who'd arranged it; his mother ran her veterinary practice from a small farm. Caron had moved back there. Perhaps she should swing by and clear the air between them.

Caron stood in a grassy enclosure, coaxing a skittish mare towards a horsebox. Julie stopped at the paddock fence and watched, full of admiration for his patience. Was it true that working with horses made you a better manager? Or was it just that horses trusted good people?

Was Caron a good person? She waited until the horse was inside before clearing her throat.

'Hi,' she said.

Caron wheeled around, a sudden smile lighting up his face. He turned back to the horsebox to bolt the door and gave a signal to the driver, who started the engine. When he faced her again, his features were more carefully composed, a firm mouth and wary brow line over narrowed eyes.

'Julie,' he said. 'I wasn't expecting you.'

'I was passing,' she said. 'And thought I'd drop by to apologise.'

'Apologise?'

'Caron, the night of the charity ball . . .'

'Yes?' he said.

'I behaved unprofessionally,' Julie said.

He closed his eyes. 'You regret what happened between us?'

Was the man in total denial? Nothing had happened between them. No sex, at least. No point in spelling that out. In any case, that was only part of the problem.

'Do you?'

'I'm glad you brought it up,' he said. 'And I'm glad you stopped by.'

'Then we're good?'

He nodded.

Colleagues, then. Nothing more. It felt like jumping into freezing cold water. Julie looked up at the grey sky, blinking fast to stop the tears that threatened to spill over.

'I think we're very good together,' he added.

'I'd better get going, then,' she said.

'Wait,' he said. 'I think we have unfinished business.'

'We do?'

He nodded towards the stables. 'I was rather hoping you'd give me the chance to behave unprofessionally as well.' He walked towards her, long, confident strides.

Julie's knees began to tremble, and she reached out for the fence to support herself. 'I'm not sure . . .'

He put a hand over hers. 'Come and see where I live,' he said.

Julie looked round at the farmhouse. 'I thought you lived with your mum.'

He shook his head. 'I live in the stables,' he said.

Julie couldn't help the bark of laughter that escaped. 'You're inviting me up to a hayloft?'

'Not exactly.' He took her right hand and raised it to his mouth, his eyes never leaving hers. 'A little apartment.' His voice dropped an octave. 'With a big, soft bed,' he added as his lips brushed her knuckles. 'And this time, no one knows and there's no pressure.'

It was tempting. So tempting. She was melting inside. Arni was staying overnight with friends. There was nothing to get back for except a cold and lonely house and a TV dinner. But did she trust Caron? How could she be sure that he was not involved in Brian Burrow's motorbike accident or the convenient discovery of the murder weapon in a pannier? Could it all be coincidence?

Julie didn't like coincidences.

She hadn't totally dismissed the idea that Caron deserved another chance; the man was too gorgeous to let go of without a fight, but not until this case was over. And then if, and only if, he could explain both his relationship with DS Wharton and the circumstances that led him to the accident involving Brian Burrow.

'I can't stay.' She slipped her hand from his. 'I'm working.'

'You won't give me a second chance?'

Julie leant forward and kissed him, backing off before he could wrap his arms around her.

'Once this case is solved,' she said. 'Let's talk.'

'You're leaving?' He sounded incredulous.

'There's someone I need to talk to, and he only works at night.'

Chapter 53

ALF

South Bank – Saturday, 30 November 2024

It was another foul night. Gusts of wind blasted the sides of the Portakabin, whopping it like a drum. The rain arrived at strange angles, rattling against the windowpanes and pooling up under the door. If it didn't stop soon, the whole site would flood. The River Tees would crest the barrage, burst its banks and scoop him up, lifting the flimsy little office from its breeze-block foundations, and he would float out to sea in his cabin. Perhaps the wind would blow him all the way to Australia.

His daughter, Naomi, had called at eleven p.m., but he hadn't made out a word she'd said after the news that her husband Jim's leave from work had been cancelled, so they'd changed their minds about Christmas.

Alf stuck an old towel under the door frame to stop the water coming in. He settled down under the strip light in an old car seat, the comfiest chair in the cabin, and the warmest when positioned right next to the single electric heater. He'd stopped off at the library on his way to work and two of the three books he'd borrowed sat on the packing crate they used as a table. The non-fiction volume was about fishing, useless now the boys weren't coming. He opened the other book, but less than a chapter in, he realised he'd read it before. The jacket was different, but the story was the same and didn't merit a second reading once you knew whodunnit.

Bloody new librarian. Judgemental and hopeless. The old one always looked out for him. Somewhere in the library computer was a record of every book he'd ever read. The old librarian would have spotted the duplication and stopped him borrowing something he'd read before. She'd have picked out a newer one by the same author, or found him a new series in the same style. He knew what he liked, and he liked what he knew. The new woman lacked boundaries, inquisitive to the point of rudeness, always badgering him to try something contemporary, something different. She'd even suggested he join their book group, but as far as he could see it was all women and he hadn't heard of any of the books they read. He'd taken the third book, the one she recommended because the book group were reading it, just to shut her up.

He opened his satchel and looked at it now. *Nested.* A woman's book, judging by the name on the cover. Written by a woman for women. Had the librarian done it deliberately? Well, she was going to regret it. He'd be giving her a piece of his mind when he took the books back and he didn't care who overheard. No more Mr Nice Guy.

A blast of wind made him look up. The door swung open, and a woman stood in the frame. Her mouth moved, but Alf couldn't make out a word against the background noise. She flashed a police badge.

Alf struggled to his feet.

'Officer?'

She mouthed something and stuck out a hand. It was cold and rain-damp, but Alf shook it anyway.

'Come in. Close the door before all the heat gets out.'

She stepped over the sodden towel and pulled the door closed.

Alf put in his hearing aids and switched them on.

'Sorry, I couldn't hear you, what with the wind. What did you say?'

'Are you Mr Alfred Pearce?'

'Yes.'

'My name is Detective Inspector Cadell.'

'How can I help you, Inspector?'

302

'I'm investigating a murder.'

Alf nodded. He knew all about it, had seen the crime scene tents go up at the boundary with the container port.

'The man who washed up in Hartlepool?' he asked.

She nodded.

'Poor bastard.' Alf sighed and shook his head. There were worse things than being alone at Christmas. Drowning was an awful way to go.

'I made a statement,' he said.

'Yes, I understand that DS Wharton came to visit you at home.'

'I'm sorry about his car.'

From her reaction he guessed that there was no love lost between the two police officers. Which made him warm to her.

'Can I get you a cup of tea?' Alf asked, pointing to the thermos. 'We can't run a kettle and the heater together, I'm afraid, but I made some up at home.'

'Just a drop,' she said. 'If you can spare it.'

He cleaned out two mugs and shared the sweet, strong tea between them.

'I don't get many visitors,' he confessed as he handed one to her.

She sat on the wooden stool near the desk, leaving the warm chair to him, took a sip and smiled. 'Aaah, just what I needed.'

'Condensed milk,' he said and tapped the side of his nose as he settled back into the old car seat. 'That's the secret.'

She took another sip, then put the mug down on the crate.

'Were you here on Wednesday the sixth of November?'

'I'm here every night.'

'Don't you get any time off?' she asked.

He shrugged. 'I like the overtime.'

She frowned and he backtracked. 'Just until Christmas.' He didn't want his employer prosecuted. 'My daughter is in Australia. I'm saving up to go and visit.' Now he said it, it sounded like a good idea. If they couldn't come to him, perhaps he could go to them.

'Where in Australia?' she asked.

'Melbourne.'

'I hear it's nice.'

He shrugged. 'I've two grandsons I barely know.'

'Is there a Mrs Pearce?' she asked.

He shook his head. 'Not anymore,' he said. 'She died.'

'I'm so sorry.'

She took another sip of tea, and they sat in silence for a while.

'May I ask you about the night of the bonfire?'

'Of course.'

'Tell me everything.'

Alf fetched the logbook from the desk.

'You can read for yourself.'

While she flicked back through the records, Alf stroked his chin and regretted not shaving before coming to work. He'd wanted to catch the library before it closed. Given his disappointing haul of books, he might as well not have bothered. He wished he'd been a little more presentable for such a lovely woman, but unlike her colleague, she didn't seem to be the sort of person to judge by appearances. In fact, DI Cadell seemed fascinated by what she was reading. It was the first time anyone had shown any real interest in his work journal.

He was proud of his logbook. None of the other security guards bothered with it, but he wrote at least half a page each night in a careful, neat hand. He took pride in being both clear and succinct. He doubted that management ever looked at it, but he liked to flick back and see how his style had evolved over the years. It was heavily influenced by what he was reading at the time.

'You have a lovely turn of phrase,' she said.

He felt the blood rush to his face and looked away.

'It was you who put the fire out?' she asked.

'I did,' he confirmed.

'And you saw a taxi leaving the area?'

'That's right.'

'Could it be this one?'

She passed him her phone. He peered at the photo of a taxi with the logo of a large bird. He put on his glasses to read the letters. Osprey Cars, not

Eagle Taxis. 'Yes, that's more like it.'

'Is there anything else you can remember?' she asked. 'Anything, however small, might be useful.'

He shook his head.

'Then let's go back to last year,' she said. 'Is there another logbook for 2023?'

He went over to the steel cabinet with the broken door. He was too ashamed to pass her the dirty old logbooks. 'Best if you tell me the date of interest and I'll find it.'

She scrolled down her phone. 'Twenty-sixth of September 2023,' she said.

Alf found the book and flicked through to the date.

'Nothing,' he said.

'May I see?' she asked.

He wiped the cover with the tea towel before handing it over.

'Strange,' she said. 'According to my records, the police were called in at one a.m. to arrest a trespasser.'

'The cable kerfuffle?' he asked.

'The what?'

'An incident involving cables,' he explained.

'Tell me more.'

Alf sat back in his seat.

'The management tried to replace security guards with computers, CCTV monitored from a control centre in Wilton, but at the first hint of trouble, they found out that some of the cameras hadn't been recording .'

'Go back a sec,' Julie said. 'What trouble?'

'A big roll of brand-new cable appeared on site, and no one knew what it was or where it had come from.'

'I'm not sure I understand why that was a problem.'

'Scrap is a dirty business. The bosses were worried someone was using the site to store stolen stuff,' he said. 'Around the same time, the phone and computer network went down.'

'How was that connected?'

'All a bit of a mystery,' Alf said, 'but it gets even stranger.'

'I'm listening.'

'Some foreign guy was caught on site at night trying to fix it.'

'Wait,' Julie held up a hand. 'You're telling me that someone broke into the site to do some guerrilla maintenance? That makes no sense.'

'Suspicion was something else had been going on for months.'

'Something that had damaged your network? Like what?'

'Search me.' Alf shrugged. 'They never got to the bottom of it. Or fixed it.' He held up a sturdy looking phone. 'We use a satellite phone now.'

Julie frowned. 'This cable that got everyone worried. What did it look like?'

Alf rummaged around in the filing cabinet until he found what he was looking for.

'It was still here when I started. I snipped off this sample to show my electrical mates. They'd never seen anything like it before.'

He handed her a fifty centimetre length of armoured cable with multi-coloured strands twisting inside. She inspected it in a way that told him she was no expert either.

'Can I borrow this?' she asked.

'Knock yourself out,' he said.

She put it in her coat pocket.

'So after the incident...what did you call it?'

'The cable kerfuffle.'

'After the cable kerfuffle, they hired you for night-shift security.'

'That's right.'

'Any trouble after that?'

Alf shook his head. 'I sometimes have to chase kids away, but nothing major.'

'Until the bonfire?'

'That's right.'

'Can you retrace your steps, show me exactly where you went on the night of the bonfire?'

Alf glanced down at her shoes. 'It's all puddles and mud out there.'

'Can't we drive?'

Alf laughed. 'Not unless you've got a Chieftain tank with you.'

She smiled. 'I'll get my boots from the car.'

The rain had stopped. The moon and stars were obscured by gathering snow clouds; only the lights of the Zagrovyl factory burned bright, an orange flame flickering at the top of the highest chimney. DI Cadell produced a powerful torch and handed it to Alf, who led the way. He took the long way round. Best to avoid tripping over sharp scrap or falling into deep troughs in the dark. They moved along the boundary fence as it turned down to the river, past where the bonfire had been, until they could see the no-man's land between the scrapyard and the container port.

The torch beam caught the sea glass and shells forming a spiral on the lid of a concrete pillbox, and she looked up at him, her eyebrows forming a question.

If it had been anyone else, he might have felt embarrassed to admit to the shrine, but somehow he felt she'd understand.

'I collect the little things my wife would have liked,' he explained.

She nodded.

'How do we get past the fence?'

He handed her the torch and showed her how to hold onto the end of the fence and slip round the embankment. Once he was on the other side, she passed the torch round to him and followed.

'I can move my things if you want,' he said.

'No need.' She shook her head. 'At least, not tonight.'

'It's no bother.'

'What was her name?' she asked. 'Your wife.'

'Grace,' he said.

'This is a lovely memorial.' She seemed about to say something else, then stopped herself and bowed her head. They stood in silence for a while.

Alf shivered. 'Seen enough?'

'On the night of the bonfire, did you come here?' she asked.

'No,' he said. 'And the next day all these things were scattered over the ground.'

She stared out across the river.

'Let's go back now.'

The torch beam caught the silver cross.

'Wait,' Alf said and reached out to retrieve it. 'I tried to tell DS Wharton, but then the kids attacked his car. I picked this up near the bonfire that night.'

He handed it to her.

She studied it in the torchlight then raised a hand to unclip a bead necklace.

'Here,' she said, handing it to him. 'Can we swap? Just a loan until I can get this back to you?'

'Sure,' he said and laid the beads in the place where the cross had been.

She sealed it in an evidence bag and slipped it into her coat pocket.

DI Cadell walked back with him to the Portakabin.

'You've been enormously helpful, Mr Pearce,' she said. 'May I take your number in case there are any further questions?'

He handed her the satellite phone and she keyed the number written on the back into her mobile.

'Thank you.'

She handed it back and nodded towards the library book propped against his satchel: *Nested*.

'I loved that one,' she said.

Alf blushed for the second time that night. Just as he'd suspected, the librarian had tricked him into taking out a book for women.

'Oh, I'm not quite sure it's my cup of tea,' he mumbled.

Chapter 54

North Yorkshire – Sunday, 1 December 2024

Julie woke early on Sunday morning, her mind racing.

Brian Burrow was – or had been – a control engineer. What exactly had he found missing from the Zagrovyl stores? Who had he accused of theft? What was the connection with the trespasser and the mysterious cable on the other side of the river?

She took four clean sheets of A4 paper from the printer, Sellotaped them together and began drawing a mind map.

She put the murder victim Dameer Ghosh at the centre, drawing a circle around his name. She added further circles as satellites around him and populated them with all the people they knew. His half-sister, Alvi Zaidi. His employer, Uzain Bagra. Sue Bell and Simon Sharp, his Zagrovyl colleagues. Further out in her solar system she added the other witnesses, people who claimed never to have met the victim: Brian Burrow, Alf Pearce. Then she drew squares with the companies: Zebra, Zagrovyl, Hartlepool Nuclear Power Station, South Bank Scrap Services, South Bank Container Port, Tiger Industrial Security.

Finally, she listed all the outstanding questions, grouping them into who, what, where, when, how, why.

That last one was the hardest. If she could figure out the motive, the rest would surely follow.

After breakfast, Julie drove back to Hutton Rudby to see if Omar Matar was home.

The lights were on, and the smell of fresh baking drifted from an open window.

Julie rang the doorbell.

A grey-haired woman opened the door, dressed in a green sari.

Julie flashed her badge. 'DI Cadell,' she said. 'I wonder if I might have a word with Omar Matar.'

'Is this about the car?'

Julie nodded.

'Come in,' the woman said. 'He's in the kitchen.'

Omar was a slight man with a smile as warm as the kitchen range.

Julie introduced herself and accepted the offer of tea.

'So, have you found the scallywags that stole my Mercedes?' he asked.

'Not yet, sir,' she said. 'But I wonder if you'd mind taking a look at a couple of pictures?'

She unlocked her phone and found the pictures Nadia had sent. As soon as he saw the photo of the pale driver he jumped to his feet, calling to his wife.

'When was this taken?' he asked.

'Earlier this month.'

'The double-crossing bastard!' he shouted.

'You know him?'

'Of course I know him. He used to work for me.'

'His name?'

'Everyone called him Tadpole,' he said.

This couldn't be a coincidence. Tad the Pole was the nickname of the IT contractor sacked from Zagrovyl for falsifying his attendance record. Brian Burrow had accused him of stealing from the stores although charges were never pressed.

Mrs Matar bustled over with a plate of warm scones and glanced at the photo on the phone. 'You're right,' she said. 'That's definitely Tadeusz Makowski.'

'He was employed by Osprey Cars?'

'On a casual basis. He had a clean licence and was happy to work odd hours, so I used him for the late-night jobs.'

'What do you know about him?'

'He came to the UK from Poland long before Brexit. He was saving up to bring his family over, so he was always looking for extra work. I think he trained as an electrician, but he did all sorts of other jobs.'

'Like what?'

'His main work was in IT, I think, but he lost his job with one of the chemical companies over some misunderstanding. I assumed he'd gone back to Poland.'

Definitely not a coincidence.

Back in the car, Julie sent CIO Latif a message.

Forgot to ask you to file another weather report.

Julie looked up the coordinates of Teesside airport and added the date that the ghost taxi went up in flames. Her phone rang almost immediately, from a number she didn't recognise.

'DI Cadell, Cleveland Police.'

'It's Nadia Latif here. How can I help?'

Julie could hear the noises of children in the background. Music and laughter too, it sounded like a party.

'The boss of Osprey Cars identified our mystery driver as Tadeusz Makowski.'

'Why does that not surprise me?'

'See if he was caught on camera around Teesside airport on the day the car was torched,' Julie said. 'You might get a better picture of him.'

'Will do.'

'And get someone out to Wynyard to talk to Simon Sharp's neighbour, Christine Bracegirdle. See if Tadeusz Makowski was the man who returned Simon Sharp's car to his house.'

'I'll check the CCTV too.'

When Julie got home, Arni's shoes were in the hall. Upstairs, his door was slightly open. She hovered outside then knocked.

'Arni? Can I come in?'

He made a strangled noise which she interpreted as a yes.

Her youngest son was lying on his bed in a foetal position, one arm covering his face.

'Are you OK?'

She sat at the end of the bed and waited.

'Eve's having an abortion on Monday,' he said.

He threw back his hand and she saw that his face was wet with tears.

'Permission to hug,' she asked.

He nodded and sat up and she gathered him in her arms and held him while he sobbed his heart out.

When the storm had passed and he was quiet, she asked, 'Fancy some dinner?'

He nodded.

They ate at the kitchen table. Julie waited until Arni had polished off a second and third helping.

'Are you OK to talk about things?'

He shrugged.

'Do you think it's her decision?'

'She says it is,' he said. 'She's seen a doctor and two separate counsellors as well as the school nurse.'

'And how do you feel?'

'Bereft,' he said. 'I think I'm losing her, too.'

Julie tried to remember her first real heartbreak, that moment when the world ends and nothing is worthwhile. But it was all long ago. She'd met Matt when they were both so very young. Most of her heartache had come later. What do you say to someone losing their first love? Do you tell them that there will be others, or is that something they can only discover for themselves? Everyone thinks that their first passion is the greatest love in history, unique to them and something that no one else can possibly understand.

The fate of the tiny foetus only added to the heartbreak.

There would certainly be better times to nurture that potential, to allow it to develop into an independent life. Human babies are like Tasmanian devils. They sneak into your life and then cause chaos, destroy your sex life, wreck your friendships, strain your marriage, upend your career. Babies are completely and utterly selfish and incomprehensible to those who don't have them. There is never a right time to have a baby, only a less bad time.

Eve was doing the right thing. She had her whole life ahead of her.

Yet despite the relief that her son was not going to be a father before he was an adult, she also shared his sadness.

'You fancy some mindless TV?' she asked.

He nodded.

'Any suggestions?'

'You choose.'

This was new. Arni usually had strong opinions. He liked gangster and horror films, genres she couldn't bear. Comedy or romance seemed inappropriate. They needed something distracting. *Nested*, this year's bestseller, had already been made into a series. Had it been released yet? She checked on her phone and almost balked at the price.

What the hell.

They sat on the sofa together, binge watching and eating ice cream and popcorn late into the night.

Chapter 55

Middlesbrough – Monday, 2 December 2024

The new week dawned clear and bright with a light sprinkling of snow on top of the frost. Today was the day Julie reported to her new unit. Before she left, she took her son a cup of tea.

Last night, Arni had begged to be allowed to take a day off school, and she hadn't had the heart to object.

'I do think you should go to school,' she said. 'But see how you feel when you wake up. I trust you to make the right decision tomorrow.'

He woke briefly when she knocked. She opened his bedroom door and put the tea on his bedside table.

'Thanks, Mum,' Arni murmured, then turned over and went back to sleep.

Minimax HQ was housed in a separate, purpose-built office in a new development to the east of Middlesbrough. More snow had fallen here, and it crunched underfoot as she walked from the car park to reception.

'DI Cadell.' ACC Bruma strode into the atrium a few minutes later. 'Welcome to the Minimax team!'

Julie shook his hand.

'Coffee?'

He pointed to an alcove with easy chairs and a coffee machine.

She selected an espresso pod and followed his lead. The smell of coffee filled the air as the machine sprang into action.

'I hear congratulations are in order,' he said, taking his drink first. 'Your team solved the case of the Hartlepool murder in record time.'

Julie avoided eye contact, adding sugar to the dark, hot liquid as it emerged from the machine. 'The case is closed,' she said.

He took one of the easy chairs and gestured for her to take the other.

'It doesn't sound as if you are particularly happy with the outcome,' he said.

'My boss is,' Julie said.

'Meaning?'

'A suspect has been arrested. Unfortunately, he's in hospital, in a coma, and may never testify.'

'So there remains some doubt?'

'May I speak frankly, sir?'

'I thought you always did,' he said. 'That's why I asked for your transfer.'

Julie met his cool grey eyes. 'You asked for me?'

'What did you think?'

'I thought I might have been foisted on you.'

He roared with laughter. 'Badge of honour round here, to fall out with Chalmers. Why don't you tell me about the accused?'

Julie took another sip of coffee, using the time to organise her thoughts.

'Brian Burrow didn't deny he was planning to meet the murder victim, and a knife that could be the murder weapon was found in his motorcycle saddlebag,' Julie said.

'Case closed.'

'Or all a bit too neat,' Julie said. 'The traffic investigation showed that Brian's accident was a hit and run. What if the driver of the other vehicle placed the murder weapon at the scene?'

'Why would anyone try to frame him?'

'I have no idea.' Julie sighed. 'What I do know is that he and the victim were both control engineers, and that two other control engineers, in India and Teesside, have died or disappeared in suspicious circumstances just this month. They were all connected with – directly or indirectly – with the same multinational chemical conglomerate, Zagrovyl International.'

'What's your alternative theory?'

'Someone, somewhere wants rid of anyone who might get in the way of a terrorist attack.'

'That sounds serious.'

'Best case is ransomware. The criminals threaten to disrupt the business unless money is paid.'

'There's plenty of precedent for that,' he said. 'Worst case?'

'Worst case is they're not interested in money, just in creating havoc.'

'Havoc?'

'An explosion or fire or toxic release leading to mass casualties.'

'Hmm.' ACC Bruma stood up. 'We definitely need to investigate this. Let's get you settled in.'

On the second floor of Minimax HQ she was met by another familiar face, the man who'd given her a tour of Seal Sands and later delivered the new computer.

'Morning, DS Vaziri,' she said.

'Welcome!' He smiled. 'Call me Vaz.'

Julie's phone rang. When she saw the caller ID she stopped.

'I'm sorry,' she said. 'I need to take this.'

Vaz smiled. 'No problem.' He opened a door. 'This is your office,' he said. 'Make yourself at home. If you need anything, I'm right next door.'

Julie closed the door and accepted the call from CIO Latif.

'Morning, boss.' A background roar of traffic made her soft voice hard to hear. She must have wheeled herself outside to make the call.

'I'm not your boss anymore,' Julie said.

'Then get me a job with Minimax, OK?'

Julie laughed. It felt good that someone missed her.

'What news?'

'That airport weather report you asked me for,' she said. 'I can confirm that a Polish national by the name of Tadeusz Makowski flew to Amsterdam and then on to Poznań.'

So he torched the taxi and walked over the fields to the airport.

'And there's more.'

'More?'

'We've got him on CCTV in Asda round about the time the clothes were stolen.'

If he wasn't the murderer, he was most definitely an accomplice.

'Could you do one more thing for me?' Julie asked.

'Anything, boss.'

She was about to ask the CIO to investigate Tiger Industrial Security, but then she thought better of it.

I'm not your boss. And you're just a civilian. I can't involve you in this.

'Hang fire,' Julie said. 'Look after yourself, first and foremost. I need to have a think how best to handle this.'

Julie ended the call and sat in thought.

Tadeusz Makowski, Tad the Pole or just Tadpole, once worked for both Zagrovyl International and Osprey Cars. He was sacked from the former for falsifying gatehouse records. It was suspected that he had also stolen material from the engineering stores, but no charges were brought.

Then he was caught trespassing in a scrapyard, where mysterious spools of cable had appeared, but again, no charges were brought.

A year later he reappears, driving a stolen taxi ferrying Dameer Ghosh to the last appointment before he's murdered. He's caught on CCTV in the supermarket where the clothes were stolen that were used to dress the deceased. The same taxi is seen leaving the crime scene after the body was thrown into the river. Finally he torches the car near the airport and leaves the country.

This was a man they needed to arrest as a matter of urgency.

Her personal phone pinged with a message from Flora. She was coming home today, her train arriving early evening. Julie texted back to say they'd meet her at Middlesbrough station and then sent a message to Arni. This was good news. Perfect timing; something to cheer them both up.

Chapter 56

Middlesbrough – Monday, 2 December 2024

Julie looked around her new workspace for the first time: the same blue carpet tiles and cream walls, but at least there was a false ceiling with light diffusers instead of the naked strip lights that flickered at a headache-inducing frequency; the same standard-issue furniture, but at least it was brand new. She sat in her chair, adjusted the height and tilt, then unpacked her laptop and connected it to the dual monitors.

The room was flooded with natural light. One large window looked north, out over the river to the chemical complex beyond, and the other faced west, towards the town of Middlesbrough. The snow was falling fast now. Big flakes settled on the rooftops, creating white pillows that deadened any noise.

Until ACC Bruma burst into the office.

'That case we discussed,' he said. 'The victim was Indian, right?'

'Dameer Ghosh. Yes, he was an Indian national.'

Vaz followed his boss.

'Did he have any connection with Kanpur?'

'He studied there.'

Vaz slipped his phone in front of her. 'Then I think you'd better see this.'

Terrorists take over chemical plant near Kanpur, India.

As Julie read, the blood drained from her face.

'What do we know?' she asked.

'Apparently they're threatening to release toxic gas to commemorate some atrocity.'

'Do we know anything about the occupied factory?'

'A place called Panki.'

Julie sank back into her chair, clutching her stomach.

'Zagrovyl International have a site in Panki,' she said. 'And a process control hub in India. They also have a high-hazard site in Seal Sands. If the terrorists have taken control of a multinational in India, there's a risk they could sabotage factories around the world.'

'An international cyberattack?' ACC Bruma said.

'What is the anniversary the terrorists are protesting about?' Julie asked.

Vaz took his phone back and clicked onto another page. 'The Union Carbide accident in India resulted in the release of several tonnes of highly toxic gas. It killed thousands and injured hundreds of thousands of civilians.'

'Which couldn't happen here,' ACC Bruma said.

'Do we want to take that risk?' Julie asked. 'Just look around you.' She pointed to the silver towers dusted in snow. 'The source of Teesside's wealth is also a source of danger. When is the anniversary?'

'The third of December,' Vaz said.

'That's tomorrow,' Julie said.

Vaz shook his head. 'Just after midnight on the night of the second to third of December. India is five and a half hours ahead of us, so that's six-thirty p.m. tonight.'

'Then we don't have much time,' Julie said.

'What do you suggest?'

Julie stood up and grabbed her bag. 'Mobilise the Cleveland Emergency Planning Unit. Prepare to declare an emergency. Tell the public to shelter in place.'

'Where are you going?'

Julie was already running down the stairs, her phone glued to her ear, calling Sue Bell.

Chapter 57

Greatham – Monday, 2 December 2024

Julie drove straight to Greatham, to the house that Sue Bell shared with her wife. Sue answered the door, rubbing sleep from her eyes.

'I tried to call you,' Julie said.

Snow was falling in big flakes, dusting Julie's hair and shoulders.

'You'd better come in,' Sue said, but her tummy was so large, there wasn't room to pass in the corridor.

'Excuse the mess,' Sue said as she backed away.

Julie entered, closed the front door behind her and followed.

'Have you seen the news?' Julie asked.

Sue filled the kettle and switched it on to boil. 'No, I was catching up on sleep.' She put both hands on her belly. 'Emma was on night shift last night and the Shrimp gets restless without her.'

The kitchen table was heaped with plates and mugs, books and magazines. Sue started moving them around.

'Now where is my phone? I switched it to silent.'

Julie watched as she put a hand to the small of her back and grimaced. Was it fair to involve Sue in this? She had other priorities.

'How long to go?'

'Baby's head hasn't engaged yet. Midwife says it'll be another week, if not two.'

Julie decided to plough on. If things went the way she feared, it was people like Sue and her baby who were most at risk.

'I need your advice,' Julie said.

At that moment another woman walked into the kitchen, her hair still wet from the shower. She was dressed in her work clothes, the blue and white uniform of a nurse.

'Change of plan,' she began. 'I've been called in to—' She stopped when she saw Julie.

'This is Detective Inspector Cadell,' Sue said. 'The good cop I was telling you about. Julie, this is my wife, Emma.'

Emma frowned. 'I hope you have a good reason for interrupting my wife's sleep.'

'CEPU are about to declare a civil emergency,' Julie said.

'What sort of emergency?'

'Precautionary,' Julie said. 'Close all doors and windows. Shelter in place.'

'What's going on?'

'Terrorists have seized control of a chemical site in India,' Julie said.

'Very sorry and all that, but India is a very long way away . . .' Emma began.

'The India site belongs to a multinational chemical company,' Julie said. 'There's a credible risk that the terrorists will be able to take control of other chemical sites around the world.'

'From India?' Emma sounded sceptical.

'An international cyberattack,' Sue said. 'Just like Brian warned.' She found her phone and enabled the alerts. The little kitchen filled with beeps.

'Fuck,' Sue said. 'I've missed five calls.'

She put the latest voicemail onto speakerphone. A man's voice, almost shrill with panic.

Sue, can you pick up? Please pick up. It's Jed. From work. We're in trouble here. Big trouble. Call me back, OK?

'What do these terrorists want?' Emma sounded exasperated.

'They're threatening to release toxic gas into the community. A revenge attack.'

321

'Revenge for what?' Emma asked.

'To draw attention to an anniversary,' Julie said. 'We're hoping it's just a publicity stunt, a hoax, a false alarm, but no one can take that chance.'

'Wait. What day is it?' Sue asked.

'Monday,' Emma said.

'No, the date.'

Emma glanced at the Advent calendar. 'Twenty-three days to Christmas,' she said.

'Of course,' Sue's voice dropped to a whisper, '1984.'

'What happened on the second of December 1984?'

'The worst accident in the world,' Sue said.

'So why haven't I heard about it?'

'Because everyone has forgotten,' Sue whispered. 'But perhaps all that's about to change.'

Julie stepped forward. 'I'm going to the Zagrovyl factory site. Tell me what I need to do.'

'I'll get dressed,' Sue said. 'I'm coming with you.'

Emma's mouth dropped open. 'No. NO!' She grabbed both her partner's hands. 'You're on maternity leave, for heaven's sake.'

'They need my help.'

'Then you can dial in like you always do.'

Sue shook her head. 'First response to a threatened cyberattack is to lock down all external access.' She squeezed her partner's hands and let go. 'The threat is not just in India or here in Teesside, but worldwide.'

'You're not going anywhere,' Emma said. 'You heard what DI Cadell said. You have to shelter in place.'

Sue Bell shook her head. 'Which way is the wind blowing?' she asked.

'I have no idea.'

'Look at the trees,' Sue said. 'It's an onshore wind.'

'So?'

'If I can convince you that we – me and the baby – will be safer at work, will you let me go?'

'That's an insane idea.'

'Hear me out, OK?'

'OK.'

'First, I have to tell you something about the accident in Bhopal.'

Emma sighed. 'If you must.'

'Forty years ago, a runaway reaction at a pesticide factory released twenty-eight tonnes of toxic gas into a densely populated area of the city. Thousands were killed and hundreds of thousands injured.'

'Christ.'

'Do you know how many of those deaths were inside the factory?'

'No.'

Sue held up her right hand and formed a circle with her index finger and thumb.

'Zero,' she said.

Emma frowned. 'How is that possible?'

'The gas rose, cooled and descended in a toxic fog that spread out far beyond the factory walls.' Sue moved her hands apart, splaying her fingers to illustrate. 'If this is a revenge attack with my factory as the source of release, then right now we're in the worst possible place. The wind will blow any gas directly towards us.'

'What do we do?'

'We don't have much time,' Sue said. 'If this cyberattack is timed to coincide with the original accident it'll happen just after midnight, India time.'

'Six-thirty UK time,' Julie confirmed.

Emma looked at the clock. 'Less than three hours away.'

'Which is why we need to move. Now.'

'If you don't think we're safe here,' Emma said, 'I'll take you to my work. To the hospital.'

'If things go wrong, all health centres in Teesside will be overrun,' Sue said. 'Please listen to me.'

She took both of Emma's hands in hers. 'I have to try and stop this terrible thing.'

'Why you?'

'There is no one else who knows the control system as well as I do.'

'What about your maternity cover?'

'Sharpie is missing.'

'Well, then, what about the bloke you took to lunch? The one you said shouldn't have been made redundant.'

'Brian is in a coma.'

'What about the support centre in India? Wasn't that the reason Brian was made redundant in the first place?'

'The only control engineer I know in India died two weeks ago.'

Emma's eyes widened. 'I can't believe this is happening.'

'If the attack started in India,' Sue continued, 'we must assume the IT/OT support centre has been compromised.' Sue moved towards the door. 'I have to go to work.'

Emma shook her head and stamped her foot. 'Look at you,' she shouted. 'You're thirty-eight weeks pregnant. Think of the baby.'

'That's exactly why I have to go,' Sue pleaded. 'At work, we have airtight toxic refuges.' She patted her belly. 'I am thinking of our baby. We'll be safe there.'

Emma narrowed her eyes.

'I know you, Sue. That's not the real reason you want to go to work, is it? You're not going there to hide away.'

Sue nodded. 'You're right. I'm going because I want to make sure nothing bad happens. Most of the victims in Bhopal were under five years old.' She moved forward and kissed her partner. 'It's because of this baby and all the other children in danger that I have to go and put a stop to it.'

'I promise to stick with her,' Julie said. 'Make sure she's safe.'

Emma took Sue's hands in hers again. 'Are you sure you're up to this?'

'Some bastard has taken over my control system. You bet I'm up to this.'

Julie drove, her mouth in a stern line.

'Why had I never heard of Bhopal before?' she asked.

'It happened a long time ago,' Sue said.

'So did Chernobyl, but everyone's heard of that.'

'I guess Chernobyl's nuclear fallout affected Europe directly,' Sue said. 'India is a long way away.'

'How many people died?'

Sue read out from her phone. 'Official statistics have 15,310 deaths and 554,895 injuries.'

'Christ.' Julie shook her head. 'That's the population of Teesside. Could it really happen here?'

'Not if I have anything to do with it.'

'The Bhopal accident happened forty years ago. Why bring it up now?'

'Ask the terrorists.'

Julie's phone rang and she answered it on loudspeaker.

'Where are you now?' Vaz spoke fast.

'On my way to Zagrovyl International,' Julie said. 'I've got the control-systems expert with me.'

'We're sending a police car from Hartlepool with some emergency kit. Call me as soon as you get there. And one more thing . . .'

'Yes?'

'Best if you enter the site incognito,' he said. 'The terrorists are warning that any police or army action will be met with – and I quote here – shock and awe.'

The car park was lit by the flashing blue light of a single police car. The uniformed officer looked horrified at the approach of the two women, his eyes fixed on Sue's belly.

'Ladies, it's not safe . . .'

'DI Cadell,' Julie flashed her badge. 'You have something for me?'

The constable handed her a large bag marked with the initials of Cleveland Emergency Planning Unit: CEPU.

'And this is the control-systems expert.'

Sue flashed her site pass at the officer. 'They called me in.'

The officer tapped his radio and turned away while he talked to someone.

'OK – you can go ahead.'

At the gatehouse the security guard let Sue through the side gate; she was too large for the turnstile. He held up a hand to stop Julie.

'Sorry, miss, you're not on my system. Code red emergency. I can't issue visitors with a site pass.'

Sue stopped on the other side of the barrier.

'Charlie, look at the size of me.'

'Any day now, eh, Sue?'

'You any good at delivering babies, Charlie?'

He blanched. 'No thanks.'

'Is childbirth part of the site first aid training?'

'I wouldn't know.'

'I can assure you that it's not, which is why I need my midwife with me.'

The guard turned to Julie. 'Are you really her midwife?'

Sue put her hand to her belly and groaned. 'I need her here, right now.'

The guard pushed a pad of paper towards Julie. 'Details here.'

Julie filled it in and signed.

'Give her a pass with full access,' Sue said.

The guard harrumphed before passing her a site pass on a lanyard.

Julie held it up to the reader. A light clicked from red to green, and she pushed through the turnstile.

The snow had stopped, but the wind was picking up as Julie followed Sue into the chemical factory.

'You OK?' Julie asked.

Sue grinned. 'Right as rain.'

'You were kidding about the pains, right?'

Sue winked. 'They come and go.'

Julie looked up at the sky. Dark clouds were gathering.

Sue used her pass to gain entry to the central control block, a low building set apart from the main production units. They entered a service corridor which gave access to offices and amenities. At the end was an air-lock. Through a glass window, Julie could see a room lined with panels containing dials and coloured lights and a wall of giant computer screens. A group of men in Zagrovyl International overalls huddled around a workstation.

'Wait here,' Sue said. 'I'm busting for a pee.'

There were two toilets, one male, one disabled. Julie wondered what it was like to work in a place where not being male counted as a disability.

The air-lock door from the control room opened and Alan Cosby strode out. The site manager stopped dead in his tracks and did a double-take at the sight of Julie.

'Who gave you permission . . .'

She put a finger to her lips and nodded at the CCTV camera overhead.

'I'm here to support Sue,' she said.

'Sue?'

Right on cue she exited the disabled toilet.

'Mrs Bell!' His jaw dropped as he took in the size of her belly. 'What the hell are you doing here?'

'Wind is blowing towards Greatham, so I reckon I'm safer inside than outside if this factory is in trouble.'

She turned her back on him, raised her pass to the reader and entered the air-lock. Once Sue had passed through the second door, Julie followed. A man broke away from the huddle and came forward to greet them.

'Sue, thank God you're here.'

Julie recognised his voice from the last message. This must be Jed.

Sue sat down on the chair he brought for her before logging on to a computer labelled ENGINEERING WORKSTATION. After flicking through several screens of code, she rolled the chair to the nearest screen with coloured graphics.

'What's up?' she asked Jed.

He ran her through the recent events.

'We downloaded a patch on Sunday morning and ever since then we've noticed some odd behaviour. Like a time lag. Everything seems to be running smoothly but given the security alert in India, I decided to go back to the old version. It won't let me. And there are other actions it won't let me perform.'

'Not sure I understand.'

'Start with the time delay. It's different on different actions,' he said. 'Here, let me show you.'

Jed tapped some keys. 'First a minor change to the set point for the control-room humidity. Almost instant. Then a change to the reactor level. A full thirty seconds before the loop began controlling.'

'Odd,' Sue said. 'It's almost as if someone is watching and approving.'

'Exactly.'

Julie walked round the room, noting the location of several CCTV cameras. The newer ones had a tiger logo – was that significant? She found a dark spot between filing cabinets and crouched down to open the bag. There was a sheet of paper with a message from Vaz.

International cyberattack in progress. Assume all normal communication channels will soon be compromised. Use the emergency equipment in the bag and call me when you can.

She took the CEPU bag back through the air-lock to the disabled toilet. At least there weren't any CCTV cameras in here. Julie unpacked the bag. Two CEPU phones. Two sets of hazmat suits with self-contained breathing apparatus. Flashlights and a pair of head torches. Tools. She hung up the larger of the two suits on the peg behind the door. Was it large enough for a pregnant woman? She doubted it. She placed the second phone behind the cistern. Using the first phone, she called the preprogrammed number. The phone behind the cistern rang. She cut the call and rang the third number.

'Julie, is that you?' Vaz sounded relieved when she answered. 'Where are you?'

'Inside the control block, Zagrovyl International.'

'Can you be seen or heard?'

'I don't think so. I'm in the disabled toilet.'

'What's happening?'

'Not sure. Sue Bell, the control-systems expert, is running some checks.'

'Zagrovyl International are being difficult,' Vaz said. 'Their senior management is in denial. Thanks to Brian's tape, I think we know more than they do.'

'OK, let's keep in touch.'

When Julie got back into the control room, the checks were continuing.

'You said there are actions the control system won't let you do,' Sue was saying. 'Show me.'

'OK, the third refrigeration pump is on standby. If I set the cooling target temperature to minus five degrees centigrade, it should start up.'

He entered the new set point. The pump symbol remained in the off position. After a pause, the controller reverted to the old set point.

'That's very worrying,' Sue said and turned to Alan Cosby, who was lurking near the back wall. 'We can't run without refrigeration. It's one of our safety systems.'

He waved a hand. 'Central Control is looking into it.'

Sue grimaced. 'Let's check all the other emergency systems,' she said. 'Start with the flare.'

Jed rolled and clicked his mouse, and the screen changed to a diagram of a thin, tall tower, with a flame symbol at the top.

'What's on fire?' Julie asked.

'It's a pilot light,' Sue explained. 'Permanently alight in case we have a process upset. This way we make sure any toxic gas that gets past the other safety systems will burn before it can do any harm.'

Sue turned back to the operator.

'Now the vent scrubber.'

'What's a scrubber?' Julie asked.

'A neutralising shower. If there's a release of toxic gas into the vent system, any vapour will be absorbed by the scrubber liquid. The flare is only the last resort if the scrubber is overwhelmed.'

Jed switched screens.

'That's odd,' he said. 'The liquid level is dropping.'

He moved over to the tannoy.

'control room one to outside one, come in, Steve.'

A disembodied voice came in over the loudspeakers.

'Steve here.'

'Check the scrubber level, will you, mate?'

'I've just made a cup of tea.'

'Tea can wait.'

'But my bacon roll can't.'

Sue took the radio from him. 'Steve,' she said. 'This is Sue Bell speaking. Check the fucking scrubber and do it RIGHT NOW.'

A door slammed as Alan Cosby left the control room.

And then the lights went out.

Chapter 58

In the darkness, an eerie silence descended over the control room. No one moved after the ceiling lights went out and the computer screens faded to black. When the emergency power supply kicked in, the noise of alarms was deafening.

'What the hell just happened?' Julie put her hands over her ears.

'Start the controlled shutdown,' Sue said.

Jed got onto the radio. 'Steve, mate. You OK?'

'I'm OK,' Steve said. 'But the pilot light on the flare stack just went out.'

'We've lost the flare,' Jed confirmed. 'The gas valve closed. I'll switch to the back-up supply and relight it.'

Sue grabbed the radio. 'What's the scrubber level, Steve?'

'What? You still want to know?'

'More than ever,' she said.

'Shit,' he said. 'It's below ten per cent.'

'There's something wrong with the control valves,' Jed shouted. 'I can't get caustic into the scrubber or gas to the flare.'

Sue spoke into the radio. 'Steve, can you open the manual bypass for the gas?'

'Doing that now.'

'Then get a water hose on and flood the scrubber,' Sue said. She turned to

Jed. 'We're moving to an emergency shutdown.'

'Emergency shutdown underway,' Jed confirmed.

The plant siren started to wail.

'Sue,' Jed rolled his chair back from the keyboard and approached the engineering workstation. 'I'm locked out.'

'Try logging in again.'

'My password no longer works.'

'You sure you remembered it right?'

'I'll try again.' Jed shook his head. 'No joy.'

'I'm logged in as an administrator, so I can reset it,' Sue said. 'OK, try it now.'

Jed shook his head. 'No luck.'

'What does the error message say?'

'It says call IT.'

Sue picked up the phone. There was no ringtone.

'Try yours,' she said.

One by one they checked the control-room phones. All were dead.

'No mobile signal either,' Jed held up his personal phone.

He went to the tannoy. 'Steve, can you hear me?'

No reply.

He tried the walkie-talkies, but all he got was a scream of high-pitched feedback.

'Bugger,' Sue said. 'And now I'm locked out too.'

The sirens stopped and all the screens went dark again.

The control-room doors flew open.

'New instructions from HQ.' Alan Cosby was back. 'We've been ordered to shut down.'

The team in the control room heaved a collective sigh of contempt.

'We're locked out of the control system,' Jed said.

'Switch to manual,' Alan said.

'We need to get into the control system to switch to manual.'

'Doesn't everything go to manual by default?' Alan asked.

Sue stared at him. 'The default is the emergency safety system.' She didn't even try to hide the scorn in her voice.

'Which triggers an emergency shutdown,' Alan insisted.

'You're way behind us. We triggered it ten minutes ago.'

'So, everything is OK?'

'Everything is far from OK,' Sue said. 'The flare is out and the scrubber is empty. We've lost all communication. We're completely blind and deaf to what's going on out there in the factory.'

Alan Cosby's face was white. 'What do we do?'

Sue handed him a phone.

'Try calling IT?'

The loudspeaker crackled and the screens came back to life.

The silhouette of a hooded figure appeared on the screen.

'Gentlemen. We have control of your factory. We've locked the turnstiles. No one enters or leaves.'

Julie and Sue stared at the screen.

'If you do exactly as we say, no one inside the factory will be hurt.'

'How dare you,' Alan Cosby shouted.

'Try anything stupid,' the hooded man said, 'and you will be killed faster than you can stop us.'

Julie grabbed a notepad and wrote.

Can they hear us?

Sue took the pen and wrote underneath: *I assume so.*

And see us? Julie wrote.

There were cameras in the ceiling. Sue switched the screen to display the view from the site cameras, toggling between them to show the full coverage.

What are you going to do? Julie wrote.

Sue's pen scratched underneath. *Cut the remote access.*

She passed the paper to Jed, who stood up and walked slowly to a tower of glowing lights. He looked to Sue, and she nodded. He pressed the power button. Nothing happened. The lights remained on. He bent to flick the switch at the wall socket. The next minute he was flying through the air in a shower of sparks and crackle of lightning. He crashed into the wall on the other side of the control room before slumping to the floor. His colleagues rushed to his aid.

The hooded man laughed. 'I think you'll find we're not that easy to stop.'

'What the hell do you want?' Alan had gone from white to red in the face.

'Just watch and listen,' the masked man said. 'Remember, I can see and hear everything you do. If any one of you tries anything stupid, like attempting to interrupt remote access again, all of you will die.'

Sue ripped the paper from the pad, crumpled it up and threw it in the wastebin.

Chapter 59

Seal Sands – Monday, 2 December 2024

The hooded man read out a statement.

On this night, forty years ago, the people of Bhopal were poisoned.
  The tragedy didn't end that night.
  The poison continues to spread through the soil and water.
  And yet, the world has forgotten about Bhopal.
  We are here to remind you.

At five minutes past midnight, you too will experience their suffering.
  A divine thunder will travel across the world as the heavens open and poison rains down upon you.
  You too will choke and gasp and fall and writhe and die.

You ask us – how do we stop this terrible thing?
  You ask us – what are your demands?
  You ask us – how do we put things right?
  And we reply, it is too late. It is forty years too late.
  All you can do now is pray.

The people of Bhopal tried reason.

They argued their case in court.
Millions were spent on lawyers – money down the drain.

The people of Bhopal tried compassion.
They cared for one another, organised clinics and barefoot healthcare.
One by one, little by little, those initiatives were strangled .

The people of Bhopal tried protest.
Hunger strikes, marches to the capital, anniversary vigils.
Promises were made, but never kept.

The people of Bhopal tried prayer.
Let's see if it works any better for you.

We do not represent the victims of Bhopal.
They are too good, too gentle, too kind.
And perhaps too sad and sick and weary.
They would never wish harm on others.
All they ever asked for was justice.

We are the angels of justice.
We are strong and vengeful.
We are radical and cruel.
We bring thunder and lightning, sledgehammers and whips, ice and fire.

We bring vengeance for the oppressed of the world.
All the people who are ignored, overlooked, despised and forsaken.
And this is just the beginning.

Sue groaned and put her hands on her abdomen.
'Are you OK?' Jed asked.
'Not feeling so good,' Sue said. 'It must be the shock.'
'I told you,' spluttered Alan Cosby. 'You shouldn't be here!'

'Julie,' Sue said. 'Can you help me?'

Julie took Sue's arm and supported the pregnant woman through the air-lock. Once the disabled bathroom door was open, Sue pulled her inside.

'I need to talk to you.'

'You OK?' Julie asked.

'Right as rain,' Sue said. 'Pissed off at those fucking nutters. We need to stop them.'

Julie showed her the contents of the CEPU bag.

'I don't think that's going to fit me.' Sue held the larger of the two hazmat suits against her belly and then threw it aside in disgust.

'At least we can communicate with the outside world,' Julie showed her the two satellite phones.

'Let's bring them up to date.'

Julie called Vaz.

'Status report,' she said. 'The Teesside site is under the control of terrorists. One man injured. We've lost all landline, wireless, radio and mobile communications and they can see and hear everything going on in the control room.'

'Any way to trigger an emergency shutdown?'

'We already tried,' Sue said. 'But they intervened and now we're completely locked out of our own control system.'

'What if we cut the utilities to the site?'

'Don't do that!' Sue said. 'The emergency safety systems need power. The scrubber and water curtain need water. If we lose utilities, the on-site diesel generators will kick in, but they're only designed to supply enough power for a safe shutdown. If the terrorists keep everything going, we'll quickly run out of diesel.'

'Any suggestions?'

'First, tell us – what's the situation elsewhere?'

'Zagrovyl International are still denying there's a problem at the Teesside site. CEPU are debating whether to evacuate vulnerable people within a critical radius and mandate a shelter in place for everyone else.'

'Trigger the evacuation immediately,' Julie said. 'Close the roads and stop all public transport.'

The trains. Flora was arriving at Middlesbrough station and Arni had promised to meet her.

'Understood,' Vaz said.

'What about elsewhere?' Sue asked.

'It's the same picture of denial at the Zagrovyl International sites all around the world. The German and US sites have sent non-essential staff home as a precaution, skeleton staff only. The picture isn't so clear elsewhere. The army have taken over the response in India and are threatening to storm the site. We're not convinced that will solve the situation. The masterminds, the terrorists driving this attack, they could be anywhere in the world.'

'Do we know what they want?' Julie asked

'For us to turn the clock back forty years.' Vaz sighed. 'Look, this isn't going to end well, do you want us to come and extract you?'

Julie looked at Sue.

'No,' Sue said firmly. 'I have an idea.'

'We'll call you back,' Julie said and cut the call.

'First, I need to eat something,' Sue said.

Julie looked in the CEPU bag, but there were no rations. She walked to the vending machine, but it only took coins. She patted her pockets but there was nothing there except a short length of armoured cable and a tiny cross-shaped multitool. Knowing that Iain Wharton would have no interest in new clues, she'd taken a deliberate decision not to book them in as evidence.

She returned to the disabled toilet empty-handed.

'I don't have any cash.'

'The free issue code for the drinks machine is 09230,' Sue said. 'Get me a hot chocolate.'

Julie brought it to her, and then went back for a coffee, selecting the option with extra milk and sugar.

They sat together on the floor.

'Any idea what these might be?' Julie produced the cross and cable from her pockets.

Sue took the cable. 'This is a piece control cable for multiple high-speed communications. And that,' she nodded at the silver cross, 'is a universal breaker key. Where did you find them?'

'The nightwatchman on the other side of the river.'

'Where Dameer . . .' Sue swallowed. 'Where he was murdered.'

Julie pointed to the multi-tool. 'This was found after Dameer's murder,' she said. 'But the mysterious cable appeared at South Bank Scrapyard over a year ago, round about the time an old friend of yours was arrested for trespass. Remember Tadeusz Makowski?'

'Tad the Pole, the contract IT guy? The guy we fired for falsifying the gatehouse records?'

'The same one Brian accused of stealing from the stores,' Julie said. 'We want to question him in relation to Dameer's murder. We have CCTV of him driving Dameer to Zagrovyl in a stolen taxi. Same taxi was spotted leaving the container port after Dameer died.'

Sue put her head in her hands. 'We should have listened to Brian. He wanted a full investigation into what Tadpole had done with all the stuff he'd stolen – it was so very specialised, not the kind of material you'd easily sell. But Alan Cosby and Marcia didn't want any publicity, so they didn't pursue it.' She looked up, eyes shining. 'Of course! It all makes sense now.'

'To you perhaps,' Julie said. 'But you'll need to explain it to me.'

'Can you close your ears and turn your back while I pee?' Sue asked.

'I can step out . . .'

'Best not let the cameras see you.'

Julie obliged, thinking back to her own pregnancies, the way her babies had pressed up against her bladder at inconvenient moments. Her babies. Flora was on her way to Middlesbrough train station; Arni was going to meet her. Had they stopped the trains yet?

When Sue had finished and flushed, Julie waited for her signal before turning back.

'Tell me again – where did you find Dameer?'

'His body was under the HMS *Trincomalee*, Hartlepool Historic Quay.'

'But you said he wasn't murdered there?'

'Crime scene is on the other side of the river.'

'Any idea how he got there?'

'It remains a mystery.'

'Did you notice any structures nearby? Like a concrete pillbox?'

Julie cast her mind back. 'Yes,' she said. 'There was a concrete cylinder with a metal lid. It stood about waist height and,' she opened her arms, 'this wide.'

Sue nodded. 'It's a ventilation and access shaft to an old tunnel.'

'Where does the tunnel go?'

'Under the river.'

Julie let out a low whistle.

'ICI built a tunnel to pipe hydrocarbons between their biggest sites at Billingham and Wilton,' Sue explained. 'Pipelines need regular integrity checks and maintenance, so the tunnel is big enough for people too. There are two additional ventilation and access shafts. The north one is on the boundary of the Zagrovyl site. The south one is between the container port and the scrapyard.'

'Is that how Dameer left the site on the afternoon he was murdered? Did he walk through the tunnel?'

'That explains what he was doing,' Sue said. 'Looking for a secret door.'

'A secret door in a tunnel?'

'A metaphor. For the terrorists to retain remote control, there must be a control route we didn't know about. Somewhere inaccessible and hidden. It's the only way to explain why our attempts to shut out remote access haven't worked.'

'You mean Dameer was working with the terrorists?'

'On the contrary. I think he was trying to stop them.'

'So why didn't he?'

'I'm not sure.' Sue shook her head. 'Maybe he was killed before he could act. Or maybe his murderer reversed whatever action he took.'

Julie scratched her head. 'This secret door. If it's not in the software, is it a physical thing?'

'Both hardware and software,' Sue replied. 'The emergency control system has inbuilt redundancy, so if one link fails, another takes over sending and receiving information.'

Julie frowned.

'Remember when Christmas tree lights were wired in series, so if one bulb blew, the circuit was broken, and all the lights went out? These days, they're wired in parallel, so you can lose a few bulbs without spoiling Christmas.'

'But you still expect to be able to turn all the lights off, right?'

'Yes. A two-way switch is on and off. But replace it with a three-way control and whichever way you turn, you open a new circuit. You can never turn it off.'

'And that's what's happening here?'

'Worse. Looks like someone has threaded a live power cable round the control cable. A booby trap to stop anyone trying to cut through.'

'That's what happened when Jed tried to turn off the remote link?'

'Yes. It makes sense now. Tadpole was always in here running new cables. Because he said it related to office IT and CCTV, we didn't take much notice – it was outside of our normal Permit to Work or Management of Change systems. Now it looks as if he was working for the terrorists. They must have been planning this for years.'

Julie had a sudden thought. 'The CCTV in the control room. Who supplied it?'

'I can't remember,' Sue said. 'Tiger something.'

'Tiger Industrial Security?' Julie said. 'Same outfit who hid what was going on at South Bank Scrap.'

Julie had a sudden memory of the night watchman with his erudite log book. He also had a satellite phone. Had anyone warned him to take shelter? She found his number on her mobile, keyed it into the keypad of the emergency phone and dialled.

No signal

Sue put her head in her hands. 'Running a secret control cable that we can't interrupt.'

'What do we do?'

'Our only hope is to access the tunnel.'

'How can you be sure this switch is in the tunnel?'

'I ran a complete network security check when we arrived on site. It's the only place it can be.'

Julie nodded. 'I'll call CEPU.' She pressed the dial button. 'They can access the tunnel from the south bank. If you explain what they're looking for, they can get someone down there to flick the switch.'

Dialling

Connecting

Call failed

Julie pressed redial.

Nothing.

She retrieved the other device from behind the cistern and tried again.

No signal

'How the hell have they interrupted satellite communication?'

'It might not be the terrorists,' Sue said. 'Could be the weather. Thunderstorms were forecast today.' Sue stood up. 'Go and get one of the operators, tell them I've gone into labour and you need help.'

Julie unlocked the toilet door and ran to the control-room air-lock. She held her pass up to the card reader, but it remained red. She knocked on the window. All the site personnel had gathered inside the control room as instructed. An operator appeared. He tried to open the air-lock from his side, but it remained stubbornly closed. All the site personnel were locked inside.

'We're locked out of the control room,' Julie shouted as she ran towards the exit.

Julie tried the outside door. It too remained closed.

'Shit, and we're locked in, too.'

Through a small pane of reinforced glass in the door, Julie blinked as lightning ripped across the dark sky outside. A peal of thunder followed.

The storm was directly overhead.

Chapter 60

Julie and Sue Bell were locked in the service corridor of a control room with no way in or out. Outside, a high-hazard chemical plant was being operated by terrorists from another country. All external communication had been cut and the back-up satellite signal lost while a thunderstorm raged. In less than an hour the terrorists planned to release toxic gas in simultaneous atrocities around the world.

'What now?' Julie asked.

'Do you want to hear my idea?' Sue asked. 'I'm not sure you're going to like it.'

'I'm listening.'

'How are you with enclosed spaces?'

Julie shuddered. 'How enclosed?'

Sue pointed to the floor drain.

Julie sized it up. 'Not sure I'll fit through.'

'Well, I certainly won't.' Sue patted her belly.

'Where does it go?'

'There's a crawl space under the building. If you follow the drainpipe, you'll come out near a culvert that channels surface water away and leads straight down to the river.'

'And then?'

'At the river there's a hut with lifesaving equipment, including self-contained breathing apparatus. Right under it is the access shaft down into the tunnel.'

'You want me to go down into the tunnel?'

'It's the only way.'

'And then?'

'Find the breaker, unlock it with the special tool, flick the switch. Crisis over.'

'I don't even know what a breaker looks like, still less how to disarm it.'

'Think of it as a big fuse box,' Sue said. 'About this size.' She gestured with her hands. 'One metre square and fifty centimetres deep.'

'Is there more than one?'

'Only one.'

'How will I find it?'

'It's probably right in the middle of the tunnel. Follow the cable.'

Julie held out her hand for the cable sample. It was as thick as her thumb, the outer plastic surface slightly ridged, following the contours of the armoured sheath that protected the multicore. She closed her eyes and committed the texture to memory.

'Just one thing,' Sue added. 'Can you swim?'

'Yes, why?'

'Tadpole stole an underwater breaker. It's possible they plan to flood the tunnel.'

'Great,' Julie said.

'But even if it doesn't fill up with water, there may be insufficient ventilation. Bad air down there, nothing to breathe.'

'Then I'll take my own atmosphere.'

'You're trained with breathing apparatus?'

Julie nodded. 'PADI – Professional Association of Diving Instructors.' The fateful family holiday. No time to dwell on that now.

'It's going to have to do.' Sue bit her lip. 'There are masks and air cylinders in the river shack.'

Julie nodded.

'I'll keep trying to raise the outside team, get them to go down the other side of the tunnel.'

'Let's hope they get here first.'

'You clear what you need to do?'

Julie shook her head. 'Let's go through it again.'

When it came down to it, Julie was the only person who could act in time. There was no way that Sue could fit through the floor drain, and the outside doors were locked. All the other site personnel were trapped in the control room, and so long as the storm raged overhead, they had no way of contacting the emergency responders outside. If Julie didn't do it, no one would. Julie put on the smaller hazmat suit.

Sue investigated the CEPU bag. She found the torches and the toolbox and set to work on the floor drain, unscrewing the fastenings and sliding the cover out of the way.

It was a tight squeeze. Feet-first, Julie got stuck halfway down. She hauled herself out and went in again, head-first this time, grabbing a joist to pull herself into the crawl space beneath the control block toilets.

Sue handed her a head torch and the silver cross.

'Go, girl,' she said. 'You've got this.'

Follow the drain to the edge of the building.

It stank down here, the foul smell of a leaking sewer pipe. There was less than a metre of space under the joists, and Julie had to slither through the mud - at least she hoped it was mud - following the drain to the edge of the building. There she turned and began kicking the side panels. One of them crumbled and she kicked a hole in it big enough to crawl through. She welcomed the rain on her face and gulped down lungfuls of fresh air.

Find the storm drain and follow it to the river.

The culvert was about half a metre wide and a metre deep. Julie slid in, feet first, bent forward at the waist until her head was below the edge, and tried to run. The water knocked her off her feet and she let the fast-flowing torrent carry her downstream, hauling herself out just before it discharged into the river. In the mist she searched for the river hut, spotting it just to her left. She kept close to the river, out of view of the site cameras, until it was directly above her.

Freezing rain was still pouring down, but she was out in the open, so she tried the satellite phone again. It was ringing. Come on Vaz.

The ringing stopped.

No signal

On the far bank she saw something move. Through the rain she could just make out a powerful torch moving along the far bank. Alf?

She tried his number.

Ringing. Yes! A connection. Hallelujah.

'Hello—' he began.

She cut him off. 'Julie Cadell, Cleveland Police. Get inside. I'm going into the tunnel. Call Minimax and get me some back-up from the south entrance.'

Hiss...'can't—'...crackle.

The connection went dead.

The light on the other side of the river waved from side to side.

Julie tried Vaz. *No signal.*

She tried Alf again. *No signal.*

In desperation, she put her hand over the head torch and signalled an S.O.S: three short, three long, three short flashes.

His torch flashed in reply: one short, one long, one short.

What did that mean? Had he got the message? No more time to waste.

Julie entered the hut. Inside she found the air cylinders and checked the gauges. The shaft entrance was identical to the one on the other side of the river, only the manhole was locked closed with three wing-nuts. One by one she opened them, lifted the lid and peered down.

The shaft was narrow. A vertical ladder set into rings of concrete that linked the riverbank with the tunnel dropped thirty metres into darkness. There was barely room for her alone; with her hazmat suit and the breathing apparatus on her back, it was going to be a tight squeeze.

What the hell was she doing? She'd passed the PADI course, but she'd hated the constriction of the mask. Anybody would be better than her. She should wait for help.

Had they stopped the trains? Had Arni and Flora got her messages? She couldn't focus on her own children. She had to think about all the children.

Thirty metres. Rungs every twenty-five centimetres, four to a metre, one hundred and twenty to descend. If she took five seconds for each rung, it would take her ten minutes to get down. Then she had to walk to the middle of the tunnel and find the breaker, use the special tool to open it, flick the switch and climb back up. It would be harder on the ascent, take longer and the effort would use more oxygen.

Best to have a reserve tank.

She lowered a full cylinder down ahead of her, playing out the rope until it hit the bottom and went slack. She tied the rope to an anchor point at the top.

The rain hammered down on the roof of the hut. She tried the satellite phone again. Still no signal. No point in putting this off any longer. She was on her own.

Julie started her descent.

As she reached the bottom of the ladder and stepped into the tunnel, something shifted in the shadows; she swung the torch round and screamed.

Julie had found Simon Sharp.

The decomposing remains of what had once been a man lay at the base of the ladder. There were no insects or carrion scavengers down here to hasten the decomposition process. Putrefaction had been slow, the bacteria from his own gut eating him inside out.

Julie turned her back on Sharpie's corpse.

Her breathing came sharp and fast. She was using too much air. She tried to remember her PADI training. A sandy beach. A blue sky. The gentle lapping of the waves.

Once her heartbeat had slowed, she found the armoured control cable, then started to follow it down the tunnel.

The River Tees narrows before it meets the sea, in a man-made channel that corrals it between the concrete banks of land reclaimed for industry. What was once low-lying marshland is now raised up, piles descending deep into the mud to support a smooth, hard surface for piers and roads and railways and buildings, the water concentrated into a channel two kilometres long, three hundred metres wide and twenty-five metres deep.

Julie was thirty metres below sea level, and five metres under the fast-flowing River Tees, in a tunnel four metres in diameter that carried pipes between Wilton and Seal Sands. She had to walk under the Tees, to the mid-point, to find the breaker switch.

It was hard going. Walking on the curved pipes that ran along the base of the tunnel, her feet kept slipping, and she fell hard, wedged for a moment between hydrogen and ammonia. She got to her feet and changed her approach, planting her feet across the largest-diameter crude oil pipe and moving sideways. The weight of the air cylinders on her back made every muscle ache.

When she'd done the PADI course, the water had supported the weight of the breathing apparatus. Jamie and Matt had carried the air cylinders to and from the boat. She hadn't realised how heavy they were.

She checked her air supply. At the rate she was breathing, she had less than thirty minutes of air.

She checked her watch. Six p.m. in the UK; 11.30 p.m. in India. If the attack was to be just after midnight, then all of Teesside had thirty minutes of air. Time was running out.

Calm down.

It was one of the phrases she hated most. When did anyone in a heightened emotional state respond well to such an instruction? Better to speed up. Get this task over and done with.

Julie fell between the pipes and the torch slipped off her head, skidded across a pipe and went out.

In the darkness, she tried to pull herself back up, but her foot was trapped.

She couldn't go any further. Her thighs were burning, back aching, twisted ankle throbbing under the water.

That's when she first noticed the water level. And the noise. Sue had guessed right. The tunnel was filling with water. Could things get any worse?

Calm down.

A sandy beach. A blue sky. The gentle lapping of the waves. A boat arriving with the diving party. Something wrong. The tears that she hadn't been able to shed then overwhelmed her now.

And suddenly, there he was beside her. Her first child. Jamie. She felt the warmth of his smile, the twinkle of his eyes in the darkness.

'You've got this, Mum.'

'I miss you,' she said.

'I know,' he said. 'I'm sorry.'

'It wasn't your fault,' she protested. 'You tried to help someone in trouble.'

'Or maybe they tried to help me,' he said.

She stopped for a moment. She'd never really considered that Jamie could be anything other than a hero. After all, the other fatality was a much less experienced diver.

'Forget the torch,' he said. 'Keep going. You're nearly there.'

Find the breaker. Use the key. Flick the switch. Crisis over.

Julie was tired. The weight of the air cylinders was dragging her down. Did she really need breathing apparatus? The water was up to her knees. Not high enough to swim in. Not high enough to provide buoyancy, to take the weight off her back. Not high enough to need this damn contraption. She began to loosen her mask.

'No,' Jamie said. 'Don't take the mask off, Mum.'

She pressed the button on the gas monitor. It lit up, a flashing red light: 6 per cent oxygen. What had they taught her? Confusion and loss of consciousness below 15 per cent oxygen. She checked the gauge on the air tank. A quarter left.

Calm.

A sandy beach. A blue sky. The gentle lapping of the waves. A boat arriving with the lifeless body of her eldest son. The ambulance ready to rush him to hospital. Stop. Let me go with him! No, *hanımefendi*. Your other children need you.

My other children need me. She must slow her breathing. Move forward steadily, do the job and then get out. Go home to them.

She took another step.

There was music in the tunnel. The songs of the holiday. Flora had made the playlist. Music Julie had been unable to tolerate ever since. Now it was back. Why?

Jamie was floating near the tunnel ceiling. '*Can't we just talk*,' he sang. He'd loved that song. They'd listened to it in the car. The song was etched on her memory, grooved into her brain.

They'd taken turns copying Khalid's falsetto. Arni won every time, making Jamie collapse with laughter.

She'd always loved that about the kids. Their excitement about finding new music. Their delight in sharing it. The way they ribbed one another for unfashionable choices, their unity in the end over a catchy tune, a strong beat, a subtle lyric. Ephemeral, those songs of the summer of 2019. Wispy fragments of melody that floated past, impossible to grasp.

'*I'm your summer girl*.' She hummed the Haim melody.

She turned to see Jamie with a saxophone.

'Walk beside me,' he said. 'Not behind me.'

He took her hand and guided it towards the wall. 'You can do this, Mum.'

She tried again. Following the cable. Stretching her arms as high and wide as they would go, scrabbling at the wall.

The back of her hand brushed against something metallic . She patted her hands across it, about a metre square and half as wide.

Like a fuse box. This must be it.

The breaker.

But where was the lock?

Her hands and feet were almost numb with cold, but her fingertips found the indentation. She rotated the cross-shaped multitool until she found the profile that matched, manoeuvring it to connect. Almost there. Just a bit further. Then . . . no!

The silver cross slipped from her hand.

She scrabbled around searching for it, breathing too fast.

Jamie took her hand. 'Reach down. Straight down.'

Julie lay on the pipes and slid her hands into the cold water. Reach down. Slow down. Shallow breaths. Don't flail around. It fell straight down and that's where you'll find it.

Her fingertips touched the silver cross on the floor of the tunnel and she scooped it back up.

'Well done,' Jamie said.

It felt nice, his rare praise. She turned on her side and let the water lift her, floating for a few minutes, gathering all her resolve.

'Try again?' he suggested.

This time she was more careful, slotting it into the lock, turning it with both hands. The cover flew open, and she recovered the silver cross before it fell again. She'd promised to return it to Alf, for the shrine to Grace. How lovely that he remembered her that way.

'I'm sorry, Jamie,' she said.

'Why are you sorry?'

'That we have no memorial for you.'

He laughed. He had such a lovely laugh, rich and deep and spontaneous.

'I'm seven octillion atoms. I'm all around you. I'm in the melody of birdsong and the breeze swishing through the trees. I'm in the perfume of flowers and fresh-cut grass. I'm in the silk of warm water that washes your skin. I'm in the taste of wild strawberries and the beat of the music you love.'

'So, you don't mind that there's no headstone?'

'I don't mind.'

'And you don't mind that there's no shrine?'

'I'm always with you, Mum,' he said. 'You can talk to me whenever you want.'

'And you don't mind about...' She couldn't bring herself to complete the sentence.

'You did exactly what I wanted.'

She breathed a sigh of relief at the warmth of his approval. There was something she should be doing, but she'd forgotten what it was. Something to do with control. Ah! Now she remembered.

'Don't you think it's ironic?' Julie asked.

'What's ironic, Mum.?'

'We used to control India.'

'You mean the British Empire?' Jamie asked. 'Or the multinationals?'

'Now they control us,' Julie said.

'You mean the terrorists?'

'It's come full circle.'

'No one should control anyone,' Jamie said.

He was right, of course, but now she'd lost her thread.

'Why am I here?' Julie asked. 'I don't want to be here. It's cold and dark and I'm confused.'

'You have to flick the switch.'

'What switch?'

'Here,' he said, and guided her hand into the open box.

She found the switch and pulled. Too stiff. Try again.

'Let me help,' Jamie said.

She held onto the switch with both hands, walking her feet up the wall, balancing her full weight on the lever. It began to move slowly and then faster, but she held on for dear life as she fell, tumbling between the pipes. She felt a sharp pain in her side. Something cracked, then popped. And then there was only darkness.

Chapter 61

BRIAN

Middlesbrough – Monday, 2 December 2024

In the intensive care unit of James Cook University Hospital, just before six-thirty in the evening, Brian Burrow regained consciousness for the first time since his motorbike accident, to find his ex-girlfriend, Betty, dozing in a chair beside him, her hand entwined in his.

He ran through a series of internal checks. The alphabet forwards and then backwards. The first twenty-six prime numbers: 2, 3, 5, 7 . . . 79, 83, 89, 97. Pi – twenty-two over seven – to twenty-six decimal places. The registration number of Magnus and all his previous motorbikes. The names of his cousins. Once the software check was complete, he turned to the hardware. Left leg, hip, knee, ankle, foot, toes. Right leg . . . ouch. Right arm . . . worse. Left arm, shoulder, elbow, wrist, hand, fingers. Well, at least he could see and hear, and one side of his body was working.

He turned to watch Betty for a while. As she started to wake, he squeezed her hand.

Her smile was the most beautiful thing he'd ever seen. She put a finger to her lips and pointed at the door. Through the glass pane, he could see a policeman outside. Then she pointed to the TV screen and turned the volume up.

'Oh, shit!' he said.

At the Zagrovyl International Teesside factory, the public alarm sirens began to blare.

Sue Bell unlocked the door of the disabled toilet and waddled over to the card reader. It clicked from red to green and let her into the air-lock.

Inside the control room, darkness fell as the hooded figure faded from the computer screen display.

'What's happening?' she asked.

A message flashed up on the screen.

REMOTE SESSION ENDED 18:34

'Four minutes past midnight in India,' Sue whispered.

The control system roared back to life, alarms wailing and beeping and buzzing and clanging, wall panels lighting up like Christmas trees.

'She's done it!' Sue shouted. 'Julie's only fucking been and gone and done it.' She started dancing with joy.

'Hey,' Jed said. 'Slow down, Sue. Right now, you're our most precious asset. Are you still fit to man the engineering workstation?'

'Can I woman it?'

He smiled. 'I'm not arguing with a pregnant woman.'

'Right, everyone.' Sue took charge. 'We're not out of the woods yet. Steve, get back outside and fill the scrubber and then let's figure out a way to reconnect the flare.'

She tapped the keys at her workstation.

'I'm back in administrative control. Resetting access for you all, overriding interlocks. OK, everyone.' She clapped her hands to get their attention. 'Here's what we're going to do . . .'

It took twenty minutes to restore control and ease the process into a managed shutdown.

'We're back in business,' Jed said.

'Back in control,' Sue agreed. 'Total control.'

Chapter 62

JULIE

Under the River Tees – Monday, 2 December 2024

Julie slowly regained consciousness. The pain in her side was agony. She brought a hand down to touch it. A rib, just a broken rib. It wouldn't kill her, but staying here might. Would it be so bad? At least she had Jamie with her. She'd missed him so much.

The water had filled the tunnel. She checked the gauge on the air cylinder. Almost empty. What was the rule of three? One third for descent and exploration, one third for the return, one third in reserve. She didn't have enough in this tank to make it back. But it didn't matter.

Jamie was floating beside her.

'Don't give up,' he said. 'Flora needs you.'

Her beautiful daughter.

'Arni needs you.'

Her lovely son.

'Dad needs you.'

Did he? Well, maybe Matt needed her not to die. Needed his ex-wife to stay alive and be the mother of his children. All three of them.

A sandy beach. A blue sky. The gentle lapping of the waves. The beep-beep of a life support machine. The hiss of the air being delivered through plastic tubes directly to her son's lungs. The doctors whispering. It's time, they said. Time to let him go, *hanımefendi*. There's no hope for him, but this way he can help someone else. Think of the other families.

The tears came again. This time the tears were not for Jamie. This time the tears were for herself. It was hopeless. She was going to die here. But at least she was with Jamie.

'I'm going now,' Jamie said.

'No, wait.'

'Follow me,' he said.

'Jamie, no!'

But he was gone.

'Jamie,' she whimpered.

She tried to follow but she kept falling. She picked herself up to make one final effort but her foot caught between pipes. This time it was trapped.

'JAMIE,' she screamed.

The dizziness came again.

She wasn't going to make it. She was out of air. Her hand made contact with something soft.

'Jamie?'

No reply. She reached out and then reeled back. The decomposing corpse of Simon Sharp must have floated away from where she'd left him. Well, beggars can't be choosers. She caught hold of his clothing to stop him floating past. If she was going to die down here, she might as well have company. They'd be found and buried together.

Wait.

If she could touch the body of Simon Sharp, then she couldn't be far from...

From where?

Think.

If her ankle had gone in between the pipes, there must be a way to get it out.

She moved her leg, backwards and forwards, until she found an angle that released her foot. The water was deep now. She swam along the tunnel, pushing Sharpie ahead of her, reaching up to pat the concrete ceiling until suddenly it opened up.

Her hand flailed around until it touched the iron rung of a ladder.

Jamie was back. 'Find the rope, Mum.'

What rope?

He guided her hand to it, helping her pull it up until the spare air cylinder surfaced.

A beam of light was shining down from the top of the ventilation shaft and suddenly Julie knew what to do.

Stay calm. Change supply. Open the valve. Breathe.

'Bye, Mum.' Jamie waved. 'You've got this.'

'Won't you climb up with me?' she asked.

Jamie smiled his wonderful smile, the one guaranteed to melt her heart.

'You know I can't,' he said. 'But I can be your guardian angel. If you're ever in danger, I'll be right there beside you.'

'I love you, Jamie.'

He was fading.

'I love you, Mum.'

He was gone.

Julie looked up, then began the long climb towards the light.

Chapter 63

Epilogue

Julie woke up in a hospital bed. She tried to sit up, but a wave of pain forced her to lie back. She pressed the bell beside her bed and a nurse appeared.

'I need to leave,' she said.

'The doctor will discharge you when you're well enough.'

'But there's an emergency.'

'The emergency is over,' the nurse said.

'Wait – how long have I been asleep?'

'I don't know. This is my first shift of the week. Right now, it's nine-thirty a.m. on Wednesday the fourth of December.'

A whole thirty-six hours had passed.

'What's wrong with me?'

'You are suffering from hypoxia, dehydration and have a broken ankle and three cracked ribs.'

The nurse plumped her pillow.

'There are some visitors anxious to see you. Feel up to it?'

Flora and Arni arrived first. She wanted to hug them tight, but her ribs hurt so badly it made her cry. She tried to tell them about their brother Jamie, how he'd been in the tunnel with her, but that made them cry, and then Flora lectured her about hypoxaemia and how lack of oxygen made you hallucinate. So, she just let them sit either side of her, each one holding a hand, and tell her how much they loved her. She wanted to ask about Eve, but she sensed that Arni wasn't ready. Time enough to catch up once she was home.

Next to arrive was ACC Bruma.

'At last,' she said. 'Someone who can tell me what's happened.'

He closed the door. 'Thanks to you, the remote control connection to Zagrovyl International was severed and the cyberattack interrupted. There was no toxic release anywhere in the world. The operator who suffered an electric shock is expected to make a full recovery. No one else was hurt. Apart from a few terrorists who didn't live to explain themselves.'

'Sue Bell. Is she OK?'

'She's fine.'

'Thank heavens.'

'Sue made contact on the satellite phone once the thunderstorm abated, but we'd already been contacted by a man on a bicycle. The nightwatchman at the scrapyard was cycling to Police HQ through the storm to alert us when a squad car picked him up.'

Alf Pearce. He'd got her message. He'd acted on it.

'We sent divers down into the tunnel from the south side to find you but you made it out all by yourself. How the hell you managed to climb back up the north shaft with your injuries, I'll never know.'

'Simon Sharp?'

'The divers recovered his body.'

'His parents?'

'They've been informed.'

Julie closed her eyes. Their only son, their pride and joy. The most terrible thing that can happen to a parent, to bury your own child. Someone had to pay for this.

'We need to track down a Polish national by the name of Tadeusz Makowski,' she said. 'Get an international arrest warrant if necessary.'

'On what charge? '

'For his part in the terrorist conspiracy,' she said.

'What terrorist conspiracy?' he said.

She stared at him.

'As far as the public is concerned, there was never any real danger,' he said. 'That's the line we've been asked to take.'

She shook her head in disbelief. 'Then arrest him for the murder of Dameer Ghosh and Simon Sharp. CIO Nadia Latif at Serious Crimes has all the evidence,' Julie said. 'But make sure she doesn't get into trouble with my old department.' She stopped and made eye contact. 'In fact, if you want me to toe the line, I suggest you bring her over to Minimax. She's good.'

ACC Bruma nodded. 'I'll see what I can do. Chalmers and Wharton have a lot of explaining to do. There will be a full investigation.'

'And,' Julie was on a roll now, 'once the charges are dropped against Brian Burrow, you might want to consider him for your -' she corrected herself- 'our cybersecurity vacancy.'

'Ideal candidate, from what I hear.' ACC Bruma smiled. 'So, you're planning to stay with Minimax?'

'Will you have me?' Julie asked.

ACC Bruma broke into the biggest grin she'd ever seen. 'Most definitely.'

Her youngest visitor was only a day old. Sue and Emma Bell brought their new baby daughter to see her.

'You told me you were two weeks away!' Julie protested.

'All the excitement made the shrimp eager to come and join the party.'

Julie took Sue's hand.

'Was everything OK? Did you make it to hospital?'

'She was born at home,' Sue said. 'Once the crisis was over, Emma collected me from work and then it all happened so fast we didn't have time to think.'

'Congratulations to both of you.'

'We're going to call her Julie,' Emma said. 'Julie Bell.'

Julie smiled. 'Nice ring to it.'

Julie was ready to sleep when the nurse appeared.

'Can you manage any more visitors?' she asked.

Julie yawned. 'Who's still waiting?'

'A DI Caron Riley and a Dr Sandy Armstrong.'

Julie shook her head and closed her eyes.

'Not right now,' she said.

She drifted off to sleep with a smile on her face.

Acknowledgements

I started writing *Losing Control* in November 2023 with the aim of publishing before the fortieth anniversary of the Bhopal Gas Tragedy. To achieve the one-year deadline, I've had enormous help – directly and indirectly – from many wonderful people who prefer not to be named.

Your secrets are safe with me.

My thanks to:

The professionals: **Development Editor** – Rebecca Jamieson, **Copy Editor** – Jenny Page, **Proofreader** – Marian Reid, **Cover Designer** – Mark Swan at kid-ethic and **Literary Agent** – Juliet Mushens.

The ~~press-ganged~~ volunteer readers: Marjory Flynn, Jane Jesmond, Effie Birch, Antony Johnston, Iain Souter, Jim Taylor and Andrew Erskine. A special thanks to Elizabeth and Neil - my expert Theakston Quiz Partners in Crime. Although many tried to help me, any remaining errors are entirely my responsibility.

Claire and Kayleigh gave me an informative tour of Hartlepool Nuclear Power Station (that steam chest really does looks like an upside-down baby elephant!). My guide to HMS *Trincomalee* in The National Museum of the Royal Navy at Hartlepool Historic Quay brought the ship to life (and nearly derailed my plot). The staff and volunteers at RSPB Saltholme Nature Reserve do a fantastic job of welcoming (and refreshing) visitors.

It was a conversation with Chris MacDonald, Steven Kedie and friends at **Manchester Libraries Crime Central** that consolidated an idea I'd been struggling with. The support of fellow writers – including the fabulous Jane Jesmond and the wonderful **Northern Crime Syndicate**: Jude O'Reilly, Trevor Wood, Chris McGeorge, Robert Rutherford, Rob Parker and Adam Peacock – kept me going.

A big shout out to the **UK Crime Club** for their help with Hartlepool surnames. My protagonist – DI Julie Cadell - was suggested by Deb Day (although I changed the spelling). Anne Hurst, Paul Robinson & Tracey Thomas (née Chipchase) gave Marcia from HR the name Chipchase. Jill Shapcott named the unreliable neighbour, Christine Bracegirdle. Nina Hesslewood kindly donated her surname to expert forensic technician Val Hesslewood. Pauline Lomax, Ann Thompson and Gemma Marie Hawkins came up with the surname for the Home Office pathologist, Dr Sandy Armstrong. Marian Highton, Claire Ferguson and Janet Gilliard named Brian a Burrow (with or without the s). Police Photographer, Rosie Patton, got her surname from Beverleigh Todd. Thanks to all the other readers who made terrific suggestions - I may be using them in DI Julie Cadell's next case!

Finally, my sincere thanks to those who tried to help me comprehend the scale of the Bhopal Gas Tragedy, including Tim Edwards, Satinath Sarangi, Rachna Dhingra, Kenneth Bloch (*Rethinking Bhopal*), Ramin Abhari (*Butterflies of Bhopal*), Indra Sinha (*Animal's People*), my colleagues at the IChemE *Loss Prevention Bulletin* and Jonathan Erskine for agreeing to visit India with me without quite realising where it might lead...

Afterword

BHOPAL

When I visited the city of Bhopal in India, site of the worst chemical accident in modern history, I was shocked to find that a dangerous, highly contaminated, abandoned factory is still standing, easily accessible to local children and grazing domestic animals. The untreated hazardous waste continues to leach into the soil and poison the drinking water.

No sane person, least of all the victims of the Bhopal accident, would ever align themselves with the sort of deranged terrorists I portray in *Losing Control*. We can never right a wrong by creating more wrongs. In *Losing Control* I wanted to draw attention to a long-forgotten tragedy.

The Accident

Just after midnight on the night of 2 to 3 December 1984 at the Union Carbide India Limited (UCIL) factory in Bhopal, India, twenty-eight tonnes of toxic gas were released into the community.

Water entered a tank containing methyl isocyanate (MIC), an intermediate used in the manufacture of pesticides, leading to a runaway chemical reaction and the release of a cocktail of highly toxic gases.

It was a cold, still night. The gas released from a chimney descended to ground level outside the factory walls and spread towards the centre of town in a dense, choking, toxic fog.

Thousands of people died that night, many of them children. Hundreds of thousands were injured, many of whom later died. The tragedy continues today.

Medical Care

The second tragedy of Bhopal was the failure of a coordinated public health response to the accident. No proper medical records were kept, and therapies of dubious value were sold to poorly educated victims.

The exact composition of the toxic gas released on the night of 2 to 3 December will never be known, but it certainly contained methyl isocyanate (MIC). Survivors of the disaster recall intense irritation to their eyes, nose and upper airways, likening it to burning chilli peppers.

It is likely that most of the early deaths, which numbered many thousands, were the result of pulmonary oedema and asphyxiation – people literally drowned in their own fluids as the body fought to protect itself.

In the survivors, residual damage to the lungs caused those affected to be breathless even at rest. Survivors with the most severe lung damage are susceptible to secondary cardiac failure.

Scarring of the external parts of the eye resulted in a reduction in or loss of vision. Severe mental health issues also resulted from the trauma [1].

New evidence [2] confirms the higher incidence of adverse health effects: neurological diseases, infections such as tuberculosis, pregnancy failures, birth defects, growth reduction in children and cancer.

The proceeds from the sale of UCIL in 1994 (US$90 million) were placed in a trust to fund a hospital in Bhopal to care for victims of the tragedy.

Very large sums of money were directed towards the building of expensive hospital facilities which were wholly inappropriate for the care of the survivors. These contrast starkly with the several community-based organisations (notably the Chingari and Sambhavna clinics) where large numbers of people from the most marginalised and needy sectors of the city were offered care in an environment of extraordinary tenderness. [1]

Compensation

No amount of money could ever compensate the survivors for their terrible trauma, loss, injury and economic destitution. But reasonable reparation could at least have alleviated some of the suffering. The third tragedy is economic.

The Government of India took over representation of the victims and their families in court. In 1989 UCC (Union Carbide Corporation) agreed to pay compensation of US$470 million (750 crore rupees). There was no criminal or punitive element to the settlement and no provision for environmental clean-up.

The money made available was wholly inadequate, calculated using a gross underestimate of the number of fatalities and the severity of the survivors' injuries. The amount payable was based on 1984 wages without adjusting for galloping inflation by the time it was paid out. The benchmark for the relative levels was motor vehicle accident compensation with the death of a child attracting a far lower level of compensation than the death of a man of working age.

Claimants had to take out loans to pay for the legal support and medical evidence required. The burden of proof was put on the poor and often illiterate victims. The court processes were formal and highly bureaucratic. Distribution was slow, in some cases taking almost twenty years.

The Bhopal Gas Tragedy Relief and Rehabilitation Department said that by the end of October 2003, judgement had been made on more than a million claims, with compensation being awarded to 554,895 people for injury (initial estimate 110,000) and 15,310 claims for deaths (initial estimate 3,000). Almost half a million victims were paid 25,000 rupees (US$550) by the Indian courts, while for deaths the average compensation was just 100,000 rupees (US$2,200).

The worst-affected survivors, those who were children at the time of the accident, had their education interrupted and opportunities blighted. There are reports of severe and widespread depression among those in their forties and fifties and an enduring lack of gainful employment.

Justice

The Bhopal factory was oversized, unreliable and uneconomic. UCIL were in the process of closing down the factory when disaster struck.

Investigations immediately after the accident uncovered a lack of hazard awareness which led to appalling operational decisions. Toxic releases were not properly investigated. Experienced people left. Inventories of hazardous material rose. Equipment ran to failure. Safety systems were compromised.

More recent analysis shows that the root cause of the accident goes back to design decisions made in the 1970s. Reaction chemistry, equipment selection, materials of construction and automation all contributed to the drift to disaster. The original process design decision to store large quantities of a highly hazardous intermediate (MIC) in a densely populated town, coupled with the lack of hazard awareness and loss of control, led to the worst industrial disaster in history.

As part of the 1989 settlement between the Government of India and UCC, all criminal charges were dropped, although this was later revoked.

In 2010 eight Indian nationals, all former employees of UCIL (including one who had already died) were convicted of causing *death by negligence*, sentenced to two years in prison and fined 100,000 rupees ($2,125). They were immediately released on bail and remain at liberty while they appeal against their conviction. It is highly unlikely that anyone will ever serve prison time.

Warren Anderson, the American chairman of UCC, the parent company, was also named as an accused and later declared an 'absconder' by the court. He died in the US in 2014 at the age of 92 without ever standing trial.

A technical analysis of the of the accident is summarised in the free-to-download October 2024 Loss Prevention Bulletin [3].

Environmental Remediation

The polluter pays principle is fundamental to environmental law. The final tragedy is that no one has accepted responsibility for cleaning up the mess created by the abandonment of the former UCIL factory in Bhopal.

In the 1989 settlement, no money was set aside for demolishing the factory, or for decontamination and remediation of the badly polluted land and adjacent waste lagoons (solar evaporation ponds).

Toxic wastes from production and related processes are known to have been dumped both on the factory premises and just outside in the three solar evaporation ponds.

In hot countries, it is common to use solar energy to concentrate liquid waste. The sun's heat evaporates the water from the surface of a pond, leaving solid waste or sludge which can be bagged for appropriate disposal (as landfill or toxic waste). However, such a scheme only works if the pond is lined and sealed with an impermeable membrane that is properly maintained. The ponds must be cleaned out or covered before monsoon rains arrive. In the absence of proper maintenance, toxic liquid can escape into the ground and enter the aquifers that supply drinking water.

It was known that the UCIL solar evaporation ponds were leaking as early as 1982. A report by the Centre for Science and Environment (CSE) in India brought together the data from soil and water samples over the years showing that high levels of mercury, chromium, lead, chlorinated benzenes and other persistent organic pollutants connected to the former factory operation continue to spread in an underground plume.

In 1994, the Indian Supreme Court allowed the parent company UCC to sell its shares in the Indian subsidiary UCIL to fund the Bhopal Hospital Trust. Once UCC no longer owned any assets in India there was no means of forcing compliance with the Indian courts.

UCC sold its 50.9 per cent stake in UCIL to McLeod Russel (India) Ltd and it was renamed Eveready Industries India Ltd (EIIL).

In one of the most bizarre and incomprehensible twists, the state government of Madhya Pradesh terminated the ninety-nine-year lease with

Eveready in 1998, took back control of the site and stopped any further clean-up.

It is not known who – apart from Eveready – benefited from the lease being revoked, but it was certainly not the survivors of the accident, who continue to be affected by polluted drinking water as well as contaminated milk and meat from grazing animals.

Forty years after the worst industrial accident in history, the children and grandchildren of the gas-affected survivors of Bhopal continue to suffer.

More information and ways to help can be found at www.bhopal.org

[1] IChemE Loss Prevention Bulletin 240, December 2014: 'Medical comment on the Bhopal tragedy', Professor Paul Cullinan: https://www.icheme.org/media/1277/lpb240_digimag.pdf

[2] BMJ Open (2023) 13(6): Long-term health and human capital effects of in utero exposure to an industrial disaster: A spatial difference-in-differences analysis of the Bhopal gas tragedy. McCord G, Bharadwaj P, McDougal L et al.

[3] IChemE Loss Prevention Bulletin 299, October 2024: https://www.icheme.org/media/27433/lpb299online.pdf

Further information on the 1984 Bhopal accident and its legacy

About the Author

A professional engineer with forty years of international manufacturing experience, **Fiona Erskine's** first graduate job was in the factory described in her memoir *Phosphate Rocks: A Death in Ten Objects*. Born in Edinburgh, Fiona grew up riding motorbikes and jumping into cold water. After studying chemical engineering at university, she learned to weld, cast and machine with apprentices in Paisley. As a professional engineer she has worked and travelled internationally. Fiona now teaches at the University of Sheffield.

You can connect with me on:

- https://fionaerskine.com
- https://x.com/erskine_fiona
- https://www.facebook.com/fionaerskineauthor

Also by Fiona Erskine

Losing Control is Book #1 in a new series featuring DI Julie Cadell. The unanswered questions will be explored over the next books in the series.

For more details, please visit my website https://fionaerskine.com/

Phosphate Rocks: A Death in Ten Objects

A long-deceased body, encrusted in phosphate rock, is uncovered during the demolition of an old chemical works. Ten unusual objects are positioned in front of the mummified corpse. Who was the victim? How did he die? What is the significance of the ten objects that surround him? And how reliable is the chief witness?

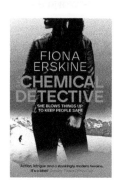

The Chemical Detective

Dr Jaq Silver is an engineer, skier and explosives expert. Working on avalanche control in the Julian Alps, Jaq stumbles across a faulty batch of explosives. She narrowly escapes death only to be framed for murder. Racing from the snowy slopes of Slovenia to the ghostly ruins of Chernobyl, can Jaq uncover the truth before her time runs out?

Milton Keynes UK
Ingram Content Group UK Ltd.
UKHW030522301024
450418UK00005B/109